RISKY BUSINESS

I picked up the tail on Broadway, just as I passed the Pigstand Coffee Shop. Despite local lore, there were no pigs present.

"Never when you need one," I said to the rearview mirror.

The tail was a black Chrysler, early '80s model. I cursed the lenient Texas regulations on window tinting. I couldn't see the car's interior worth a damn. Problem number two with driving a VW bug: unless your tail is driving a very old Schwinn with less than ten gears, you can pretty much forget losing them.

They weren't interested in hanging back, either. I hadn't even had enough time to say a "Hail Mary" before the Chrysler pulled around the intervening cars and went into high gear, coming around on my left. When I saw the shotgun window roll down I remembered why they call it the shotgun window. Then I yanked the wheel, hard.

I'll say this for the VW. It handles sidewalks a lot nicer than your average Chrysler. I was across two front lawns, a parking lot, and into an alley before the enemy managed to pull their boat around.

After ten minutes without seeing the Chrysler I slowed down to 50 in the 20 zone on Nacodoches and took inventory. That's when I noticed the new ventilation in the ragtop. Three holes the size of .45 bullets . . . the nearest one about six inches south of my head.

**Bantam Books by
Rick Riordan**

Big Red Tequila
The Widower's Two-Step
The Last King of Texas
The Devil Went Down to Austin

Big Red Tequila

Rick Riordan

Bantam Books
New York Toronto London Sydney Auckland

BIG RED TEQUILA
A Bantam Book / July 1997

ISBN-0-553-57644-5

Published simultaneously in the United States and Canada

Bantam Books are published by Bantam Books, a division of Random
House, Inc. Its trademark, consisting of the words "Bantam Books" and
the portrayal of a rooster, is Registered in U.S. Patent and Trademark
Office and in other countries. Marca Registrada. Bantam Books, 1540
Broadway, New York, New York 10036.

PRINTED IN THE UNITED STATES OF AMERICA

OPM   10 9 8 7 6

Dedication

To Haley Michael Riordan, *bienvenido* and a good
beginning

Acknowledgments

Many thanks to Glen Bates of the ITS Agency, Officer Sandy Peres of the San Antonio Police Department, and Corporal McCully of the Bexar County Sheriff's Department for their insights, Shelley Singer for her counsel, the Presidio Hill School gang for their support, Erika Luckett for her advice on the finer points of Spanish, Gina Maccoby and Kate Miciak for their help bringing to print the final draft, Jim Glusing for his stories, Lyn Belisle for her encouragement, and especially Becky Riordan, without whom none of it would have happened.

Big Red Tequila

1

"Who?" said the man occupying my new apartment.

"Tres Navarre," I said.

I pressed the lease agreement against the screen door again so he could see. It was about a hundred degrees on the front porch of the small in-law apartment. The air-conditioning from inside was bleeding through the screen door and evaporating on my face. Somehow that just made it seem hotter.

The man inside my apartment glanced at the paper, then squinted at me like I was some bizarre piece of modern art. Through the metal screen he looked even uglier than he probably was—heavyset, about forty, crew cut, features all pinched toward the center of his face. He was bare-chested and wore the kind of thick polyester gym shorts only P.E. coaches wear.

Use small words, I thought.

"I rented this apartment for July fifteenth. You were supposed to move out by then. It's July twenty-fourth."

No signs of remorse from the coach. He looked back

over his shoulder, distracted by a double play on the TV. He looked at me again, now slightly annoyed.

"Look, asshole," he said. "I told Gary I needed a few extra weeks. My transfer hasn't come through yet, okay? Maybe August you can have it."

We stared at each other. In the pecan tree next to the steps a few thousand cicadas decided to start their metallic chirping. I looked back at the cabby who was still waiting at the curb, happily reading his *TV Guide* while the meter ran. Then I turned back to the coach and smiled—friendly, diplomatic.

"Well," I said, "I tell you what. I've got the moving van coming here tomorrow from California. That means you've got to be out of here today. Since you've had a free week on my tab already, I figure I can give you an extra hour or so. I'm going to get my bags out of the cab, then when I come back you can let me in and start packing."

If it was possible for his eyes to squint any closer together, they did. "What the fuck—"

I turned my back on him and went out to the cab. I hadn't brought much with me on the plane—one bag for clothes and one for books, plus Robert Johnson in his carrying cage. I collected my things, asked the cabby to wait, then walked back up the sidewalk. Pecans crunched under my feet. Robert Johnson was silent, still disoriented from his traumatic flight.

The house didn't look much better on a second take. Like most of the other sleeping giants on Queen Anne Street, Number 90 had two stories, an ancient green-shingled roof, bare wood siding where the white paint had peeled away, a huge screened-in front porch sagging under tons of red bougainvillea. The right side of the building, where the in-law's smaller porch stuck out, had shifted on its foundations and now drooped down and backward, as if that half of the house had suffered a stroke.

The coach had opened the door for me. In fact he was standing in it now, smiling, holding a baseball bat.

"I said *August,* asshole," he told me.

I set my bags and Robert Johnson's cage down on the bottom step. The coach smiled like you might at a dirty joke. One of his front teeth was two different colors.

"You ever try dental picks?" I said.

He developed a few new creases on his forehead. "What—?"

"Never mind," I said. "You got moving boxes or you just want to put your stuff in Hefty bags? You strike me as a Hefty-bag man."

"Fuck you."

I smiled and walked up the steps.

The porch was way too narrow to swing a bat, but he did his best to butt me in the chest with it. I moved sideways and stepped in next to him, grabbing his wrist.

If you apply pressure correctly, you can use the *nei guan* point, just above the wrist joint, in place of CPR to stimulate the heart. One of the reasons Chinese grandmothers wear those long pins in their hair, in fact, is to prick the *nei guan* in case someone in the family has a heart attack. Apply pressure a little harder, and it sends a charge through the nervous system that is pretty unpleasant.

The coach's face turned red; his pinched features loosened up in shock. The bat clattered down the steps. As he doubled over, clutching his arm, I pushed through the door.

The TV was still going in the main room—a washed-up *Saturday Night Live* comedian was guzzling a light beer, surrounded by five or six cheerleaders. Nothing else in the room except a mattress and a pile of clothes in the corner and a tattered easy chair. On the kitchen counter there was a mound of old dishes and fast-food cartons. The smell was somewhere between fried meat and sour wet laundry.

"You've done wonders with the place," I said. "I can see why—"

When I turned around the coach was standing behind me and his fist was a few inches from my face, coming in for a landing.

I twisted out of its way and pushed down on his wrist

with one hand. With the other hand I slammed up on the elbow, bending the joint the wrong way. I'm sure I didn't break it, but I'm pretty sure it hurt like hell anyway. The coach fell down on the kitchen floor and I went to check out the bathroom. A toothbrush, one towel, the new *Penthouse* on the toilet tank. All the comforts of home.

It took about fifteen minutes to find a roll of garbage bags and stuff the coach's things into them.

"You broke my arm," he told me. He was still sitting on the kitchen floor, with his eyes tightly closed.

I unplugged the TV and put it outside.

"Some people like ice for a joint problem like that," I told him, moving out the chair. "I think it's better if you use a hot-water bottle. Keep it warm for a while. Two days from now you won't feel anything."

He told me he'd sue, I think. He told me a lot of things, but I wasn't listening much anymore. I was tired, it was hot, and I was starting to remember why I'd stayed away from San Antonio for so many years.

The coach was in enough pain not to fight much as I tucked him into the cab with most of his stuff and paid the cabby to take him to a motel. Leaving the TV and easy chair in the front yard, I brought my things inside and shut the door behind me.

Robert Johnson slunk out of his cage cautiously when I opened it. His black fur was slicked the wrong way on one side and his yellow eyes were wide. He wobbled slightly getting back his land legs. I knew how he felt.

He sniffed the carpet, then looked at me with total disdain.

"Row," he said.

"Welcome home," I said.

2

"Was fixing to evict him one of these days," Gary Hales mumbled.

My new landlord didn't seem too concerned about my disagreement with the former tenant. Gary Hales didn't seem too concerned about anything.

Gary was an anemic watercolor of a man. His eyes, voice, and mouth were all soft and liquid, his skin a washed-out blue that matched his guayabera shirt. I got the feeling he might just dilute down to nothing if he got caught in a good rain.

He stared at our finalized lease as if he were trying to remember what it was. Then he read it one more time, his lips moving, his shaky hand following each line with the tip of a black pen. He got stuck on the signature line.

He frowned. "Jackson?"

"Legally," I told him. "Tres, as in the Third. Usually I go by that, unless you're my mother and you're mad at me, in which case it's Jackson."

Gary stared at me.

"Or occasionally 'Asshole,'" I offered.

Gary's pale eyes had started to glaze over. I thought I'd probably lost him after "legally," but he surprised me.

"Jackson Navarre," he said slowly. "Like that sheriff that got kilt?"

I took the lease out of Gary's hand and folded it up.

"Yeah," I said. "Like that."

Then the wall started ringing. Gary's eyes floated over listlessly to where the sound had come from. I waited for an explanation.

"She axed me for the number here," he said, like he was reminding himself about it. "Told her I'd change the name over to you t'morrow."

He shuffled across the room and pulled a built-in ironing board out from the living-room wall. In the alcove behind it was an old black rotary phone.

I picked it up on the fourth ring and said: "Mother, you're unbelievable."

She sighed loudly into the receiver, a satisfied kind of sound.

"Just an old beau at Southwestern Bell, honey. Now when are you coming over?"

I thought about it. The prospect wasn't pleasant after the day I'd had. On the other hand, I needed transportation.

"Maybe this evening. I'll need to borrow the VW if you've still got it."

"It's been sitting in my garage for ten years," she said. "You think it'll run you're welcome to it. I expect you'll be visiting Lillian tonight?"

In the background at my mother's house I heard the sound of a pool cue breaking a setup. Somebody laughed.

"Mother—"

"All right, I didn't ask. We'll see you later on, dear."

After Gary had shuffled back over to the main part of the house, I checked my watch. Three o'clock San Francisco time. Even on Saturday afternoon there was still a good chance I could reach Maia Lee at Terrence & Goldman.

No such luck. When her voice mail got through

explaining to me what "regular business hours" meant, I left my new number, then held the line for a second longer, thinking about what to say. I could still see Maia's face the way it looked this morning at five when she dropped me off at SFO—smiling, a sisterly kiss, someone polite whom I didn't recognize. I hung up the phone.

I found some vinegar and baking soda in the pantry and spent an hour cleaning away the sights and smells of the former tenant from the bathroom while Robert Johnson practiced climbing the shower curtain.

A little before sunset somebody knocked on my door.

"Mother," I grumbled to myself. Then I looked out the window and saw it wasn't quite that bad—just a couple of uniformed cops leaning against their unit in the driveway, waiting. I opened the front door and saw the second ugliest face I'd seen through my screen door so far today.

"You know," the man croaked, "somebody just handed me this complaint from one Bob Langston of 90 Queen Anne's Street. Guy's a G-7 at Fort Sam, no less. Assault, it says. Trespassing, it says. Langston claims some maniac named Navarre tried to karate him to death, for Christ's sake."

I was surprised how much he'd changed. His cheeks had hollowed out like craters and he'd gone bald to the point where he had to comb a greasy flap of side hair over the top just to keep up appearances. About the only things he had more of were stomach and mustache. The former covered his twenty-pound belt buckle. The latter covered his mouth almost down to his double chins. I remember as a kid wondering how he lit his cigarettes without setting his face on fire.

"Jay Rivas," I said.

Maybe he smiled. There was no way to tell under the whiskers. Somehow he located his lips with a cigarette and took a long drag.

"So you know what I tell the guys?" Rivas asked. "I say no way. No way could I be so lucky as to have Jackson Navarre's baby boy back in town from San

Fag-cisco to bring sunlight into my dreary life. That's what I tell them."

"It was tai chi chuan, Jay, not karate. Purely defensive."

"What the fuck, kid," he said, leaning his hand against the door frame. "You just about kimcheed this guy's arm off. Give me a reason I shouldn't treat you to some free accommodations at the County Annex tonight."

I referred him to Gary Hales's and my lease agreement, then told him about Mr. Langston's less-than-warm reception. Rivas seemed unimpressed.

Of course, Jay Rivas always seemed unimpressed when it came to my family. He'd worked with my dad in the late seventies on a joint investigation that didn't go so well. My dad had expressed his displeasure to his friends at SAPD, and here was Detective Rivas twenty years later, following up on low-priority assault cases.

"You made it out here awfully quick, Jay," I said. "Should I be flattered or do they normally send you out for the trivial stuff?"

Rivas blew smoke through his mustache. His double chins turned a beautiful shade of red, like a toad's.

"Why don't we go inside and talk about that," he suggested, his voice calm.

He motioned for me to open the screen door. It didn't happen.

"I'm losing air conditioning, here, Detective," I said.

We stared at each other for about two minutes. Then he disappointed me. He backed down the steps. He stuck the cigarette in his mouth and shrugged.

"Okay, kid," he said. "Just take the hint."

"Which is?"

Then I'm sure he smiled. I could see the cigarette curve up through the whiskers. "You get your nose into anything else, I'll see you get some nice cellmates downtown."

"You're a loving human being, Jay."

"To hell with that."

He tossed his cigarette onto Bob Langston's "God Bless Home" welcome mat and swaggered back to where the two uniforms were waiting for him. I watched their unit disappear down Queen Anne Street. Then I went inside.

I looked around my new home—the bubbled molding on the ceiling, the gray paint that had started peeling away from the walls. I looked down at Robert Johnson. He was now sitting in my open suitcase and staring at me with an insulted expression. A subtle hint. I called Lillian's number with the thirst of a man who needs water after a shot of mescal.

It was worth it.

She said: "Tres?" and ripped away the last ten years of my life like so much tissue paper.

"Yeah," I told her. "I'm in my new place. More or less."

She hesitated. "You don't sound too happy about it."

"It's nothing. I'll tell you the story later."

"I can't wait."

We held the line for a minute—the kind of silence where you lean into the receiver, trying to push yourself through by sheer force.

"I love you," Lillian said. "Is it too soon to say that?"

I swallowed down the ball bearing in my throat. "How about nine? I've got to liberate the VW from my mother's garage."

Lillian laughed. "The Orange Thing still runs?"

"It'd better. I've got a hot date tonight."

"You'd better believe it."

We hung up. I looked over at Robert Johnson, who was still sitting in my suitcase.

"Deal with it," I told him.

I felt like it was 1985 again. I was still nineteen, my dad was alive, and I was still in love with the girl I'd been planning on marrying since junior high. We were going seventy miles an hour down I-35 in an old VW that could only do sixty-five, chasing down god-awful tequila with even more god-awful Big Red cream soda. Teenage champagne.

I changed clothes again and called a cab. I tried to remember the taste of Big Red tequila. I wasn't sure I could ever drink something like that again and smile, but I was ready to try.

3

Broadway from Queen Anne to my mother's house was lined with pink taco restaurants. Not the run-down family-owned places I remembered from high school—these were franchises with neon signs and pastel flamingos painted along the walls. There must have been one every half mile.

Landmarks in downtown Alamo Heights had disappeared. The Montanios had sold off the 50-50 Bar, my father's old watering hole. Sill's Snack Shack was now a Texaco. Most of the local places like that, named after people I knew, had been swallowed by faceless national chains. Other storefronts were boarded up, their half-hearted "For Lease" signs weathered down to illegibility.

The city was still a thousand kinds of green, though. In every block the buildings were crowded by ancient live oak trees, huisaches, and Texas laurels. It was the kind of rich green you see in most towns only right after a big rain.

It was sunset and still ninety-five degrees when the cab turned down Vandiver. There were none of the soft afternoon colors you get in San Francisco, no hills for shadows, no fog to airbrush the scenery for tourists on the Golden Gate. Here the light was honest—everything it touched was sharply focused, outlined in heat. The sun kept its eye on the city until its very last moment on the horizon, looking at you as if to say: "Tomorrow I'm going to kick your ass."

Vandiver Street hadn't changed. Sprinklers cut circles across the huge lawns, and wraithlike retirees stared aimlessly out the picture windows of their white, post-WW II houses. The only difference was that Mother had reincarnated her house again. If I hadn't recognized the huge oak tree in front, the dirt yard covered with acorns and patches of wild strawberry, I would have let the cabby drive right past it.

Once I saw it, I was tempted to drive past anyway. It was stucco now—olive-colored walls with a bright red clay tile roof. The last time I'd seen the house it looked more like a log cabin. Before that it had been pseudo-Frank Lloyd Wright. Over the years Mother had become close with several contractors who depended on her for steady income.

"Tres, honey," she said at the door, pulling my face forward with both hands for a kiss.

She hadn't changed. At fifty-six she could still pass for thirty. She wore a loose Guatemalan dress, fuchsia with blue stitching, and her black hair was tied back with a festive knot of colored ribbons. The smell of vanilla incense wafted out the door with her.

"You look great, Mother." I meant it.

She smiled, dragging me inside by the arm and steering me toward the pool table at the far end of her huge living room.

The decor had shifted from late Bohemian to early Santa Fe, but the general theme was still the same: "put stuff everywhere." Shelves and tables were overloaded with antique knives, papier-mâché dolls, carved wooden boxes, replica coyotes howling at replica moons, a neon cactus, anything to attract the eye.

Around the pool table were three old acquaintances

from high school. I shook hands with Barry Williams and Tom Cavagnaro. Both had played varsity with me. They were here because my mom loved entertaining guests with pool and free beer. Then I nodded to Jess Makar, who had graduated when I was a freshman. Jess was here because he was dating my mother.

They asked the standard polite questions and I answered them, then they resumed their game and Mother took me into the kitchen.

"Jess is aging gracefully," I told her.

She pursed her lips and glared as she turned around from the refrigerator. She handed me a Shiner Bock.

"Now don't you start, Jackson," she said.

When she called me that, the name I took from my father and grandfather, I never could tell whether she was scolding me or the whole line of Navarre men. Probably both.

"You could at least give the man a chance," she said, sitting down at the table. "After the years I had to put up with your father, and then years of getting you through school, I think I'm entitled to my own choices for once."

Since her divorce my mother had made a lot of choices. In fifteen years she'd gone from the pecan pie baking champion of the Wives of the Texas Cavaliers to a freelance artist who preferred big canvases, younger men, and New Age.

She smiled again. "Now tell me about Lillian."

"I don't know," I said.

Expectant pause, waiting for an admission of guilt.

"You knew enough to come back," Mother prompted.

What she wanted me to say: I'd marry Lillian tomorrow, at the drop of a hat, just based on the letters and calls we'd exchanged since she'd phoned me out of the blue two months ago. Mother wanted to hear that, and it would've been true. Instead, I drank my Shiner Bock.

Mother nodded as if I'd answered.

"I always knew. Such a creative young woman. I always knew you couldn't stay away forever."

"Yeah."

"And your father's death?"

I looked up. The air of frenetic energy that usually swirled around her like a strong perfume had dropped away totally. She was serious now.

"What do you mean?" I asked.

Of course I knew what she meant. *Had I come back to deal with that too, or had I put it behind me?* Mother stared at me, waiting. I looked down at my beer. The little ram on the label was staring at me too.

"I don't know," I said. "I thought ten years away would make a difference."

"It should, dear."

I nodded, not looking at her. In the next room someone sunk a billiard ball with a heavy thud. After a minute my mother sighed.

"It hasn't been too long for you and Lillian," she told me. "But your father—that's different. Leave it be, Tres. Things have changed."

Fifteen minutes later, after three attempts at automotive CPR and lots of strong language, my VW convertible coughed itself back to life and chugged fitfully out of the driveway. The engine sounded bad, but no worse than it had a decade ago, when I had decided it would never make the trip to California. The left headlight was still out. A cup I had been drinking beer from in 1985 was still wedged between the seat and the emergency brake. I waved to my mother, who hadn't aged in two decades.

I drove toward Lillian's house, the same one she had lived in the summer I left.

"Things have changed," I repeated, halfway wishing I could believe it.

4

"Now I know I'm in love," Lillian told me after she tasted her drink.

The perfect margarita should be on the rocks, not frozen. Fresh-squeezed limes, never a mixer. Cointreau rather than triple sec. No tequila but Herradura Anejo, a brand that until a few years ago was only available across the border. All three ingredients in equal proportions. And without salt on the rim it might as well be a daiquiri.

I sat next to Lillian on the couch and tried mine. It had been a few years since I'd worked behind a bar, but the margarita was definitely passable.

"Well, it's not Big Red . . ." I said ruefully.

Lillian's smile was brilliant, a few new wrinkles etched around her eyes. "You can't have everything."

Her face had a little too much of everything, just as I remembered. Her eyes were slightly large, like a cat's, the irises flecked with too many browns and blues and grays to call them only green. Her mouth was wide, her nose so delicate it bordered on being sharp. Her light brown hair, which she now wore shoulder-length, had so many blond and red streaks it looked off-color. And she had too many freckles, especially noticeable now when she had a summer tan. Somehow it all worked to make her beautiful.

"It sounds like your day was hell, Tres. I'm impressed you're still standing."

"Nothing an enchilada dinner and a beautiful woman won't cure."

She took my hand. "Any one in particular?"

I thought about it. "Green or chicken mole."

She slapped me on the thigh and called me names.

We knew better than to try making reservations at Mi Tierra on a Saturday night. You just throw yourself into the crowd of tourists and native San Antonians in the front room, wave money, and hope you get a table in under an hour.

It was worth it. We got seats close to the bakery, where trays of cinnamon-smelling *pan dulce* in neon colors were brought out of the ovens every few minutes. The Christmas lights were still up along the walls, and the mariachis were as thick as flies, only much fatter. I threatened Lillian with having them play "Guantanamera" at our table unless she let me buy dinner.

She laughed. "A dirty trick. And me a successful businesswoman."

She had promised to show me her gallery the next day. It was a small place in La Villita she co-owned with her old college mentor, Beau Karnau. They mostly sold Mexican folk art to tourists.

"And your own art?" I asked.

She looked down briefly, smiling still but not so much. Sore subject.

Ten years ago, when I left, Beau Karnau and Lillian had been talking big about her career—New York shows, museum exhibitions, changing the face of modern photographic art. As soon as the world rediscovered Beau's genius (which they'd apparently appreciated for about three months during the sixties) Lillian would ride his coattails to fame. Now, ten years later, Beau and Lillian were selling curios.

"I don't get as much time as I did in college," she said. "But soon. I have some new ideas."

I decided not to push it. After a large waiter with an even larger mustache came to take our order, Lillian changed subjects.

"How about you? Now that I've got you out here without a job, I mean. It can't be that easy without an investigator's license."

I shrugged. "Some legal firms like that—informal help for the messy jobs, no records on the payroll. I've got a few leads. Maia has lots of friends of friends."

The minute I said her name I wished I hadn't. It landed in the middle of the table between us like a brick. Lillian slowly licked some salt from the rim of her glass. There was no change in her face.

"You could always get a job evicting wayward tenants," she suggested.

"Or I could help sell art for you."

She gave me a lopsided smile. "When I have to pin a customer in a joint lock to buy my work, I'll know it's time to put down the camera and the paintbrush for good."

The waiter returned quickly with a bowl of butter and a basket the size of a top hat filled with handmade tortillas. Unfortunately Fernando Asante came up to our table right behind him.

"I'll be damned!" he said. "If it isn't Jack Navarre's boy."

Before I could put down my half-buttered tortilla I was shaking hands with him, staring up at his weathered brown face and a row of smiling, gold-outlined teeth. Asante's hair was so thin and well greased, combed back from his forehead, that it could've been drawn on with a Marksalot.

I stood up, introducing Lillian to San Antonio's eldest city councilman. As if she didn't know who he was. As if anybody in town who read the *Express-News* tabloid section didn't know.

" 'Course," Asante said. "I remember Miss Cambridge. Fiesta Week. The Travis Center opening, with Dan Sheff."

Asante had a gift for names, and that one fell onto the table like another brick. Lillian winced a little. The councilman just smiled. I smiled back. An Anglo man had come up behind Asante and was waiting patiently with that distracted, brooding expression most bodyguards develop. About six feet, curly black hair, boots and jeans, T-shirt and linen jacket. Lots of muscles. He didn't smile.

"Councilman. You made it into the San Francisco paper a while back."

He did his best modest look. "The Travis Center opening. Millions in new revenue to the city. Friends called me up from all over the country, said they saw the coverage."

"Actually it was that piece about the secretary and you in Brackenridge Park."

Lillian suppressed a laugh by choking on her margarita. Asante's smile wavered momentarily, then came back different—more of a snarl. We were all quiet for a few seconds. I'd seen him give that look plenty to my dad in the years they had been at each other's throats. I was downright proud to see it turned on me. I figured wherever my father was he would probably be biting the end off a new cigar and laughing his ass off about then.

Asante's large friend felt the change of mood, I guess. He moved around to the side of the table.

"Love to have you join us for dinner," I offered. "Double date?"

"No thanks, Jack," the councilman said. That was the second time today someone had called me by my father's name. It sounded strange.

"I hear you're in town for good." He didn't seem to like the sound of that. "It can be tough finding jobs down here. You have any trouble, let me know."

"Thanks."

"Least I can do." A politician's grin smoothed over his

face again. "Not every day a Bexar County sheriff gets shot down. Your dad . . . that was a bad way to go."

Asante kept smiling. I was counting the gold caps on his teeth, wondering how hard they would be to break off.

"I always wished I could do something more for your family, Jack, but, well, you left town so fast. Like a jackrabbit, heard that shot and boom, you were in California."

A young orange-haired woman in a glittery dress came up behind Asante and waited at a respectful distance. Asante glanced back at her and nodded.

"Well," he said, patting his belly. "Dinnertime now. Like I said, you need anything, Jack, let me know. Nice to see you again, Miss Cambridge."

Asante's fan club followed him to a table nearby. My enchilada dinner was probably very good. I don't remember.

Around midnight Lillian and I drove back to her house with the VW top down. The stars were out and the air was as warm and clean as fresh laundry.

"I'm sorry about Asante," she said after a while.

I shrugged. "Don't be. Coming home is like that— you have to face the assholes too."

She had taken my hand by the time we pulled into her driveway. We sat there listening to the *conjunto* music from the house next door. The windows were lit up orange. Beers were being opened, loud talking in Spanish, Santiago Jimenez's accordion wailing out "Ay Te Dejo En San Antonio."

"Tonight was hard anyway," Lillian said. "We're going to need time to figure things out, I guess."

She raised my hand to her lips. I was looking at her, remembering the first time I had kissed her in this car, how she looked. She had been wearing a white sundress, her hair cut like Dorothy Hamill's. We had been sixteen, I think.

I kissed her now.

"I've been figuring things out for ten years," I told her. "It's got to get easier from here."

She looked at me for a long time with an expression I couldn't read. She almost decided to say something. Then she kissed me back.

It was hard to talk for a while, but I finally said: "Robert Johnson will be mad if I don't bring him these leftovers for dinner."

"Enchiladas for breakfast?" Lillian suggested.

We went inside.

5

Everything with Lillian was familiar, from her linen sheets to the citrus scent of her hair when I finally fell asleep buried in it. I was even hoping I might dream of her for a change, the way I used to. I didn't.

The dreams started out like a slide show—newspaper photos of my dad, *Express-News* headlines that had burned themselves into my memory that summer. Then it was a late spring evening in May of '85 and I was standing on the front porch of my father's house in Olmos Park. A battered gray Pontiac, probably a '76, tinted windows and no license plate, was pulling up by the curb as my father walked from the driveway to the front door, carrying two bags of groceries. Carl Kelley, his deputy and best friend, was a few steps behind him. For some reason I remember exactly what Carl was holding—a twelve-pack of Budweiser in one hand and a watermelon in the other. I was opening the front door for them, my eyes red from studying for my last round of freshman final exams at A & M.

My dad was at his very heaviest—nearly three hundred pounds of muscle and fat stuffed into oversized jeans and a checkered shirt. Sweat lines running down his temples from the rim of his brown Stetson, he lumbered up the steps with a cigar drooping off the corner of his mouth. He looked up and gave me one of his sly grins, started to say something, probably a wisecrack at my expense. Then a small hole blew open in the grocery bag in Dad's right arm. A perfect white stream of milk sprouted out. Dad looked momentarily puzzled. The second shot came out the front of his Stetson.

Fumbling for his gun, Carl hit the ground for cover about the same time my dad hit the ground dead. Dad was three months away from retirement. The watermelon made a bright red starburst as it exploded on the sidewalk. The gray Pontiac pulled away and was gone.

When I woke up alone in Lillian's bed the *conjunto* music from next door had stopped. The cranberry glass night lamp was on, making the squares of moonlight pink against the hardwood floor. Through the open bedroom door I could see Lillian standing naked in the living room, her arms hugging her body, staring at one of her photos on the wall.

She didn't seem to hear me when I called. When I came up behind her and put my arms around her shoulders, she stiffened. Her eyes never left the photo.

It was one of her early college pieces—a black and white photo-collage of animals, human faces, insects, buildings, all of it hand-tinted and merged into one surrealistic mass. I remembered the December weekend when she'd been putting it together for her end-of-term project. I'd done my best to distract her. We'd ended up with photo scraps scattered all over the bed and clinging to our sweaters.

"Naive," she said, absently. "Beau used to take me out into the country—we'd be shivering all night in sleeping bags on some godforsaken hilltop in Blanco for one shot of a meteor shower, or we'd trudge through twenty acres of pasture outside Uvalde so we'd be in just the right position at dawn to catch the light behind a windmill. He used to say that every picture had to be taken at the greatest possible expense. Then I'd look back at my old collages like this one and think how easy they'd been."

"Maybe naive gets a bad rap," I said.

We stood there together and looked at it for a minute.

"It just feels strange," she said. "You being here."

"I know."

She leaned her head against me. The tension in her shoulders didn't go away.

"What else is it?" I said.

She hesitated. "There are complications."

I kissed her ear. "You asked for me to be here. I'm here. There's no complication."

Until Lillian looked around at me I didn't realize her eyes were wet.

"When you left San Antonio, Tres, what were you running from?"

"I told you. The rest of my life stuck in Texas, the idea of marriage, the careers everybody else wanted me to take—"

She shook her head. "That's not what I meant. Why did you go when you did, right after your father's death?"

I hugged her from behind and held on tight, trying to get lost in the citrus smell of her hair. But when I closed my eyes against her cheek, I still saw the old newspaper photo of my father, the caption that I knew by heart. *"Sheriff Jackson Navarre, gunned down brutally on Thursday evening in front of his Olmos Park home. Deputy Sheriff Kelley and Navarre's son watched helplessly as the assassins sped away."* My father's face in the photo just smiled at me dryly, as if that caption was some private joke he was sharing.

"Maybe because when I looked around town," I told Lillian, "all I saw was him dying. It was like a stain."

She nodded, looking back at her photo-collage. "The stain doesn't go away, Tres. Not even after all these years."

Her tone was bitter, not like Lillian. I held her a little tighter. After a while she turned around and folded herself into my arms.

"It doesn't have to be a complication for us now," I whispered.

"Maybe not," she murmured. But I didn't need to see her face to see that she didn't believe me.

She didn't let me say anything else, though. She kissed me once, lightly, then more. Soon we were back in the linen sheets. I wasn't sleeping again until almost dawn, this time with no dreams.

6

I was back at 90 Queen Anne at nine the next morning to meet the movers. Robert Johnson gave me an evil look as I walked in the door, but decided to call a truce when he heard the sound of aluminum foil being peeled away from my leftovers.

He has a system with enchiladas. He bats them with his paw until the tortillas unroll. He eats the filling first, then the tortillas. He saves the cheese for last. This kept him occupied while I did the first hour of my tai chi set, at which point the moving truck gunned up the driveway and scared him into the closet.

Three guys wearing baseball caps and leather weight belts were trying to figure out which way to fold my futon frame to get it through the door when the phone rang. I pulled down the ironing board and picked up the receiver.

Maia Lee said: "Hey, Tex. Ridden any good bulls lately?"

The background noise placed her immediately. It was Sunday morning at the Buena Vista.

"No," I said, "but me and the boys are hog-tying a futon even as we speak. It's an uppity little filly."

"You cowpokes sure know how to party."

I could picture her standing in the dark green entry hall of the bar, the receiver balanced between her shoulder and chin. She'd be wearing her business clothes—blazer and skirt, silk blouse, always in light colors to show off her flawless coffee-colored skin. Her hair, chocolate-brown and curly, would be tied back. Behind her I could hear Irish coffee glasses rattling, the unmistakable clanging of cable car bells.

"Listen," Maia said, "I wasn't really calling for a reason, if you're busy."

"That's okay."

In my doorway the futon seemed to be holding its own. One mover was wedged against the wall and another was trying to extract his leg from between two of its slats. The third guy had just figured out that the bolts could be loosened. An ice cream truck drove by, providing us with a momentary soundtrack: a very warped recording of "Oh, What a Beautiful Mornin'."

"It's a whole 'nother world down here, Maia," I said.

She laughed. "I remember telling you something like that, Tex. But everything's going all right? I mean . . ."

"It's okay," I told her. "Being home after so long is like—I don't know."

"Coming out of amnesia?"

"I was thinking more along the lines of infectious skin diseases."

"Hmph. You don't pick your home, Tres. It just is."

Maia knew about that. Take away the Mercedes and the law practice and the Potrero Hill loft, and Maia's most important possession was still a photograph of an unpainted Sheetrock shack in Zhejiang Province. Logic had nothing to do with it.

"Some things you don't choose," I said.

"Isn't that the truth."

I'm not sure either of us bought it. On the other hand, I figured it was as close to an understanding about what had happened between us as we would ever get.

She told me she was on her way to interview a client whose teenage son had been charged with setting part of the Presidio on fire. It was going to be a long morning. I promised to call in a few days.

"Drink one of those frozen strawberry margaritas for me," she said.

"Infidel," I said.

By noon the movers had everything out of the truck and into the living room without any major accidents. I gave them directions back to Loop 410. Then I headed down Broadway toward downtown.

Ten minutes later I turned up Commerce and started looking for street parking. Fortunately I was used to San Francisco traffic. I U-turned across three lanes and beat a Hilton valet to a nice meter spot without so much as a fistfight, then walked south into La Villita.

The place hadn't changed over the last few hundred years. Except for being cleaner and having higher rents, the restored four square blocks of original settlement were not much different than they'd been back in the days of the Alamo. Tourists wandered in and out of the white limestone buildings. A family of large Germans, severely overdressed for the heat, sat at a green metal table in the sun outside one of the cantinas. They were trying to look like they were having fun on their vacation, mouths open, fanning themselves with menus.

I wandered down the narrow brick lanes for almost twenty minutes before I found the Hecho a Mano Gallery, a tiny building in the shade of a huge live oak behind the La Villita Chapel. The gallery didn't seem to be getting much business at the moment. I came in the door just as a glass paperweight flew past, banging into the wall and rattling a few framed pictures of Guatemalan peasants.

A male voice around the corner of the entryway said: "God *damn* it!"

A loud disagreement followed.

"Lillian?" I called, loudly.

I looked around the corner, cautious for more flying objects. Lillian was standing up at a small wooden desk near the opposite wall. She was pressing her fingertips against her temples and glaring at a man who looked nothing at all like the Beau Karnau I remembered.

What I remembered from the few times Beau had condescended to shake my hand a decade ago was a short, burly brunette with a crew cut, black clothes, and a face smoothed over with acne scar tissue and smugness. Now in his late fifties, Karnau looked more like one of the Seven Dwarfs. He sported a potbelly, a scraggly gray beard, a receding hairline, and a braided ponytail. He'd traded in the black clothes for a gaudy silk shirt, boots, and jeans. His forehead was almost purple with anger.

"God *damn* it," he shouted. "You *can't*."

Lillian saw me, told me with a shake of her head that she wasn't in danger, then looked back at Karnau and sighed in exasperation.

"Jesus Christ, Beau! You're going to kill somebody with your tantrums."

"Tantrums my ass," he said. "You *will* not do this to me again, Lillian."

He crossed his arms, huffed, then seemed to notice me for the first time. Judging by his sour face he must not have been impressed by my rugged manliness.

"This must be Mr. Wonderful," he said.

"Dr. Wonderful," I corrected. "Ph.D., Berkeley, '91."

"Har-de-har."

How can you fight against lines like "har-de-har"? I looked back at Lillian.

"Beau," she said slowly, staring down at her desk, "can we *please* talk about this later?"

Karnau shifted his weight from foot to foot, obviously thinking of the most withering comment he could make. Finally he decided to make a grand silent exit. Arms still crossed, he stormed past me to the front door, slamming it shut behind him.

When Lillian's facial expression told me she had depressurized I came over to the desk. I waited.

"Sorry," she said. "That, of course, was Beau."

"Your great inspiration," I remembered. "Your biggest fan. Your ticket to—"

She cut me off with a look. "Things change."

"Mm. My finely honed deductive skills tell me he was slightly miffed at you."

She sat on the edge of her desk and made a dismissive gesture. "He's been getting like that over a lot of things."

"You want to say what?"

She gave me a tired smile. "Nothing. I mean I didn't want to get you involved in this yet. It's just—I've decided to pull out of the business. I want to do my own work full-time, without Beau. I'm getting tired of selling to vacationing Midwesterners."

"It's about time."

She took my hand. "I figured the time was right, after we talked last night. Time to get back on track in a lot of ways."

I came closer. After a few minutes Lillian's mood had improved enough for her to give me a tour of the gallery.

They specialized, she told me, in "Border Morbid." The main room was devoted to ceramic Day of the Dead sculptures by artists from Laredo and Piedras Negras. There were skeletons playing guitar, skeletons making love, mother skeletons nursing baby skeletons in cribs. Every scene was thickly glazed in primary colors, hideous and comical.

"I've been saving this one for you, Tres," Lillian said.

The statuette was tucked away on a corner podium—a dead man's road trip. The skeletal driver had his arm around his skeletal girlfriend. They were both grinning of course, holding up miniature tequila bottles as they careened along in a bright orange car that looked suspiciously like my Volkswagen.

"Lovely," I said. "So this is the way you remember our road trips?"

Lillian stared at it without replying, a little sad. Then she smiled at me.

"Take it," she said. "A housewarming gift. At least this car won't break down on you."

"We are not amused," I grumbled.

I let her wrap it up in tissue paper for me anyway. If nothing else it would be good for scaring the bejesus out of Robert Johnson.

Beau came back with a salad-in-a-box forty-five minutes later. He had gone from inflamed to smoldering, but still said very little. He just nodded when Lillian said she was leaving early.

When we got back to Lillian's house that afternoon a new silver BMW had pulled up over the lawn and parked sideways across her driveway. A well-built blond man in a disheveled Christian Dior suit was sitting on the trunk, waiting.

He'd put on a few pounds since high school but it was definitely Dan Sheff, former water polo team captain for the fighting Alamo Heights Mules, heir to the multimillion-dollar Sheff Construction empire, jilted ex-hunk of Miss Lillian Cambridge. By the angle of his tie it was fairly easy to see that he'd gotten a little too happy at happy hour. It was also obvious he was not there to welcome me to town.

7

"I want to talk to you," he said, meaning me.

Dan was speaking clearly enough but he was listing slightly to port. Lillian had gotten out of the car first and was standing in front of him with her hands out. It was hard to tell whether she was trying to hold him back or catch him if he fell.

"I think I've got a right to talk to him," Dan told her.

"This isn't fair, Dan," Lillian said.

"You're damn right."

She was trying to corral him back toward the BMW, but he wouldn't move. He looked at her and for a few seconds his expression wavered between angry and injured. He put out his hands.

"Lillian—"

"No, Dan!" she said. "I want you to go."

The Rodriguez brothers next door were out on their porch, drinking beer in their tank tops and swim trunks. They watched us, grinning. One circled his temple with his finger and said something in Spanish I couldn't catch. The other one laughed.

I touched Lillian on the shoulder.

"I can talk to Dan if he wants," I said.

She looked back at me, her face incredulous. "Tres, no. I mean, you don't have to do that. Dan, leave now."

She pushed him back. He wobbled a little but didn't fall over.

"I'm not leaving until I get my say," he said.

Dan and I looked at Lillian.

"I don't believe this," she snapped. She gave us both a withering scowl as she retreated toward the house, then slammed the screen door behind her. One of the Rodriguez brothers opened a new beer.

"I just want to know something." Dan rubbed the side of his face with two fingers that had gold rings the size of walnuts. "I want to know what makes you think that you can come back to town after ten fucking years and act like you're Christ Descended. You ditch this town, you ditch Lillian, you run away from the whole fucking scene, and then you come back and expect everything to be waiting for you just like it was. You ever heard of burned bridges, Navarre?"

Sheff was getting warmed up now, almost sober. As he talked he got faster and angrier, slapping one hand into the other to make his point. His perfectly combed hair had come unraveled, one little curl hanging down in his face Superman style.

"You want an answer?" I said.

"Some of us stayed in town, man. Some of us don't run away from people we care about. We've been building something, Lillian and me, for six months now. What the hell gives you the right to come out of nowhere and stomp on that now?"

I thought about what to say to that. Nothing came to mind.

"You're pathetic," Dan said. "You can't make a life for yourself out there; go someplace else and leave us alone. You don't get another chance here."

I exhaled, looking over at the Rodriguezes, who seemed highly entertained, then back at Dan.

"Pathetic might be a little strong," I said.

"Fuck you."

"Lillian called me, Dan," I said, trying to keep my voice even. "Not the other way around. If you were building something, I think it was collapsing way before I got here."

In itself, that didn't strike me as that much of an insult, but there were at least two months of pent-up anger in Dan's first punch. I admit I wasn't ready for it. It caught me square in the stomach.

You don't ever want to fight an emotionally distraught person, especially one who's in good physical shape. What they lose in coordination they gain in power and unpredictability. When he hit me I had to ignore the nausea and the instinct to double over in order to avoid a haymaker swing that would've caught me in the head.

I slid down under the punch on my left leg, a little awkwardly, and used my right leg to knock Dan off his feet with a sweep-kick. He didn't know to roll, so he fell on his back pretty hard.

I got up and backed away. My gut felt like a piece of sheet metal that was hardening as it cooled.

Dan scrambled up and started toward me. I held up my palms, offering a truce.

"This is stupid, Dan," I said.

He tried one more punch but this time I was ready for it. I stepped out of the way and let him punch air. After that he just stood there for a minute, breathing heavily.

"God damn it," he said. "You got no right."

He turned and started back toward his car. From the way he walked, his lower back must've been in a lot of pain.

The windows of his BMW were tinted almost black, so it was only when Dan opened the door that I saw the older woman with bright gold hair sitting in the passenger seat. Her face rested in her left hand as if in total mortification. As the door slammed Dan was growling to her: "Don't start!"

Then he drove over half the Rodriguezes' front lawn

and over the curb getting back on the street. The BMW swerved slowly down Acacia like a drunk shark. The Rodriguez brothers looked at me and grinned, raising their beer cans in a salute.

Lillian was in her bedroom, pretending to read.

"Just a little man-to-man talk?" she asked coldly. "Did you mark off your territory for him?"

"Lillian—" I started. I stopped, realizing I sounded like Dan had a few minutes before.

She threw down her magazine. "I don't like being told to go to my room while the big fellas fight it out, Tres."

"You're right. I should've let you handle it."

"You think I couldn't have?"

No answer would've worked, so I didn't try one.

She got up and looked out the window. Finally, she walked over to me and put her arms around my waist. Her eyes were still angry.

"Look, Tres, this hasn't been a real great day for me. I think I need a hot bath and a night alone with a book."

"I love you," I said.

She kissed me as lightly as you'd kiss a Bible.

"I think we should talk more tomorrow," she said quietly. "I don't want any more surprises from my past."

I closed the front door quietly on my way out.

Back at home, I checked my newly installed answering machine. Mother had called twice, upset that I hadn't given her a report yet on my first date with Lillian. Bob Langston had left a cryptic message threatening me with bodily harm and legal action.

I unwrapped the ceramic skeleton-driven car Lillian had given me and put it down on the carpet in front of Robert Johnson. He hissed at it, puffing up his tail as thick as a raccoon's, then walked backward into the closet, still staring at the new monstrosity.

Two days back home and I'd managed to mess up my fragile relationship with Lillian, aggravate my mother, traumatize my cat, and make at least three new enemies.

"Just about par," I told myself.

There was only one other thing I could possibly stir up to make myself feel worse. I called directory assistance and asked for Carl Kelley, retired deputy sheriff, my dead father's best friend.

8

"I'll be damned," he said. "I never thought I'd hear from you again, son."

Years of smoking hadn't been kind to Carl Kelley's voice. Every word sounded like it was being scraped across a metal file as it left his throat.

Before I could tell him why I had called, he began a long gravelly sentence without periods, telling me about all the people he and my father had known who were now either dead, in the hospital, or afflicted in their old age with ungrateful children. I got the feeling Carl was living alone now and probably hadn't gotten a phone call in a long time. I let him talk.

One of God's little jokes: as soon as I had reached Carl on the phone the TV program somehow switched from baseball coverage to a rerun of Buckner Fanning's morning sermon from Trinity Baptist. I had dragged the phone across the living room as far as the cord would reach and was now trying to reach the television controls with my foot, hoping I could either turn the set off or find another channel. So far Buckner was thwarting my efforts. Tan and immaculately dressed, he was smiling and admonishing me to accept God.

"Yeah," I said to Carl at the appropriate moments. "That sounds pretty bad." After a while Carl presented me with an opening. He asked me what I was doing back in town.

"If I were to want some case files on Dad's death, who would I talk to?"

A long pull on a cigarette. A rumbly cough. "Christ, son. You've come back to look into that?"

"No," I said. "But maybe now I could read about it fresh, more objectively, maybe put it behind me."

I could hear him blow smoke into the receiver.

"Not a week goes by I don't see him in my sleep," Carl said, "lying there like that."

We both got quiet. I thought about that eternal five minutes between the time my father had fallen to the ground and the first paramedic unit had arrived, when we'd stood there, Carl and I, watching the groceries roll down the sidewalk with the lines of blood. I'd been completely frozen. Carl had been the opposite. He'd started pacing, rambling about what Jack and he had been planning on doing that weekend, how the hunting was going to be, what Aggie jokes Jack had told him the night before. All the while he was wiping away tears, lighting and crushing cigarettes one after the other. A jar of jelly had rolled into the crook of my father's arm and nestled there like a teddy bear.

"I don't know about putting it behind you," Carl said.

Buckner Fanning started telling me about his latest trip to the Holy City of Jerusalem.

"Who would I talk to to see the files, Carl?"

"It's in-house, son. And it's been too long. It just ain't done that way."

"But if it was?"

Carl exhaled into my ear. "You remember Drapiewski? Larry Drapiewski? Made deputy lieutenant about a year ago."

"What about for SAPD?"

He had a coughing fit for a minute, then cleared his throat.

"I'd try Kingston in Criminal Investigations, if he's still there. He was always in debt to Jack for one favor or another. There was an FBI review of the case a few years back too. I can't help you there."

I remembered neither Drapiewski nor Kingston, but it was a place to start.

"Thanks, Carl."

"Yeah well, sorry I can't help much. I thought you were my son calling from Austin. He ain't called in over a month, you know. For a minute there, you sounded like him."

"Take care of yourself, Carl."

"Nice way to spend an afternoon," he said. "You kept me talking all the way up to *60 Minutes*."

I hung up. I couldn't help picturing Carl Kelley, sitting in some house alone, a cigarette in his withered hand, living for television shows and a phone call from Austin that never came. I sat for a minute, Robert Johnson instantly on my lap, and we watched Buckner talk about spiritual healing. Then I turned off the set.

9

"Little Tres?" Larry Drapiewski laughed. "Jesus, not the same seven-year-old kid who used to sit on my desk and eat the custard out of the middle of my donuts."

As soon as he said that I had a vague memory of Drapiewski—a large man, flat-topped red hair, friendly smile, a sweating face that looked like the Martian landscape. His big hands always full of food.

"Yeah," I said, "only twenty years and a lot of donuts later nobody calls me 'little.' "

"Join the club," the lieutenant said. "So what's on your mind?"

When I told him why I was calling he was quiet for an uncomfortable amount of time. An oscillating fan on his desk hummed back and forth into the receiver.

"You understand everybody has looked at this," Larry said. "Half the departments in town, the county, the FBI. Everybody wanted a piece of this. You want to find something that nobody's caught before, it isn't going to happen."

"Does that mean you won't help?"

"I didn't say that."

I heard papers being moved around on the other end of the line. Finally Larry swore under his breath.

"Where's a pen?" he asked somebody. Then to me: "Let me have your number, Tres."

I gave it to him.

"Okay," he said. "Give me a couple of days."

"Thanks, Larry."

"And, Tres—this is a personal favor. Let's just keep it personal."

"You got it."

He cleared his throat. "Yeah, well, I owed your dad a lot. It's just that the Sheriff is sensitive to taxpayer dollars being used on, let's say, nonessential work. It also doesn't help if it's about one of his predecessors who beat him in three straight elections, you know what I mean?"

I checked with SAPD next. After a few minutes of being transferred from line to line, I finally got Detective Schaeffer, who sounded like he'd just woken up from a nap. He told me Ian Kingston, formerly with Criminal Investigations, had moved to Seattle two years ago and was presently overseeing a large private security firm. Kingston's ex-partner, David Epcar, was presently overseeing a small burial plot in the Sunset Cemetery.

"Wonderful," I said.

Schaeffer yawned so loud it sounded like somebody was vacuuming his mouth.

"What was your name again?" he asked.

I told him.

"Like in Jackson Navarre, the county sheriff that got killed?"

"Yeah."

He grunted, evidently sitting up in his chair.

"That was the biggest pain in the ass we've had since Judge Woods took a hit," he said. "Fucking circus."

It wasn't exactly a show of sympathetic interest. Seeing as I was out of other options, however, and had to say something before the detective fell back asleep, I decided to give Schaeffer my best song and dance. Much to my surprise, he didn't hang up on me.

"Huh. Call me back in a week or so, Navarre. If I get a chance to look at the files, maybe you can ask me some questions."

"That's mighty white of you, Detective."

I think he was snoring before his receiver hit the cradle.

By sunset it still wasn't cool enough to run without getting heat stroke. I settled for fifty push-ups and stomach crunches in the living room, then held horse stance and bow stance for ten minutes each. Robert Johnson lounged across the cool linoleum in the kitchen and watched. Afterward I lay flat on my back with my muscles burning, letting the air conditioner dry the sweat off my body and listening to the dying hum of the cicadas outside. Robert Johnson crawled onto my chest and sat there looking down at me, his eyes half-closed.

"Good workout?" I asked.

He yawned.

I unpacked a few boxes, drank a few beers, watched the fireflies floating around in Gary Hales's backyard at dusk. I tried to convince myself I wasn't fighting any kind of compulsion to call Lillian. Give her some time. No problem. It was just a coincidence that I kept staring at the phone.

I started digging through my box of books until I found Lillian's letters wedged in between the Snopes family and the rest of Yoknapatawpha County. I read them all, from her first in May to the one that had arrived last Thursday, just as I was packing. Reading them made me feel much worse.

Irritated, I dug around in the box some more, looking for some lighter reading material—Kafka maybe, or an account of the Black Plague. What I found instead was my father's scrapbook.

It was a huge canvas-covered three-ring binder stuffed with just about every insignificant piece of writing he'd ever scribbled but was too lazy to throw away. There were yellowed drawings he'd done for me when I was five or six—stick figures of armies and airplanes that he'd used to illustrate his drunken Korean bedtime stories to me. There were letters that had never been mailed to friends who had long since died. There were pages of notes on old cases he'd been pursuing that meant nothing to me. There were grocery lists.

I still have no idea why I'd taken the scrapbook from his desk after the funeral, or why I'd kept it, or why I decided to look at it again now, but I sat down on the futon with it now and started flipping through. In several places I'd dog-eared interesting pages, most of which I'd forgotten about. One of them caught my attention.

A yellowed piece of spiral paper, the kind of scrap my dad was always leaving around the house, filled with rambling reminders to himself. It appeared to be a list of notes for a trial testimony he was making against Guy White, a suspected local drug trafficker. Then at the bottom it said: *Sabinal. Get whiskey. Fix fence. Clean fireplace.*

This page had bothered me the first time I read it and it bothered me now, though I wasn't sure why. It wasn't just Guy White's name. I remembered White's drug trial vaguely, then later some speculation that White's mob connections might have been behind my father's murder, but Dad's testimony notes revealed no shocking secrets. The seven words Dad had scrawled at the bottom of the page bothered me more. They sounded like a reminder of what to do next time we went to the family ranch outside Sabinal. Except we only went to Sabinal at Christmas, for deer season, and the notes were written in April, a month before Dad died.

I finished off my six-pack of Shiner Bock while I read, and felt almost grateful when my father's shaky cursive started to blur.

I'm not sure when I actually fell asleep, but when I woke up it was full dark and the phone was ringing. I almost impaled myself on the ironing board trying to get to the receiver.

"Hello—" I said. My mind was fuzzy, but I could hear the sounds of a bar in the background—glasses clinking, men talking in both Spanish and English, a jukebox playing Freddy Fender. No one said anything into the receiver. I waited. So did the caller. He waited much too long for a typical prankster, or an honestly confused drunk with a wrong number.

"Leave," he said. Then the line went dead.

Of course it was just the fact that I was half-asleep, probably still half-drunk, and that I'd been thinking about things way too much. But the man's voice sounded familiar to me. It sounded a little like my father.

10

The next morning I made the mistake of practicing tai chi sword in the backyard. By nine o'clock I had served as breakfast for a small army of mosquitoes and scared the neighbors half to death. The woman next door came outside in a blue terry-cloth bathrobe around eight-thirty, dropped her coffee cup when she saw me swinging the blade, then went back in and locked the door. She left the coffee cup broken on the back porch. Across the alley, two pairs of large dark eyes were following my movements cautiously through the miniblinds on the second floor. Finally Gary Hales shuffled out in his pajamas and asked me, in a listless voice, what I was doing. He might've been sleepwalking for all I could tell.

I stopped to catch my breath.

"It's a kind of exercise," I said.

He blinked slowly, looking at the sword. "With big knives?"

"Sort of. It makes you exercise very carefully."

"I reckon so."

He scratched behind his ear. Maybe he was trying to remember why he'd come outside.

"You think maybe it's better if I don't practice out here?" I suggested.

"I reckon maybe," he agreed.

Before I went inside, I looked up at the people behind the miniblinds and pretended to stab at them with the sword. The lifted slat flicked down instantly.

After a shower I tried Lillian's number and got her answering machine. I figured she was in transit to work, so I tried an old number for Carlon McAffrey at the *Express-News*.

I was bounced back to the main operator for the newspaper, who told me Carlon was now working for the Friday entertainment section. She transferred the call.

"Yo," McAffrey answered.

"Yo?" I said. "Is that the way all you slick entertainment writers answer the phone, or do you just have trouble with words over one syllable?"

It took him three beats to place the voice.

"Navarre, do the words 'piss off' mean anything to you?"

"Not when you hear them as often as I do."

"Hang on," he said.

He covered the phone for a second and yelled at someone in his office.

"Okay," he said. "So where the flying fuck have you been the last decade or so?"

Carlon and I had been in high school together, then had worked for the A & M newspaper in college. He'd played the star journalist while I, one of the very few human beings ever to major in both English and physical education, had written a sports editorial column. Young and stupid, we drank to excess and terrorized the cows of Brian, Texas, by pushing them down hills while they slept with their legs locked. After I moved out to California my sophomore year we had eventually lost touch.

"Believe it or not," I said, "I'm back here seeing Lillian."

Carlon whistled. "Sandy over at the society page is going to love that. She's been getting a lot of mileage out of Lillian and ole Dan the Man Sheff lately."

"You put my picture on the same page as the debutantes and I'll rip your nuts off."

"I love you too," he said. "So why the warm and friendly call, if not to fill me in on your romance?"

"Tell me about the newspaper morgue. I'm looking for information on my father's murder and the investigation."

"Mm. That was what, '84?"

" '85."

He asked someone behind him a question I couldn't catch.

"Yeah," he told me, "anything before 1988 is still on microfiche. After that we joined the computer age. Public access, but it would be a lot faster if I got one of the mole people down in Archives to round it up for you."

"That would be great, Carlon."

"So you owe me. What else is new? Now tell me why you're digging up family history, Navarre. I thought you wanted nothing to do with that."

The tone of his voice told me the question was more professional than personal.

"Ten years makes a difference," I said. "Especially if I'm back here to stay."

"You got something new on the case?"

"Nothing that would work for the entertainment section."

"I'm serious, Tres. You got anything on the case, I'd like to know."

"This from a man whose biggest scoop in college was a breakthrough in onion-growing technology."

"Some friend," Carlon said, and hung up.

I tried Lillian's studio and got Beau Karnau instead. At first he pretended not to remember me. Finally he admitted that Lillian was not in.

"When do you expect her?" I asked.

"Day after tomorrow."

I was silent for a moment. "I don't think I got that."

"Yes you did," Beau said. I pictured him smirking—it wasn't a pretty image. "She went on a buying trip to Laredo, left a message on the studio machine this morning. I might add it's the least she can do after stabbing me in the back like she's doing."

"Yeah, you might add that, mightn't you?"

"The least she can do. Drops everything in my lap, thinks she can actually make a living—"

He had more to say but I put the receiver down on the ironing board. He might be talking to himself for hours before he figured out I was no longer there.

When my mind started aching this bad I knew it was time to abuse my body instead. I put on running shorts and a Bay to Breakers T-shirt, then headed down New Braunfels toward the Botanical Center. The really hot part of the day was yet to come, but after two miles I was drenched in sweat. I found a little stand that sold coconut *paletas* and bought one, letting the icy chunks of fruit slide down my throat as I sat in the shade of a pecan tree near the entrance to Fort Sam Houston.

I stared across at the army base, wondering if Bob Langston was in there somewhere, laughing about a prank call he'd made to me last night. I hoped that was the case.

When I got back to Queen Anne the phone was dead from being off the hook so long. Evidently Beau had finally got tired of his own voice. I put the receiver back in the cradle.

I did push-ups and crunches, then decided to tackle cleaning the kitchen. The memory of Bob Langston lived on in the fruit keeper of the refrigerator, where several black bananas had turned into oblong mounds of mush. He'd also left two sandwich bags filled with some kind of meat slices, congealed in what I assume had been a barbecue sauce. Not even Robert Johnson was interested.

The place was looking almost clean by that evening when the phone rang.

"I'm very close to being pissed off," Jay Rivas said. "In fact, I'm downright perturbed, Navarre."

"I'm not a qualified therapist," I warned him. "Maybe there's some kind of inferiority complex for incompetent bald fat men with large mustaches."

"Or maybe there's some kind of asshole who keeps smearing his shit all over town where I have to step in it."

I sighed. "Do you have a point to make, Jay?"

He blew smoke into the phone. "Yeah, kid, I got two points. First, yesterday evening you assault a young man whose family is heavyweight on the Chamber of Commerce. Said young man will not press charges, otherwise you and I would be having this chat in person right now. Second, I hear about you digging for information on a ten-year-old murder, bothering people who have better things to do than help you come to terms with your fucking manhood."

I counted to five before answering. "You're talking about my father's murder. I think I've got a right to know."

"You had a right to know ten years ago," Rivas shot back. "Where the fuck were you when it mattered?"

There were a lot of things I wanted to say to that, but I waited. Finally Rivas swore under his breath.

"Look, Navarre, let me save you some time. *On* the record, nobody can prove who whacked your old man, okay? You're not going to get the goddamn case files, but if you did, that's what they'd tell you. *Off* the record, it's no big secret. Your dad spent the last two years of his life putting thumbscrews on the mob in Bexar County. It's one of the few things he did well. The mob finally hit back. Nobody can prove it; everybody knows it. That's the short and shitty truth, and after all this time nobody's going to do any time for the killing. So unless you got some indisputable reason why this case needs to be looked into again, which you don't, and the goodwill of the SAPD, which I promise you you don't, then you lay off. Go marry your high school sweetheart and get a nice job teaching college somewhere, but stay the hell out of my sight."

He hung up.

I stared at the wall for a while, seeing Jay Rivas's face. I thought about Lillian's sudden trip to Laredo, the way our reunion wasn't quite going as I'd planned, the way Maia Lee had sounded on the phone, and the way people kept sending me these loving phone calls. When I put my fist through the Sheetrock, I missed the stud by less than an inch.

I think it surprised me more than it did Robert Johnson. Clearly unimpressed, he stared up at me from his nest of freshly unpacked clothes on the futon. I checked for broken knuckles.

"Ouch," I told him.

Robert Johnson got up and stretched. Then he showed me the kind of sympathy I was used to. He left the room.

11

Yielding to Robert Johnson's hungry cries Tuesday morning, I walked to Leon "Pappy" Delgado's grocery on the corner of Army and Broadway. The rest of the block had gone up for lease years ago, but it restored some of my sense of universal justice to see Pappy's Christmas lights still blazing around the pink doorway of his dilapidated adobe storefront.

My father, always suspicious of any store larger than two thousand square feet, had been a patron of Pappy's for years, but since I had spoken no Spanish when I left San Antonio and Pappy knew little English, we had never said a word to each other beyond "*Buenos tardes.*"

He was amazed, maybe a little suspicious, when I started talking to him *en Español*. He rubbed his paddle-shaped nose, perplexed, then gave me a crooked grin.

"San Francisco," he said. "You talk just like my wife's brothers now, Señor Tres."

As I searched in vain for Robert Johnson's brand of

food, Pappy told me about his seven boys and two girls. The youngest had just had her confirmation. The oldest was in the Air Force now.

I looked in my wallet after paying for my two small bags of food. It was a sobering moment.

"So what are you doing back in town, Señor Tres?" asked Pappy.

"It would seem," I said, "that I'm looking for a job."

"Always need counter help," Pappy said, grinning.

I promised to keep it in mind.

Back at home, I found the list of leads Maia had given me and started making calls. After an hour on the phone, I had talked to a dozen voice mail services, one receptionist who couldn't spell my name but was free on Saturday night, and two personnel directors who promised not to throw my résumé in the trash if I mailed it in.

"And you say you're a paralegal?" the last man on the list asked me. He had graduated from Berkeley with Maia.

"Not exactly."

"Then—what is it that you do?"

"Research, investigation, I'm bilingual, English Ph.D., martial artist, congenial personality."

I could hear him tapping his pencil.

"Maia employed you for what, then—discussing literature? Breaking arms?"

"You'd be surprised how few people can do both."

"Uh-huh." His enthusiasm was not overwhelming. "Do you have a Texas P.I. license, then?"

"My work for Terrence & Goldman was more informal than that."

"I see—" His voice seemed to be getting farther and farther away from the receiver.

"Did I mention I was a bartender?"

To prove it I started giving him the recipe for a Pink Squirrel. By the time I got to the sugar on the rim he had hung up.

I was taping over the hole in my wall and pondering

my limitless job opportunities when Carlon McAffrey
called from the *Express-News*.

"Shilo's," he said. "One hour. You're buying."

When I got there at one o'clock the little downtown
deli was still packed with businessmen gorging themselves on the pastrami and rye lunch special. The air
was so thick with the smell of spiced meats you could
get full just breathing it.

Carlon waved at me from the counter. He'd put on at
least twenty pounds since I'd seen him last, but I could
still recognize him by his tie. He never wore one with
fewer than twelve colors. This one had enough pastel to
repaint half the West Side.

He smiled and pushed a thick manila envelope across
the counter toward me.

"When the mole people start digging they don't mess
around. I got everything, even some copy from the
Light. We inherited most of their archival material
when they went defunct."

The first thing I pulled out was a picture of my dad,
taken the last year he had campaigned for sheriff. Those
gray, mischievous eyes stared back at me from under the
rim of his Stetson. He had an amused look on his face.

I always wondered how anyone could see a photo
like that and willingly vote this man into public office.
Dad looked like the quintessential third-grade class
clown, only older and fatter. I could imagine him cutting off little girls' ponytails with his school box scissors, or throwing spitwads at the teacher's back.

The counter waitress came by. I decided to skip the
lunch menu and go straight for Shilo's cheesecake, three
layers thick, any of which by itself would've been the
best cheesecake in the world. I ate it while I skimmed
through the rest of Carlon's envelope.

There were lots of headlines about my dad's last big
project in office—a multi-department sting operation
against drug trafficker Guy White that had eventually
gone down as the most expensive failure in Bexar
County law enforcement history. According to the
articles, the case against White was finally thrown out

of court on a ruling of entrapment, just weeks before
my father's murder. Dad won lots of friends on the federal level by telling the press that the FBI had botched
the whole operation.

There was an ongoing series of "guest editorials"
from the *Light* written by another of my father's great
admirers, Councilman Fernando Asante. He blasted my
father for everything from abuse of police power to
poor taste in clothes, but mostly Asante focused on the
Sheriff's opposition to Travis Center, a proposed hotel-
tourist complex for the southeast side of town. Back in
'85 Asante was making Travis Center the centerpiece of
his first campaign for mayor—pushing the idea that the
complex would generate tourist dollars in the poor,
largely Hispanic section of the city. My father opposed
the project because it would require the annexation of
county lands, and more importantly because it was
Asante's idea.

Then there was a report on the fall '85 election
results, which Dad didn't live long enough to see. The
voters showed a healthy sense of humor by voting
against Asante for mayor five to one but approving his
Travis Center bond initiative by a landslide. Now, ten
years and umpteen million dollars later, Asante was still
just a councilman and Travis Center was finally complete. I'd seen it from above on my plane's final
approach—a huge bulbous structure, hideously painted
pink and red, cutting a gash in the hills on the edge of
town like a giant flesh wound.

Finally there were stories about the assassination.
There in black and white were all the front page headlines I had nightmares about, plus pages of follow-ups
I'd never had the stomach to read. The murder scene,
the investigation, the memorial services—all reported
on in microscopic detail. Several articles talked about
Randall Halcomb, the closest thing to a real suspect the
FBI ever discussed in public. An ex-deputy, Halcomb
had been fired by my dad for insubordination in the late
seventies, then arrested in 1980 for manslaughter. Halcomb was paroled from Huntsville a week before my

dad's murder. Convenient. Only by the time the FBI found him, two months after Dad's death, the ex-deputy was curled up in a deer blind in Blanco, shot between the eyes. Inconvenient.

The last thing in Carlon's files was a photo of my father's body covered with a blanket, his hand sticking out the side like it was reaching for a beer, while a grim-faced deputy held up his hand to block the camera, a little too slow.

I resealed the envelope. Then I stared at the neon beer signs over the bar until I realized Carlon was talking to me.

"—this personal vengeance theory," he was saying, "just some ex-con with a score to settle. That's bullshit. Christ, if Halcomb was acting alone, how come he turned up with a bullet between his eyes once the Feds start looking for him?"

I ate a piece of cheesecake. Suddenly it tasted like lead.

"You've been doing your homework, McAffrey. You stay up last night reading these?"

Carlon shrugged. "I'm just saying. There had to be a cover-up here."

"Maybe that's the journalist in you talking."

"My ass. Your dad was murdered and nobody ever did time for it. Not even a fucking trial. I'm just trying to help."

Years of good living had softened Carlon's face a little, but you could still see the hard edge in his smile. His eyes were cold and blue. There was energy there, self-confidence, a harsh kind of humor. Nothing that might pass for compassion. He was still the same college kid who pushed cows down hills for fun and laughed shamelessly at racial jokes and broken limbs. He came through for his friends. He probably meant what he said about helping. But if you couldn't use it for fun or profit it meant very little to Carlon McAffrey.

"Halcomb had his own motive," I reminded him. "Assuming he's the one who did the shooting, he wouldn't have needed anyone pulling his strings."

Carlon shook his head. "My money's on the mob. My sources at the SAPD tell me I'm right."

"I heard that from the SAPD too. Doesn't exactly inspire my confidence."

"Your dad died right after he brought Guy White in for trafficking, Tres. Don't tell me that was coincidence."

"Why should the mob target a retiring sheriff? That would be pointless. The charges against White had already been thrown out."

Carlon wiped a piece of sauerkraut off his cheek. He was looking over my shoulder now, toward the booths on the east wall of the restaurant.

"Good question," he said. "Go ask him."

"Who?"

Carlon pointed with the bottom of his beer bottle. "Guy White, man."

The booth Carlon was pointing at had two men in it. The one with his back toward me was a skinny, middle-aged Anglo whose mother dressed him funny. His slacks rode up at the ankles, his beige suit coat was too big around the shoulders, and his thinning brown hair was uncombed. He had finished his meal and was now tapping a quarter slice of pickle absently on his plate.

The man sitting across from him was much older, much more carefully dressed. I'd never seen Guy White in person, but if this was him the only thing white about him was the name. His skin was carefully bronzed, his suit light blue, his hair and eyes as rich and dark as mole sauce. He had to be the best-looking man over sixty I'd ever seen. Mr. White was about halfway through with a club sandwich and appeared to be in no hurry to finish the rest. He was chatting with the waitress, smiling a Colgate smile at her, gesturing every so often toward his associate across the table. The waitress laughed politely. Mr. White's poorly dressed friend did not.

"He comes in here twice a week to be seen," Carlon told me. "Clean-nosed celebrity these days—bailed the symphony out of bankruptcy, goes to the Alamodome for all the games, supports the arts, gets his picture taken with Manuel Flores at charity garden shows.

Gone downright respectable. If something new came up in your dad's case, something that screwed White's public image to hell, that'd make a nice story."

I shook my head. "You expect me to walk over there right now and confront him?"

"Where's that old college try? The Tres Navarre *I* knew would go up to an ROTC captain during live ammunition practice and tell him his girlfriend—"

"This is a little different, Carlon."

"You want *me* to do it?"

He started to get up. I pushed on his shoulder just enough to sit him back down on his stool.

"What then?" Carlon said. "You asked me for the files. You must have some kind of theory."

I took one more bite of cheesecake. Then I stood, put the manila envelope under my arm, and left my last twenty on the counter.

"Thanks for the info, Carlon," I said.

"Suit yourself," he said. "But you want this thing covered in a friendly way, you know where to come."

I looked back at him one more time as I left. He had pocketed my twenty and was ordering another beer on the *Express*'s expense account. For a minute I wondered why he had never gone into straight news reporting. He seemed disturbingly well suited for it. Then it occurred to me that he was probably thriving right where he was, catering to the interests and appetites of the city in the entertainment section. That thought was even more unsettling.

12

Twenty minutes later I'd reparked my VW at the top of the Commerce Street Garage, one row down from the dark green Infiniti J-30 in Guy White's reserved monthly space.

I knew White parked in the garage because it was the only logical place to park if you're going to Shilo's. I knew he had a regular space because ten minutes earlier a nice parking attendant had shown me the list of monthly parkers. In fact he'd shoved it in my face, exasperated, trying to convince me that *my* name, Ed Beavis, was *not* registered. Normally I would've bribed him for the information I needed, but poverty makes for creative alternatives.

A few more minutes of waiting and the elevator door shuddered open. Mr. White's skinny associate in the ill-fitting beige suit walked out first, bouncing car keys in his right palm. He wasn't any handsomer from the front. His face had that sandblasted look farmers tend to get—dark pitted skin, permanently squinting eyes, features worn down to nothing but right angles. Mr.

White strolled a few steps behind, reading a folded newspaper in one hand and smiling contentedly like there was nothing in there but good words.

We started our cars. Making no effort to hang back, I followed the Infiniti out of the garage, then onto Commerce and east for a mile to the highway. I couldn't see anything through the silvered rear window of Guy White's car, but once in a while my friend the driver would glance back at me in his sideview mirror.

Tailing someone well is extremely hard. It's rare that you can strike the right balance between being far enough away to look inconspicuous and being close enough not to lose the subject. A full ninety percent of the time you'll lose the person you're tailing because of traffic or stoplights, nothing you can do about it. Then you have to try, try again, sometimes for seven or eight days.

That, of course, is assuming you don't want to be seen. Tailing someone badly is very easy.

When I got about fifteen feet behind the Infiniti in the center lane of McAlister, the driver looked in his side mirror and frowned. I smiled at him. He said something to his boss in the backseat.

If they'd sped up they could've easily left me in the dust, but they didn't. I guess one guy in an orange Volkswagen wasn't their idea of terrifying. The Infiniti kept cruising at an easy fifty mph, finally taking the Hildebrand Exit and turning left onto the overpass. I followed it into Olmos Park.

Mansions started rising out of the woods and hills. Bankers' wives jogged by in warm-up suits that cost more than my car. The natives seemed to smell my VW as it went by. It looked like their noses weren't pleased.

We passed my father's old house. We passed the police station. Then we turned off Olmos Drive onto Crescent and the Infiniti pulled into the red brick driveway of a residence I knew only by reputation: the White House.

It wasn't just called that because of the man who lived there. The facade was an exact replica—wraparound porches, Grecian columns, even the U.S. flag. It was an egomaniac's dream, except the whole building was scaled down to about half the size of the original. Still impressive, but after you looked at it for a while, it somehow seemed pathetic. It was a Volvo trying to look like a Mercedes, a Herradura bottle filled with Happy Amigo tequila.

I pulled over on the opposite side of the road, where the cactus and wild mountain laurels sloped down toward an old creek bed. The driver of the Infiniti got out and started walking toward me. Mr. White got out next. He brushed some invisible speck off his powder-blue suit, then folded his newspaper under his arm and began walking leisurely toward his front door, not looking back.

The skinny guy came down the presidential lawn and across the street. He put his right hand on the side of the car and leaned in toward me. When his coat fell open I got a pretty good view of the .38 Airweight in the shoulder holster.

"Trouble?" he asked. The number of vowels and syllables he packed into that one word told me he was a West Texas boy, probably hailed from Lubbock.

"No trouble." I gave him a winning smile.

Lubbock ran his tongue around his lips. He leaned in closer and gave me a short laugh. "I'm not asking if you *got* trouble, mister, I'm asking if you *want* it."

I feigned bewilderment, pointing to my own chest. Lubbock's face turned into one big sour pucker.

"Shit," he said, a three-syllable word. "You a retard, mister? What the hell you want following us like that?"

I tried another dashing smile. "How about a few minutes of Mr. White's time?"

"That's about as likely as pig shit."

"Tell Mr. White that Sheriff Navarre's son is here to see him. I think he'll agree to talk."

If the name Navarre meant anything to Lubbock, he didn't show it. "I don't give a damn whose damn son you are, mister. You'd best get out of here before I decide—"

"You've never been a highway patrolman."

He scowled. It didn't improve his looks any. "What?"

Before he knew what had happened, I'd grabbed the handle of his .38 Airweight and twisted it, still in its holster, so the barrel was angled into the side of Lubbock's chest. His arms jerked up instinctively, like he was suddenly anxious for his armpit deodorant to dry. All the tight lines in Lubbock's face loosened and most of his color seemed to drain into his neck.

"When you're stopping somebody in a car," I explained very patiently, "you never wear a shoulder holster. Much too easy to reach."

Lubbock raised his hands, slowly. His mouth was twitching in the corner.

"I'll be goddamned," he said. Too many syllables to count.

I got the Airweight free of its holster, then opened the car door. Lubbock stepped back to let me out. He was smiling in earnest now, looking at the gun I had leveled at his chest.

"That's the ballsiest son-of-a-bitch move I've seen in a while, mister. I'll be damned if it wasn't. You just put yourself in so much deep shit you don't even know."

"Let's go see about getting you that raise," I suggested.

The front door was painted white, with a bathtub-sized piece of beveled glass in the center. Lubbock led me through into a spacious entry hall, then left to a pair of double oak doors and into a private study. Somewhere along the way he must've pressed a security buzzer with his foot, but I never saw it.

Things were going very well until the guy behind the coat rack clicked the safety of his gun off and stuck a few inches of barrel in my neck.

Lubbock turned around and repossessed his .38 Airweight. He never stopped grinning. The man behind me stayed perfectly still. I didn't try to turn.

"Good afternoon," I said. "Is Mr. White at home?"

"Good afternoon," the man behind me said. His voice came out smooth as honey over a sopapilla. "Mr.

White is at home. In fact, Mr. White is about to kill you if you don't explain yourself rather quickly."

I put my hand over my shoulder, offering to shake.

"Jackson Navarre," I said. "The Third."

I counted to five. I thought that was it. I started to make peace with Jesus, the Tao, and my credit card agencies, then I heard the safety click back on. Guy White took my hand.

"Why didn't you say so?" he asked.

13

"Would you pass me the Blue Princess, Mr. Navarre?"

Guy White pointed with his trowel to the flat of baby plants he wanted. I passed them over.

For his gardening ensemble, White had changed into a newly-pressed denim shirt with the sleeves rolled up, Calvin Klein jeans, huaraches on his perfectly tanned feet. He'd traded the 9mm Glock for pruners and trowel. Shadows from the brim of his wicker hat crisscrossed his face like Maori tattoos as he knelt over a five-foot plot of dirt, digging little conical holes for his new babies.

Next to me on the hot stone bench, a jar of sun tea Guy White had brought out with us ten minutes before was already dark amber. Sweat was starting to trickle down my back. My butt felt like a fried tortilla. I looked longingly at the nearby patio, shaded with pecan trees, then at the swimming pool, then at Guy White, who was smiling contentedly and humming along with the drone of the cicadas and not sweating at all.

I'd liked him better when he was holding a gun on me.

"I'm quite excited about these," he told me. He broke one plastic container off the flat of plants and turned it upside down to shake the roots loose. "Do you know about gardening, Mr. Navarre?"

"It's not my specialty. That's some kind of verbena?"

"Very good."

"It was associated with sorcerers in medieval times." White looked pleased. "Is that so?"

He carefully placed the verbena into its new home and patted down the dirt. The little clusters of flowers were cotton candy blue. They matched Mr. White's ensemble perfectly.

"This is the first year the Blue Princess variety is available," he explained. "From England. It's only being offered commercially in South Texas. Quite an opportunity."

I wiped the back of my neck. "You always do your planting in the middle of the afternoon?"

White laughed. When he sat back on his heels I realized for the first time what a large man he was. Even with me sitting and him kneeling we were almost eye level.

"Verbena is a hearty plant, Mr. Navarre. It looks delicate but it demands full sunlight, aggressive pruning, well-drained soil. This is the best time to plant it. Many people make the mistake of pampering their verbena, you see—they're afraid to cut the blooms, they overwater or overshade. Treat verbena with gentleness and it mildews, Mr. Navarre. One can't be afraid to be aggressive."

"Is that your business philosophy too? Is that the way it was ten years ago?"

Not a wrinkle marred Guy White's face. His smile was the smile of the Redeemed, of a man with no troubles in this world or the next. "I think, Mr. Navarre, that you may be operating under some faulty assumptions."

I spread my hands. "It wouldn't be the first time. Maybe you could set me straight?"

"If I can." His digging had uprooted a six-inch earthworm, and when White stabbed his trowel into the dirt it cut the worm neatly in half. White didn't seem to notice. He removed his leather gloves and took a long drink from his glass of ice tea before speaking. "I had nothing to do with your father's death, my boy."

"I feel better already."

White shook his head. "I'm afraid if you've inherited Sheriff Navarre's stubbornness there's little point in our talking."

"He made your life uncomfortable for several years. There are plenty of people who still say you got away with his murder."

White pulled his gloves back on and started troweling the second row of Blue Princess. Under the shadow of his hat brim, his pleasant smile didn't waver at all. "I've been the convenient answer for many criminal questions in the past, Mr. Navarre. I'm aware of that."

"In the past."

"Exactly. Would you hand me the 19-5-9, please?"

"Pardon?"

"The fertilizer, my boy, next to your foot. You may not know that in recent years I've done my best to give back to the community. I'm pleased to be thought of as a good citizen, a patron for many causes. I've been actively cultivating that role, and I much prefer it to the undeserved reputation I had in my younger days."

"I'm sure. Murdering, drug dealing—hardly the sort of thing you can talk about at the Kiwanis Club."

White stabbed his trowel back into the dirt, up to the handle this time. He was still smiling when he looked up, but the lines around his eyes revealed just a bit of frayed patience.

"I want you to understand me, Mr. Navarre. Your father never made my life as difficult as it was after he died, when I was subjected to all sorts of scrutiny, all sorts of witch-hunters looking for someone to blame for his murder. I've worked for many years since then to build back my position in the community, and I am not anxious to have that position compromised with groundless speculation that should have been put to rest long ago. I hope I'm being clear?"

While White was talking, Lubbock had ambled across the lawn. He was now standing respectfully a few yards away, holding a cell phone and waiting to be summoned forward. White let him wait.

"Do we understand each other?" White asked me, very quietly.

I nodded. "How was it you used to kill your rivals, anyway—bullets through the eyes? I forgot."

For an instant White's face froze. Then, slowly, his smile rebuilt itself. He let out his breath. "You really are a great deal like your father, my boy. I wish you luck."

He almost sounded sincere. It wasn't exactly the response I'd been expecting.

"Maybe you should be trying to help me, then," I suggested.

White ignored the comment. He got up and brushed the dirt off his Calvin Klein's, then seemed to notice Lubbock standing there for the first time.

"Ah," he said, "now if you'll excuse me, my boy, I must take this call. Emery here will see you out."

Emery handed Mr. White the phone and nodded for me to follow him inside. I got up from the stone bench.

"Mr. White," I said.

White had already dismissed me. He was chatting pleasantly with his caller about the weather in Vera Cruz. Now he looked back, taking the phone away from his ear.

"Just so you understand me: If you're lying, if you killed my father, I'll personally mulch you into your own garden."

He smiled as if I'd wished him happy birthday. "I'm sure you will, my boy. Good day."

Then he turned away, unconcerned, and resumed his phone conversation about the pros and cons of Mexican real estate. He walked into his garden.

Emery looked at me and laughed once. He patted me on the back like we were old friends, then led me back toward the White House.

14

"Now *this* I like," my mother said.

She had come over to the apartment around eight o'clock, minus Jess, who was watching the Rangers game. For five minutes she'd commented on my new home's "interesting Spartan look," sprayed essential oil to cleanse the place's aura, and looked around halfheartedly for anything she could compliment. Finally she'd spotted the Mexican statuette Lillian had given me.

The minute Mother picked it up, Robert Johnson hissed and backed into the closet again. Looking at the statue, thinking about my last talk with Lillian, I had a similar reaction.

"I think he wants you to have it," I said. "It fits your decor better anyway."

Mother's green eyes sparkled mischievously. She dropped the statuette into her massive gold lamé purse. "I'll trade you for dinner, dear."

Then we walked down to the corner of Queen Anne and Broadway.

Sad but true. I'd lived in San Francisco for years, gone to Chinatown almost daily, but I'd never found lemon chicken as good as the kind they serve at Hung Fong. Maia Lee would throttle me for speaking such sacrilege, since I'm including her own family recipe in the comparison, but there it is.

The restaurant had doubled in size since I'd been there last, but old Mrs. Kim was still the hostess. She greeted me by name, not fazed a bit by the fact I hadn't been there in a decade, then gave us our favorite table under the neon American and Taiwanese flags entwined on the ceiling. It was Tuesday night after the dinner rush and we had the place to ourselves except for two large families at corner booths and a couple of guys who looked like basic trainees eating at the counter. Five minutes after we ordered, the tablecloth was buried under platters piled with food.

"Isn't it odd that Lillian left for Laredo the day after you arrived?" Mother asked. Mother had dressed informally tonight: a brilliant gold and black kimono over a black cotton bodysuit. Every time she reached over the table the gold and amber bangles around her wrists slid down over her hands and caught on the lids of the covered dishes, but she didn't seem to mind.

"All right," I said. "So we had a small fight. Not even a fight, really."

I told her about Dan Sheff, hunk from hell. Mother nodded.

"I remember his mother from the Bright Shawl." She waved her chopsticks dismissively. "Horrid woman. Never trust anyone named Cookie to raise a child properly. Now what else happened?"

I shrugged. "That's it."

She frowned. "It doesn't sound like anything worth leaving town over."

"Beau Karnau probably had something to do with it. He seems to like capitalizing on emotional stress."

"You just be persistent," she advised. "Here, I'll read the tea leaves for you."

Actually I'd been drinking beer, but Mother was

never one to let technicalities stop her. She poured me a cup of tea, drank it herself, then turned the cup over on a napkin. I could never figure out whether she was playing a game for her own amusement, or whether she really had a system for making sense of the sediment from beverages, but she studied the little brown flecks intently, making meaningful "hmm" sounds.

The basic trainees at the counter looked over briefly while she was doing her divination. One made a joke under his breath. Both laughed.

"Not good, my son," Mother said in her best gypsy accent. "The leaves spell 'Adversity.' A troubled time is ahead."

"Profound," I said. "And so unexpected."

She tried to look offended. "Scoff if you must."

"I must, I must."

At the end of dinner Mother insisted on picking up the tab. Since I was down to spare change and a few maxed-out credit cards, I didn't argue too hard. The two men at the counter paid for their meal and walked out behind us.

When you train long enough in tai chi, you get to a point where your eyes and ears start feeling like they wrap around you 360 degrees. You have to develop this unless you want to get hit over the head from behind while you're protecting yourself in front, or turn a few inches too far and run yourself through on your opponent's sword. My senses switched into that mode the minute we walked out of the restaurant, but I wasn't consciously worried until we got to the corner of Queen Anne.

Mother was talking about the sorry state of the arts in San Antonio. The two men from the restaurant were coming up behind us, but they seemed to be at ease, joking to themselves, not paying us much attention. The neon lights from Broadway dropped into darkness once we walked onto my street. The two men stopped talking, but turned the corner with us. Without looking back, I could tell they were quickening their pace. They were about twenty-five feet behind us now. My apartment was at the end of the block.

"Mother," I said casually, "keep walking."

She had just been warming up on the subject of limited downtown gallery space. She glanced up at me, puzzled, but I didn't give her time to say anything. Instead, I did an about-face and went back to meet our new friends.

They didn't like their timing being messed up. When they saw me coming toward them they stopped, momentarily off-balance. Both were in their mid-twenties, with bland, square faces. They wore jeans and untucked denim shirts. Both had crew cuts. Their upper body development made it obvious they were bodybuilders. They were trying hard to be twins, but one was a red-headed Anglo, the other a Hispanic with a tattoo on his forearm—an eagle killing a snake.

When I was five feet away they moved apart slightly, waiting for me to act. Behind me I heard my mother call, more than a little nervous: "Tres?"

"Tres?" the one with the tattoo mimicked. The red-head grinned.

"Either you're following us to get your tea leaves read," I speculated, "or you've got something to say to me. Which is it?"

I let Tattoo come closer, putting his chest close to my face. He was still grinning. Red moved around to my left.

"Yeah sure," said Tattoo. "We heard you're one of those faggots from San Francisco. That true?"

He was about six inches away.

"You asking me to dance?" I blew him a kiss.

He almost decided that was worth punching me for, but Red stopped him.

Behind me I heard Mother call my name again. She was trying to decide whether she should come back for me or not. I knew she would eventually walk over and give these goons a piece of her mind. Whatever went down, I needed to make it happen before she did that.

"How hard you want to make this, buddy?" said Red. "I'd hate smashing a guy's face in front of his own mom. The message is simple: Get the fuck out of town. Nobody wants you here."

"And whom are these joyous tidings from?" I said. I slid my left foot back slightly, rooting my weight more solidly.

"Anybody you want to guess." Red sneered. "Just go back to Pansyland if you want your face in one piece."

"And if I don't," I said, "I suppose Tattoo here will chest-bump me all the way out of town?"

"You little shit—" Tattoo moved forward, meaning to grab my shirt with both hands.

The thing about bodybuilders is that they tend to be top-heavy. They can be incredibly strong, but their overdeveloped chests make their center of gravity, which should be right around the navel, much higher and surprisingly easy to unbalance. It's also easier to grab someone who has lots of muscles; it's like walking around with built-in handles all over your body.

I swept my forearms up under Tattoo's wrists before they connected and redirected his arms out. When he was wide open, I brought my left leg up and knee-kicked him in the groin. Then I pushed. He went backward stiff as a cut tree. Red got my left elbow in his nose as he came in to tackle me. I grabbed him by his triceps and twisted my waist, shifting his momentum so he flew over my knee and landed on top of his friend instead of me.

"Tres!" my mother called. She was coming toward us now.

Tattoo wasn't used to having his balls kicked. He stayed doubled over, communing with the pavement. But Red got his balance much more quickly than I'd expected. He came at me, more cautiously this time, taking a boxer's stance, right fist out. I let him miss twice, turning my body in quarter circles out of the line of his punches. That screwed up his guard. He tried a left hook but forgot to follow with his right. It was easy to step inside the punch, turn into his chest as I grabbed his wrist, and send him flying over my shoulder.

Holding on to his arm, I twisted the joints so he had no choice but to roll over on his stomach or snap a bone. I put my knee into his back, then pinched down on the nerve just below the elbow joint with my thumb. He yelled.

"You want me to hold this until you black out?" I asked. "Or do you want to tell me a little bit about yourself?"

"Go fuck yourself," he groaned.

It must've taken a lot of stamina for him to speak. Or maybe he just knew that his buddy wouldn't be down on the ground forever. In fact, Tattoo was staggering to his feet now, and we both knew I couldn't pin Red down and deal with Tattoo at the same time.

I didn't like it, but I twisted Red's arm sharply. He screamed. Maybe I broke it, maybe I didn't. But I had to give him something to worry about while I was busy with his *compadre*.

Tattoo was still walking funny. He tried his best to get me in a wrestler's hold, but I slid underneath and hit him in the gut with my shoulder. I pushed up and forward, lifting him off his feet. He fell backward again, harder this time.

I stepped back toward my mother, catching my breath. Her face was hard to read. Her eyes were very wide, but not exactly frightened. It was more the look of someone who had believed in ghosts for years, but had finally had one shake her hand.

Red and Tattoo were still on the ground, cursing.

I asked my mother for a pen and paper. She stared at me, then rummaged in her purse. On a large magenta Post-it note, I wrote: RETURN TO SENDER. Then I signed my name.

I stuck it on the front of Red's shirt.

"Thanks anyway," I said.

Before they could decide they weren't so badly hurt after all, I took my mother's arm and we walked down Queen Anne. I got her into her car before she decided it was time to talk.

"Tres, what exactly—"

"I'm not sure, Mother," I said, a little harsher than I meant to. "I'm sorry you got involved. It's probably some friends of Bob Langston, the old tenant I had to kick out. Rivas said he was Army. So were those guys, probably. That's all."

I must not have sounded very convincing. Mother kept looking at me, waiting for a better answer.

I felt tired, the hazy crashed feeling you get when adrenaline stops flowing. I tried to muster up a smile.

"Look, it's fine."

She turned and stared through the windshield. "You're my only boy, Tres."

She has tremendous strength, my mother. Despite all her eccentricities, she can harden to steel in sixty seconds flat in a crisis. I don't think I've ever seen her cry, or look as shaken as she had a few moments before. Now she smiled at me, reassuringly. When I bent and kissed her on the cheek, I could feel the slight tremble in her skin.

"Call me tomorrow," she said.

After she drove away I went inside and locked the door. Robert Johnson sniffed my legs for the strange odors of Red and Tattoo while I sat in the dark and called Lillian's number.

Her answering machine didn't pick up after ten rings. Lillian should have been home from Laredo by now. It was almost ten o'clock. She was there, I decided glumly, choosing to ignore the phone.

I stared at the coffee table, at the packet of old news clippings Carlon McAffrey had given me that afternoon, my father's grinning face still on top. Looking at his picture, I realized how badly I needed to see Lillian tonight. I needed something clean and physical with her that wasn't part of our past. I pushed the news clippings onto the floor.

Then I went to the refrigerator and got two items I'd picked up at Pappy's Grocery in a moment of whimsy: a six-pack of Big Red and a bottle of tequila. I went out to the VW. A summer thunderstorm was coming in over the Balcones Escarpment, but I took the top down anyway. Then I drove toward Monte Vista, thinking about the future.

15

There is no place in San Antonio quite as lonely as the Olmos Basin. You can drive across the dam road at night, looking over an ocean of live oaks, and see no sign of the city that surrounds you. Just you, your car, and the dam. Unless you are my mother's old high school chum, Whitley Strieber. Then I guess you have the UFOs to keep you company.

Tonight, diffused flashes of lightning illuminated the Basin, turning it from black to deep green. Thunder rolled over the tops of the trees like oil over the surface of a hot pan.

Up and down Acacia Street, dogs were barking at the storm. Lillian's house was dark except for the small cranberry glass lamp she kept on her bedstand. Fuchsia light seeped out through the closed miniblinds. Her car was in the driveway.

Next door five or six Rodriguez children, fearless and unattended, roller-skated up and down the sidewalk in semidarkness, screaming with joy every time the thunder cracked. The music from inside their parents' living room was muted tonight, as if in deference to the storm.

I pulled up to the curb and got out, carrying my Big Red and tequila up to the front porch. Two grinning Rodriguez children almost sideswiped me as I passed them.

In the basket Lillian used for mail was a stack of letters and ad circulars. Two newspapers on the porch. She could've come in through the back. Or maybe she hadn't taken her own car to Laredo; maybe she was still gone. I thought about whose car she might've taken to the border instead, and I didn't like the options I came up with.

The buzzer didn't work. I knocked as loudly as I could on the frame of the screen door but it was very possible she wouldn't hear me. The wind was picking up. Ripped from their branches, petals from Lillian's crape myrtle and antique rosebush were thrown across the yard like pink confetti.

After three knocks I tried the door and found it open. "Lillian?"

I put my six-pack and Herradura bottle down on the coffee table and called her name again. There were magazines strewn around the floor by the couch, typical of Lillian's "read and dump" method.

Still the only light was the pink glow under the bedroom door. I stuck my head in slowly, half expecting her to be curled up under the covers. An unmade bed, a half-open underwear drawer, but no Lillian.

An uncomfortable burning sensation started building strength in my chest.

I checked the back room, then the kitchen. A small AM radio was talking to itself on the cutting board. The sinkful of dishes wasn't surprising in itself, but they'd been scrubbed and never rinsed.

Possibilities started occurring to me that I didn't want to entertain. I checked the front door again, then the windows for signs of forced entry. Nothing obvious, though very little would've shown up on the scuffed and scarred doorjamb, and the window latches were woefully easy to work open. The stereo equipment was untouched. The answering machine had been turned off. No messages to replay. Computer disks and files were strewn around her desk, but no equipment seemed to be missing. Someone had been looking for something here recently in a messy fashion, but it could easily have been Lillian. I checked for toiletries in the bathroom and looked in her closet. No signs that she'd packed for a trip, but no definite proof that she hadn't.

Then I heard the clump of skates on the hardwood floor behind me. One of the Rodriguez children rolled into the bedroom doorway and grabbed the doorjamb to steady herself. She had stringy hair and small dark eyes, glittering as she looked at me. She was wearing a red and white striped dress with teddy bears on it.

I must have had a startled look on my face. She giggled.

I was still trying to frame a question when she skated back toward the front door, letting out a happy squeal as if she expected to be chased. She turned at the door and looked back, grinning mischievously.

"Do you know Lillian?" I asked, still in the bedroom doorway.

I'm not great with kids; I can't handle the eerie resemblance they bear to human beings. She cocked her head like a curious dog might.

"You're not the same man," she said.

Then she was gone, the screen door slamming behind her.

Now what the hell had that meant? I should've followed the child and asked her more questions, but the idea of chasing a group of prepubescents on roller skates down the sidewalk in the dark was more than I could handle just then.

Maybe she was talking about Dan Sheff. The neighbors would have seen him here many times, no doubt. Or maybe she'd seen someone else come into the house. I turned and stared at Lillian's bed. The burning feeling got stronger in my chest.

"Wait for tomorrow morning," I told myself.

Maybe she had decided to stay an extra night in Laredo; maybe she was on her way back right now. I pictured her coming home and finding me in her house uninvited, or learning that I'd questioned the neighbors on her comings and goings. The "I was worried" argument wouldn't carry much weight with a woman who had recently accused me of trying to control her affairs.

I weighed that against the unlocked door, the unread mail and newspapers, the half-washed dishes. I didn't like it. On the other hand, it wasn't totally out of character for Lillian to leave any of those things in her wake.

I locked the front door behind me.

The thunderstorm was directly overhead now, but there was no rain, just churning dry electricity. The Rodriguez children had finally abandoned the street. Exhausted as I was, I still couldn't face the idea of going back to Queen Anne and trying to sleep. I drove back to the Olmos Dam, then parked the car where there really wasn't a shoulder and sat on the edge of the drop-off with my bottle of Herradura, my feet dangling above the treetops.

I watched the storm move south for almost an hour. I tried not to think about where Lillian was, or about my earlier soiree with Red and Tattoo, or about the package of clippings on my father's murder. It felt like there was a huge slow spider crawling back and forth inside my head, trying to connect those things with tenuous, unwelcomed threads. Every time something started taking shape, I took another drink of tequila to wash it away.

I'm not sure how I got home, but when I woke up early Wednesday morning the ironing board was ringing. I yanked it down from the wall and fumbled with the receiver.

"*Hola, vato,*" the man on the other end said, then he insulted me rapidly in Spanish.

I rubbed my eyes until the walls came into focus. It took my brain a second to switch languages, then I placed the voice.

"That doesn't sound like a real hygienic position, Ralph," I said. "Haven't you guys heard about AIDS?"

Ralph Arguello laughed.

"So I heard right," he said. "You're back in town and speaking *Español,* no less. How the hell am I supposed to insult you to your face now?"

If there had been a spider in my head last night, this morning it felt like the thing had crawled into my throat and died. I sat on the floor and tried not to throw up.

"So how's the pawnshop business, Ralphas?"

I'd known Ralph since varsity in high school. Even then he was a con man of epic proportions. He'd once stolen the coach's pickup truck and sold it back to him in a different color, so the legend went. About the time I went off to college Ralph had started buying pawnshops all around the West Side, and by the time I'd gotten my BA, I'd heard rumors that Ralph was worth a million dollars, not all of it from honest loans.

"How do you feel about visiting my side of town today?" Something in his tone of voice had changed. It made me wish I could concentrate more on his words without the pounding in my head.

"There's a lot going on right now, Ralph. Maybe we could—"

"Yeah," he interrupted, "I heard about Lillian, and I heard she's out of town. This isn't exactly a social call."

I waited. It didn't surprise me that Ralph knew all this, any more than that he'd known I could now speak Spanish. Ralph could just drive through town and news would cling to him the way lint clings to velvet. Still, the mention of Lillian's name woke me up fast.

"Okay," I said finally. "What is it?"

"One of my girls just showed me a purse she found out on Zarzamora a few nights ago. It'd been run over a couple of times. The driver's license says 'Lillian Cambridge.' "

16

By the time I parked the VW on the curbless street in front of the Blanco Cafe, my hangover had been replaced by a colder kind of nausea. I was afraid I'd go completely numb with it if I didn't keep moving.

A sign inside the grimy window of the cafe read *"Abierto."* I stepped over two emaciated brown dogs that were snoring in the doorway and went in.

The air inside was thick, lubricated with the smell of peppers and old grease. It was only seven-thirty in the morning, but at least twenty men crowded the counter along one side of the tiny room to wolf down steaming fried *migas* and black coffee. Huge waitresses, their hair the color of chorizo, were shouting at each other in Spanish. They carried plates the size of hubcaps four at a time from the kitchen. It was the only place in town I knew where you could get a meal two plates wide that cost under three dollars.

Some of the men at the counter looked over at me,

their brown eyes sleepy, slightly annoyed when they saw I was a gringo. Then they went back to their *migas*.

Only one person was sitting away from the counter. At a yellow Formica table in the back corner, under a huge black velvet painting of a Mayan warrior, Ralph Arguello was drinking a Big Red. He was grinning at me.

"*Vato,*" he said, then motioned for me to come back.

If John Lennon had been born Hispanic and then overfed on buttered gorditas, he would've looked like Ralph. His hair was long and tangled, parted in the middle and tied back in a ponytail, and his eyes were invisible behind the sheen of his thick round glasses. Ralph's face was as round and smooth as a baby's, but when he smiled, there was a demonic glee there that made men nervous.

Ralph dressed more expensively than Lennon ever had, though—today he was wearing a white linen guayabera that almost managed to hide his belly and a gold chain around his neck so thick you could lock up a bicycle with it.

He held out a meaty hand. I shook it.

Then he sat back, still grinning. His black eyes swam around beneath several inches of prescription glass. Maybe he was looking at me, maybe at the stack of business papers in front of him. I couldn't tell.

When he spoke it was in Spanish.

"You remember Jersey and those other *pendejos* came after me for slashing their tires?"

I was thinking about Lillian, about her empty bedroom lit up the color of blood. I wanted to scream at Ralph to get to the point, but that wasn't the way he worked. He talked in circles and you just had to hang on for the ride.

I sat down.

"Yeah," I said. "They came at us outside Mr. M's, didn't they, right after school."

" 'Us'?"

He laughed—a small, sharp sound like a cat's sneeze. "You could've walked," he said. "Never figured out why this scrawny white boy was stupid enough to back up my Mexican ass against four redneck linebackers."

"I knew someday you'd be rich and famous," I suggested.

"Damn right."

"And there were only three of them."

Ralph shrugged. "That's what I said. Ain't that what I said?"

He shouted at the waitress for two more Big Reds. Then he leaned forward and put his elbows on the table, his smile gone. I caught the distinct, heavy smell of bay rum on his clothes.

"So last night," he said, "I'm talking to this girl who owes me some . . . back rent, you know?"

I nodded. Ralph paused while a waitress clunked two sweating soda bottles in front of us.

"And this girl says she's low on cash but she's come across some credit cards maybe I can use. I tell her maybe so. Then I see the name on the cards and it rings a bell. I think about you."

Ralph spread his hands in a "what could I do?" gesture.

"She's a good lady, this friend of mine, but you know, sometimes she needs encouragement to stay honest. So we talk for a while about how she really found this stuff, but it seemed to me like she was telling the truth—out on Zarzamora like I said."

Ralph put the wallet on the table. It was a Guatemalan billfold, now stained and muddy, embroidered with blue and green trouble dolls. It was Lillian's. Ralph took out several credit cards, then her license. Lillian's face stared up at me from the yellow Formica—a bad picture, washed out and unfocused, but it still captured her lopsided smile, her amused multicolored eyes.

"Was there any money?" I asked.

Ralph shrugged. "Cash evaporates fast with this lady friend of mine; you know how that is. But yeah, I think there probably was."

"Then the wallet wasn't stolen. She dropped it, or somebody dropped it."

"*Vato*, billfolds full of credit cards and money don't

sit very long in the middle of the road. Especially my side of town. Couldn't've been dropped too long before my friend picked it up—a little before midnight on Sunday, say."

"Could you find out anything else?"

Ralph showed his teeth. "Maybe I could ask around. Sunday night not too many white girls are strolling around the West Side, *vato*. If it was really her that dropped it, could be somebody saw her."

The cold from the Big Red bottle was going into my fingers now, spreading up my arm toward my chest. I was trying to imagine Lillian on Zarzamora late at night, or other ways her wallet could have traveled there without her. I thought about the sudden trip to Laredo that Beau had told me about, the unused car in the driveway, the half-wrecked house.

"I can't pay you anything, Ralphas," I said.

He grinned, tapping Lillian's Visa card against the Formica. "Maybe I'll just put it on the lady's tab if you find her, eh? Now tell me what's going on."

"I wish I knew."

But he waited, and twenty minutes and two Big Reds later I had told him everything that had happened my first week in town.

Talking to Ralph was like talking to a priest. He knew how to listen. He'd heard the sins of man so many times nothing could shock him. His grin never changed. With the priest, whatever you said went straight to God. With Ralph, it went straight into public domain. Therein lay the absolution. At least I figured the rest of the town would listen. With God I wasn't so sure.

"Hard to go to Laredo for three days without your wallet," Ralph said when I'd finished. "Hard to disappear anywhere, unless somebody makes you disappear."

I couldn't even nod.

Ralph studied Lillian's Visa card. He said: "Your friend Detective Rivas was in El Matador night before last. He mentioned about your dad's death. Said you wanted to kick up some very old dust in a lot of people's faces."

"Rivas is full of shit."

"*Vato*," Ralph said, "you think about putting two and two together, eh?"

When he said what I'd been thinking, it made it seem less outrageous. That made me want to shut out the idea even more.

"Why would somebody take Lillian to get at me? What the hell for?"

Ralph spread his hands. "You think about your papa's enemies—Mr. White's *familia*, one; the whole city council, two; half the SAPD, three. Some paranoid people with things to lose, man. If you scared somebody bad enough—"

"How?" I interrupted, a little louder than I meant to. "I don't have shit on anybody, Ralphas."

For a moment the talking at the counter died down. One of the waitresses glanced over, frowning. Ralph just sat back lazily and shrugged.

"Maybe somebody doesn't see it that way, *vato*. The question is, what now? You play good boy? Wait around for orders?"

I wanted to hit something. Instead I just stared at Ralph's black floating eyes.

"He was my father, Ralphas. What was I supposed to do?"

Ralph nodded. "Eh, *vato*, you don't have to tell me—" Then his voice trailed off.

An older Mexican man had come into the cafe and was walking toward our table. His balding forehead was shiny with sweat. He was a large man, probably used to people getting out of his way, but he shuffled toward Ralph like there was a heavy collar around his neck.

Ralph didn't offer him a chair. He just grinned. The man looked at me uncertainly; Ralph waved his hand in a dismissive gesture.

"Don't worry about him," he told the man in Spanish, then to me: "Only speakie *Inglés*, eh, *compadre*?"

I shrugged my shoulders and tried to look lost. It wasn't hard.

I half listened while the man told Ralph about his money problems. He needed to pay the mortgage; he'd been sick and unable to work. Ralph listened patiently, then pulled out a straight razor and set it on the table. Almost absently, he unfolded the polished blade from its well-worn black leather sheath and stroked it with his little finger. Still in Spanish, he said, "She's your wife. If I hear about you getting drunk again, or yelling, or threatening her boys, I will slice your fingers off and make you eat them." He said it calmly.

Then Ralph laid out ten fifty-dollar bills on the table next to the razor. The man tried to keep his hands from shaking as he scooped up the money. He didn't succeed.

When he'd left, Ralph looked at me.

"My newest stepfather." He smiled. "Like I was saying, you don't have to tell me about dead fathers, *vato*. I been the man in my family since I was twelve."

Then he put away his razor.

As I left the Blanco Cafe, the whole West Side was coming to life. More working men poured in for *migas* and coffee. Old Mexican grandmothers, each one as large as my VW and twice as loud, lumbered down the street from market to market, haggling as they went. And Ralph sat at his table in the middle of it all, grinning.

"I got twelve pawnshops to check on before noon, *vato*," he called after me. "Not bad for a poor boy, eh?"

I drove away thinking about twelve-year-olds with razor blades, about white women alone on Zarzamora Street in the middle of the night, about a hole in a brown Stetson hat.

Conjunto music was crying on every car radio up and down Blanco.

17

After an hour of tai chi and a shower, my thoughts weren't exactly clearer, but I'd regained my balance somewhat. Tai chi is good that way. It teaches you to yield before you advance. You let events push you around for a while, you keep your footing, then you push back. And I was pretty sure now where to start pushing.

By noon I was back in La Villita, standing on the porch of Hecho a Mano Gallery and trying to work my Discover card across the sidebolt. I've never been very good with the trick, but this time the old oak door gave up almost immediately. It swung open with the same relieved "Arrrr" that Robert Johnson makes in the sandbox.

I closed the door behind me. A sign had fallen off the windowsill that read: *"Out to Lunch——B."*

Never a truer word, I thought.

The lights were off in the main room, but huge blocks of sun came in from the craftsman windows. It was enough to see that the place was a disaster. Podiums had been turned over. Skeleton statues lay in colorful pieces on the stone floor, hip bones not connected to the thigh bones. The drawers were upside down on top of Lillian's big oak desk.

I checked the framing room and the rest room. Both trashed. A twenty-pound wooden milagro-studded cross from Guadalajara was sticking out of the shattered computer monitor. Photographic prints of cowboys had been ripped out of their frames. Even the toilet paper dispenser had been kicked open.

I picked up a black spiral binder from a mount of papers fluttering around under the ceiling fan. Lillian's datebook. I moved into the shadows of the bathroom and started reading.

Inside, on the July page, one note indicated the day I was coming into town. It was starred and circled. Under Sunday night, the last time I'd seen her, Lillian had written *"Dinner 8."* Not surprisingly, there was no mention of a trip to Laredo for Monday morning. In fact, no other dates at all.

I flipped back over the last few months. March and April were full of "Dan" messages, especially around Fiesta Week. Then they stopped. Lillian's last date with Dan, at least the last one she'd recorded, was for the River Parade in late April. My number in San Francisco was written a few spaces after that. Maybe I should've been flattered, but something about the timing bothered me.

I flipped ahead. Lillian had scribbled random phone numbers and reminders on the memoranda page at the back of last year, but that was it. None of the information jumped out at me. I ripped out the page anyway.

I went back into the framing room and dug around in the ruined prints. Somebody had bashed open a locked storage closet in the corner and strewn its contents around. About the only thing interesting was a canvas portfolio, three by three, with the initials "B.K." on it. The laminated leaves were bent and torn. One had a rather large shoe print on it—no grooves, pointed toe, a boot.

The portfolio made for sad reading. On the first page, *ArtNews* and *Dallas Herald* articles from 1968 announced Beau's arrival on the photographic scene: "New Visions of the West," "Fresh Perspectives on Ancient Vistas," "Dallas Native Follows Dream." The last one took a rags-to-riches angle: the tragic death of Beau's father, Beau's childhood with a well-meaning but alcoholic mother, his determination to work his way through community college in Fort Worth, buying film for his photography classes instead of food when he had to. The interviewer seemed to think it was charming that Beau had actually been on welfare. In the middle of the articles Beau's picture stared back at me—young, dressed in black, his Nikon slung over his shoulder, and the beginnings of smugness on his face.

I flipped through several more pages of his photos—abandoned ranch houses, steers, dew on barbed wire. The announcements for new shows and the glowing reviews got fewer and further between. The last two articles Beau had clipped were from the *Austin American-Statesman* in 1976. The first, a lukewarm gallery review, commented sadly that "the refreshingly energetic, naive quality of Karnau's earlier work has all but disappeared." The second, Beau's letter to the editor, detailed exactly what the reviewer could do with her comments.

Beau's more recent photographs, from his days as an assistant art professor at A & M to the present, looked like they could have been taken by Ansel Adams if Ansel Adams had downed enough tequila and dropped his camera enough times. More abandoned ranch houses, more steers, more dew on barbed wire. Finally, on the last portfolio page, was a glitzy-looking flier for "The Authentic Cowboy: A Retrospective by B. Karnau." A weathered cowboy peered out at me, trying to look authentic.

The opening was scheduled for July 31 at Blue Star, this Saturday. The list of underwriters showed how much Beau had relied on Lillian's social connections: Crockett, her father's bank; Sheff Construction; half a dozen other blue-blooded businesses and foundations. I folded up the flier and pocketed it.

I was just about to put aside the portfolio when I noticed the way the front cover felt between my fingers—a little bit thicker than the back cover, a slight bulge on the inside of the canvas. I found an X-Acto knife on the floor and delivered by cesarean two eight-by-tens sandwiched between squares of cardboard.

The photos were identical—an outdoor shot, taken at night. Three people were standing in knee-high grass in front of an old Ford truck, its doors open and headlights on. One of the people was a tall skinny man with his face turned away from the camera. His slicked-back blond hair and his white shirt almost glowed in the headlights. The other two people, whoever they were, had been carefully cut out of the picture with a razor blade. Nothing was left of them but vaguely human-shaped holes, side by side, slightly apart from the blond man.

From the angle of the shot, and a huge out-of-focus tree branch in one corner of the photo, it looked like the photographer had been uphill from the scene and fairly far away, using a telescopic lens.

The quality of the prints wasn't bad, but the texture of the paper was wrong for photographs. Looking closely, you could tell they had been laser printed rather than developed. On the back of both photos someone had written "7/31" in black pen.

I was just folding the prints to fit in my pocket when keys rattled in the studio's front door lock.

I moved to the door of the framing room and listened. Two steps, a moment of stunned quiet, then Beau Karnau cursed under his breath. He kicked something that shattered. A ceramic skull in a pink sombrero came skittering to a stop at my feet and grinned up at me.

When I came out into the doorway Beau was standing with one lizard-skin boot planted on an overturned podium, surveying the damage. His balding forehead was bright red and yellow. It matched his silk shirt beautifully.

I cleared my throat. He cleared about three feet, straight backward.

"Ah!" he said. Out of some reflex he grabbed his ponytail and pulled it like a ripcord.

When he recognized me he didn't exactly relax, but his face shifted gears from scared shitless to pissed. For a minute I thought he might charge me.

"What the fuck—" he said.

"You were expecting the maid?" I asked. "Looks like you had quite a morning rush."

"What the fuck are you doing here?" he said, louder this time.

"Who did you think I was just now, Beau? You damn near wet your boots."

His eye twitched. "What the hell do you think, Mr. Goddamn Smart-ass? I come back from lunch and you've wrecked my place. How should I act?"

"Like you know better," I said. "Like you're ready to tell me what it's got to do with Lillian."

Beau swore at me. Then he made the mistake of coming up and pushing my chest.

"Where the hell do you get off—"

Before he could finish the sentence he was sitting down. From the tears in his eyes I'd say his balls connected with the stone floor pretty hard. I put my foot on his left kneecap and pressed down, just hard enough to keep him sitting.

He said: "Uhm."

"Lillian is missing," I said. "Now I find out her studio is trashed."

"*My* studio," he said. He packed a lot of hatred into those two words.

I put a little more pressure on the knee.

"Jesus!" he yelled. "You break into my goddamn place, you assault me, you blame me when that little princess runs out on you—leave me the hell alone!"

"Lillian never made it to Laredo," I told him. "I don't think she ever planned on going. What I'm trying to decide now is if she really left a message Monday morning or if you lied to me. I need to know that, Beau."

I give him credit. Beau didn't scare easily. Or at least he wasn't scared of me. His neck veins were so purple I thought they'd explode, but he kept his voice even.

"Believe what you want," he said.

"What were they looking for, Beau?" I gestured at the ruined artwork all around us.

"I don't have a clue," he said. "Nothing."

I took out one of the photos I'd found and dropped it on his chest.

"Nothing?"

All I saw in his eyes was his opinion of me, and I already knew that.

"So it's a cut-up picture," he said. "Your girlfriend does photo-collages. You expect me to get excited?"

He said it a little too fast, like it was an answer he'd practiced in the mirror many times, just in case he needed it someday.

"I expect some real answers," I said. "Like why did Lillian decide to leave the gallery?"

I waited. Beau's face was tightly controlled, but the pressure on the knee ligaments must've been pretty bad. Little sequins of sweat were starting to pop up all over his forehead.

"When I was starting," he said, almost under his breath, "I didn't have shit. You know that? Not wealthy parents, not college, nothing. Lillian had everything, including ten years of my time. Now she's just giving up. The hell with me. The hell with years trying to build up a name in the business. You want to know why she's leaving, you're asking the wrong person, asshole. I stuck with her; you didn't. If you ask me, it's a little late to show up now and decide you're her goddamn protector."

We stared at each other. Judging from Beau's expression, I had the option of breaking his kneecap and finding out nothing more, or letting him up and finding out nothing more. Maybe I was having an off day. I took the photograph off Beau's chest, then I let him up.

Beau got to his feet warily.

I looked around the ruined gallery, then picked up a

skeleton trumpet player from the floor, dusted him off, and tossed him to Beau. He missed the catch. The unfortunate musician landed between Beau's boots and broke neatly in half.

"A man without friends should get a deadbolt," I suggested. "I have a feeling, when these people visit you again, they're going to lack my charm."

Beau kicked the broken statue away. Under his breath he said: "I *have* friends, asshole."

I saw the next line coming, so we said it together: "You're going to regret this."

"That was good," I said. "You want to try it in harmony now? I'll go up a third."

His next riposte was just as creative: "Fuck you."

"You artistic types," I said admiringly. Then I walked out, closing the door carefully behind me.

Without looking back I strolled across the plaza, around the corner of La Villita Chapel, then turned into a side alley. Even at midday, the shadows under the old villas and live oaks were deep and easy to hide in. I had a great view of the front and rear exits to the gallery I leaned against the cool of a limestone wall and waited to see what would happen.

Thirty minutes later Beau came out the rear entrance of the gallery. He closed up shop and headed across Nueva, still walking like a man with saddle sores. I followed about a block behind. The moment I stepped out of the shade of La Villita the summer air wrapped around my shoulders like a heavy cat. Everything smelled like warm asphalt, and fifty feet in front of me Beau's shape became watery from the light and the heat.

It wasn't until he stopped on the corner of Jack White and stood there for a minute that I realized I'd made a mistake. A car I knew pulled up briefly to the curb, the passenger's door opened, Beau got in, and the car pulled away, heading south.

The VW was three blocks away, hopelessly far. I couldn't do anything but stand on the corner watching Dan Sheff's silver BMW disappear down Nueva Street, just another mirage in the midday glare.

18

I was starting to feel slightly depressed until I got home and saw the police cruiser in front of Number 90 again. Gary Hales, still in his pajamas, was out front, listing backward at about the same angle as his house. He was talking to Jay Rivas and the two uniformed cops, probably telling them how I came and went at all hours and played with swords in the backyard.

Gary shuffled back inside and Jay greeted me warmly as I got out of my car.

"Little Tres," he said. "What a fucking pleasure."

"Jay," I said. "If I knew you were coming I'd've half baked a cake."

He motioned toward the house. The two cops hung back under the pecan tree, trying not to sweat out of their uniforms. When we got inside Robert Johnson took one look at our guest, puffed up to twice his size, did a somersault, then ran into the bathroom. I was sorry I hadn't thought of it first.

"He likes you," I said.

Rivas looked disdainfully at my futon, then decided to stand. I started hunting through my bags for a fresh T-shirt.

"Late night last night, Navarre?" he speculated. "You look like a pile of shit."

I let that pass. I brushed my teeth, splashed some water in my face, laminated my armpits into submission with extra strength Ban.

Rivas didn't like being kept waiting. He went over to the wall and lifted my sword out of the rack. He looked at it, snorted, dropped it on the floor. Then he picked up Carlon's packet of news clippings from the carpet.

"Funny thing," he said. "Seems like just yesterday we were having this conversation about you staying the fuck out of trouble. But it sounds like you got the monopoly on stubborn and stupid."

I put on a UC Berkeley T-shirt and walked up to Rivas. Calmly, I took the packet out of his hands and put it back on the table.

"You want to tell me about last night," he said, "or do you maybe want to think about it in a cell for a while?"

"You want to tell me what the hell you're talking about? Then maybe I can be more help."

"Lillian Cambridge," he said.

"I'm interested."

"You're deeply in shit."

If he was waiting for me to display mortal terror, he was disappointed.

"You'll have to be more specific, Jay. I'm usually in deep shit."

"How about this," he said. "Mom and Dad Cambridge expect daughter Lillian for dinner every Sunday night. Lillian's a good kid. She does that kind of thing. She doesn't show—she doesn't answer the phone all night or all yesterday. Worried parents call the police. Seeing as Dad is the president of Crockett Savings and Loan and can throw a few million dollars around, the police tend to take his concerns to heart. Are you following this so far or should I talk slower?"

"It'd be easier if I could watch your lips move, Jay, but keep going."

"We check out her house this morning. It's been trashed, looks like the lady in question left in a hurry, maybe not under her own steam. Then we find out from the neighbors that an orange VW convertible was parked in the driveway late Monday night. There's just millions of those still running around town. Little neighbor girl gives a pretty good description of the guy she saw in Miss Cambridge's house. Little girl's parents recall this same guy having a fight in front of the house Sunday afternoon. Is this starting to sound familiar?"

"I don't guess these attentive neighbors noticed anything more subtle, like somebody tearing up her house on Sunday, or carrying her away at gunpoint."

"You got something to say, I'm listening."

"Jesus Christ," I said.

I went to the kitchen and got a Shiner Bock. It was either that or beat the crap out of Rivas. At the moment, a beer sounded more constructive.

"Jay, let me see if I can get through to you on this. I admit I came back to town because of this lady, but are you suggesting I waited ten years and then moved back two thousand miles to abduct an old girlfriend?"

Rivas had one lazy green eye that weighed anchor and drifted astern when he stared at you. It just heightened his resemblance to a hairy reptile.

"You got a temper, Navarre. Old boyfriend meets new boyfriend—sparks fly. Things happen."

I looked out the grimy kitchen window. Outside, the afternoon had officially begun. Warmed up to about a hundred and five degrees, the army of cicadas in the pecan trees had started humming. The two cops were still standing in broad sunlight in my front yard, melting. Every living thing with more brains than them was crawling under a rock or into the air-conditioning to sleep.

Then a second cruiser pulled up. This one said "Bexar County Sheriff's Deputy" on its side. I had to smile as a big man with flat-topped orange hair got out, frowning at the SAPD. My landlord was probably staring out his window too, calmly shitting in his pants.

"Jay," I said, "I appreciate the extent to which you're fucking up this investigation. That takes real talent. I'm also impressed with the way you follow me around. Whoever's paying you for that should give you a bonus."

Rivas held up one finger, like a warning. "Your dad was way smarter than you, Navarre, and he had more connections. Still—look where it got him. You should think about that."

I drank my beer. I smiled in a friendly way.

"You're a piece of shit, Jay. My father scraped you off his boots twenty years ago and you're still shit."

He started walking toward me.

I glanced behind him and said: "If you've got a reason to arrest me, Detective, I'd love to hear it. Otherwise leave me the fuck alone."

"Sounds reasonable to me," said Larry Drapiewski.

Whatever Rivas was going to do, he stopped himself. He looked around at Drapiewski, who was leaning in the doorway. Drapiewski was so big I wasn't too worried about the AC escaping. His left palm was resting casually on his nightstick. In his other hand was the largest *benuelo* I'd ever seen. It looked like a half-eaten Frisbee.

"Lieutenant," said Rivas, forcing out the word. "Can I help you with something?"

Drapiewski grinned. There was a coating of sugar around his mouth.

"Just a social call, Detective. Don't let me interrupt anything. I always like to see you city pros at work."

Rivas snorted. He looked at me, then back at the door.

"Maybe another time," he said. "But, Tres, you want to talk about your father, how he played around with people's lives, screwed their careers to hell, I'd be happy to have that conversation. You've got a lot to be proud of, kid."

Then he started toward the door.

"And, Jay," I said.

He turned.

"Pick up the goddamn sword."

It was worth it just to see his face. He didn't pick it up. He wanted to say something. I wanted him to say it.

Then Drapiewski said: "Good-bye, Detective," and moved his bulk out of the doorway.

Rivas took the out.

When the door closed, Drapiewski just looked at me, his bushy red eyebrows raised. Cautiously, Robert Johnson came out of the bathroom, lured by the shower of sugar and crumbs that was falling from the deputy's *benuelo,* then tried to climb Drapiewski's pants. I don't think Drapiewski even noticed.

Larry took a thick bundle of police reports from under his arm and dropped it on the coffee table. "Want to tell me about it?"

19

By the time I'd told Larry Drapiewski my tale of woe he had relieved me of my leftover lemon chicken, four Shiner Bocks, a couple of beef fajitas, and half a box of the former tenant's Captain Crunch, dry. Robert Johnson sat on his lap, sniffing the food, but was careful to stay away from the big man's mouth.

"Holy hell," Drapiewski said. He put his boots up on the coffee table and the room suddenly seemed smaller. "Lillian Cambridge? As in Zeke Cambridge's daughter? I guar-un-tee you, if this goes down as a kidnapping, this town will be boiling by tomorrow morning. That's some large dollars moving, son."

I'll give him this, the deputy got my mind off my problems. Now I was thinking about my empty refrigerator and my empty wallet. I was hoping to God that Larry didn't want something else to eat.

"*If* it goes down as kidnapping?" I said.

Drapiewski shrugged. "Just seems strange I haven't heard about it over the telex yet."

"Some kind of waiting period?"

He laughed, sprinkling Captain Crunch across Robert Johnson's fur. Robert Johnson vaporized from his lap and reappeared on the kitchen counter, looking indignant.

"That's a damn myth, son. The network treats it just like an APB, puts it all over South Texas. You wait twenty-four hours to report something like that, usually the missing person is dead."

Then he realized who we were talking about.

"Sorry," he said.

I swallowed. "What about Guy White?"

Larry kept looking at me. "It was a damn stupid thing to do, pushing yourself in his face. You don't do that to somebody who's had as many people killed as Mr. White has. But if you're talking about your lady friend disappearing on Sunday, and you didn't see White until Monday afternoon—"

"I know. The timing's wrong."

I must not have looked too convinced.

Larry leaned forward, lacing his thick fingers around his beer bottle. "You know how many true abductions San Antonio has had in the last decade, son? I remember exactly two—both kids, neither had anything to do with the mob. If there was any suspicion of kidnapping, ransom demands, anything like that, the Feds would become lead agency immediately. So I can only assume there's reasonable evidence to let Rivas keep this in-house, to stick with the idea that Lillian disappeared of her own free will."

"Bullshit," I said.

Larry looked at me. "You sure?"

It irritated me that I couldn't answer. "So why is Rivas on the case? And into everything else I touch?"

Drapiewski raised his eyebrows. "There's some fine, decent people at SAPD. Honest cops."

"And Rivas is not among them," I suggested.

Drapiewski smiled.

"So," I said, "either he's screwing with me for personal

reasons or because somebody's pulled his strings—but either way he's screwing with me."

"Listen, son, Zeke Cambridge will *get* the police to do a damn good job, Rivas or not. Eventually they'll have to bring the Feds in on this and things will happen."

"Like they did with my father?" I said.

Larry looked at me the way people do to somebody who grew up while they weren't looking. He laughed again. "Holy hell, Tres, I don't believe you. That face you just made—that's your dad's 'shit list' expression, plain and simple."

There was such honest pleasure in his voice I had to smile. For a second it didn't matter that Lillian was missing, or that my father's murder was coming back like the worst acid flashback. You heard Drapiewski laugh and you knew there had to be a nice clean joke in there somewhere. But it only lasted a second.

"Karnau and Sheff?" I asked.

He didn't smile at that. He looked back down at the two photos I'd shown him—the ones with human figures cut out.

"I don't know," he said. "I'll look into it, but I doubt there's much to find. Either way, there's nothing you can do except sit tight."

"I can't stay out of this, Larry."

He did me a favor and acted like he hadn't heard that. Instead he got up and appropriated the last Shiner Bock from the refrigerator. Then he found my tequila and brought that back to the table too. We sat there listening to the cicadas and passing the bottle. Finally Larry leaned back, stared at the bubbled molding on the ceiling, and started laughing under his breath.

"Your father—you ever hear that story about the one-balled flyboy?"

"Yes," I said.

"It was my first goddamn time in the field," he went on. "Found myself out behind an old ranch house with this screaming son-of-a-bitch Navy pilot wearing nothing but his Justin shitkickers and a 12 gauge."

Drapiewski laughed, scratching his acne.

"He'd come home from Kingsville early, I reckon, snuck into the sack naked to surprise his lady, and laid a big kiss on something that hadn't shaved in a week. By the time I got there he was dragging his girl across the back forty and hollering. He'd chased that Mexican salesman all the way to the property line before he shot him in the leg. The Mexican was just on the other side of the barbed wire with most of his thigh gone, bleeding all to hell, and this old flyboy couldn't decide who to shoot next, me, the Mexican, the wife, or himself. I thought right there—'This is it, first and last day on the job.'

"Then your father comes huffing up behind us like a Hereford bull, two more deputies behind him. And he just starts cussing out the flyboy like there's no tomorrow, saying 'Goddamn fool, why'd you go and let that Mexican get across the line 'fore you shot him?'

"That naked pilot just looks at him confused and your father tells him: 'You shoot him *off* your property, that's attempted murder, you idiot. You shoot him *on* your property, Texas law says that's trespassing.' Then the sheriff pulls out his notebook and says: 'I'm starting to write this up, boy. You best get that Mexican back over that fence before I get to my incident description.' And you should've seen how fast that flyboy ran. But soon as he started, your father had his .38 in his hand. I never seen anything come as fast as that—first shot blew the 12 gauge right out of the old boy's hand. Second one went straight between his legs and took his left ball clean off."

Drapiewski swore in admiration and downed a few more ounces of my Herradura.

"So the old boy jumps about six feet up like a shot jackrabbit and falls over. And your father comes up to him and says: 'That first shot was for waving a 12 gauge at my deputy. The second was for being so goddamn stupid.' After we got that Mexican fixed up he sent your daddy a case of champagne every Christmas for fifteen years. That was your daddy, Tres."

The story had evolved a lot since I'd last heard it, years ago, but I didn't bother pointing that out. I just took the bottle from Larry and finished it off.

There didn't seem to be much to say after that, so Drapiewski turned on the afternoon talk shows and waited while I read through the police files.

Paper-clipped to the coroner's report were three black and white pictures of something that had once been my father's body. The corpse looked massive on the metal table, washed out and unreal in the harsh fluorescents, like a stag caught in headlights. The exit wounds, two surprisingly small holes in his chest and forehead, were circled in black Marksalot. It took me a few minutes to focus on the words of the report after putting down the photos, but once I read them there were no surprises about the cause of death.

The other files traced a series of dead-end leads in the case. The Pontiac used in the drive-by was found among the burned-out shells of stolen cars that littered the West Side each week, then traced to a retired Buttercrust baker who had actually watched it get stolen from in front of his house. The baker told the police bitterly he'd just assumed it was another creditor repo and hadn't even bothered to report it. Things looked up briefly for the investigation when the old man tentatively IDed the thief as Randall Halcomb, the ex-deputy who'd been arrested by my father for manslaughter, then been paroled a week before my father's murder.

That line of questioning ended two months later in a deer blind outside Blanco, where Halcomb was found in a bloody fetal position with a .22 hole between his eyes. His body was badly decomposed by the time a local rancher stumbled across it, but the coroner estimated the time of death to be no more than a week after my father's.

Heavy pressure on Guy White and the other known drug traffickers in South Texas, trying to connect them to the murder, yielded exactly nothing. White had gotten most of the attention. Every agency in town had conducted raids on White's properties, tied up his assets in court, slammed anyone who associated with him for the smallest misdemeanor, all to no avail in the Navarre case. Just like Rivas had told me: Everyone suspected the connection; no one could prove it.

The compiled list of my father's other enemies and Halcomb's associates also yielded nothing.

Finally, the investigation turned back to Randall Halcomb. The revenge motive was nice and clean, the timing and the ID that connected Halcomb to the Pontiac very convenient. The fact that some other party had killed Halcomb was a minor glitch. Maybe Halcomb was killed for reasons unrelated to the murder. Maybe my father's friends in the department had gotten to Halcomb before the Feds could. It had been known to happen. Either way, the FBI liked dead murderers, probably a lot more than they had liked my father. They sold it to the press as a vengeance killing, classified the case as "ongoing," and quietly shelved it.

It was eight o'clock and getting dark before I resealed the folder and handed it back to Larry, minus a few items I'd lifted while his head was in the refrigerator. My eyes felt like melting ice cubes.

"Well?" he said.

"Nothing," I said. "At least nothing that makes sense yet."

"Yet?"

Drapiewski took his boots off the coffee table, walked stiffly to the refrigerator, then finding it empty, decided it was time to leave. He took his gun and his hat off the table and stood looking at me.

"Tres, Rivas is right about one thing—you don't belong in this. Let them find the young lady. Let me look into Karnau and Sheff for you. You put yourself in the way and it won't help anything."

My look must've told him something. He swore under his breath, then fished out a card and tossed it on the table.

"Your father was a good man, Tres."

"Yeah."

Then Drapiewski shook his head, as if I hadn't heard:

"The kind of man who could get you to take your own gun out of your mouth when you figured nothing else mattered."

I looked up at Drapiewski's greasy, fifty-year-old adolescent face. He was smiling again, like he couldn't help it. Maybe I hadn't heard him right. For a second, I had imagined him in a dark room somewhere, staring down a gun barrel.

"You need something," he told me, "call that number. I'll do what I can."

"Thanks, Larry."

After he left I took a lukewarm shower, then looked again at my father's notebook. I reread his notes for the testimonies against Guy White, the cryptic reminder at the bottom: *Sabinal. Get whiskey. Fix fence. Clean fireplace.* It still made no sense. I closed the notebook and tossed it on the table.

My girlfriend was missing. The other love of her life, who hadn't been a love of her life for several months, was driving around town with her business partner. And I was sitting on my futon reading my father's old grocery lists.

I decided to make my perfect day complete. I called my mother and asked for a loan. She was, of course, delighted. I felt about as good as that flyboy who'd just kissed something hairy.

20

In my dreams that night I was hunting with my father at the family ranch in Sabinal. It was Christmas break, my seventh-grade year, one of the coldest winters South Texas ever had. The mesquite trees were bare as TV aerials, and the brush was a dull yellow-gray that matched the clouds. I was kneeling in an orange parka, holding a .22 rifle my father had given me as a gift that morning. The barrel was slightly warm from ten rounds of fire.

My father, next to me, was also dressed in hunting clothes. He looked like a fluorescent tent for six. His Stetson tilted over his eyes so all I could see were his huge bristly jowls, his nose webbed with red veins, his crooked wet smile half-hidden by a battered Cuban cigar. The mist from his breath mixed with the smoke. In the cold sharp air he smelled like a good meal that was burning.

Out in the clearing the javelina still quivered. It was a huge animal, all black hair and tooth, much too large and mean to kill with a .22. I'd shot it first out of surprise, second out of anger, then again and again out of desperation to finish the job. All the while my father just watched, only smiling at the end.

Finally the beast stopped dragging itself along the ground. It made a thick, liquid sound. Then even that stopped.

"Meanest animal on God's earth," my father said. "And the dirtiest. What you reckon you should do now, son?"

He could talk like a Harvard graduate when he wanted, but when he tested me, when he really wanted to distance himself, he put on that accent. The familiar, cracker barrel drawl was easy and slow the way a cottonmouth snake is slow, moving toward you in the river.

I said: "Can we use it?"

My father chewed his cigar.

"You can fix up some mighty fine javelina sausage, if you've got the mind to."

He let me take the knife and stood back as I moved up to the warm carcass. It took a long time to gut the thing. From the moment I touched it, my skin began to crawl, but I ignored the feeling at first. I remember the steam from the innards and then the indescribably bad smell—a sour blast of fear, rot, and excrement that beat the worst inner-city alley. That was my first lesson—the gas that a newly dead animal exudes. It nearly knocked me down, nearly forced me to double over, but then I saw my father watching sternly behind me, and knew I had to go on. I'd made my choice.

After gutting it I tied its feet and pulled it through the brush. Now the itch was intolerable. My father watched as I struggled to get the javelina into the bed of the pickup. My eyes were watering; my entire body crawled. Small red bites were breaking out on my arms like an acid wash. Finally, in desperation, I turned to my father, who was still standing a good distance away. In pain, humiliated, I waited to hear what I had done wrong.

When he spoke it was almost kind.

"Every hunter needs to make that mistake *once*," he

said. "And he never makes it again. You get too close to a javelina that's just shot, the first thing you get is the smell for a good-bye present. But that's not the worst."

He dropped his cigar butt and smashed it into the dirt with one huge boot. When he spoke again, the pain was crawling across my scalp, under my armpits, around my groin. It caused a dull roar in my ears.

"The body heat," my father said. "It cools off right fast, and all them little fleas, all them chiggers and ticks and every other form of varmint that breeds in that hide, looks for the nearest warm thing to jump on to. You're it, son. Don't never approach a dead thing until it's as cool as the ground, son. Not ever."

I couldn't ride back in the truck. I had to walk behind it as my father led me home. I spent one day in the shower, another day bathed in cortisone. And I'd never fired a gun since that Christmas. The other lesson, the one about avoiding the dead, had been harder to learn.

Then the scene of the dream changed from Sabinal to the A & M campus. I saw Lillian at eighteen, leaning in the doorway of her freshman painting class, barefoot, her hands behind her. Her denim overalls and her short off-blond hair were both flecked with red acrylic.

A week earlier we'd had another one of our epic fights. I'd stormed out of the Dixie Chicken in the middle of dinner. Lillian shouted at my back that she'd never talk to me again. Now she just stared at me as I walked closer.

When I came up to her she brushed my face with her fingers, lightly, and left sticky red acrylic streaks on my left cheek. Then, keeping a straight face, she decorated the other side, like war paint. She laughed.

"Does this mean I'm forgiven?" I said.

Her eyes turned bright green. She put her head so close to mine that her lips brushed my chin as she talked. Her breath smelled like cherry Life Savers.

"Not even close," she said. "But you can't get rid of me. Remember that next time you walk away."

The phone was ringing.

I woke up sideways on the futon with the receiver

already in my hand. The blinds above me were open and sunlight was pouring onto my face as strong and hot as gasoline. I squinted. Before I could make my voice work, Robert Johnson was on my head talking for me.

"Mur," he said.

Maia Lee said, "Oh, good, Robert Johnson, you're home."

"Sorry," I croaked. "Should I get off the line?"

She laughed. The sound was a hard one to wake up to; it brought back Sunday mornings on Potrero Hill, drinking Peet's coffee, watching the fog recede from the Bay. It made me remember a city for runaways where you didn't have to think about the past, or home, or who had disappeared from your life.

"You're a hard person to get in touch with, Tres," Maia said.

I sat up, knocking over the empty tequila bottle. Then I looked across the room and noticed the kitchen window.

Maia was waiting for a snide remark. When I didn't offer one, her tone changed. "Tres?"

I walked into the kitchen as far as the phone cord would go. The rusty metal frame window above the sink was hanging wide open at a crazy angle. Its bottom hinge had been neatly pried away, so the ancient turn-crank that was supposed to hold the window shut could be stripped.

"Tres?" Maia said again. "What is it?"

I sat on the kitchen counter and stared out into the crape myrtles. A few of their pink petals were floating in yesterday's coffee cup next to the soap dish. A few more were smashed into the single muddy footprint that was in my sink—no grooves, pointed toe, a large boot, maybe a ten and a half wide.

"Maia," I said, "how much time have you got?"

21

I blamed Robert Johnson for not being a Great Dane. Maia blamed me for being a heavy sleeper.

"I told you so often," she complained, "if a burglar had ever come in while we were sleeping—" She caught the *we* part of that statement a little too late. Her voice tangled on it like silk on barbed wire.

When she spoke again it was in her professional tone, careful and even. "All right. Tell me the whole story."

I told her what little I'd learned about my father's death. I told her about Lillian's disappearance, my talk with Guy White, the threats against me, Beau Karnau's mystery photos and his ride with Dan Sheff, the boot print at the gallery and in my sink.

Maia was silent for a minute. Behind her somewhere, a foghorn sounded.

"Did they take anything? These photos you found, for instance?"

"Whoever it was came and left quickly. I don't think

they were looking for paperwork. None of it was touched. Nothing else was taken."

"Not even your life."

I tried to believe there was no disappointment in her voice.

"It's nice to be loved," I said.

After she had fumed silently for a while, she said: "Tres, your friend Drapiewski is right. Leave this to the police. Get the hell out of there."

I didn't answer.

"But naturally," she said, "you're not going to."

I didn't answer.

She sighed. "I should've left you where I found you—tending bar in Berkeley."

"I was the best person you ever trained."

"You were the only person I ever trained."

It's hard for a Texan to argue with someone who insists on sticking to the truth. Robert Johnson jumped onto the counter and started smelling the boot print in the sink. He gave me an insulted look that was probably a close approximation of Maia's expression right then. Two against one.

"All right," Maia said, "let's assume, even if I don't agree, that you pull on the two ends of this, Lillian's disappearance and your father's death, and you find out they connect somewhere in the middle. That would mean someone besides this dead convict—"

"Halcomb."

"—it would mean someone besides him was involved in the killing ten years ago, and is now nervous about your questions. Whoever it is, they're worried enough to threaten you, perhaps to kidnap someone you—someone you know, but not willing to kill you. Why?"

I picked a crushed crape myrtle petal out of the sink and looked at it. Thinking about why I was alive this morning didn't help the empty acidic feeling the tequila had left in my stomach. The half memory of somebody looking down at me in the night had started to crawl across my skin like the smell of dead javelina and the sticky feel of red acrylic paint.

"I don't know," I said. "Why does someone search the art gallery, then Lillian's house, then my apartment? Why does Dan Sheff hang around Lillian's front yard ready to beat up new boyfriends when Lillian's datebook declared the relationship dead months ago? Why does Sheff give Karnau a ride? I don't know yet."

Maia hesitated. "Tres, I know you want to find the connection between this and your father."

"But?"

"But maybe there isn't one."

I stared at the ceiling. Just above the stove, there was a water stain in the shape of Australia, bowing in the middle like it was desperately clinging to the bottom of the world. When I spoke I tried to keep my voice even.

"You think I want it that way?"

"You want it to be your problem and your responsibility to fix," she said. "I know you. But maybe Lillian was into something all by herself. It happens, Tres."

I know you. The three most irritating words in the English language. When I didn't answer, Maia muttered a few curses in Mandarin. I think she switched the receiver to her other ear.

"All right then," she said. "Let's talk about your father. Do you really think one of his political enemies could be involved?"

For a moment I envisioned Councilman Fernando Asante in an extra large brown leisure suit trying to squeeze himself through my kitchen window, his Lucchese boot in my sink, his well-fed belly wedged between crape myrtle branches. It almost cheered me up.

"Even in Texas the politics aren't usually that colorful," I told her. "Asante, the most likely candidate, has enough trouble just keeping his dick in his pants."

"The drug trafficker, then, the man whose house you so debonairly barged into at gunpoint?"

I had to think longer about that one. "If it was Guy White, I can't figure his logic. Why murder a retiring sheriff, especially when you know you're going to get the heat for it? And why get nervous about me now when the Feds couldn't find anything?"

"You don't sound convinced."

"Maybe it's worth another visit."

She paused. "But you can't just walk up to a Mafia boss twice in one week and start shaking him down for information on assorted felonies—"

I was quiet.

"Oh, Christ," she said. "Don't even think about it, Tres."

"It's either that or retrace some leads from these police files I stole."

"Excuse me?"

"Okay, you didn't hear it."

"Christ," she said.

"Urrr," said Robert Johnson, in sympathy.

"This is information about my father. I consider it an inheritance."

"Insanity was your only inheritance, Navarre."

I protested. "I worked hard for my insanity, Ms. Lee. Nobody handed it to me on a silver platter."

"How the hell did I ever fall for you?" she wondered.

Things were awkwardly quiet for a while after that.

Finally Maia sighed. "Tres, I'm thinking about a time you were lying in an alley off Leavenworth with a Balinese knife in your lungs—"

"Grazed them, actually."

"—because you insisted on going to talk to a crazy hashish dealer by yourself."

"It would've been fine if the illustrious April Goldman had been straight with me."

"You would've been dead if she hadn't sent me after you."

"Good old Terrence & Goldman. Your bosses must miss me," I said.

A little more Mandarin swearing. Then Maia made her final plea bargain. "Is this friend of yours any good in a fight?"

I laughed. "Ralph, you mean? Ralph is a sneaky son of a bitch who fights about as fair as a cornered weasel."

"Good. Will you take him along?"

"Ralph has business interests. He likes a low profile."

"I don't want you going into this any further alone, Tres."

"Maia, I'm not exactly living across the Bay Bridge anymore."

She hesitated. "Then what if I were to come down there?"

Silence on my end.

"What happened to a nice clean break?" I asked. "The quiet acceptance of my choice to move?"

Maia thought about that. "Have you ever known me to lie, Tres?"

"Only to get what you want."

She didn't argue the point.

I stared at the ceiling. "I'll be fine. Besides, this is my hometown. They can't touch me here."

"You're a true asshole, Navarre."

"So I've been told." But she'd already hung up.

I picked up an old *Texas Monthly* with Anne Richards on the cover and shook it. Anne revved her white motorcycle and dropped the notes I'd stolen from Drapiewski's files.

There were a dozen or so Xeroxed faces of men who had been under investigation by the FBI—various cons who were at large around the time of the shooting, some of whom had been put behind bars by my father and who possibly knew Randall Halcomb, the probable stealer of the Pontiac used in the drive-by. The faces stared back at me, telling me nothing.

Finally I took out the last page of Lillian's datebook and looked at it again, at the third line where she'd erased a phone number and a street address in the Dominion.

I put on my best clothes, my Sunday visiting T-shirt and my least torn jeans, then headed out to pay a call at the Sheff family mansion.

22

The Dominion is where your ordinary run-of-the-millionaire Texan dreams of going when he dies. George Strait lives there, along with a few congressmen, a few Howard Hughes types, and anyone else willing to pay six or seven figures for a design-your-own mansion on a spacious lot of former sheep ranch land. No black sheep, obviously.

It was a thirty-minute drive from Queen Anne, forty with the VW fighting a hot north wind. As I passed Loop 1604 the land opened up and you could see the storm coming in. Blue-black clouds rolled off the Balcones Escarpment in a perfect line. The pastures turned dark green. A dry white branch of lightning cracked off from the sky and hit the horizon, then evaporated. I did what any sensible person would do. I put on my sunglasses.

When I pulled up to the development gates I stopped right in the entrance and got out to put up the ragtop. The condition it was in, it wouldn't stop the rain but it might slow it down. And putting the top up here was just the kind of non-thinking thing a Dominion resident would do—not rude exactly, just not realizing anybody else of importance could possibly exist in your space. Two Cadillacs pulled up directly behind me and waited. Nobody honked. The security guard wavered in the doorway of his little booth, not sure whether he should yell at me or help me. I could be a rich person in disguise. I could be a friend of George's. I was wearing Ray•Bans in a rainstorm.

I got back in my car and drove up to the guard, slowly. I tried to look mortally bored.

"Hey," I said.

He had a vibrating smile, this guy, like it would jump right off his face. He was younger than me. Probably his first week on the job. The white uniform and his twitchy eyes made him look like the ice cream man after a nervous breakdown.

"Your destination, sir?" he said, laying petal-soft hands on the car door. He tried to hide his distaste when he caught a whiff from inside of the VW. It had been doused by plenty of rainstorms before now, and some parts had never completely dried.

"Yeah," I said, yawning. "Two——Aw shit, two——"

I snapped my fingers helplessly. I gazed off like I was having a flashback.

Behind us the Cadillacs were starting to get impatient. The one in front flashed its high beams. He had places to go, golf games to start.

"Two——"

I almost thought it wouldn't work. Then the second Cadillac honked. The guard jumped.

"200 Palamon?" he offered, almost in tears. "The Bagatallinis?"

I grinned. "Yeah."

"Yes, sir, straight up, past the ninth green, your first right."

"Good deal."

And I drove through, wondering who the poor Bagatallinis were if they kept sorry company like me. Maybe I should drop by.

I'd been in the Dominion a few times before. Once, in the last days of their marriage, I'd been sent by my mom to pick up the Sheriff when he was puking Cuba Libras into somebody's million-dollar cactus garden after a social hobnob. But I didn't know the place well enough to locate the Sheff house on the first try.

After two passes around the swan pond, however, I finally found it. It was a modest place by Robin Leach's standards—two white stucco wings that met in a three-story-high point at the center, the middle portion all glass so you could see the coliseum-size living room and the interior balconies that looked down on it. The front yard was all rocks. I looked at the glass house. I looked at the million stones in the yard. I shook my head. The joke probably hadn't even occurred to them.

Dan Sheff's silver BMW was parked a little ways down the hill. A brown Mercedes and a restored cherry-red '65 Mustang were in the driveway. So was an honest-to-God chauffeur, black suit and all, washing the cars.

It wasn't his first week on the job. He met me at the curb before I'd even taken off my shades.

"Can I help you?"

He was a small Anglo man, lean and well muscled, the kind of guy who's five feet five with an extra six inches of attitude on top. The plastic sheen of his face told me nothing. He could've been anywhere between thirty and fifty.

"I don't think so," I said. "I usually wait until after the storm to wash my Mercedes."

I've never seen anybody smile without making wrinkles somewhere on their face, but this guy managed it, briefly. Then he was Mr. Impassive again.

"Thursday morning like clockwork," he said. "I get paid anyway, man. And your business is with—?"

"Mr. Sheff," I said.

He gave me a quick scan from my Triple Rock T-shirt to my jeans to my deck shoes, which over the years, I admit, had come to resemble a pair of baked potatoes more than footwear. Mr. Impassive was not in awe.

"Which one?" he said.

"Dan."

He didn't even smile. "Which one?"

Ah. A family with as many confusing duplicate names as mine.

"Junior," I ventured.

If he'd said "which one" again I would've had to flog him with my Ray•Bans. Fortunately he just lied to me.

"Not here," he said.

I guess he didn't expect me to buy it, because he didn't move. He kept his chest between me and the house as if his chest were an obstacle at least the size of Kerrville.

I glanced over at the BMW.

"Dan's taking public transportation these days? Or maybe carpooling in the neighbors' Lexus to save gas?"

"Mr. Sheff doesn't make appointments at home," he said. "Unless you're a friend—"

The idea must have amused him. He made a small sound in the back of his throat that either meant he had a hairball or he was laughing.

"He'll want to talk to me," I said. Then I tried to walk past him.

His hand wrapped around my biceps like a torque wrench. I tried to look suitably impressed, which wasn't hard. He liked that. The smooth smile came back.

"No visitors unannounced," he said.

I stood still, offering no resistance. "Not a bad grip for a guy who must drive power steering."

"I bench three-fifty cold, six reps."

I whistled. "I drink twelve ounces cold, six reps."

"I mean it, man. You leave now."

I sighed, resigned. I seemed to think about it.

No matter how strong your grip is, it's always unconnected where the thumb meets the fingertips, and the thumb is the weakest part of the lock. The trick is to twist against it fast enough to break out. It's really pretty easy, but it looks impressive. I was halfway up the sidewalk before he realized he didn't have me anymore.

He came at me again, but he had a serious disadvantage. He was on the job and I wasn't. In a bar fight I would've thought at least twice about taking this guy on, but even the toughest employees are usually hesitant about cold-cocking somebody in front of their rich boss's house, at least not without permission. I had no such restrictions. He tried to grab me with both arms. I stepped underneath and flipped him into the gravel.

Then I stepped onto the porch and rang the doorbell, or rather I pulled it—a huge brass chain that would've made Quasimodo homesick, connected to some ridiculously tiny-sounding chimes. As if to compensate, a thunder-lightning combo exploded directly overhead. Raindrops as big and warm as poblano peppers started to fall.

Meanwhile the chauffeur was sitting up, brushing the white dust off his black suit. You'd've thought he got flipped every day by the calm look on his face. He just stood up and nodded.

"Aikido?" he asked.

"Tai chi."

"How about that." Then he cleared his throat and looked at the front door. "You mind if *I* make the introductions, man? I don't feel like job-hunting today."

"You got it." I told him my name. For an instant his face changed expressions. Then it smoothed over again.

When Cookie Sheff answered the door, the chauffeur told her: "Tres Navarre to see Mr. Dan Jr."

It only took the society matron a few awkward seconds to warm up her best smile. Then she held out her hands in welcome, as if I were late for tea and had been presumed dead.

"Good gracious, yes," she said. "Please come in, Tres."

23

"You'll have to excuse the house," Cookie Sheff said. "The maid doesn't come until noon."

Maybe the flagstone floor needed to be scrubbed, or the walk-in fireplace vacuumed. I looked up at the ceiling fans, three stories above. Maybe they needed dusting. Other than that I couldn't see much for the maid to do.

"Please . . ." Mrs. Sheff said, waving me toward the white leather couch. I opted for a pigskin chair instead. Cookie perched across from me on the very edge of her seat.

"Well." She slid her withered hands around a half-finished Bloody Mary. "What can I get you?"

Mrs. Daniel Sheff, Sr., had unnaturally golden, unnaturally smooth hair that fit around her head like a Roman helmet. Her bright red lipstick went well over the real boundaries of her lips. Her eyebrows were similarly enhanced. The makeup looked like a waterline that had been drawn at the height of a flood. Since that

time, however many decades ago, Cookie Sheff's face
had receded.

She was the picture of aging gracefully—graceful if
you didn't count the kicking and screaming and the
surgery. She was also the woman who had been sitting
in Dan's car in front of Lillian's house last Sunday.

"I came to ask about Lillian, ma'am," I said. "I
assume the police have been by already?"

The Bloody Mary froze halfway to her lips.

"Lillian?" she said. "Police?"

"That's right."

She shook her head, trying to smile. "I'm afraid I
don't . . ."

"That would surprise me, ma'am," I said, "unless
you've sworn off phones since you were PTA president
at Alamo Heights."

The smile turned to stone. "I beg your pardon."

"My mother used to tell me that you could boil every
piece of gossip in town down to just seven numbers—
Cookie Sheff's phone number."

When she spoke again, after apparently swallowing
her tongue several times, her voice had all the charm
and affection of a drugged bobcat.

"Oh, yes," she said, "your mother. How is the old
dear?"

"She looks great."

Her drink was quickly reduced to red ice cubes.

"Tres," Cookie said, taking on a patient, mildly
chastising tone, "perhaps it should occur to you that a
certain . . . quality of people do not wish their family
crises aired so openly."

"Meaning I should've called instead of dropping by?"

"Meaning," she said, "that the Cambridges are my
very dear friends."

"Soon to be family?"

She looked satisfied. "So you see why perhaps your
coming here was not in the best taste."

"I feel just awful, ma'am. Now where is your son,
please?"

She sighed quietly, then stood up.

"Kellin?" she called.

Mr. Impassive, already immaculate in a fresh black uniform, appeared instantly from an interior doorway, a full Bloody Mary in hand. He walked like he enjoyed the sound his boots made against the flagstones.

"See Mr. Navarre out, please," Cookie said.

Kellin looked at me and nodded. Maybe a faint smile—permission to kill at last.

Then on one of the balconies above me, Dan Jr. appeared, fashionably dressed in a maroon velour housecoat-looking thing. His hair was sticking up on both sides.

I waved at him and smiled. "Dan," I called up. "Thought we might have a talk."

His face compacted. Before he said anything he looked at his mother, who shook her head.

"What the hell do you want, Navarre?" he said.

"To find Lillian," I answered. "You interested or not?"

"Danny," said Mrs. Sheff, "do you think it's a good idea to talk to this man?"

Her voice was soft, sweet and cold as Blue Bell ice cream. Her tone implied that the right answer was "no," and the wrong answer would probably mean no allowance for a week.

Dan thought about it. Then he looked at me. I smiled, letting him see a little of my amusement. That did it.

"Come on in the office, Tres," he said. Then he disappeared from the balcony.

The slight shake of Mrs. Sheff's head told me there would be a Conversation at the family dinner table tonight. Then she gave me a look that was meant to suggest no dessert for the rest of my life. She took her Bloody Mary and exited up the nearest staircase.

"Come on," said Kellin.

He led me into a smaller room, not much bigger than my apartment, really. Above the fireplace on the right was a recent oil painting of Cookie, minus the wrinkles. Opposite it, on the left wall, was a huge black and white enlargement of a young Dan Sr. dressed for war—Korea, probably. Directly between them, Dan Jr. pulled out the chair behind an oiled mahogany desk. Behind him, outside a heavily curtained picture window, a true South Texas storm was raging, brief and violent. I could see my VW on the street, its roof fluttering, threatening to peel off. Small newly planted trees along the sidewalk were bent to the ground.

"Have a seat," Dan said.

He'd combed his hair but was still drowning in maroon bedclothes. In his hand was a drink that looked like plain orange juice. I sat down across from him and waited.

After a minute of staring at me he said: "Okay. What the hell is it?"

"You know about Lillian."

Either he was a great actor or his anger was genuine. His knuckles curled up white. "I know that you show up, and a day later she's gone."

"When did you see her last?"

Dan looked at me with red eyes, then looked down at the desk. He ran his hand through his hair and a lick of blond sprang back up like a canary wing.

"You goddamn know when," he muttered. "And you were still there when I left. That's what I told the police, not that they have a fucking clue. If it was up to me you would've been put away by now, Navarre."

"Danny," I said, "we agree about something."

He made a sound like a bull that's been zapped with the same cattle prod once too often. "Don't call me that. And we don't have shit in common."

"The police don't have a clue. I agree with that. I didn't come all the way back to Texas to see Lillian disappear and then watch the police fuck up the investigation, Dan. Think about that."

He didn't look very convinced. Shadows from the rain crawled across his face along with guilt, frustration, and some other things I couldn't read. He looked down at a more recent picture of his father on the desk, Dan Sr. the way I remembered him when I was in high school: a big man in flashy clothes, the football team's biggest patron, or the cheerleaders', anyway. That was before he'd come down with his well-publicized cases of Alzheimer's and Parkinson's. Now, from what Lillian had told me, the old man was upstairs somewhere, silently withering down to a husk while the best and prettiest nurses money could buy looked on.

"There was a time he'd say something and the police would jump," Dan said, almost to himself. "You remember that, Kellin?"

Behind me Kellin said nothing.

"Now . . . shit," said Dan. "They tell me not to get too worried. 'She might be out of town,' they tell me. Shit."

I thought about that. "Your mother said the Cambridges want to keep it quiet for a while, downplay things."

Dan snorted, like that was a good joke.

"Downplay things," he echoed.

I leaned forward and picked up the picture of his dad. The silver frame must've weighed ten pounds. It was just about the coldest thing I'd ever touched. "Only child, right?"

"If you don't count my fifteen cousins."

"And they're all dying to inherit a piece of the business," I suggested. "Must be tough on you."

"What the fuck do you know about it?"

His shoulders slumped; the anger in his face loosened up into melancholy.

It was time to change tack.

"What did Beau Karnau say to you yesterday, Dan?"

I'm not sure what kind of reaction I was expecting, but it wasn't what I got. I've never seen a man turn molten red so fast. Dan was on his feet and if the desk had been any narrower he would've had his hands on my throat. As it was he just leaned toward me and shouted.

"What the *fuck* is that supposed to mean?" he spat.

Kellin had come up next to me to monitor the situation. I decided it was time to stand up, slowly and calmly.

"Look, Dan, I want to find the lady, that's all. You want to help, great. You want to tell me Beau Karnau got a lift from the gallery in somebody else's silver BMW yesterday around one o'clock, I don't have time to argue with you. *Lillian* might not have that kind of time."

Dan stared at me. I couldn't tell whether his expression was incredulity or outrage. For a minute we were all totally still, listening to the thunder.

Then Dan shut down almost as quickly as he'd blown up.

"Lillian," he echoed. The red trickled out of his face. He slid back into his chair with one long exhale. "Jesus, I need a drink."

Maybe Jesus wasn't listening but Kellin was. He took away the orange juice and replaced it quickly with a tumbler of bourbon. Instead of drinking it, Dan pressed the glass against his cheek like a pillow and closed his eyes.

"Beau called me," he said finally. "He wanted—some money. He said Lillian had made his life difficult by leaving, that he needed a few thousand dollars as a loan."

"Why you?" I asked.

I waited. Dan moved the bourbon to his lips.

"Things weren't always smooth between us—Lillian and me," he said into the glass. "Sometimes Beau helped me get things back on track. Flowers, telling me her plans, that kind of thing."

"The crazy sentimental fool," I said.

Dan looked up and frowned. "Beau is all right. He's been Lillian's friend for years. He would never do . . . anything to Lillian, nothing bad."

I'm not sure who he was trying to convince, himself or me. Judging from his tone of voice I don't think he succeeded either way.

"So you agreed to see Beau yesterday," I said.

Dan looked up at me and said nothing. The rain was dying down. Lightning flashed, and I counted almost to ten before the thunder. Dan scowled as he drained the bourbon from his glass.

Afterward he looked up at me in surprise, as if I'd just appeared there. He seemed to ask himself a silent question, then nodded. He brought out a square leather account book from the desk.

"How much?" he said.

I stared at him.

"I'll hire you, asshole," he said. "Lillian said you did this for a living, this . . . stuff. I'll pay you to find her. How much?"

I felt a little slimy just for being tempted, but I shook my head. "No."

"Don't be a prick," he said. "How much?"

I looked at Kellin. Kellin stared back, his face about as expressive as Sheetrock.

"Look, Dan," I said, "I appreciate it. I promise you I'll find her. But I can't take your money."

Then I turned to leave before I could change my mind.

"Navarre," he called after me.

I turned around in the doorway. From across the room Dan looked about ten years old, dwarfed behind his father's huge mahogany desk, drowning in oversized maroon robes, his blond hair in disarray as if Dad had just come by and tousled it.

"You know what it's like," he said. "Living in the Old Man's shadow, I mean? You know about that, at least."

It was some kind of peace offering, I guess. Looking back, maybe I should've taken it.

"Like you told me," I said, "we don't have shit in common."

Kellin walked me to the door, where Mrs. Sheff was waiting to see me off. That brilliant hostess smile must've been sitting in a glass in some other room, because when she spoke she hardly opened her stern little mouth at all.

"Mr. Navarre," she said, "I would highly recommend that you avoid my household in the future unless you are invited."

"Thank you for the hospitality, ma'am."

I stepped out onto the front porch. The rain had stopped and the clouds kept rolling south toward the Gulf of Mexico. Ten minutes from now there would be nothing left of the storm but bent trees and wet cars drying in the sun.

"I care deeply about my family," Cookie told me. "I have a sick husband and a very dear son to look after, along with the reputation of the entire Sheff family."

"And a rather large construction firm."

She gave me the slightest sour nod. "I will not allow our family, or our friends, to be dragged through the mud."

"One question, ma'am," I said.

She just looked at me.

"Are you normally a spectator at your son's fistfights?" I asked. "Somehow I would've thought you'd fight them for him."

For a woman of good breeding, Cookie Sheff did an excellent job of slamming the door in my face.

24

I waited almost two hours on the shoulder of I-10 South with no company but my AM radio before Dan's BMW sped by at a leisurely eighty-five miles per hour. By a combination of good luck and bad traffic, my talk-show host and I managed to keep up with Mr. Sheff as he headed toward downtown.

It had been a sobering moment when I had tuned into WOAI and hadn't turned it off immediately. Here it was two hours later, still on. I kept telling myself it was nostalgia for those torturous trips to Rockport with my parents. Surely I couldn't be interested in this stuff. Surely I wasn't approaching thirty.

"The problem with this country," Carl Wiglesworth was saying, "is the socialists who are running our schools."

Ah, Texas. For a moment I wished Maia were there. She would've gone into the cutest little apoplexy over Carl.

On the way downtown I watched Dan's taillights from a hundred yards back and thought about my

quality time with the Sheffs. First there was the problem
of somebody—the cops, the Sheffs, maybe even the
Cambridges—trying to downplay things. For some
reason, Lillian's disappearance hadn't yet gone down as
a potential kidnapping.

Don't worry, she might just be out of town.

No way would Rivas pull that shit on a big-name
family without a seriously good reason and a seriously
greased palm. If he *had* pulled back the reins on the
investigation, somebody with heavy clout had made it
happen.

Then there was Dan. He was lying about Beau. And
he wasn't exactly stable. Maybe it was just Lillian's disappearance that had gotten to him, but I had the feeling
there was more wrong with Dan Sheff's life than one
lady could cause, unless that lady was his mother.

I still needed Dan alone, away from Kellin and a
thirty-second Dominion Security response time, to ask
him why he was pursuing a relationship that Lillian's
datebook had pronounced dead months ago.

But first, we did our day at the office.

It started at a huge construction site where Basse
Road met McAlister Highway—a half-finished strip
mall on the grounds of the defunct Alamo Cement
Company, right down the street from my mother's
house. Dan pulled in next to a trailer with Sheff Construction's black and white logo on its side.

I looked around at the changed terrain and said:
"God damn."

Of course my mother had told me about the real
estate changes in the old neighborhood, even sent me
some news clippings from time to time, but still I wasn't
prepared for what I saw.

The Alamo Cement Company had been the largest
single piece of private property in Alamo Heights for as
long as I could remember. Its front borders along
Tuxedo and Nacodoches had been carefully sculpted
with acres of trees, trails that nobody ever hiked, and
shady groves that were strictly for show behind a
square mile of storm fencing. Only if you went around

back, next to the Basse Road train tracks, did you see the uglier side of the cement business—four beige smokestacks and a massive wedge of factory, dusty trucks, and freight cars that never seemed to move, floodlights that stayed on twenty-four hours and made the place look like a rocket launch site on a particularly desolate part of the moon. In the center of the quarry the Latino workers lived in an area dubbed Cementville, a collection of shacks so squalid that they could have been directly transplanted from Laredo or Piedras Negras.

Of course hardly any of the wealthy Anglos in the neighborhood ever saw that part. We'd just seen the Cementville kids at school—dirt-poor worker children, dark and hungry-looking, dropped with the greatest irony into the richest public school district in town. They would sit on the steps of the high school, clustered together for protection, surrounded by Izod shirts and new Cutlass Supremes. Ralph Arguello was one of the few who had broken out of the pack by playing football. Most of them had simply disappeared back into the quarries after graduation.

Now, four years after the land had been sold off, only the factory itself had yet to be developed, and it looked like the Sheffs were about to remedy that. The shell of the building and the smokestacks were still there, as were a few broken-down freight cars and trucks, and about twenty odd acres of weeds surrounded by barbed wire. Everything else had already changed. The road to McAlister Highway went right through the old plant grounds past a huge man-made canyon, once the quarry, now lined with million-dollar homes. The shacks of Cementville had been swept away in favor of a golf course, a church, several restaurants. The strip mall Dan's company was constructing was right in the shadow of the old factory.

Dan got out of the BMW and spent about five minutes talking to the foreman. The foreman talked slowly, going over a blueprint, and Dan frowned and nodded a lot, like he was pretending he understood. Then, to the foreman's visible relief, Dan got back into the Beamer and left.

"A day's work well done," I said, figuring we'd be on our way back to the Dominion now.

Only we drove the wrong way—onto I-35 and then south, almost to the city limits, then exited into a war zone of apartment projects. The last time I'd passed them, fluorescent seventies' daisies had adorned the sides of the buildings. Now it was scrawling neon spray paint advertising the *Alacranes* and the *Diablitos*.

"The youth of America is the key," Carl told me. "When will we stop accepting these deviant lifestyles that are destroying our kids?"

"Go deviance," I told the radio.

Not looking like a tail was getting difficult now. It hadn't been easy to begin with in an orange monstrosity like mine. But when you've covered thirty miles from one side of town to the other, it's almost impossible. Fortunately for me, Dan seemed about as aware of his surroundings as a dug-in armadillo. Otherwise I might as well have flashed my high beams and waved a lot.

We drove through the projects, past a mixture of condemned industrial lots and sickly pastures grazing sickly cattle, toward a glass and prefab office complex that looked about thirty seconds old. It squatted defensively in the wastelands of the far South Side, surrounded first by thick, ridiculously out-of-place rows of salvias and petunias, then on the outside by a more honest ten-foot fence topped in barbed wire. A huge white stylized "S" in a black circle was emblazoned on the front gates.

Dan parked in the handicap space and walked through the front doors like he owned the place. He did. I pulled off the road next to a pasture and tried to look inconspicuous.

Think cow, I told the VW.

Carl and I had a nice long chat about local politics while we waited. He told me the socialist environmental types at the Edwards Aquifer District would probably bring about the end of Western Civilization. Then he mentioned the new bond initiative for a fine arts complex that Councilman Fernando Asante had recently pushed through in special election. Carl was skeptical.

"The last thing the taxpayers need," he said, "is another city-funded Travis Center pork barrel."

Then he read the figures on how many double-digit points Asante's popularity had gone up since that first brainchild of his—Travis Center—had opened on the edge of town. Proof positive, Carl said, that the voters have been deluded. Another pork project like that, combined with Asante's new push to be the "law and order" candidate, and old Fernando might actually attain his dream of mayorhood. Carl was even more terrified by that thought than I was.

Dan came out after about an hour and stood at the door with an older Hispanic man. White hair, white mustache, dark blue suit.

Dan's body posture told me he wasn't thrilled with his employee. He stood back as they talked, arms crossed, shifting his weight impatiently from foot to foot. The white-haired man spread his hands in a placating gesture. He did most of the talking. Finally Dan nodded. Gold rings flashed as they shook hands.

We drove north again until Dan's BMW turned onto I-10, heading toward home. I exited at Crossroads Mall, then drove back to Alamo Heights.

"Money," said Carl. "It all boils down to money, my friends."

I drove through Terrell Hills, past the Country Club, then into the forested shade of Elizabeth Street. Tall white houses and old old money. I had a flashback to Senior Party (Alamo Heights had been too cool for a prom back then) when I'd driven down this street bringing Lillian a dozen roses and a dozen balloons for her mother.

"She likes balloons," Lillian had said.

"You're not just setting me up, are you?"

She laughed, then kissed me for a long time. So I brought balloons.

Sure enough, Lillian's mother and I became fast

friends after that, bonded by balloons, much to the chagrin of Mr. Cambridge. Until June fifth in 1985. That night at 8 P.M. I was supposed to meet the Cambridges for dinner at the Argyle with an engagement ring for Lillian. That night at 8 P.M. I was on a Greyhound somewhere outside El Paso, heading west. I hadn't seen Lillian's parents since.

The beige Spanish villa hadn't changed, just sunk a little deeper into the forest of pyracantha. The rough-hewn oak door barely registered my knocks.

"Oh, my," said Mrs. Cambridge.

She tried to frown at me but it wasn't in her nature. The ice melted between us in a matter of seconds, then my neck was wet with her tears, my cheeks well kissed, and my hands filled with ice tea and banana bread. She made the best banana bread. We sat down in her small shadowy den, surrounded by photos of Lillian and a dozen bird cages filled with parakeets, while Mrs. Cambridge began patting ten years of stories into my kneecap.

"Then after college," she was saying, "it was so difficult for her. Oh, Tres, I know it's not your fault, but—well."

Mrs. Cambridge had always been a thin woman, but now she was almost skeletal. Age had left her eyes milky and her skin spotted with chocolate. She held on to my knee like I might disappear any minute. She gave me a genuine smile.

If scum had knees, I was scum. She could've called me any name she wanted, just not that smile again. Her love for me closed up my throat like alum powder.

"Mr. Karnau took such an interest in Lillian's work, you know. They used to go on trips in the country, photographing everything under the sun." She pointed proudly to Lillian's hand-tinted photos on the wall. When she mentioned Karnau she tried to keep her tone lighthearted. I think it was an effort for her. "I didn't know—a young lady and such an older man together alone in the woods, but well—they had such high hopes for the gallery. They needed to have that chance, I suppose. Still, she wasn't really happy."

Mrs. Cambridge had begun crying silently again, wiping away tears with the back of her hand as if it were an old-established habit to cry while you entertained. The parakeets chattered around us.

"Lillian was discouraged, you know, because her own work wasn't selling. More and more it became a business to her, not something she enjoyed. Then she and Daniel had their falling out . . ."

When she mentioned Sheff's name she glanced at me guiltily, as if she might've hurt my feelings.

I tried to smile. "Go on, please."

More knee patting.

"I don't know, Tres. When she said she was talking to you again, after all this time, I didn't know. Ezekiel, of course, well—"

She let that go unsaid. I remembered Mr. Cambridge's booming voice quite clearly.

I looked at Mrs. Cambridge. Her smile was as watery as her eyes.

"I'm sorry," I said, "but what have the police said?"

"I have to let Ezekiel handle that, Tres. I just can't—"

I nodded, accepting her hand in mine.

"And the Sheffs?"

Even Mrs. Cambridge had trouble making it sound genuine. "They've been very sweet."

For several minutes we were quiet, holding each other's hands. Her birds chattered. Then she closed her eyes and began to rock, humming a song I couldn't discern.

When she looked at me again, she seemed to have a secret thought. Smiling weakly, she rose from the couch and went over to the grandfather clock in the corner. From the bottom of the pendulum closet she extracted a Joske's shoe box tied with an ancient ribbon. She brought the box back, setting it on my lap. She removed the lid, then held up a yellowed photograph printed on the thick paper they used in the 1940s. It was black and white but had been lovingly hand-tinted, like the kind of photos Lillian did.

A rakish-looking pilot stared out at me, young and confident. On the back of the photo, in faded blue ink, it said *Angie Gardiner + Billy Terrel*. Vaguely, I remembered Lillian telling me about this man. It had always seemed to me, though, that Lillian considered Terrel almost a myth, someone her mother had made up.

"My first husband," Mrs. Cambridge said. When she looked at me then, I could see the multiple colors in her irises, like Lillian's, and in her smile that vaguest hint of mischief that Lillian mixed so well with love. It was hard to look at.

"Lillian's father doesn't like me to keep these things around. He discourages me from talking about it." Then she added, like a well-worn litany: "Ezekiel's a good man."

"Mrs. Cambridge," I said, "Lillian may be in a lot of trouble. I'm not sure how much the police can help."

She looked at the picture of Billy Terrel. "Lillian couldn't understand when you left. She'd never lost someone like that before. Then so many years later, to have a second chance, like it was all a mistake . . ."

I didn't know what else to do. I bent over and kissed her cheek, very lightly. Then I knew it was time to go.

"I'll find her, Mrs. Cambridge," I said at the door.

I don't think she heard me. Before I could turn away, I saw her hugging that old shoe box, trying to smile and humming along with the bright and senseless chatter of a dozen parakeets.

Then I went out to the car to tell Carl Wiglesworth what was really wrong with the world.

25

I was just making Robert Johnson's usual Friskies taco lunch when Larry Drapiewski called from the Sheriff's Department.

"I'm pretty sure I don't want to tell you this," he said. "Beau Karnau had a restraining order issued against him last year—to stay away from Lillian Cambridge."

I put down the heated flour tortilla and spooned the chicken Friskies over it. Normally I would've sprinkled cheese on top, but we were out. Then I did my best to convince Robert Johnson that his food dish really was full. I shook it. He stared at me. I pretended to sprinkle cheese. He stared at me.

"You get that, son?" Larry said.

"Unfortunately, I got it."

"The way one of the reporting officers remembers it, Karnau kept showing up at Miss Cambridge's house drunk, yelling at her, threatening her. He would go on about how she owed him big and couldn't leave the business. Broke a window once. Never actually struck her."

I stared out the unhinged kitchen window. "What about since last year?"

"The order was rescinded at Miss Cambridge's request in December. No further complaints. Could be old history. There was never any—"

"Okay, Larry. Thanks."

I could hear him tapping his pencil. "Damn it, son—"

"You're going to tell me not to jump to conclusions. Not to fly off the handle."

"Something like that."

"Thanks, Larry."

I hung up.

Robert Johnson was chewing on my ankle. I shook my fist at him. Clearly unimpressed, he started to bury his Friskies taco under the kitchen rug.

When I called Carlon McAffrey at the *Express-News* he sounded like he was in the middle of an especially noisy sandwich. I asked if he'd heard anything interesting lately.

Carlon belched. "Like what kind of 'anything'?"

"You tell me."

"Jesus, Tres, I'll show you mine if you show me yours. What the fuck are you talking about?"

I took that as a no. "Okay. How about the name Beau Karnau?"

Carlon covered the phone and shouted to somebody behind him. After a minute, without reducing the volume, he shouted back into the phone. "Yeah. Karnau's got a photography opening Saturday, Blue Star, some cowboy shit. Why, should I be there?"

"Please no," I said. I could hear Carlon clacking the address and time into his computer calendar.

"Come on, Navarre," he said. He was trying for the "old buddy" treatment now, the syrup in the voice. "Give me something I can use. I've been talking with some people about Guy White, working up that angle on your dad's murder. You thought any more about it?"

"I haven't been thinking in terms of things you can use, Carlon."

"Hey, all I'm saying is we could help each other out.

You come up with something that sells copies, I'll see about getting you compensated for the exclusive."

"You've got the sensitivity of a rottweiler, McAffrey."

He laughed. "But I'm a hell of a lot better-looking."

"Sure. I'll get you a bitch for Christmas."

Then I hung up.

At least I knew Carlon didn't have a clue about Lillian. Otherwise he would've barraged me with questions, and if Carlon didn't know, it meant nobody had talked to the press at all. I grabbed my car keys, left Robert Johnson looking mournfully at his buried lunch, and headed into the afternoon heat.

I had visited Zeke Cambridge at his bank exactly twice in the years that I'd dated his daughter. The first time was when I was sixteen, just before my first formal date with Lillian. I remember sitting in Mr. Cambridge's office in a two-ton leather chair that smelled like cigars, waiting nervously while this monstrous man with a white marble face, green eyes, and an undertaker's suit checked my driver's license. Then he explained, very politely, that he'd been quite a Navy marksman in his younger days and had no compulsion at all against firing at intruders in his home or young men who sat on his daughter's bed. He patted me on the shoulder, offered me a butter toffee from his desk, and told me to have a good time. Of course that was before he knew me.

On my second visit, after Lillian and I had broached the subject of marriage, Zeke Cambridge didn't check my driver's license. He didn't offer me a butter toffee. He just reminded me that he had been quite a Navy marksman in his younger days and had no compulsion at all against firing at young men who married his daughter and then failed to get a good job following college. He gave me a multiple choice test as to what my major at A & M was—petroleum engineering, pre-law, or business. He was not amused when I answered "None of the Above."

"He really likes you, in his own way," Lillian told me afterward.

In the later months of our relationship she had tried to

blame her father's bad temper on the savings and loan crisis, which had hit Crockett S&L just as hard as any.

"He just takes out all the bad investments on the people around him, like you," Lillian explained.

"Sure," I said. "And he's used 'punk' for the last three years as a term of endearment."

Whatever bad investments Mr. Cambridge might've made back then, he seemed to be doing pretty well these days. Crockett Savings and Loan had moved its corporate offices from a small strip mall in Alamo Heights to a four story glass and brick office building on Loop 1604, and Grace June, the old secretary with the beehive and the horn-rims, had been replaced in the front office by a young blonde in a silk blouse and Claiborne skirt. I nodded at her, told her I was expected, and walked on through.

"Um, but—" she started to say behind me.

The two-ton leather chair was still in Mr. Cambridge's office. His plaques from all the right clubs still hung on the wall—Rotary, Republican State Steering Committee, Texas Cavaliers. The butter toffees were still on his desk. Only Zeke Cambridge had changed.

He looked smaller than I remembered, less ogreish. His black suit fit a little looser and his rectangular face had started to sag at the corners. His pointed nose, one of the only things Lillian had inherited from him, had collapsed into a network of red veins.

Mr. Cambridge looked up from a stack of legal papers as I came in and started to ask me a question. When he saw that I wasn't the secretary, he scowled and got up from his chair, a little unsteadily.

Then he showed the other thing Lillian had inherited from him—his temper.

"What the hell are you doing here?"

Behind me, the secretary barely stuck her head in the door, as if she were afraid of having it shot off. "Mr. Cambridge?"

He glared at her over the top of his bifocals, then back at me.

"It's all right, Cameron. This won't take long."

Cameron closed the door. I think she made sure it was locked. Zeke Cambridge stared at me for a long time, then grudgingly gestured me toward the leather chair. He threw his bifocals onto the stack of papers.

"What right do you have coming into my office, boy? Haven't you done enough damage?"

There was a time when those words would've been bellowed loud enough to shake the furniture. I would've apologized for bringing Lillian home late, for using my horn in the driveway, for wearing the wrong clothes in front of their friends, just for fear of being murdered by this man. Now when he spoke, the words were more like hammer strikes on a saw blade, loud but shaky, so watery they were almost absurd in their force.

"I had a feeling you would've refused to see me, sir."

"You're damn right."

"It's about Lillian."

His jawline trembled slightly. "Of course it is."

"Mrs. Cambridge told me—"

He banged his fist on the desk. "Haven't you done enough to my family, damn it?"

The framed pictures didn't rattle. The bowl of toffees didn't move. He sank down into his chair and pounded the desk again with even less force. The anger in his face dissolved into simple frustration.

"Leave my wife alone."

It was strange being able to meet his stare. His green irises had washed down to olive over the years, and his lower lids had loosened so they could barely contain the moisture in the corners of his eyes.

"Mr. Cambridge, I want to help."

"Then leave. Go the hell away."

"If you'd tell me what the police said, maybe I could—"

"The police said nothing. They talk about Laredo. They talk about Lillian being an adult. I've been convinced . . . to wait."

"By the police?"

He glared up at me, his jaw still shaking. "By many people."

"But you don't believe they're right," I said. "Neither do I."

"What I believe is that Lillian had a chance at happiness, boy. What I believe is that you took that away from her—again." He spoke like a man who had just swallowed sour milk.

The words weren't new to me. They brought back years of Thanksgivings, Christmases, birthdays where the conversation had always eventually turned to what I wasn't doing for Lillian. The only difference was that Mrs. Cambridge wasn't here now to steer the conversation someplace else. And this time, maybe, I couldn't argue with him.

Mr. Cambridge nodded, as if agreeing with my thoughts. "They said it might be because of you. The police said that. If it is, boy—"

"Detective Rivas said this?"

Cambridge waved his hand dismissively. "If it is—"

He didn't have to tell me about his younger days in the Navy. I heard the threat just fine.

"Sir, I'd like to have your help, but I'll find Lillian with or without it."

"So help me God, if you interfere—if you make it any harder to get my girl back—"

"It is true she had a falling out with Dan?"

His head was trembling more now. "Nothing that couldn't be mended."

"And you knew that Lillian was leaving the gallery she shared with Beau Karnau?"

He liked hearing Karnau's name about as much as a diminished chord. "She made the right decision— leaving that gallery. It was never right for her. But God damn it, I've always supported her. I never said a word. I'd do anything for my family, boy. I've seen them through. What have you done besides making the hard times worse for her?"

I don't know why. Something in his tone made me uncertain which "her" he was talking about. I thought about Lillian, refusing to say a negative word about her father, hugging him when he came in the door, blaming his terminal bad temper on investments. I thought about Angela Cambridge, probably still sitting in her dark room surrounded by her parakeets, crying, hugging an old shoe box full of dead memories. Then I thought about Zeke Cambridge coming home to that every night for forty years, his determined green eyes eventually washing out with old age, fading a lot faster than that photograph of a pilot who'd never come back. Investments, my ass.

I didn't say anything, but when I looked him in the eye again he heard the pity as clearly as I'd heard his threats. Face trembling, he slapped his stack of legal papers and his bifocals off the desk.

"Get the hell out," he said, his voice surprisingly soft.

I stared at the cracked armrest of the leather chair. I swear I could still see the impressions a sixteen-year-old's nervous fingers had made there, waiting for his driver's license to pass inspection. When I looked back up I almost hoped to see the marble features I remembered, the fierce disapproval. Instead, I saw an old man whose last shot at dignity was making the bowl of butter toffees rattle on his desk.

I got up to leave.

As I closed the door Zeke Cambridge kept staring straight ahead, looking more like an undertaker than ever, one who was getting old and angry and still hadn't successfully buried his first client.

26

Just to piss off Jay Rivas, I spent the rest of the afternoon at SAPD looking through the blotters for any recent mention of the names in Drapiewski's police files. They can't keep you out of the blotters, but they didn't have to like it. My charming guide, Officer Torres, kept glaring at my jugular and making little growling noises in the back of her throat. I almost asked her if I could put a bow on her neck and send her to Carlon McAffrey for Christmas.

After that I visited the mole people at Carlon McAffrey's much-touted newspaper morgue, then the County Bureau of Records.

Never let them tell you an English Ph.D. is useless. True, I don't get many calls to discuss the dirty jokes in *The Canterbury Tales,* even if that was my dissertation topic, but I can research rings around your average P.I. Terrence & Goldman always loved me for that. By five-thirty when the clone of my third-grade teacher kicked me out of Records, I'd whittled Drapiewski's list of twelve FBI suspects in my father's murder down to four viables, or at least questionables. Three others were in Huntsville for life without parole. Four were dead. One was awaiting trial on federal charges. None of them were going anywhere for quite a while, nor could they have been up to anything since I had come back to town. I looked at my four possibles, trying to imagine one of them behind the wheel of a '76 Pontiac with Randall Halcomb. I waited for a volunteer to jump out at me. Nobody raised his hand.

I picked up the tail on Broadway, just as I passed the Pigstand Coffee Shop. Despite local lore, there were no pigs present.

"Never when you need one," I said to the rearview mirror.

The tail was a black Chrysler, early eighties model. I cursed the lenient Texas regulations on window tinting. I couldn't see the car's interior worth a damn. Problem number two with driving a VW bug: Unless your tail is driving a very old Schwinn with less than ten gears, you can pretty much forget losing them.

They weren't interested in hanging back, either. I hadn't even had enough time to say a "Hail Mary" before the Chrysler pulled around the intervening cars and went into high gear, coming around on my left. When I saw the shotgun window roll down I remembered why they call it the shotgun window. Then I yanked on the wheel, hard.

I'll say this for the VW. It handles sidewalks a lot nicer than your average Chrysler. I was across two front lawns, a parking lot, and into an alley before the enemy managed to pull their boat around. Thank God for my high school years, revving around these streets with Ralph like we were James Dean's drunk and ugly younger brothers. I still knew the turns and I took them. Another good thing about the VW: The engine's in the back so you aren't blinded when it starts burning to hell and billowing black smoke.

After ten minutes without seeing the Chrysler I slowed down to fifty in the twenty zone on Nacodoches and took inventory. That's when I noticed the new ventilation in the ragtop. Three holes the size of .45 bullets on the left side, three identical holes on the right side. The nearest one was about six inches south of my head. I hadn't even heard them.

"So much for not being willing to kill me," I said, cursing Maia Lee.

I'd like to say I was calm when I got back to Queen Anne. The truth was, when I found that Robert Johnson still hadn't eaten his Friskies taco, I kicked it across the living room. The dish, that is, not Robert Johnson.

"Enough is enough," I told him.

Something under my dirty laundry in the closet said: "Row."

Then the phone rang.

I must have sounded like a man who'd just gotten shot at and spurned by his pet, because Ralph Arguello paused for a second before responding: "Mother of God, *vato*. What *cavron* spit in your *huevos* this morning?"

Behind him, the sounds of the Blanco Cafe were all much louder than they had been that morning—more shouting waitresses, more customers talking, more blaring *conjunto* from the jukebox.

"I've had a great day, Ralph," I said. "Somebody just drilled me a skylight in the VW with a .45."

There were a lot of ways somebody could respond to that. For Ralph there was only one choice: he laughed long and hard.

"You need a beer and a shot of real tequila," he suggested. "Come out with me tonight."

"Maybe another time, Ralphas."

I could almost hear his Cheshire cat grin over the phone.

"Even to a little cantina where your lady friend was on Sunday night?" he said.

Silence. "What time?" I asked.

27

Ralph's maroon Lincoln slid down South St. Mary's like a leather-upholstered U-boat.

" 'Scuse me if I hit a few pedestrians," he said. He laughed. I didn't. With the black window tinting, the moonless night, and the haze of bay rum and mota smoke in the car, I couldn't see a damn thing out the front windshield. And I didn't wear prescription glasses. Ralph just smiled and took another hit off his cigar-sized joint.

We turned down Durango and cruised through a neighborhood of neon-colored clapboards. Their front yards, not much bigger than Ralph's backseat, were decorated with cola caps in the trees, statues of saints in the painted gravel, plastic milk jugs filled with colored water along the sidewalks. An old lady in a worn-out muumuu stood in the orange square of porch light on her front steps, slicing potatoes and watching us as we passed by.

Ralph sighed like a man in love. "Home again."

I stared at him. "You were raised North Side, Ralphas. You went to Alamo Heights, for Christ's sake."

His smile didn't waver. "All that means is my momma cleaned for a better class of folk, *vato*," he said. "Doesn't mean shit about where your home is at."

On the corner of Durango and Buena Vista we pulled into a gravel lot outside the world's smallest outdoor cantina. Three green picnic tables squatted on a red concrete slab. In the back, a stack of fruit crates and an old Coca-Cola cooler passed for the bar. The whole place was ringed by a low cinder-block wall and covered by sagging corrugated tin, strung with the obligatory Christmas lights. Nobody had bothered to put up a sign for the cantina. It just naturally radiated *conjunto* music and the promise of cold beer.

Ralph put down the mota and picked up a S & W Magnum, almost invisible in the dark. It disappeared under the linen folds of his olive-green extra-large guayabera. He smiled at me.

"Subtle," I said.

"Last offer," he said. "You want a piece, I got that nice little Delta in the glove compartment."

I shook my head.

"More trouble than it's worth," I said. "That shit causes bad karma."

He laughed. "Somebody going to spill your karma right out the back of your head, my friend, you think like that."

Lydia Mendoza's voice, badly recorded fifty years earlier and still sexy as hell, drifted across the patio with the smells of tobacco and cumin. All three tables were crowded with men in dirty blue work shirts with their names embroidered on the pockets. Their brown faces were worn and hardened like pieces of driftwood. They sat and smoked, watching us as we walked to the bar.

"*Que pasa,*" Ralph said, totally unfazed by their stares. One of the men smiled like a jackal, lifted his beer bottle very slightly, then turned back to his friends. Someone else laughed. Then they ignored us.

Ralph dragged two green metal stools up to the fruit crates and nodded to the bartender.

"Tito," he said. "*Dos* Budweisers."

For a minute I was convinced Tito was a work of taxidermy. Nothing moved—his thick frown, his eyes, his huge frog-shaped body. Tattooed arms hung limp at his sides. Under the yellow silk shirt his chest didn't move. I was tempted to borrow Ralph's coke spoon and hold it under Tito's nose just to see if he was really breathing. Finally, very slowly, Tito's eyes drifted over to me and fixed there. Somewhere in his chest he made a sound like a motor boat engine getting stuck in mud.

"*¿De donde sacaste el gringo?*" he said.

Ralph drank his beer, then looked at me like he'd never seen me before.

"Who," he said, "this guy? Wants to break into the pawn business, man. Teaching him everything I know."

Tito didn't exactly react, but he let his eyes slide off me like bird shit off a windshield. Behind us, one of the drinkers finished a joke about a gringo lawyer and a donkey. His friends laughed.

"So," Ralph said. "I heard about that white woman last Sunday."

Tito had solidified again. He gave no response at all, just stared at Ralph blankly.

"Your friend is making me nervous, Ralphas," I said in English. "Could you tell him to calm down?"

A tattooed cobra on Tito's forearm twitched almost imperceptibly.

"*No se,* man," Tito told Ralph. "I just open the beers."

Ralph took his glasses off and cleaned them on his shirt. When he did, he let Tito see the .357 clearly. Then he smiled.

"Man," he said, "how long we known each other? What was that loan I did you, anyway? Three grand?"

Tito stayed blank, but the cobra twitched again.

I looked back at the other customers. Three of the tougher ones at the end of the nearest table were paying more attention to us now. They sat slightly apart from the others, not quite as weathered-looking, not laughing at the jokes. The only grease on these three was carefully applied to their hair. Their work shirts were open over striped tank tops, stretched tight over their pects.

When I glanced at Ralph, he was already looking at me. His slight nod told me he knew about the competition. Meanwhile Tito wasn't talking. He produced two more beers. He turned up the knob on Lydia Mendoza. Then he played taxidermy.

"Well," said Ralph, "that's a real pisser, Tito. A lady with some class walks into this shithole and you don't even want to remember it, man. That's bad."

"Huh," said Tito. He looked about as intimidated as a stoned mule.

Then a dirty gray rag appeared in his hand. He started making lazy circles across the top of the counter. Maybe he thought he was cleaning it.

Ralph looked over at me and started talking loud enough to be heard at the tables.

"So this friend of mine was here last night, like I said. And he tells me a couple of the regulars here were talking about this lady that came in Sunday. It was a big joke over a couple of beers, he says. But you know, *vato,* these *hotos* can't keep anything in their heads longer than a few minutes unless it's somebody else's *pendejo.* I guess we're shit out of luck."

"Ralphas," I said. I was wondering if he'd laced his joint with something more potent. His will to live, and for me to live, seemed pretty damn weak at the moment. He just held up his fingers to placate me and kept talking.

"Yeah," he said. "Tito, man, you ought to think about cattle for this place. Eat and drink less than these *cavrons* but more intelligent, and you could at least make *barbacoa* when you got tired of them."

It got very quiet. Then one of the tough guys started to get up. He was chewing on something, maybe a stick. When he smiled his front two teeth flashed silver. His two *compadres* kept their seats, but they turned around to stare at us. Tito's other patrons had frozen like mice under a cat's paw.

Ralph stayed calm, a little too calm for my tastes. He gave the guy with the silver teeth a smile like they were long-lost friends.

"So, Tito," Ralph said, not looking at the bartender. "How you feeling, man? You want to tell me anything? Like is this the guy she was with?"

Tito still didn't look like he wanted to chat with us. He shrugged very slightly.

"Eh, *chingado*," Silver-teeth said. "Maybe we should do you up some *barbacoa*, huh? Maybe you got enough fat to fry."

Ralph spread his hands in a friendly gesture. "A man can only try, my friend. Or maybe if you got a story for me, we can hear that. Then we can all have another beer."

"You want a beer?" Silver-teeth leaned over and broke his bottle on the cinder-block wall. Then he held up the jagged neck and smiled.

"Shit, man," said Ralph. He was already holding his revolver, eight inches of black steel that reflected the colored Christmas lights beautifully. "You want to play with me you got to get better toys."

Then he fired twice, which from a .357 is only slightly less impressive than a cannon barrage. Beer bottles exploded on the table, sending glass fragments and brown foam into the faces of Silver-teeth's pals. There was one yelp of pain, then silence. Silver-teeth almost fell back over the edge of the wall. The rest of the bar patrons stayed very very still.

"That's how you break glass," Ralph told them. "Now, who wants to tell me something?"

I wouldn't have believed that Tito could move so fast. He had the double-barrel half out of the Coca-Cola cooler and was turning toward Ralph when I slammed the metal seat of my stool into his face. Crude but effective. Tito's nose flattened like a paper tent and he went down.

Ralph whistled. "They teach you that in kung fu class?"

I shrugged.

Then I stepped back around the bar and unloaded the shotgun. Tito was making his motor boat sound again, blowing red bubbles against the red cement.

"*Hijo*," said Silver-teeth.

Ralph smiled and turned the gun on him. "So what's your name, *vato*?"

"Carlos, man."

"You got a bedtime story for us, my friend Carlos?"

Carlos's dark face drained out until it was the color of heavily creamed coffee. He dropped his broken bottleneck and held up his empty palms. He said: "You're looking for Eddie, man. He ain't here tonight. And I swear to God, I just heard about it."

Carlos's two friends were getting up now, wiping the blood and foam out of their faces. One had an inch-long fragment of beer glass sticking from his forehead like a rhino horn. I don't think he even felt it, but he was pissed as hell.

"Jaime," Carlos murmured. "Cool it, man."

But Jaime wasn't interested. He came at Ralph fast and stupid. Fortunately for him, Ralph was in a good mood now. Instead of putting a bullet in his face, Ralph just implanted the tip of his boot in Jaime's gut. In slow motion, the wounded man curled up at Ralph's feet like a faithful old dog.

Ralph turned back to Carlos. "Okay. Let's try that again."

Carlos swallowed.

"Eddie Moraga," he said. "I heard he was in here a few nights ago with this lady. He's a friend of Tito's, man, a regular here."

Under my feet, Tito started making wet, half-conscious grunts.

"And?" Ralph asked.

"That's it."

Ralph waited, smiling.

"Shit, man," Carlos pleaded, "a friend told me about it. I don't know."

Ralph's next shot took out a healthy chunk of concrete in front of Carlos's left foot. By sheer luck, none of the fragments killed anybody.

"You'd better tell me about Eddie," Ralph suggested.

I thought I was hearing beer pouring off the tables from the broken bottles. Then I saw the stream coming out the bottom of Carlos's jeans.

"Jesus, man," he said. "Eddie's ex-Air Force. He's a construction worker. What the fuck else do you want?"

I handed Ralph the photos of suspects from Larry Drapiewski's files. Ralph glanced at them, then held them up for Carlos to see, one at a time, leisurely.

"Which one is he?" Ralph said.

Carlos looked, then shook his head, almost reluctantly. "No, man. None of these. He's about twenty-six, crew cut, kind of light-skinned. Tattoo. Heavy on top, you know? Pumps iron. Drives a green Chevy. Eddie's here most nights by this time, man. I don't know where the fuck he is."

Tattoo. Construction worker? Wait a minute. I rapped on the bar to get Carlos's attention.

"This tattoo," I said. "About here, eagle and a snake?"

Carlos glanced over at me, then nodded, very slowly.

"Que padre," said Ralph. "Now how about the story?"

Carlos addressed Ralph's gun as he talked. "Eddie comes in Sunday night, I don't know when, late. He's got this girl by the arm, kind of skinny but good-looking, sort of blond hair. And she's stumbling like she's really wasted, so Eddie jokes with us that she's got to go puke. She had jeans and a black shirt on, nice tits. So they go back to the Porta-John and he waits for her to come out. The pay phone's right over there, you know? So he makes a call. Says to us he can't stick around. But the funny thing is this lady kicks Eddie on the shin as they're going back to the car, and we all start laughing. Then he sort of slaps her, you know, cuts her across the eye with his ring, and they get in the car. That's it."

He said it matter-of-fact, like it happened every night at Tito's. I swallowed. Maybe I would've gotten more emotional, but something about Ralph and that .357 kept me cool and sober.

"How did the girl act?" I asked. "Besides wasted."

Carlos looked at me like the question was in Japanese. "Her? Shit, I don't know. Like they always act, you know? Pissed off, I guess—arguing, hitting him."

Instead of using my stool on him, I said: "Did it cross your mind she might be in trouble?"

He almost laughed at that, then he remembered the gun.

"With Eddie every lady's in trouble," he said. "She didn't scream or help or anything, man. Nothing like that."

"Did Eddie have a piece?"

Carlos looked helpless. "I didn't even think about it, man. I don't think so. I know he carries sometimes. He does some work for some friends of his sometimes; that's what I hear."

"What friends?" Ralph said.

"I don't have any idea, man. That's the truth. He just said—yeah, he said one thing. That he had to get up early tomorrow, 'cause the lady had to make a phone call for him. That's it, man."

Monday morning, when Lillian had supposedly left her message with Beau about Laredo. I pictured her making it with a gun pressed against her neck. I pictured Beau not giving a damn.

That's when I heard sirens in the distance, coming from downtown. Ralph yawned. He slid off his stool. Then he stretched his arms leisurely and put the gun away.

"You see Eddie," Ralph said, "tell him he's been dead since Sunday. Rigor just hasn't set in yet."

Lydia Mendoza had finished her last song, but nobody changed the tape. We walked out to the

parking lot in silence, then we disappeared down
Durango in the maroon U-boat. On the dashboard, the
tip of Ralph's joint hadn't even gone out yet.

After a few minutes I said: "You know this Eddie?"

He shook his head. "You?"

I nodded. "I had to kick him in the balls outside
Hung Fong."

Ralph glanced over at me, impressed. We drove a few
more blocks in silence.

"Why would you take a girl you'd just kidnapped to
a bar?" I said. "It'd make more sense to get out of sight
and stay there."

"You afraid the lady was with him by choice?"

I didn't say anything. Ralph smiled. "No, man. Guys
like this Eddie, they don't need to make sense. Long as
they make a good show."

I thought about that. Then I said: "Just this morning
I told a friend of mine in California how you like a low
profile, Ralphas. That was before I saw your Annie
Oakley routine."

Ralph laughed. "You know how many bar fights and
shootings go on in this side of town every night, *vato*?
That *was* low profile."

"Oh."

Ralph inhaled about an inch of the mota, then blew it
out through his nose. We drove for a long time. But
when I closed my eyes I saw Tito's pulverized face, Lillian with a bloody eye, a red cement floor chipped and
splattered on. And still Ralph looked out his window,
watching the multicolored yards of the South Side and
sighing like a hopeless romantic. A romantic with blood
on his boots.

"Besides," Ralph said after a while, "I always wanted
to be Annie Oakley, man."

We both laughed about that for a long time.

28

Three hours later I should've been asleep on the futon with Robert Johnson snoring on my head. Instead I was crouching outside a chain-link fence in the weeds.

"No accounting for intelligence," I told the cow next to me.

She grumbled in agreement.

Except for my bovine friend and occasional gunshots from the nearby apartment projects, it was quiet. The guard inside the glass doors of Sheff Construction looked about as excited to be here as I was. His mouth was open. He had his feet up on the desk, his face lit up blue from the portable TV on his belly. In the binoculars his name tag said "Timothy S."

I'd circled the grounds and watched for almost forty-five minutes before I was relatively sure that Timothy S. was alone in the building. From there it was easy.

"Cover me," I told the cow.

Two minutes to clip along the base of the fence and roll under, then thirty seconds across the petunias and up to the side of the building. Contact paper on the bathroom window, a small muffled break next to the latch, and a minute later I was inside standing on the urinal.

Once my eyes adjusted to the dark I slipped into the hallway. Down on the left, I could hear Lucy and Ricky having it out on the guard's TV set. I went right, into a room of work cubicles. On my way through I put a garbage can in the doorway, just in case the guard decided to do something radical like patrol the area.

A door in the back said "D. Sheff." It wasn't locked. After a few minutes inside I saw why. Dan had no computer on his desk, no files in the cabinet, no paperwork of any kind except a few dog-eared novels. There was a decanter of Chivas in the side drawer of the desk and a Looney Tunes glass like the kind Texaco used to give with a fill-up. The closet was less friendly: an extra Bill Blass jacket, no matching slacks, and a box of .22 ammunition, no matching gun.

I slipped out of the office and tried another door. This one said "T. Garza." And it was locked, for a few seconds anyway.

Once inside I sat down in Garza's leather chair, behind his oak desk, and looked at his picture of the wife and kids. An attractive Hispanic woman in her forties, two sons about six and nine. Garza stood behind them smiling, a thin, athletic-looking man with silver hair and mustache, a nervous smile, eyes as dark as an East Indian's. He was the man I'd seen Dan arguing with in front of the office that afternoon.

His desk drawers were unlocked and the computer terminal was still on. Damn accommodating. At least it seemed that way until I was denied access to every file I tried to open.

I studied the dimmed screen. If I were an ordinary schmuck I would've spent the next few hours hunting for passwords in Garza's desk and file cabinets. Instead I took out the disk my big brother had traded me six months ago for a pair of Jimmy Buffett tickets.

"Mr. Garza," I said quietly, "meet Spider John."

Good old Garrett. When my half brother wasn't smoking pot or following Jimmy Buffett around the country, he made innocuous system extension programs for an Austin computer firm called RNI. When he *was* smoking pot and following Jimmy Buffett around the country, he made not-so-innocuous programs like Spider John. I never figured out how it worked. Garrett had talked to me about weaving temporary logic webs around command functions until I went cross eyed. Finally I'd said: "Give it to me in three words or less."

Garrett gave me one of his toothy grins. "Ganja for computers, little bro."

Whatever it did, when I put the disk in and Spider John's black web wove across the screen, to the muted tune of "Havana Daydreamin'," Mr. Garza's computer suddenly smiled at me and mellowed out something considerable. Anything I punched in for a password seemed perfectly groovy now. MICKEY MOUSE, I typed. COOL, it said, and showed me Sheff Construction's personnel files.

Eddie Moraga was listed on the payroll as a half-time carpenter. No health benefits. No special duties noted, such as abducting women from their homes or intimidating English Ph.D.s in front of Chinese restaurants. Twelve thousand dollars a year. But that wasn't including a ten-thousand-dollar monthly item labeled "expenses."

A carpenter with an expense account. Not since Jesus, I figured.

I tried to access a description for that field, hit another roadblock, typed EAT ME for a password. Even then the computer didn't offer much of an explanation for what Sheff Construction expected Eddie to spend his petty cash on, just a familiar address—HECHO A MANO GALLERY, 21 LA VILLITA WAY. The expense account had been drawn on at the end of each month for the last year, in regular cash installments, and was authorized by the man whose chair I was borrowing—Terry Garza. The date for the next withdrawal was marked "7/31." I took out the two cut-up photos I'd retrieved from Beau's portfolio. They were marked on the back in black pen: "7/31."

I looked up at Garza's picture.

"Supporting the arts?" I asked him.

Garza's picture smiled back, looking a little nervous.

I typed a few more insults for passwords and started skimming through the Sheffs' financial spreadsheets. There wasn't much to look at—very few jobs had been done this year, very little money was coming in. In fact, Sheff Construction seemed to have been surviving until last year on one bread-and-butter contract alone: Travis Center. Hmm.

I looked at the company profits for the last decade. From '83–'85 there hadn't been any. Just some fairly massive debts, probably some fairly nervous corporate creditors. Then, almost overnight, the debts disappeared quietly and completely. In their place had been the Travis Center project.

Sheff's long and healthy profit margin for the past decade until last year suggested that Travis Center had gone way over budget and way behind schedule. Your tax dollars at work. But now Travis Center was completed and it looked like Sheff Construction was heading back into the red.

I looked at their projections for next year—there was only one pending deal. The entire resources of the company were already committed to building the city's new fine arts complex. Sheff Construction had done their cost estimates based on the bidding price the city had approved, figured their payroll based on that income, and had a pretty good estimated timetable for their subcontractors. They would be back in the black again easily.

The only problem was that the bidding process for the fine arts complex project, according to my radio chum Carl Wiglesworth, hadn't even started yet.

I stared at the computer screen, wondering how Sheff had monopolized a huge city works project like Travis Center. And, more importantly, how they could be so damn sure they would get the next one. I was just about to ask the computer those questions when the office door swung open.

"Before I call the security guard," the man in the doorway said, "maybe you'd explain why you're sitting at my desk."

Terry Garza didn't look as good as his picture. His silver hair was flat on the left side and he had red lines on his cheek like he'd just been sleeping on a corduroy-covered pillow. He was wearing the same dark blue suit pants he'd had on that afternoon, half untucked from his gray Justins. His shirt was wrinkled and his tie was hanging loose around his neck. In the picture he also wasn't holding a tiny silver .22.

I shut down Spider John and spit out the disk. Then I stood up very carefully.

"Sorry," I said. "I talked to Dan earlier, said I'd be coming by tonight. I thought he'd cleared it with you. Tim out front didn't mention you were still here."

I held up my key chain, as if it were proof that I'd come in legitimately. I looked innocent, meeting Garza's stare.

Garza's dark eyes narrowed. The gun lowered a few inches, then came back up again.

"I don't think so," he said.

"Maybe if I was wearing a tie?"

A smile flickered across the left side of Garza's mouth. "Timothy is his last name. Sam Timothy. Nobody calls him Tim."

"Shit. Missed the comma."

"Yeah."

Garza motioned for me to come around the desk, turned me around, then did a pretty professional job of patting me down with one hand. He took the computer disk out of my pocket.

"They teach you frisking in contractors' school?" I asked.

He gave me another half smile. We were buddies now. Then he went around the desk to reclaim his leather chair and left me standing on the other side. His face looked calm, still half-asleep, but his dark eyes were alert, maybe a little anxious. They got more anxious when they saw Beau Karnau's photos on the desk. Garza looked quickly from me to the photos, to the computer, then back at me.

"So," he said thinly, "who have we got here?"

"We've got Jackson Tres Navarre. No comma."

Garza stared at me for a minute. Then he actually smiled all the way. "No kidding."

I didn't like the way he said that. Garza must've read my expression. He just shrugged.

"You made Dan angry this morning, Mr. Navarre. So I said to him, 'I'll keep my eyes open.' I close my eyes for a while and—" He snapped his fingers, then pointed at me. "I just think that's funny."

He met my eyes and tried to look relaxed, like he was in charge. His teeth were as white as his mustache. His fingers had tightened on the gun a little too much for my taste.

"Hysterical," I agreed. I looked down at the family picture on his desk. "No other place to sleep, Mr. Garza? Problems at home, maybe?"

Garza's smile hardened. His face turned the rusty color of Hill Country granite.

"Let's talk about you," he said.

I was thinking about options for leaving Garza's office without a police escort or a bullet in my anatomy. At the moment the alternatives seemed slim. I decided, for the moment, to confuse him with the truth.

"Dan wanted to hire me," I told him. "We talked this morning about Lillian Cambridge."

Garza stroked his mustache. "Do you always start a job by investigating your boss, Mr. Navarre?"

"Only when I have questions."

Garza leaned back in his chair. He propped one foot on the edge of the desk. I couldn't help noticing the bottom of his boot—no grooves, pointed toe, maybe a ten and a half wide.

"Such as?" he asked.

"For starters, how you got the contract on Travis Center, and how you managed to win the fine arts complex before the bidding process even started. Last I checked, fixing city contracts was a legal no-no."

Garza said nothing. His smile had frozen.

"I'm also wondering who the two missing people in that picture might be, who the blond guy is, and why it might be worth ten thousand dollars a month to Sheff Construction. I keep thinking, if I were Beau Karnau, and my art wasn't selling so well, and I somehow came across evidence that my studio partner's fiancé was up to some very profitable, very illegal insider deals with city contracts—well, I might just be tempted to take some photos of him and whoever his partners were. I might just blackmail the hell out of them."

Garza rested the butt of his little silver gun on the top of the desk. In the light of the computer screen it looked blue and translucent, like a water pistol.

"Is that all, Mr. Navarre?"

"Except for one thing. What size boot do you wear, Mr. Garza?"

I smiled. Garza smiled. Keeping one eye on me, Garza slipped my disk into the computer.

"Eleven wide, Mr. Navarre. As to the rest, assuming you have any business asking, you'd have to talk to Mr. Sheff."

"Which Mr. Sheff? The comatose one or the one with the Looney Tunes glass in his desk? They both seem equally well informed about the family business."

Garza shook his head, obviously disappointed in me. He showed me the hand that wasn't holding the gun, palm out. "You see these?"

"Fingers," I said. "I count five."

He smiled. "Calluses, Mr. Navarre. Something you don't see much these days. A blue-collar man who's made a decent living—that's a dying breed, a dinosaur." He tapped the family photo with the side of his gun. "Worked construction since I was fifteen, don't have much formal education, but I manage to support my family pretty well. I like my employers for giving me that. And I don't have much patience for privileged young Anglo shits who break into my office at three in the morning and try to tear it all up."

He was still smiling, his knuckles white on the gun. Legally, we both knew, he could shoot me right now for trespassing and the biggest complication he would face would be how to dry-clean the rug. Then Spider John wove its web across the computer screen one more time to the tune of "Havana Daydreamin'."

"Now let's see what you've got here," Garza said. "Before I erase it, and decide whether or not I need to erase you."

That's when I saw the car.

When the headlights got near enough to shine through the window behind Garza's desk, Garza glanced around briefly and scowled, probably wondering who the new early morning visitor could be. But he was more worried about me. He turned back to the computer screen. I couldn't see anything but headlights, getting big very quickly.

Let's see what happens when it turns toward the gate, I thought.

Stupid, Navarre. The car didn't turn toward the gate. I stood there frozen and watched it come straight through the fence, past my friend the cow, through the petunias, and down my throat.

I think I rolled toward the doorway before the window exploded. I don't remember. When I opened my eyes, a few hundred years later, I was wedged between the wall and Garza's overturned desk, about four inches shy of having been pressed into a human tortilla. The back of my head felt like it had rubbed off against the carpet. Somewhere close by, Terry Garza was groaning. His eleven wide boot was in my face.

From floor level all I could see of the car that had nearly killed us was the ruined front end—radiator steam hissing out in several places, blue metal and tangled chrome teeth that looked like they were trying to eat Garza's desk. I could smell gasoline. Finally I looked above me, hazily, and saw three small holes. It took me a while to realize that two of them were the security guard's nostrils. The third was the barrel of his gun.

"Jesus Christ," Timothy, S. was saying. He was pointing the gun at me but looking into the car. "Jesus fucking H. Christ."

I tried to sit up, to see what he was seeing. It wasn't one of my better ideas.

"Don't even do shit, God damn it," Timothy, S. said. The quivery sound in his voice told me he was very close to breaking, even closer to blowing my face off.

I sat back and jarred Garza's boot. Garza groaned.

Timothy, S.'s nostrils kept dilating. His face had gone totally yellow now, even his eyes.

"Jesus H. Christ," he said again. Then he threw up.

"The driver is dead?" I asked.

The guard looked at me and tried to laugh. It came out as a yelp. "Yeah. Yeah, you might could say that, shithead."

Very slowly I put up my hands.

"Look," I said. "I need to get up. You smell the gasoline, right?"

Timothy, S. just stared at me, his gun leveled.

Okay, I thought. I kept my hands in plain view while I got up. Then I hobbled out from behind the desk, bent over like a question mark. Garza kept moaning from underneath a pile of books and unpotted plants.

I looked over at where Garza's office wall had been.

The car was an old blue Thunderbird convertible, or it had been before it was driven through the wall. The hood was crumpled like a contour map of the Rockies. The windshield was shattered. Somebody had tied the wheel straight and laid a slab of granite over the accelerator. The T-bird probably would have barreled right on through the building it if hadn't lost an axle when it jumped up onto the foundation.

The driver's seat was occupied.

My intestines started dissolving and trickling down into my shoes. I could still see the eagle killing the snake on Eddie Moraga's forearm. Eddie was wearing the same denim shirt he'd had on the night he attacked me

outside Hung Fong. Except for that he was hard to recognize. A person can be that way when his eyes have
been tunneled out with a pistol at point-blank.

I'm not sure what happened after that. I do know
that when the police arrived, the guard and I were sitting in the broken glass, staring into space, talking like
old friends about the living and the dead. Garza
groaned like a chorus in the corner. I didn't care about
Detective Schaeffer asking me questions. I didn't even
care when Jay Rivas arrived, dragged me into a room,
and slapped me across the side of the face. I just spat
blood and teeth and kept staring into the headlights
that I still saw coming at me, running over everything
and everyone that mattered.

29

Chen Man Cheng once said that if your movements were refined enough you should be able to practice tai chi in a closet. He never said anything about doing it in a jail cell.

When I rose to meet the new day with my usual exercise routine, my head was pounding, my stomach was empty and sore, and my mouth had swollen to the size of a small cantaloupe. The stink of old urine and semen from the bunk mattress had rubbed off on my clothes. My tongue tasted like Robert Johnson's food dish. In short, I was looking and feeling my best as I started my first set.

"What the fuck is that?" my cellmate said.

One of his parents had obviously been a Weimaraner. He was incredibly thin and desperate-looking, with splotchy skin and a face that was almost all nose. He hunched over in the top bunk, staring down at me with a pained smile. He wheezed when he spoke.

Maybe I could've moved my mouth enough to respond to his question, but I didn't try. It was taking all my concentration just to keep from falling over or throwing up. After the first set he lost interest and laid back down.

"Goddamn nutcase," he wheezed.

By the time I started my low form routine I'd managed to work up a good sweat. I'd like to say I felt better. The truth is my mind was just clearer and more able to appreciate how screwed up things really were.

We had the talented Mr. Karnau, whose photographs, even if they were poo-pooed by the art world, were still fetching ten grand a month from certain interested patrons. It seemed a lot to pay for an original Karnau, unless the shot was one the buyers didn't want publicized, and the payment was blackmail money to protect—say— some illegally contracted construction jobs worth millions. Then a little payoff, a little abduction, maybe a little murder, started looking cost-effective. And Beau had started this line of work last year about the same time Lillian had demanded out of their business. Back then Beau had gotten sufficiently violent to warrant a restraining order. Now that Lillian wanted out of the business again, she had disappeared altogether.

We had the dashing Mr. Sheff, who seemed eager to lead his company to greatness as soon as his mother combed his hair and tied his shoes. I couldn't see a nineteen-year-old Dan initiating the Travis Center scheme ten years ago. I could barely see a twenty-nine-year-old Dan carrying on the family tradition now by fixing the bidding on the new fine arts complex. Nevertheless, he'd lied to me about Beau, had just about gone apoplectic when I mentioned the name, and he certainly had a strong desire to claim Lillian as his territory months after Lillian started having other ideas. Either Dan Jr. or someone else in Sheff Construction— his mother, or maybe Garza acting on his own—had arranged Karnau's payment, then Lillian's kidnapping, then Garza's desperate search for whatever it was they wanted so badly. And Sheff Construction wasn't in this alone. There had been two people cut out of Karnau's blackmailing photo, and two copies of it in his portfolio, which meant somebody else was getting Karnau's bill too. Maybe that somebody was getting pissed at their partners in Sheff Construction. Maybe that's why Eddie Moraga came back to work last night dead.

But there were too many maybes.

All night long I'd been dreaming about Eddie Moraga's blue T-bird, except it was me behind the wheel, or sometimes Lillian. She would look at me and say: *"I've been saving this for you, Tres."* Only one answer made sense to me about why Lillian disappeared when she did, and why Garza would want to ransack her house, her gallery, then my apartment. Lillian had given me something for safekeeping, something I'd inadvertently given away.

I finished tai chi about the time the guard brought breakfast.

I tried to eat powdered eggs from a plastic tray. The pain in my mouth was so bad with every bite I might as well have tried chewing on staples. Above me the Weimaraner seemed to be nuzzling his breakfast to death. I held up the rest of mine and he snatched it instantly.

When I heard the metal gate buzz at the end of the hallway and two pairs of shoes coming my way, I figured Rivas was coming to gloat. Maybe he'd found some sadistic friend to bring along this time. I put on my best mean and stoic look, tried not to drool out of my busted mouth, and stood to face them.

It was worse than I had imagined. When the guard slid back the door I was standing face-to-face with my mother. She instantly grabbed my cheeks for a kiss and sent a wave of hot lava from my gums all the way to my toenails.

"Oh, Tres," she said, "I'm sorry."

Through tears of pain I managed to nod.

Mother had come prepared. Her vanilla essence was so strong it even dissolved the stench of the cell. She'd pulled a colorful Guatemalan patchwork cloak around her to ward off the institutional green. She was wearing so much Mexican silver jewelry I imagined she could've hidden several metal files in there without arousing much suspicion. Fortunately I didn't need to find out.

She stood there, sadly shaking her head. Then she said: "Let's go home."

Still dazed, I shuffled out behind her into the light and bureaucracy of the Bexar County Jail Annex. Three or four pounds of paperwork later, they brought us into a conference room that was empty except for a table and four chairs. In one of those chairs was Homicide Detective Gene Schaeffer, looking as sleepy as he'd sounded the first time I'd talked to him on the phone five days ago. In the second chair was a fifty-year-old incarnation of a Ken doll, dressed in a summer-weight white Armani suit.

"Tres," my mother said, looking at the Armani Ken doll, "this is Byron Ash. Mr. Ash has agreed to represent you."

It took a minute for the name to sink in. Then I raised my eyebrows. "Lord Byron," formerly of the King Ranch, probably the most high-profile corporate lawyer in South Texas. It was said that when Byron Ash sneezed, the price of oil fell and state judges caught pneumonia. My mother would've had to mortgage her house just to pay his consultation fee. I looked at her in amazement. For some reason, she didn't seem at all pleased with her accomplishment. In fact, she seemed almost sour.

"I'll explain later, dear," she muttered.

Ash smiled slicker than Texas crude. "We were just discussing this unfortunate incident with Detective Schaeffer, Mr. Navarre. And although criminal law is not my specialty, it would seem to me—"

He turned that smile on Schaeffer, started talking, and fifteen minutes later I was a free man. I'm not sure exactly what happened. Ash established that I was not at present charged with anything. Certainly I was not under suspicion in the Eddie Moraga homicide. The Sheffs had decided not to press charges against me for trespassing. Therefore I could not be held. Ash used the word "liability" a lot. Schaeffer made a lame admonition for me to "stay available for questioning." I made a lame promise to "stay out of police business." Rivas never showed up.

Mother took one arm, Byron Ash took the other, and we walked outside onto the steps of the Annex. The morning sky was overcast and a hot wind pushed dried pecan leaves across the sidewalk like little canoes. The scent of advancing rain hung in the air like aluminum. I'd never smelled anything so good.

I didn't think it was possible for me to have any more surprises that morning. One dead body, almost two including myself, breakfast in jail, and a high-priced lawyer shaking my hand just about filled my quota. But when I spotted Mother's Volvo, where she'd illegally parked it on North San Marcos, most of my internal organs folded into a slipknot and pulled themselves taut.

Byron Ash strolled down to the Volvo, shook hands with the woman waiting there, said "No problem," then strolled away.

My mother sighed. "I asked her to wait."

For a minute I stopped thinking about images of the dead and started wondering whether my fly was unzipped, whether I'd washed all the blood out of my hair in the cell sink. My mother pushed me forward, like she used to do in junior school cotillion dances. I felt absurd and awkward, mostly stunned.

Maia Lee gave me a dazzling smile.

"I almost thought you'd make it a whole week without me, Tex."

30

Maia looked great, of course. She was wearing all white silk—blazer, blouse, and pants—and her skin glowed like hot caramel. Her hair was tied back in a rich brown ponytail. As usual she wore no makeup or jewelry, and when she smiled you could see why she didn't need any.

I opened my mouth to say something, but all that came out was mumble. I think it would've been mumble even without the busted mouth.

"Don't try to talk, Jackson," said my mother.

Maia's eyes glittered. She touched my jaw lightly with her fingertips. There was no pain, but I flinched. Slowly, her smile dissolved. She took her hand away.

I wasn't used to people being glad to see me. My look was probably harsher than it should've been. I was in pain. I was angry. I resented the way it felt to see her again. I didn't like the way my eyes kept drifting down to the cut of her blouse against her collarbone.

Maia's face closed up.

"After our talk I got concerned," she said. "I had

some vacation time coming. It wasn't a problem. When I couldn't find you at your apartment—"

She nodded at my mother.

I looked at Mother, who folded her Guatemalan cloak over her arm and sighed.

"Tres, I just wish ..." Mother let that statement hang, as if I should be able to complete it myself. "You remember Sergeant Andrews, of course."

I nodded, not really remembering which ex-boyfriend that was. Maybe Andrews was the one who had dated my mother for a few months after her divorce, before she had exploded into full Bohemian. As I recall, he'd shown up one night with roses and a couple of T-bones and found her burning patchouli incense over a spread of Tarot cards. He never came by much after that.

"Sergeant Andrews was good enough to call me." Mother made it obvious that *some* people had not been. "Ms. Lee insisted on helping. She suggested Mr. Ash."

Mother was resentful. Maia had interrupted a perfectly good maternal rescue operation and now Mother was obliged to stand apart from her, avoid eye contact, and do her best to look hurt. She crossed her arms and hugged her silver and Guatemalan prints tight.

If Maia noticed, she ignored it. She met my eyes again and tried to make her tone light as she spoke. "So," she said, "here I am."

All three of us feeling wonderful, we rode north on McAlister toward my mother's dentist's office while the rainstorm came through. After ten minutes my mother, never one for prolonged silences, tried to break the ice. She put on a cassette of Buddhist chants.

"Chinese mysticism is so fascinating," she told Maia. "I've been studying it for years, off and on."

Maia had been staring out at the rolling live oak forests along the highway. She pulled her eyes away and smiled absently at my mother.

"I'll have to take your word for it," she said. "Is there a good place to get *huevos rancheros* on the way, Ms. McKinnis? I'm afraid I'm starving."

I could almost see my mother cringing closer to the

driver's side window. We listened to the windshield wipers for the rest of the drive.

I should have insisted on going home immediately, but I was tired, and it felt good, just for the moment, to be carried along, lying down in the backseat of my mother's car for the first time in twenty years. I let myself be carried right into Dr. Long's office. My dentist from elementary school, Dr. Long was older and grayer now, but his hands were just as big and clumsy inside my mouth as I remembered.

"Well," he said, "anything for a friend."

Then my mother smiled her warmest smile. Dr. Long smiled back and immediately cleared his afternoon appointments. Through a haze of anesthetics we had a great one-sided discussion about the advances in porcelain grafting technology. When he poured me out of the chair and into the waiting room, around five o'clock, he didn't even offer me a lollipop.

The first word I said was: "Vandiver."

Mother looked overjoyed. At least until I walked into her house and started rifling through her knickknack displays for the Mexican statuette that Lillian had given me a week ago at the gallery. I finally found it on top of the piano, the two skeleton lovers in their hideously glazed orange car parked contentedly between a book of Zen poetry and a horseshoe. I repossessed the statuette, then walked out to Mother's Volvo again.

I said: "Home."

It took my mother a few minutes to realize I meant Queen Anne Street. Then, looking pained, she asked Jess Makar to meet us there when he had liberated my impounded VW. Fifteen minutes later Mother dropped Maia and me off at Number 90, and was almost convinced she could leave us there safely when Jess drove up in my car. The .45 holes in the ragtop flapped wildly.

"Tres—" she said. She started to get out of the car for the third time.

I just shook my head and kissed her cheek. Jess

nodded at me, gave Maia a long look, then climbed into the passenger seat.

"Tres—" she said again.

"Mother," I mumbled, "thank you. But go home now. It's okay."

"And Lillian?"

I couldn't meet her eyes. I couldn't look at Maia either as we went up the steps.

After I had made sure that no one had been in the house, I stretched out on the futon. I stared at the water stain of Australia on the ceiling. Maia stood over me, hugging her arms.

"Byron Ash?" I said.

Maia shrugged very slightly. "He owed me a favor. His son and I were at Berkeley together."

"I don't remember his name on that list of job possibilities you gave me."

Maia managed a smile as she sat down next to me.

"Not *that* big a favor, Tex."

Eventually I slept, me and my hollow-eyed chauffeur driving a Thunderbird blindly into some dreams about men with little silver guns, Looney Tunes glasses full of bourbon, and pictures of authentic cowboys. I'm not sure, but I imagined Maia keeping watch over me all night. I think she kissed me once, very lightly, on the temple. Or maybe I just dreamed that too. At the time, I wasn't sure which thought was more disturbing.

31

When I woke up the next morning all the police records and news clippings were stacked in neat piles around Maia's bare feet. She'd changed into a beige sundress, and her hair was loose around her shoulders. Robert Johnson sat on her lap, sticking out his tongue at me.

"So which one is Halcomb?" Maia said.

She looked up and smiled. I tried to focus on the mug shots she was showing me.

"Halcomb?" I repeated.

I tried to lift my head. It throbbed, but the swelling around my jaw had gone down to nothing larger than a Mexican lime. My new teeth felt slick like the side of a pool. I looked up at Maia's very awake face.

"Shit," I mumbled, "I can't believe you're here."

It almost felt good to resent something so familiar for a change. I'd forgotten the way she woke me up with her pop quizzes, always at the bedside, fully dressed no matter how early I tried to rise, ready to pummel me with questions about cases I was working on, world politics, the PG&E bill. I stared glumly at Maia's coffee mug.

"Wait a minute," I said, catching the scent. "You brought Peet's?"

She raised her eyebrows. "You get none until you talk to me."

"That's inhuman."

"Talk," she ordered.

I muttered some of her own Mandarin curses, then sat up and straightened my T-shirt.

"All right. That one's Randall Halcomb."

I pointed to the mug shot of a scraggly-looking man—shoulder-length blond hair, darker beard, thin face, a nose that had been broken at least once. Halcomb's eyelids were heavy and his mouth upturned at the corners, as if he had been pleasantly stoned when he was booked. He looked much too content to steal a Pontiac, or to drive it past a sheriff's house with the intent to kill.

"One of the others could've been Halcomb's accomplice in the drive-by," I said. "There had to be at least two people in the car—one to drive, one to shoot. All those guys knew Halcomb in prison, all are still alive and free as far as I can tell, and if you don't give me that coffee now I'll have to kill you."

"You can try."

She poured me a cup only after she had poured a little more into Robert Johnson's saucer.

"He definitely does not need caffeine," I warned her.

"You're just jealous," she said.

Maybe it was true. The traitor required exactly the right mix of Blend 101 and whole milk, a recipe only Maia had had the patience to master. He lapped at his cafe au lait and stared at me smugly.

"So," said Maia, "maybe one of these men was involved in your father's death and got past an FBI investigation."

"Right."

She shook her head. "Or maybe the FBI knew what

they were doing, Tres. Maybe this line of suspects goes nowhere."

I drank my coffee.

On the table in front of me, the *Express-News* head-lines for the Thunderbird murder glared in lurid color. Detective Schaeffer was answering questions. Terry Garza was looking battered, trying not to look terri-fied. Garza told the paper that yes, the dead man Eddie Moraga had worked for Sheff Construction, but that Moraga had been laid-off several months ago. Right.

Eddie's face had been fuzzed out of the newspaper photos just enough to titillate the gentle reader. You could vaguely see the dark holes of his eyes. *"The trade-mark execution style of a well-known South Texas crime syndicate,"* one caption declared. Guy White's name was mentioned. The nature of the death would lead to speculations about mob involvement. This would be a PR nightmare for Sheff Construction. There was no mention of me, which might explain why Carlon McAffrey wasn't sitting in my lap yet.

I spent a few minutes bringing Maia up-to-date on what I'd learned from Mr. Garza's computer. When I finished she stared at her bare feet for a minute, flexing her toes against the stack of police reports.

"Mr. Sheff is involved with some bad people," she said. "These fixed city contracts—I've seen two cases like it before in the Bay Area, Tres. Both times the mob was behind it. They give the construction firm an assur-ance that the city project will go to them with the price tag they want, and with no labor problems. The mob provides the bribery and the arm-twisting; in return, they cut themselves in for several million. The project always goes way over budget and behind schedule. Huge profits all around."

I stared at her. "And you know about this because—"

She shrugged. "One of those cases, I was defending the contractor. We won."

"Terrence & Goldman, always fighting the good fight."

"Tres," Maia said, "if Beau Karnau messed up a profitable arrangement between Sheff and the mob by trying blackmail, and if Sheff's people got blamed for letting it happen—or botching the payoff . . ."

She looked down at the picture of Eddie Moraga's corpse.

I nodded, trying to believe it. I remembered Dan Sheff behind his father's big desk, looking nine years old, his hair sticking up like canary wings. I tried to imagine him playing some kind of hardball game with Guy White's organization—making millions illegally off fixed bids on city projects, then ordering his employees to kill, abduct, wreak havoc on any who might find out, all while he was drinking Chivas from a Foghorn Leghorn glass.

Then the living-room wall rang. Maia frowned. I pulled down the ironing board and took the receiver.

"Mr. Navarre," the man said.

It took me a minute to recognize Terry Garza's voice. It sounded like someone had mixed it with a few quarts of water, like Garza had been driving around all night in the same Thunderbird as me and was getting a little shaken up by the company.

"I think it's time we talked," Garza said.

I looked at Maia.

Her eyebrows came together. She silently mouthed: *What?*

"I'm listening," I said into the phone.

"No. In person," Garza said. "This has to be in person."

"Because you want me to bring the statuette."

I waited for him to confirm it. Obviously Garza didn't feel it was necessary.

"I'm a good employee, Mr. Navarre. I told you that. But I didn't sign on for this. I have a family—"

"Who shot Eddie Moraga?"

Behind Garza I heard the drone of highway traffic, the background buzz of a pay phone connection.

"Let's just say two parties are interested in what you have, Mr. Navarre. When the other party breaks into your apartment in the middle of the night, you won't wake up the next morning. Do you understand that?"

I looked at Maia.

"I'll be at Earl Abel's tomorrow morning at seven," Garza said. "I tell you what you need to know about your girlfriend, you give me what I need to smooth things over. We might be able to get things . . . back to normal."

"If your employers don't release Lillian Cambridge, there's not going to be any normal."

Garza exhaled sharply. Or maybe it was a nervous laugh. "We need to have a talk, Mr. Navarre. We really do."

He hung up.

I stared at Maia. She looked at me, her eyes intensely black.

"Tell me," she said.

I looked down at the front page of the paper again, where Eddie's dead face was a circle of fuzz in the bottom corner. I told Maia what Garza had said. She mixed cream into her coffee by turning the cup in little horizontal circles.

"Garza's desperate to set things right before he becomes the next sacrificial lamb," she said.

I nodded.

Maia studied me over the top of her cup. "You still think we're not dealing with the mob?"

"It's convenient. Homicide will look at how Moraga was killed, then they'll bring in Vice, then the FBI task force. Pretty soon everything is focused on Guy White. Just like it was ten years ago, with my father's murder."

Maia paused, choosing her words carefully. "Tres, I want you to think about this. What if this is separate from your father's death? What if you've walked into something that has nothing to do with that, or your questions about the investigation, something that isn't your fault?"

I stared at her. When I swallowed, it felt as if I were back in the dentist's chair, someone's big awkward hands rearranging my mouth, sending muted but persistent jabs of pain down the nerves of my jaw. "Do you think that would matter now?"

She lowered her eyes. Her voice grew hard around the edges. "I think it should. Lillian has had her own life, Tres, and she can create her own problems. You're both grown-ups now. Maybe you should start thinking about it that way."

"Grown-ups," I repeated. "So why the hell are you following me around like my damn mother?"

I guess I deserved it. At least the coffee had cooled off a little before she threw it in my face. Then, since there wasn't really any place to go to get away, Maia walked out the back door and sat down on Gary Hales's patio.

I took a long shower and changed before I went out to apologize. I put the ceramic road-trip statuette on the table and sat across from Maia. We both stared at it. The two skeleton lovers grinned back at us from the front seat of their little orange car. A few blocks away the ice cream truck went by, playing a warped rendition of "La Bamba."

"This is hard," I told Maia. "I'm sorry."

Her eyes were only a little red. I could almost convince myself it was just from the sleepless night.

She forced a smile. "I liked you better with the busted mouth."

"You and half of Texas," I said.

I noticed Gary Hales looking out his bedroom window at us, his face so drooping and soft with amazement it seemed about to melt off. I waved. After another minute of silence Maia picked up the statuette and turned it around. The skeletons in the convertible kept grinning, grotesque and shiny white.

"If you're right, somebody wants this back very badly," Maia said. "And not just for the artistic quality."

"So let's assume the obvious."

"Yes."

I let her do the honors. The statuette hit the pavement. I'm not sure what I was expecting to find inside when the ceramic car cracked open. At first I didn't see anything but clay. Then I nudged it with my toe and the back seat broke neatly open along a crack as thin as a piggy bank slot. Maia picked up the small silver disk by the edges and held it up to her eye, looking through the hole like a monocle.

"Don't suppose you have a CD-ROM drive?" she said.

When I heard the slow shuffle of my landlord's feet I looked up.

"I reckon you'll be cleaning up that mess now?" Gary Hales asked mildly.

"I reckon," I said.

32

"Bats?" I said.

"Bats," said my half brother Garrett.

"I'll admit," I said, "it's a word I often think of when your name comes up."

"I'm not shitting you, little bro. You have to see this. It's fucking unreal."

I covered the receiver and looked over at Maia. "How'd you like to take a little road trip?" I asked her.

She stared at me. "What?"

"Just to Austin. My brother wants to show us the sights."

Maia's arms folded. "How many 'no' reasons do you want? Detective Schaeffer wants you in town, your car stands out on the road like a neon advertisement, you've been shot at and almost run over—"

I uncovered the receiver.

"We'd love to," I told Garrett.

"Cool," he said. "You remember what the Carmen Miranda looks like?"

"That would be kind of difficult to forget."

"The bridge at eight, little bro."

Instead of terminating my life, Maia compromised with me. She agreed to go to Austin; I agreed to let her rent a car for the trip. By early afternoon we were heading north on I-35 in a brown Buick so nondescript it was almost invisible. Maia kept having to honk at people to keep them from drifting into us on the highway. By the time we passed Live Oak I was convinced we were not being tailed.

"I would've preferred a white Cadillac," I protested.

"Asshole," she said.

When we hit Selma I discovered that the universe as I knew it had come to an end—the old Selma Police Department building had been turned into a bar and grille. For decades the terror of all motorists wanting to drive above fifty-five and a half mph, the town had finally cashed in its speed trap reputation for tourist dollars. The sign out front promised free appetizers with any proof of moving violation. And that was only the first surprise. The I-35 corridor was almost nonstop developments now. There were outlet malls where cow pastures and ranch houses had once been, fast-food restaurants in knolls once filled with barbed wire and stands of mesquite trees. As we moved along the edge of the Hill Country I found myself less and less sure where I was. Even the few remaining cattle along the side of the highway looked confused.

When we stopped for a late lunch at a restaurant I remembered on the San Marcos River we found the place had closed four years ago. So we settled for a loaf of bread, a jug of wine, and a billboard of Ralph the Swimming Pig in the park across from Wonder World. Paddleboats went by on the river; a few unambitious wet suit divers braved the ten-foot-deep green waters; Ralph the Swimming Pig and Maia kept looking at me.

"You haven't told me what you're thinking," Maia said.

I chewed on my bread and cheese and watched the river. It had taken me a few minutes to realize why I felt so bad being here again. Then I'd remembered that time with Lillian, Christmas break, when we'd gotten stupid drunk and gone skinny-dipping around midnight just a few yards upriver from here with a band of coked-up bluegrass players. The water had been so cold our lips turned purple. I remembered Lillian. Then I looked at Maia, sitting there in the sunlight, her eyes almost gold. The part of my mind that was trying to put the facts together felt like it was threading a needle with a pair of cooking mitts on.

"Tres?"

"Yeah, I know. I just don't have an answer yet."

She ran her finger along the edge of her wineglass. "Do you want to hear mine?"

She waited. I kept eating flavorless bread.

Maia looked back down at her wineglass and swore under her breath, something about me being a stupid white devil. "Damn it, Tres. Do you think Lillian gave you that statue accidentally? Do you think she didn't know what would happen when it turned up missing? How can you keep seeing her as just the *victim*?"

I stared out at the river. "Maybe."

"Maybe," she repeated. "What if, just maybe, Lillian disappeared on purpose? If it were me, once I realized the person I'd been trying to blackmail was really the mob, I'd admit I was in over my head and I'd run like hell. Maybe first I'd send up the only distress signal I could think of—to you. How are you going to know the truth when you see it?"

"The truth." I looked at her. "Maia, I know you're trying to help. The truth is you're distracting the hell out of me."

I think I wanted it to sound angry, but it didn't come out that way.

Maia started to answer, then pressed her lips together. For a moment she looked cold in the sunshine, hugging her knees and curling up her toes under her beige sundress.

"Tell me to go home then," she said.

I looked down. We sat silent for a while and threw bread to some sickly-looking ducks. Sometimes they ate it. Most of the time they just stared at us and let the pieces hit them in the face. No points for intelligence. At the moment I empathized.

"Okay, then," Maia said. "Tell me you'll come back."

The paddleboaters laughed. Ralph the Pig grinned at me. I looked at Maia's sad half smile and listened to the devil talking on my shoulder. I was chasing ghosts through a town I barely remembered, dealing with people I could barely see through emotional scar tissue. Maia could be right. I'd only made things different for the worse. And a beautiful woman was offering me escape from the first twenty years of my life. It would've taken a stupid man to tell Maia Lee no.

"No," I said.

Maia just nodded. She gave me a hand and pulled me up.

We looked at each other for a minute. Then she turned and headed toward the car.

I beaned a mallard with the last of the bread. He stood there for a minute with the same dazed expression I probably had. Then he honked and went skittering into the San Marcos River like he'd seen a ghost.

33

Around eight we pulled into the Marriott parking lot off Riverside in Austin and walked down to the water. You could barely see the city because of the sunset. Town Lake was a half-mile sheet of corrugated silver. Beyond it, behind a few wooded hills, downtown blazed with a dozen mirrored office buildings I'd never seen before. About the only things that looked the same as in 1985 were the red dome of the Capitol and the white UT tower.

The cement underside of the Congress Avenue Bridge echoed with chatters from a few million bats and only slightly fewer sightseers. When I spotted Garrett, he'd just pulled his wheelchair up to a newly erected plaque that honored the "bats of Austin" and was staring with distaste at the army of camera-toters. His tie-dyed shirt was stretched a little tighter these days and he'd gone almost completely gray, but he still looked like the love child of Charles Manson and Santa Claus, minus the legs.

"Man," he said, by way of greeting, "this is worse than fucking Carlsbad. They've *discovered* this place."

We shook hands. Garrett looked at Maia for a moment longer than he needed to, scratching his beard. Then he nodded.

"Last time I was here," he said, "it was me, couple of Hell's Angels, three kayakers, and a lady with a poodle. Now look at this shit."

He led the way down the grassy slope, waving gnats out of his face and running over as many people's feet as he could. Maia and I followed a few yards back.

"That's—" Maia started to whisper. She looked at me, then at Garrett's rainbow-clad back.

"Yeah, my half brother."

"You didn't mention—"

"That he's so much older than me?"

Maia glared at me.

"We got about five minutes," Garrett called back to us. He swung his chair around and squinted up at the top of the bridge, where the stone arches made a honeycomb of little caves. "Then the little peckers start coming out thicker than pig shit."

A line of retirees was standing in front of us, watching the bridge with binoculars. When we sat down on the grass knoll I found myself staring at a row of old butts in pastel prints. I exchanged looks with Garrett. He grinned.

"Yeah," he said. "Kind of gives you a different perspective of the world, doesn't it?"

Maia sat down between us, her left arm pressing against mine just slightly, very warm. She smelled like amber. But of course I noticed none of that. She put her other hand on Garrett's armrest.

"So, Garrett," she said, "Tres tells me you can break into high security networks with half your RAM tied behind your back."

Garrett laughed. He had more teeth than any human being I'd ever known, most of them yellow and crooked. Maia smiled back at him like he was Cary Grant.

"Yeah well," he said, "my little brother tends to exaggerate."

"He also says you could be running the world if you didn't spend so much time at Jimmy Buffett concerts."

Garrett shrugged. But he had a pleased gleam in his eyes.

"A man's got to have a hobby," he said. "Just please no jokes about wasting away in Margaritaville. That one got old faster than Ronald Reagan."

Maia laughed. Then in a very quiet, very passable voice she started singing "A Pirate Looks at Forty." Garrett kept smiling, but he looked at Maia as if he were reevaluating her.

"My theme song these days," Garrett said.

"Mine too."

It was the first and only indicator I'd ever had of Maia's age. Garrett showed his teeth, all hundred of them.

"So, Tres," he said, "where'd you meet this lady again?"

With that he took out a joint and lit up.

Paranoia was not a concept that existed in Garrett's mind. I'd seen him smoking pot in shopping malls, restaurants, just about anywhere. If questioned he would talk poker-faced about his "prescription." Nobody ever wanted to argue much with a paraplegic. The line of retired sightseers froze when the smell of the mota hit them. They glanced back nervously at Garrett, then dissolved. We no longer had butts obstructing our view of the bridge.

Maia and I both refused the joint, politely. Then Garrett spent half an hour telling us about his last Parrothead tour of the South, his asshole bosses at RNI, the impending collapse of Austin society at the hands of Silicon Valley transplants.

"Damn Californians," he concluded.

"I beg your pardon," said Maia.

Garrett grinned. "You can come into the state, honey. It's just this ugly bastard you brought with you."

I showed Garrett a hand gesture. Maia laughed.

It got dark and cool. God poured grenadine on the

horizon. Finally, when he was ready to talk business, Garrett said: "So what's all this about, little brother?"

I told him. For a minute Garrett blew smoke. He stared at me, then at Maia's legs. His expression told me he'd just reevaluated my IQ downward a hefty percentage.

"So you and Maia are looking for—"

"Lillian," I said.

"More or less," said Maia.

Garrett shook his head. "Unreal."

"Can you look at the disk for us?" I asked Garrett.

Cameras flashed as the first few bats flitted overhead like sparrows with hangovers. Garrett glanced up at them, shook his head to indicate that the real show hadn't begun yet, then turned back to us. He pulled his tie-dyed shirt back down over his belly.

"I don't guess you want my advice," he said.

"Not really," I said.

"Sounds to me like this is your old girlfriend's gig," he said. "Turn this shit over to somebody else and walk, little brother."

Somebody on the bridge shouted. When I looked up, a woman in pink was leaning over the railing with her arms dangling into a steady stream of bats.

"They *tickle*!" she shouted to her friends. People laughed. More cameras went off.

"Fuckers," said Garrett. "The flashes disorient the hell out of the bats. They run into cars and shit. Don't they know that? *Fuckers!*"

The last word he shouted into the crowd. Only a few people turned around. Nobody wanted to argue with him, maybe, but nobody wanted to pay him any attention, either.

"Tres?"

In the twilight Maia's face was losing its features, so it was hard to guess her expression, but her arm still pressed against mine warmer than ever. She waited for me to say something. When I didn't, she turned to Garrett.

"Can you look at it, Garrett?" she asked.

His scowl softened. Maybe it was Maia's hand on his armrest. Maybe it was the joint.

"Sure," he said. "Whatever. But it seems to me you got to get a life, little brother. Picking at old wounds—fuck, if I spent my life with that they'd've locked me up by now."

He met my eyes only for a second, then he laughed and shook his head. Whatever pain was there, it had been buried a long time ago under drug abuse, wildness, testiness, and arrogance—all the Navarre family values.

I couldn't help it. I tried again to imagine Garrett at those dark railroad tracks twenty years ago. The confident train-hitcher, the intractable hippie, running away from home for the twentieth and last time—the one time he'd sprinted to the freight car and missed the rungs. I tried to see his face, pale with shock, looking desperately at the black glistening lake where his legs had been. I tried to imagine him for once without that cultivated son-of-a-bitch smile. But he'd been alone then and he was still alone with it. There was no way to imagine what Garrett had said or thought two decades ago, staring at those wet rails that had mercifully sealed the blood flow. He'd been alone and conscious for more than an hour by the time my sister Shelley found him.

"Old wounds," he said now. "Fuck that."

Then the bats came out for real. Cameras stopped flashing. People's mouths dropped. We all just stared at the endless cloud of smoke drifting east into the Hill Country, smoke looking for a few jillion pounds of insects to eat.

Garrett smiled like a kid at the matinee.

"Un-fucking-real," he said.

In ten minutes more bats passed over our heads than the total number of people in South Texas. Somewhere in that time Maia had taken my hand and I hadn't pulled it away.

The tourists unfroze. Then one by one, growing bored with the bats, they drifted off to the parking lot. Maia and I stayed perfectly still. Finally Garrett wheeled his chair around and pushed himself up the hill. Maia stood and followed him. Then I followed her.

It was hard to miss Garrett's VW safari van. In the dark, the mound of plastic pineapples and bananas that was hot-glued to the roof made the van look like it had hair. When we got closer I saw that the paint job was just the way it had been years ago, rows of Ms. Mirandas along the sides, all in outrageous Caribbean dresses.

"They don't dance like Carmen no more?" Maia suggested.

Garrett grinned at her as he slipped his chair into the lift grooves. "Will you marry me?"

A few minutes later we were sitting on beanbags and drinking Pecan Street Ale from Garrett's cooler. My eyes teared over from the smell of mota and very old patchouli. Garrett had booted up his "portable" computer—several hundred pounds of wires and hardware that had years ago taken over the van's backseat and whose generator required most of the luggage compartment. Then he stuck in our mystery CD.

Garrett frowned. He thought about it for a minute. He tried a few commands. He cracked open some files and looked inside.

"Slice and dice," he pronounced. "Easy to fix if you've got the other disk."

Maia looked at me, then at Garrett. "The other disk?"

"Yeah. You split your data between two disks. The program to reassemble it's pretty simple. But you read one disk alone, it's all nonsense codes, man, scrambled eggs. Pretty safe way to store sensitive stuff."

I took a drink of my Pecan Street and thought about that. "So you can't tell anything about what's on there?"

Garrett shrugged. "It's big. That much data usually means detailed graphics."

"As in photographs."

Garrett nodded.

Maia stared at the dingo balls around Garrett's windows.

"Garrett," she said, "if I was using photos to blackmail somebody—"

He grinned. "You just keep looking better, honey."

"If I was, why a CD? Why not just keep the negatives?"

Garrett took a long drag on his joint. His eyes glittered. You could tell he was enjoying figuring out the devious possibilities.

"Okay. You can't encrypt negatives. You can't lock them so that nobody but you can make copies. Somebody finds them, then they'll know exactly what they're looking at, right? If it was me, shit yes, I'd scan everything in, keep that as my master print, then shred the negatives. You got your two disks, you got your program to reassemble. In a couple of minutes you can print up as many hard copies as you need, or, even better, upload those suckers onto the net and pretty soon they're printing out at every news desk and police station in the state, if that's what you want. But if somebody comes looking through your stuff, unless they're very good or they know exactly what they're looking for, they don't find shit."

Garrett stopped and took another hit. "So who's got the other disk?"

I took out a flier that had been folded in my pocket for a long time. I looked at the date—July 31, tonight. Nine to midnight. Driving like bats out of hell, we could be there just when things started cooking. No offense to the bats.

Besides, Garrett was leering at Maia's legs again and about to offer her another beer. If I didn't make a counteroffer we'd be here all night.

"You like art openings?" I asked her.

34

Even with the windows rolled down at ten at night the Buick felt like the inside of a blow drier. I sat shotgun and watched the subdivisions go by while a cold triangle of sweat glued my shirt to the back of my seat. The smell of dead skunks and brushfires blew through the car.

I guess I was being too quiet. When we passed Live Oak, Maia finally reached out and touched my arm. "You still thinking about Garrett?"

I shook my head.

In fact I hadn't thought about much else since we'd left Austin. I'd been foolish to think I'd get away from Garrett without one of his lectures. While Maia retrieved the rental car from the Marriott parking lot, Garrett had given me his philosophy on old girlfriends. Then for the millionth time he'd cataloged Dad's offenses against the family: how Dad had basically abandoned Garrett and Shelley after their mother had died, left them with his abusive second wife for years while he went out drinking, politicking, falling in love with whores and Junior Leaguers. How Garrett took to running away and Shelley took to abusive men.

"By the time he married your mom it was too fucking late to make any difference," Garrett said. "Shelley and I were out of the house and your mom was too damn nice to change him. She never told you the last straw, did she? You were in what—tenth grade? The bastard took your mom to some party at the McNay Museum, then disappeared. When your mom and her friends finally found him, he was down in the woods by the old fish pond screwing the lights out of Junior Leaguer number seven. He just smiled, zipped his pants, and went back into the party to get another drink."

Garrett laughed weakly. Then he looked down at where his lap should've been. "Let the bastard stay dead, little brother. It's the only thing that's ever given me a sense of justice."

Maia exited in downtown San Antonio. We drove past the decaying mansions of the King William District, then across East Arsenal where the San Antonio River flowed by sluggish and polluted with tourist leftovers. Its banks this far south were empty except for the crack addicts.

When we pulled up in front of Blue Star the gravel lot was already full to bursting with BMWs and Ferraris. Women in evening dresses did coke on the hoods of their cars; men in black sweated in the heat and drank champagne on the old loading docks of the renovated warehouses. An apathetic handwritten sign in front of one of the larger galleries announced Beau's opening upstairs at a loft space called Galleria Azul, perched at the top of a narrow iron fire escape.

Inside the gallery, halfhearted Western swing warbled from a few wall speakers. Somebody had put an old saddle on the table next to the sign-in book.

Twenty or thirty people were drifting around the room looking at bad photos of authentic cowboys. One of the guests was wearing a starburst Jerry Garcia tie, clipped with a wrinkled green press pass that had been old during Watergate. He came up next to me from behind the beer keg and quietly belched garlic.

"The beer is free," Carlon McAffrey said, "but these little sandwich things suck."

In one hand Carlon had a spiral notebook pinched between two fingers and a stack of canapés in his palm. He handed me his cup of Lone Star from the other hand so he could shake with Maia.

"Carlon McAffrey," he said. "You're not Lillian."

Maia smiled. "Likewise, I'm sure."

Carlon nodded. He was nice enough to puff his cheeks out for the next belch, holding it in.

"You hear about your buddy Sheff?" he asked me. "Somebody made his office into a drive-through morgue last night."

"I heard."

Carlon waited. I looked disinterested. Finally Carlon's blue eyes detached from my face and made a circuit of the people in the room, looking for new prey.

"Okay," he said. "I've seen ranches, I've seen cows, I've seen Councilman Asante schmoozing it up in back. So far I see nothing worth a headline."

I looked around the corner, into the back room of the gallery. Sure enough, against the side wall, his beer set casually on top of a metal sculpture, Fernando Asante was holding court. He had on an after-hours outfit—black jeans, white silk shirt over his huge belly, a denim jacket with the Virgin Mary embroidered in sequins on the back and on the breast panels. Two plump ladies in satin dresses stood on either side of him. A few businessmen laughed at his jokes. The curly-haired Anglo bodyguard I'd seen at Mi Tierra lounged nearby. He was the only one who didn't look enchanted to be in Asante's presence.

What the hell. I gave Carlon back his beer.

"Keep your eyes peeled, Lois Lane," I told him. "I have to go say hello to somebody."

I looked at Maia to see if she was coming.

Maia looked at Fernando Asante, who was laughing at his own joke and patting the rump of the nearest satin cherub. Then she looked at Carlon, trying to eat canapés out of his palm. She let me steer her toward the back room.

Asante gave me his best gold-toothed smile as we came up. He gave Maia a head-to-toe appraisal and seemed to find her a good risk. When he nodded at his fan club, they excused themselves in unison, all except for the bodyguard.

"Jack," Asante said. "Good to see you again, boy."

He loosened the silver Texas-shaped bola around his neck. He offered me a well-manicured hand to shake. I declined.

"Councilman," I said. "Hell of an outfit. That jacket weep on holy days?"

He just smiled and shook his head, then leered at Maia. "I like patronizing the arts, ma'am. I always do admire beautiful things."

Maia smiled warmly. "You must be Mr. Asante."

Asante looked gratified. His face just oozed Charming Elder Statesman.

"That's right, princess," he said. "And you are?"

"Endlessly amused by the tabloid stories Tres reads me," she cooed. "Is it true, the one about you and your secretary in the same pair of underpants?"

Asante's pupils dilated down to pinpoints. His genitals probably followed suit. Somehow he managed to keep his smile intact.

"I can see Mr. Navarre has been around you a little too long, princess," he said.

Maia leaned close, as if to tell him a naughty secret.

"Actually I taught him everything he knows. And if you call me 'princess' again I'm going to throw up on your Virgin Mary."

"Speaking of nausea," I said, "I didn't know you were a fan of Beau's work, Mr. Asante. Do you know him?"

He wasn't quite sure who to look at now. He regarded Maia like a dog might look at a snake, trying to determine how dangerous this little thing was. The bodyguard had moved a little closer, just enough to share the gallon or two of Aramis on his chest. My eyes began to tear.

Asante looked from Maia to me. "Why, Jack? You looking for an autograph?"

"Just curious," I said. "I wanted Beau's professional opinion on some photos I've come across."

I waited for a reaction, but I might've been talking about the Rangers' chances in the finals.

A man in a yellow silk shirt and black genie pants came up to us, apologized, and peeled a red sticker off a sheet of labels. He pointed to a photo behind the councilman. "This one, Mr. Asante?"

The photo was about eight by eleven, with Beau's name scrawled at the bottom. It showed an abandoned ranch house on a hill overlooking the Texas plains. In the nighttime sky behind the house was a bloated full moon and a single meteor streak. In the foreground, rusty iron gates rose up; the name "Lazy B" was arced across the top in black metal cursive. One gate was open and unhinged.

Asante looked back at it lazily. "Sure, son. That's fine."

The gallery employee marked the picture sold, apologized again, and left.

"Lazy B," I said. "That stand for 'Bastard,' maybe?"

Asante ignored me. "Good bargain. I'm told it's one of Karnau's best, one of his older shots," he said to Maia. "I always buy something, long as it's small and priced to sell."

He leered at her like that was a private joke. Then he looked back at me.

"And how's the job market for you, son? Haven't given up yet?"

"Actually," I said, "I was wondering if your friends at Sheff Construction could find me some work."

Asante stared. "Pardon?"

"I figure there'll be a lot of money in this new North Side arts complex you're planning. Biggest pork barrel since Travis Center, bigger maybe. I also figure it's a sure thing Sheff will get the contract. That's your arrangement with them, isn't it?"

Asante looked at his bodyguard, nodding that he was ready to move on. The Aramis Man came and stood next to me.

"Misinformation is a dangerous thing, Jack." Asante said it almost blandly. "The City grants contracts by anonymous bidding. When we approve a bond package for a new project, we only then look for the right firm— goes through numerous committees and the Chamber. I really have very little to do with it. Does that clear things up for you?"

"Shucks," I said. "No kickbacks or anything?"

Asante couldn't have smiled colder.

"You know if I were you, Jack," he said, leaning forward to deliver some private advice, "I'd take this young lady back to California. I'd go back where the prospects are better, the life expectancy is longer."

He showed me his gold teeth. Up close, his breath smelled like used motor oil.

"I'll file that in the proper place," I promised.

Asante took his beer from the top of the statue, nodded politely to Maia. "Good night, Jack."

He walked away with his bodyguard in tow.

Maia raised her eyebrows. She looked like she was about to exhale for the first time in ten minutes when Carlon came up, hands still full, and nudged me with his elbow. "Okay. Back window, now."

I stared at him.

He kept walking toward the back of the room, not waiting to see if we would follow. When we caught up he was standing on the tips of his huaraches, peering down through a tiny metal-barred window into the alley behind the warehouse.

"Okay," he said, "Dan's blond, right, drives a silver Beamer?"

"Yeah."

Carlon frowned. "You want to tell me why he's delivering a sack lunch to Beau Karnau in the alley?"

Maia and I looked out. It took a few seconds for our

eyes to adjust to the darkness outside before we saw the
two figures, one blond, sitting with arms folded on the
hood of the silver BMW, the other a balding brunette,
visible because of his stark white tux shirt. Sure enough,
Beau was holding a brown lunch bag, shaking it in Dan
Sheff's face like he was unhappy with it.

"Maybe Dan forgot to pack a dessert," I said.

Dan just sat there, silent. In the shadows, I couldn't
see his face, but his body looked stiff, tense with anger.
Then, while Beau was midsentence yelling at him, Dan
delivered the same haymaker swing he'd tried on me in
Lillian's front yard last Sunday. This time it connected.

Beau went over backward and the lunch bag spilled
thick green bricks of cash across the alley, into the light
from the gallery windows.

"Or maybe he didn't," said Carlon.

35

After Dan Sheff's taillights disappeared down East Arsenal and Beau started staggering back through the alley, Carlon paid the gallery owner with the yellow shirt and the genie pants fifty dollars for the use of his office. It was probably the most money the gallery owner had seen all night.

We waited less than five minutes before Beau came in to clean up. His tux shirt was stained and half-untucked from his Jordaches, his left hand was cupped over the eye Dan Sheff had just punched, and he was cursing somebody's great-grandmother. I stepped in next to him and slapped his good eye with my open hand.

I probably could've just punched him, but I was in a bad mood. The palm strike in tai chi is arguably the most painful attack. It's a soft strike, the way a whip is soft. Sometimes it takes a layer of skin off. I didn't want any more stand-offs with Mr. Karnau.

Beau's cursing cut off in a startled grunt. Now blind, he stopped walking, but I kicked his legs out from under

him and kept him going forward, directing his fall into a
director's chair. The chair groaned but didn't break.

"Shit," said Carlon.

I took the brown paper bag off the floor where Beau
had dropped it and spilled the contents on the desk in
front of Carlon. The green bricks were stacks of fifties.
For a second I thought Carlon would have a coronary.

Beau stayed very still, both eyes covered, head
down. He sounded like he was struggling to remember
the tune of a song. When he finally looked up out of
two swollen eyes, he had to stare at me for two minutes before he realized who I was. Blood washed
through his face. He thought about getting mad, then
seemed to realize he didn't have the energy for it.

"Great," he mumbled. "Wonderful."

I touched his right eye. He winced.

"Dan decided to charge some interest this time," I
observed. "What's the problem, Beau? Eddie couldn't
be your delivery boy this time?"

"Tres—" Maia began. I ignored her.

With a pair of rapidly swelling eyes it was hard for
Beau to look mean, but he was trying his best. I took
the ceramic steering wheel from the broken road-trip
statuette out of my pocket and tossed it in Beau's lap.

"I didn't plan on it, but it seems I've started collecting
your stuff."

Karnau's face was paralyzed for a moment, then
there was a glimmer of recognition. "What the hell—"

"Beau," I said, "let me give you some perspective
here. I have one disk; you have the other. Without both
of them, I'm betting you don't have shit to keep the
people you've been blackmailing from eating you alive.
You want to talk about that?"

"I *don't*—" he started to yell.

Then he just stopped and stared at me. He brought his
fingers to his temples and started making little circles
with them.

Maia said: "Mr. Karnau? It would be best if you
talked to us."

He focused on her, dazed. Then his face hardened.

"You sound like a fucking lawyer," he said finally.

Maia tried a smile. "I'm not representing anyone."

That made Beau laugh, a shrill little sound.

"Wonderful," he said. "That's all I need."

He picked up the ceramic steering wheel and threw it back at me. "I don't have shit to say to you. And I don't have a clue what you're talking about."

I looked at Maia.

" 'I'm not representing anyone,' " I repeated. "Great line. Opened him right up."

Maia shrugged.

Carlon was sitting behind the owner's desk, chewing slowly on a canapé. He was using one of Beau's unmatted prints for a beer coaster. His blue eyes reminded me of a buzzard's—the way they look on while the bobcats are finishing up a carcass, hungry, patient, highly interested.

"So where's your dad's murder come in?" he wondered.

Beau's forehead turned maroon. "Who the fuck is this?"

"We've got a lawyer," I told him. "And we've got an entertainment writer from the *Express-News* ready to go for your jugular. What I suggest, Beau, is you just answer yes or no when I ask you something. You tell me you don't know what I'm talking about one more time, I'll make sure Carlon here spells your name right in the Sunday edition. Got it?"

Beau decided to stand up. I planted another red hand print on the side of his face. He sat back down, in slow motion. His head bent down into his hands.

"I'll kill you," he mumbled, without any conviction at all.

"The photos on the disk," I said. "They show the same thing as the cut-up prints in your portfolio—a night meeting in the woods, three people, something that happened between them bad enough to warrant ten thousand a month in blackmail."

I think he nodded. It was so slight I could hardly tell.

I picked up some of the money on the desk. "The 7/31 payment was due today, but there's a lot more here than ten grand. And Dan must know you've lost one of the disks. I'd say you made a deal to sell him the other. You close your accounts and run; he gets insurance that the photos are out of circulation. Only you stalled him tonight. Maybe that's why he hit you."

"Fuck off."

"I'll take that as a yes. Where the hell is Lillian, Beau?"

Beau was shaking slightly, his head in his hands. It took me a minute to realize he was laughing. When he looked up his eyes had turned into puffy slits.

"You're a fucking joke," he said. "Still playing her goddamn protector."

My throat tightened. "You want to explain that?"

"She's real good at that—getting people to protect her. I tried it for years. Sheff tried it. If you're lucky maybe she's dead and buried, Navarre. Maybe that's where she is."

Maia had a hell of a grip. It was only her grip on my elbow joint that kept me from disassembling Karnau's face. She held me in place until my forearm started losing circulation.

Then she leaned close to my ear. "Come on," she murmured. "Enough."

We left Beau collapsed in his director's chair, still shaking like he couldn't control his body. I took the bag of money.

We walked past the frowning owner in the yellow shirt and the genie pants, down the metal stairs, and into the parking lot of Blue Star where the black-dressed men were opening another bottle of champagne. It wasn't until Maia took my hand that I realized how hard it was clenched.

We walked Carlon to his car—a new turquoise Hyundai parked in the loading zone with a fake police light on top. He took a silver flask off the front seat, drank half, then passed it to me.

"Remind me to put you back on my Christmas list, Navarre. I don't ever want you pissed at me."

I sampled the stuff and grimaced. I stared at him.

"Jesus. Big Red and tequila?"

He shrugged. "Breakfast of champions, Navarre. You gave me the recipe."

"You ever thought about growing up, Carlon?"

He snorted. "Highly overrated, man. I'll wait for the video."

I offered Maia the flask. She shook her head.

"Now tell me the story." Carlon stopped just short of rubbing his hands together in anticipation. "I've got a gallery review to write."

"No story," I told him.

Carlon looked dazed, as if he were translating the two words. Then he laughed. "Right."

I stared at him.

"Wait a minute," he said. "You bring me out here so I can see a high-profile businessman making a payoff to the guy who's blackmailing him for—what, ten large a month? You bring up Lillian. You bring up—" He paused, then smiled very slowly as he made the final connection. "Shit. You said *Eddie*. That corpse the mob drove into Sheff's office wall. Eddie something. And you tell me *no story?*"

He laughed. I didn't.

"Twenty-four hours," I said.

"What the fuck for?"

"Lillian's in this somehow, Carlon. Publishing anything might kill her."

He thought about that for a bit. "What else do I get?"

I was tired and irritated. I stepped a little closer to him, then picked up his Jerry Garcia tie with two fingers and admired it.

"My name back on your Christmas list," I reminded him.

Carlon hesitated. He was breathing so shallow now I couldn't even smell the garlic. His pale blue eyes looked at me steady, calculating. We could've been doing a business deal.

Finally he shrugged. "Like I said before, I'm just trying to help."

I nodded, swallowed the taste of Big Red tequila out of my mouth, and threw the flask back into Carlon's car. "I knew that, Carlon. I knew that."

36

It was midnight when Maia and I left Blue Star. Seeing as how neither of us had eaten in six hours and most of the town was closed down, I had to swallow my pride along with three chorizo and egg *taquitos* at Taco Cabana. At least I didn't compromise myself enough to try the neon pink chain locations. I drove Maia to the original *cocina* on San Pedro and Hildebrand, still a sleepy wooden shack that gave no indication of the million-dollar franchise it had spawned.

"Why is it orange?" Maia asked the cook behind the counter.

She had stayed with her habitual favorite, *huevos rancheros*. The plate was overflowing with eggs and *pico de gallo*, beans, handmade tortillas, and grease. The cook frowned, not understanding the question. I tried to explain the virtues of Tex Mex over Cal Mex to Maia. I was feeling contentedly native again when I turned to the confused cook and said in Spanish: "She doesn't understand why it looks different. I told her it's more cheese, more lard in the beans."

I tried to get fancy with the vocabulary. The cook yawned.

"Man," he said, "either you're from California or you're a fucking Cuban. Nobody says *habichuelas* for *frijoles*."

Shamed into silence, I made a mental note of the vocabulary problem and retreated quickly with my pile of tacos.

"What did he say?" asked Maia.

"He said you'll be quiet and eat it if you know what's good for you."

We sat under the ceiling fans on the patio and watched the occasional VIA bus grind down an otherwise deserted street. A vagrant stopped for a minute to admire our midnight breakfast. He was dressed in a ragged brown Cowboy Bob outfit complete with bandolera and toy pistol, his eyes unfocused and milky. I handed him my last taco. He grinned like a five-year-old and ambled on.

I was thinking about Lillian, trying to remember how she'd acted and what she'd said the day before she disappeared. But when I called up her face it was blurred with images of her at sixteen or nineteen. It scared me how fast she was dissolving into an old memory again. However much I kidded myself about knowing her, I couldn't even guess about her last few years. I couldn't discount the idea that she might be involved in what had happened, maybe deeply involved.

She had asked for court protection against Karnau last year, only to go back into business with him. She'd broken off her relationship with Dan Sheff last spring, then reestablished contact with me a few days later. She had brought me back to town, told me she loved me, given me something people were dying over, then vanished.

I wadded up my taco tinfoil and made a basket in the trash barrel. I tried to focus on translating the mariachi music on the kitchen radio. Maia had evidently been looking at me for a while, following the same train of thoughts. Her expression was soft and resigned.

"We need to know," she said. "You need to see her through somebody else's eyes, Tres."

She took my hand. I stared out at San Pedro, then gave Maia directions to Lillian's house on Acacia Street.

The *conjunto* and beer were still flowing at the Rodriguezes' when we drove past. The windows were lit up orange again. The yelling and the breaking glass inside told us that a spirited family discussion was under way. Maia parked the Buick around the corner, then we walked up the alley and slipped into Lillian's backyard.

No police tape on the back door, no sign that the police had ever been here. In two minutes we'd worked open a lock on the guest bedroom window and stepped inside. Maia's ten-pound key chain came in handy once again. Along with a Swiss Army knife, and minicanister of capsaicin, and keys to most of the Western world, she kept a pencil flashlight in her purse for just such an occasion as a friendly B & E. In the thin beam of its light, Lillian's living room looked about the same as I had left it a week ago—trashed, but not alarmingly so. At least, not alarming to me.

"Yuck," whispered Maia. "Is this normal?"

"Yes," I said. Then reluctantly: "Maybe. I don't know."

A screen door screeched opened at the Rodriguez place and a puppy yelped as it was shoed outside. Some woman cursed in Spanish: "*You* feed the damn thing." Men laughed. The bass was turned up.

"I don't think you need to whisper," I told Maia. "We could take clogging lessons in here and the Rodriguezes would never notice."

We checked Lillian's computer first. There was a half-finished spreadsheet for the gallery on file, a few word-processed business letters, a few standard software applications. The only disks on her desk were blank. She had no CD-ROM drive, much less the capacity for creating such a disk. The only thing we learned was that the Hecho a Mano Gallery wasn't even making enough money to bother recording.

In the corner of the main room was a board and cinder-block bookshelf that dated back to our college days. Maia and I pulled out books on everything from O'Keefe to Christo, unread textbooks with forgotten pressed flowers inside, five or six years worth of *Sunset* and *Texas Monthly,* all smelling like mildew and Halston. Finally Maia opened a white photo album and shone her flashlight on the first page. In the little yellow halo of light, Lillian and I stared up at us. I was wearing a tuxedo; she wore a red silk kimono over her black pantsuit, holding a peacock feather. The outfit, of course, had been a gift from my mother, an act of revenge as Lillian and I were preparing to go to my father's sixtieth birthday party, back in my first year in college. I'd like to say that I remembered the rest of the details about that night. The truth is I didn't. I looked at my own confident, very young smile, the way Lillian looked up at me with her head slightly tilted toward my shoulder. I couldn't imagine myself ever having been there. Maia flipped the page quickly—pictures of Lillian's family, several of us, all old and faded, a few of Lillian's paintings. Maia closed the book.

"There's nothing here," she whispered. She got up and moved on.

When I followed Maia into the bedroom she was shining her flashlight on Lillian's white wicker baby carriage. It was lined with red gingham and filled with rows of antique porcelain dolls. Ever since junior high, that carriage had been in Lillian's bedroom wherever she lived. I remember feeling nervous the first time I'd kissed her on her bed, looking over her shoulder at all those little porcelain eyes.

"It's my mother's." Lillian had laughed, biting my ear. "Family heirloom, Tres. I can't get rid of it."

I touched the gingham blanket. There was a small bundle tucked underneath. I brought it out. Ten letters postmarked from San Francisco, each carefully refolded and placed back in its envelope. Before I could put them away, Maia took the stack, noticed the address, then dropped them lightly back into the doll collection.

"So that's what happened to all my stamps," she said.

She shone the flashlight right in my eyes as she turned away. I tried to believe it was an accident.

After a few minutes in the bathroom, Maia found a cigar box full of assorted junk—door handles, rubber bands, costume jewelry, and a rather large diamond engagement ring.

Maia held up the ring and examined it. Finally she said: "Can I assume you didn't mail this too?"

I stared at it, wondering how many years I would have to work for something like that, assuming I ever got a job. Maia's expression was tightly controlled, but from the cold fierceness in her eyes I guessed she was pondering where on my face she might most effectively embed the engagement ring.

It was a strange feeling, sitting on Lillian's bathroom floor, having a stare-down with my former lover by the light of her pencil flashlight. Then the police siren sounded. It was a few blocks away and probably had nothing to do with us, but it reminded us where we were. Ten minutes later we were back in Maia's Buick, heading out of Monte Vista.

I said nothing except to direct Maia through town until we were crossing the Olmos Dam. Then I said: "Wait. Pull over."

Maia frowned. She looked at the narrow road that sloped off a hundred feet into the Basin on either side. "Pull over where?"

"Just pull over."

I got out and leaned against the hood of the Buick, which was only slightly warmer than the air. Tonight there was no storm coming through. It was clear and orange with light pollution, with the only visible stars right at the top of the sky. I wasn't sure why I wanted to be here again, without even the defense of a tequila bottle, but I wasn't ready to go home either, wherever the hell that was. Maia got out of the car, uncertain at first what to do.

She sat down next to me, followed my gaze. "I used to look at the stars out in the countryside, after my father went away."

Went away, she still called it. I tried hard to imagine her as a six-year-old child, crying as her father was dragged away by the Red Guard for reeducation. I tried to picture her as a teenager, before she'd been reeducated herself by her English-speaking uncle, then taken to America, leaving the rest of the family to suffer the consequences. But it was the opposite problem I had with Lillian, who I always saw in the past. With Maia, I couldn't imagine her any other way than she was now— sensual, adult, as carefully polished as teak wood.

"In my home village outside Shaoxing," she continued, smiling sadly, "there was this huge old plum tree I used to sit in. I'd look up at all those millions of stars and envy them."

"Yeah," I agreed.

She shook her head. "No. I envied them because there were so few. I used to dream about being in such a small population, being alone and silent like that, with a few glorious centimeters between you and the next person. You don't understand what a billion means unless you're Chinese, Tres, and you don't appreciate zero."

I wanted to argue. I stared at Maia's face, watching her force herself not to cry. I thought about death and absence and memories as foggy and sore as a tequila hangover. Even stone sober I couldn't figure out why I'd come home, but I thought I appreciated zero pretty damn well. Before Maia could stand up and walk away, maybe for good, I put my hand on the back of her neck very gently and pulled her forward.

The dam was nearly deserted, but I think two cars went by before I opened my eyes again. The second one passed with the horn blaring, someone yelling insults at us that faded into the dark with the taillights. Maia's eyelids were still wet on my cheek. She didn't say anything, but guided my hand under her blouse, up her back. Her skin was cool. My fingers traced her spine all the way to her shoulder blades, then undid her bra with a single twist.

Her laugh was shaky, the end of a silent crying spell.

"You must've been a terror in high school," she said into my ear.

"I'm a terror now," I said, but it was muffled.

I held her underneath her blouse and slid down into the smell of amber and the taste of salty skin, thanking God and Detroit for the wide smooth hood of the Buick.

37

Around 1:30 in the morning, the only light in San Antonio was from streetlamps, stars, and my landlord's TV. Looking upstairs at the one blue eye in Number 90's paralyzed face, I wondered what was on television at this time of morning that was so interesting. Or maybe, since Gary was half-asleep all the time, he didn't need to be all asleep any of the time. I think Abraham Lincoln said that.

I'm not sure whether I felt worse or better with Maia leaning up against me, her arms around my waist as we walked to the front porch. I simply didn't care at the moment about anything except lying down on my futon and going comatose.

That was before I realized that my futon was already occupied.

I should have known when Robert Johnson failed to scold me at the door. I think Maia sensed it first. She froze with her hand halfway to the light switch even before I heard the snick of the revolver cock.

"Everything on the floor in front of you," he said.

The flashlight beam that hit our faces was from no pencil-thin model. I squinted, blind, and raised my hands. Maia dropped her purse. Her key chain hit the floor like a small bowling ball.

"Okay." His voice was slightly familiar now. "Kneel."

We did.

"You going to knight us, buddy?" I said. "It's usually done with a sword."

The air moved. Maybe I could've dodged the kick if I hadn't been so tired and so blind. As it was I just had time to turn my newly corrected teeth to keep them from getting rebroken before our guest's foot stamped Doc Maarten on the side of my face.

I managed to get back on my knees without crying out. My cheekbone didn't feel broken, but everything was fuzzy now. The left side of my face was going to look like a rotten tomato in the morning.

"That's strike one," he said. Then he turned on the lights.

The redhead was holding the Colt .45 in his left hand because his right arm, the one I'd broken outside of Hung Fong's last week, was in a cast. He looked like he hadn't shaved or slept or even bathed since that encounter. The lit fuses in his eyes told me that this was a man who'd already pulled the pin and had decided this was as good a place as any to stand until he blew up.

"Tell us what you want," said Maia.

She spoke the way she would to a distraught client, and I waited for it to backfire the way it had with Beau. This time, though, it seemed to work. Red lowered the gun slightly. He kept his eyes on me.

"You know," he said. "And don't even fucking tell me it's not here. You don't want to know what strike two is."

I found myself wondering if his eye sockets could really be that dark blue. His face looked so old and leprous now I started to doubt he was the same man who'd attacked me last Tuesday.

I showed him that I was going for my shirt pocket, then

with two fingers extracted the disk Garrett had given me. It had scrambled photo data on it, all right—pictures of Garrett's last fishing trip with the New Mexico branch of the Hell's Angels. I threw it at Red's feet.

"Rough week?" I asked.

"Tres, shut up," Maia hissed.

Now Red had a problem. With only one hand, he couldn't pick up the disk and hold the revolver at the same time. He pointed the gun at Maia.

"Get up."

He made Maia pick up the disk and come toward him, keeping the Colt .45 aimed at her chest where he couldn't possibly miss. I didn't think Maia would try anything, and even if she did I wasn't sure I'd be in much shape to help, but I paid close attention to her body anyway, looking for any sign she was tensing up.

It didn't happen. She slipped the CD into Red's jacket pocket, then knelt down again. Red seemed to relax to a temperature just under a rolling boil.

"Okay. You want your tea leaves read now, Navarre?"

"More than once a month is bad karma," I said.

His laugh was more like a brief facial spasm. "Nobody's going to break any arms tonight. Nobody's going to write any fucking messages on my shirt or put their fucking elbow in my face."

"Okay," I said.

I looked at Maia out of the corner of my eye. We came to an understanding. We were both looking for a sign that Red was ready to kill. As long as he kept talking we were all right, but more than four seconds of silence meant he would fire. If that happened we went for him, and one of us died for sure, but maybe not both of us.

"You ever been hit by a black talon?" he said.

"Once almost," Maia said.

"Nasty little fuckers," he continued, looking at me as if I'd said it. Red tried to scratch his face, then remembered he was holding a gun. I think it was only then that I realized he was drunk as well as desperate. So his reflexes would be a little slower. At three feet with black talons from a .45, I wasn't exactly relieved.

He said: "Once they open up they don't leave much of your chest cavity, man. Makes a ragged son-of-a-bitch hole. One guy I saw got it from the police, he just screamed until his lungs came out his throat."

I nodded. "Not as quick as bullets through the eyes, then?"

That registered in his face like a cattle prod. He aimed the Colt at my head.

"So we're going to put things right," he said, as if he were just ending a pep speech to the team. "We're going to give this back, I'm going to get my ass out of this town, and you maybe get to live."

None of us bought that, not even Red. He shrugged. "If this isn't the disk, it's going to be a lot more fun, man. A lot more fun for your lady here."

I stared at him, trying to look cooperative and unimpressed at the same time. The way my face was contorting on the bashed-in side, I probably looked more like Dill the Cat.

"You and Eddie worked for Sheff," I said. "That's who we're going to?"

The idea amused Red so much he decided to kick me again, this time in the gut. When I got my face out of the carpet, a few centuries later, I saw one and a half redheads with guns hovering in front of me, smiling.

"Now unless you've got more questions, let's go."

We left in Maia's car. Whatever Gary Hales was watching on television, it must've been more interesting than your run-of-the-mill abduction at gunpoint. He never even looked out the window.

I played chauffeur while Red sat in back, his .45 aimed lazily at Maia's head. We turned off Eisenhower onto that stretch of Austin Highway where the strip malls that hadn't been abandoned yet housed head shops, heavily barred pawn and liquor stores, beauty salons that still had faded pictures of beehive models in the windows.

Every few seconds I glanced back at Red in the

rearview mirror and watched his eyelids drooping. Once, when his chin dipped an inch, I almost made a move. Before I'd even taken my hand off the wheel, the Colt barrel was in my ear.

"Don't," he said, no sleep in his voice at all.

I smiled in the mirror, then concentrated on the road.

It must've been 2 A.M. The drunks were starting to stumble out of taverns like the Starz N Barz or the Come On Inn to find their cars to sleep in, preparing to wait out the unendurable six hours until the bars would open again. Bikers clustered in the parking lots, invisible except for the glint of Harley steel and the orange tips of their joints.

"Next left," Red said.

We passed a row of mobile home parks and pulled into one where the plywood sign on the Cyclone fence out front said "Happy Haven." The gravel and strips of corrugated steel and broken patio furniture that littered the courtyard said something else entirely. There were five other cars in the lot, all in various stages of disassembly. The courtyard was lit only by a yellow car repair lamp draped over the branch of a dead elm tree.

I handed the Buick keys to Red, then he and Maia got out first. We walked to the third trailer, a dented white and green metal canister that looked like an oversized hatbox. Red opened the screen door, then waved me inside.

This time I knew something was wrong the instant the air hit my face. It was cold as a meat locker inside, and it smelled just about as bad. Refrigerated animal waste overpowered the other smells of bourbon and cigarettes. It was also pure black except for the yellow square of light from the door we'd opened. Somewhere off to the right, a window unit air conditioner hacked and wheezed to keep the room under sixty degrees. I tried not to gag. Then I went inside and began talking as if there were really someone there.

"Long time no see," I said to the blackness.

Maia followed my lead, then rolled away to the left. I went right and nearly tripped over something soft and wet. As I slid down against the cheap wood paneling on the wall, I could feel a few dozen splinters shooting up into my arm. I made myself not move.

Red was only two steps behind us, but he was in the light now and we weren't. It only took two or three seconds for him to realize something was very wrong and decide to blow holes in the dark with his Colt. In that time both Maia's feet hit his kneecap at a ninety-degree angle. The cartilage snapped like celery. Red shot a two-foot-wide hole in the trailer roof as he staggered forward. Before he could shoot again with better aim I got his good forearm in "play biwa" posture. It's called that because when you twist the two bones of the forearm across each other and keep twisting, they snap with a sound resembling a plucked string on a Chinese lute. At least that's what Sifu Chen had told me. It sounded more like a percussion instrument to me.

Red screamed and dropped the gun. But he didn't go down until I double-chopped his neck just below the jawline. Then he melted into the shag carpet and started snoring.

Maia was already crouching down in the corner with Red's .45. She closed the front door of the trailer with her foot. After a few minutes staying absolutely still, listening to the air conditioner whine, I groped up the wall until I found the light switch.

The first thing I noticed when the light came on was the color of my hand. Then the thing I was sitting on. I'd thought it was a waterbed mattress, the way it gave under me, but waterbeds aren't covered in blue silk and they don't have white hair. I got up, turned it over, then made a face as contorted as the corpse's.

Terry Garza was four hours early for our appointment. Blood had flowed out of his neck so freely it had finally blossomed and crusted over into a huge, grotesque rose on his neck. The *anticucho* skewer that had brought it into bloom still sprouted from the center.

I tried to remind my stomach that it belonged inside my rib cage, not my mouth. It didn't listen very well.

Look someplace else, I told myself. I stared at the flower-patterned sofa Garza had rolled off of, the stripped mattress in the far corner, the three empty beer cans rattling on top of the air conditioner. There was nothing else in the trailer.

Maia unfroze more quickly than I did. Without speaking, she retrieved her keys and purse from Red, then killed the overhead light. With her flashlight and a handkerchief, she started going over Garza's body, checking pockets, looking at his hands and feet. Garza's face had a twisted, almost puzzled expression. His eyes stared out the ragged skylight Red had blown in the roof. At the moment Garza looked like he had even more questions than I did.

"Don't hold your breath," I told him.

Garza held his breath.

If anybody in Happy Haven had heard the shot, or cared about it, we hadn't had any indication of it so far. Nevertheless, my internal timer was telling me it was past time to leave. I used Red's flashlight to make a quick check of the kitchen while Maia examined the dead man.

Under the silverware tray in the left kitchen drawer was a six-month lease to Terry Garza of Sheff Construction.

When I got back to Maia she was looking at a photograph she'd found on the dead man. She frowned when I interrupted her train of thought by showing her the lease.

"Chez Garza."

She looked at me, nodded as if I'd said something of absolutely no consequence, then looked back down at the photo.

"Hello?" I said.

"I apologize," she said at last. "Maybe you should tell me more about your father's murder."

She handed me the photo. It was almost identical to the one I'd seen in Karnau's portfolio, but in this one, the blond man's face was turned toward the camera. I still didn't recognize him. The two missing figures were slightly closer to him. On the back "6/21" was written in black pen.

"Last month's bill from Mr. Karnau," I said.

Maia starting complaining in Mandarin about my ignorance. "—facial hair fooling you again. Look at the bone structure of the cheeks, the eyes."

I looked more closely at the face of the blond man. It was thin, with deep-set eyes, crooked nose. Clean-shaven and short slicked-back hair. I imagined him with longer hair, curly, and a darker beard.

Suddenly I realized what the blackmail had been about. The revelation wasn't exactly uplifting.

"Randall Halcomb," I said.

"With his killers," Maia agreed.

38

I got no sleep the rest of the night. At sunrise I was lying on my futon memorizing the ceiling and getting cold from Maia's breath condensing on my skin. Finally I extracted myself from underneath her arm and got up.

Robert Johnson looked amazed that, for once, I was the first one out of bed. He immediately began playing tackle football with my feet as I tried to walk toward the kitchen. I would've cursed at him except I knew he'd curse back loud enough to wake Maia. I stumbled here and there, righting the coffee table, picking up clothes, putting the fallen paperbacks back on the kitchen counter. I struggled into some underwear and stood in front of the bathroom mirror for a while, picking wood paneling out of my arm, then reapplying Mercurochrome to my busted cheek.

"What a looker," I told myself. Robert Johnson stared at me from the lid of the toilet and yawned.

I slipped into shorts and a sweatshirt, then did a solid two hours of tai chi on the back porch, starting with the low stance to shock my muscles into working. After a while the thighs and calves unknotted and I got too sweaty even for the mosquitoes.

I was just starting to feel better when the neighborhood woke up for Sunday. The two pairs of eyes reappeared in the upstairs window across the alley and stared at me through the miniblind slats. The lady next door came out to read her paper on the patio again. This time I hardly warranted a second look. She kept her coffee cup firmly in hand and tightened her terry-cloth robe. Then she smiled wickedly as she let a small herd of Chihuahuas out the back door. For the last half of my set, they threatened me from their side of the fence, yapping insanely and popping up into the air like a tireless row of Mexican jumping beans. Meanwhile their mother read aloud to them from Roddy Stinson, repeating the funny bits.

I tried to be grateful for the challenge to my concentration. *Think emptiness, Navarre. Blue water trickling down through your body. Cultivate the chi.* This morning, all I cultivated was a headache and the need to pee like a racehorse. I said my silent apologies to Sifu Chen and went inside.

Maia was making the last of the Peet's coffee. Her hair was blown into a mass on one side of her head, as if she'd been walking on the beach. She was wearing my last clean T-shirt. She looked up, smiled, and for a second burned the images of dead bodies out of my mind. But only for a second.

"You look like hell, Navarre. And you just about wore this poor girl out last night."

"I'm always great in the sack after getting the shit kicked out of me."

"I'll remember that." She pulled me closer by the elastic of my shorts, then kissed my face. I winced.

"Speaking of last night—" I said.

She smiled, a little sad. "Leave it alone for a while, Tex. Okay?"

I sat down with coffee at the counter, pushed Robert Johnson's butt out of my face, and stared at the .45

Maia had taken from Red, the stacks of fifties I'd taken from Beau Karnau, the crumpled photo of Randall Halcomb we'd found on Terry Garza's corpse.

I didn't like the connections I was coming up with. Ten years ago my father somehow finds out about the scheme to fix the contract on Travis Center. Before he can make it public, the people behind the plan use Randall Halcomb to silence the Sheriff. Then, before the FBI can track down Halcomb, his employers silence him too.

Maia and I looked at each other.

"First rule of assassination," I told Maia, "kill the killer."

Maia frowned. "And Beau Karnau just happens to be there with a camera—in a field in the country in the middle of the night. That's a hell of a coincidence."

I agreed. It didn't make sense. Neither did the fact that blackmail payments for a ten-year-old murder had only been happening for the last year.

I rubbed my eyes. "We need to know about Guy White. Whether the mob's really in this, or whether it's just convenient for somebody to make it look that way. We need to know what the police have on Garza's murder, and Moraga."

"And Lillian," said Maia quietly.

I stared out at the crape myrtles. Maia came closer. She put her hands lightly on my shoulders.

"First, you need to eat something," she said. "Then we'll see about the police."

I rubbed my eyes again, pondering how to make breakfast from one beer and some baking soda. Thinking about my empty refrigerator led me to thinking about Larry Drapiewski's card sitting in my medicine cabinet.

I looked at the time—9:00. Almost a civilized hour. If I made it sound urgent enough, he could be here in under thirty minutes, but only if I was prepared to discuss police matters in the serious businesslike manner to which he was accustomed. Which meant only one thing.

I peeled a few fifties off Beau Karnau's stack.

"First," I told Maia, "we go grocery shopping."

39

I wasn't sure whether Pappy Delgado was glad to see me or just happy to meet Maia. I harbored illusions that the old grocer took an interest in my well-being. It was probably closer to the truth that he took an interest in Maia's white culottes and brown legs. Whichever, it was a slow morning in his little pink Christmas-lighted store, and Pappy decided to give us a guided tour of the produce aisle.

On the way he helped me correct my Californian *Español* so I sounded more like a Tejano than a Cuban. *Sandia* instead of *patia* for watermelon *agua fresca*. Forget *guinea* for banana. He seemed endlessly amused to be schooling the gringo. Finally, while Maia was picking out avocados, Pappy nodded his huge nose her way and grinned at me.

"*Y la chica?*" he whispered.

I told him he was a dirty old man. He just grinned and told me he bathed daily, preferably not alone.

I called Drapiewski from the pay phone at the corner of New Braunfels and Eleanor and told him we had things to talk about and *pan dulce* to eat. He grudgingly agreed to come over.

"You want to give me some context here, Navarre? What's the problem?"

"Heard about the murder at Sheff Construction? You guys had some deputies on the scene, I remember."

He was silent.

"Okay, how about Terry Garza dead on Austin Highway? We called it in anonymously last night."

He was still silent.

"Can I take that as a yes?" I asked.

"Holy hell," Drapiewski said. Then he hung up on me.

Back at Queen Anne, I heated up the *pan dulce* Pappy's wife had made in the back of the shop that morning and added a little butter and cinnamon. By the time they were out of the oven, Drapiewski was at the door. He wasn't in a jovial mood.

Before he said anything he took a fistful of *pan dulce* and sat on the futon. On impact, it sank a few feet into the foundation. Robert Johnson was flushed out from underneath and belly-crawled all the way to the closet.

"All right," said Drapiewski. "Now what the fuck is this about homicides?"

Then Maia came out of the bathroom. Larry turned redder than he already was and pulled off his hat. He started to get up.

"Sorry," he said. "Didn't know you had company."

Maia smiled and motioned him to stay seated.

"That's all right, Lieutenant. I'm enchanted—I didn't know anyone apologized for saying 'fuck' anymore."

"Ah—" Larry said.

Maia laughed, then introduced herself. One hand shake and Larry was in love. He grinned cinnamon and butter. He tried to make room on the futon for her and just about goosed himself with his nightstick.

Since he'd totally forgotten he was supposed to be pissed at me, I decided to help him out. "Homicide, Larry? You were saying?"

He tried to scowl at me. Maybe it was for Maia's benefit.

"I checked the telex on Garza a few minutes ago. Nothing's even been posted yet."

Maia sat back as much as she could on the two inches of the futon not occupied by Drapiewski's body. "Is that unusual?"

"What's unusual is that I hear about it from your friend here first." His eyes bored into me with all the accusatory power of a faithful hound dog I'd just kicked. "I also followed up on Karnau this morning—had one of my deputies swing by his apartment, then his studio. They were both empty, like Karnau's left town."

Maia and I looked at each other. Larry waited.

"So you want to tell me?" he asked.

I told him. By the time I got to last night's soiree in Terry Garza's trailer, Drapiewski didn't look too happy. When I'd finished he put his hands together like he was praying and pointed them at me.

"You walked out on a murder scene after removing evidence."

"That's one interpretation," I admitted.

"And the only solid evidence you have about this construction scam you obtained during a B & E at Sheff's offices, which pretty much ruins it for the courts."

I nodded.

Larry's huge red eyebrows came together. He exhaled.

"Son, you probably just ruined the best chance we'd ever have to string Guy White up by his balls for murdering your dad. I would've given anything, anytime in the last ten years for that chance and you just—" He stopped, collected himself. I could tell he was counting silently. "All right, let's say you broached this whole thing as a hypothetical. Okay, fine. I'm not obliged to follow up. But here's my hypothetical advice: Get your ass down to SAPD and cooperate like hell."

"That's it?"

He exploded. "God damn it. You better believe the FBI will be in this sooner or later. When that happens they'll take one look at the way you've screwed up the scene, and your ass will be flying at half-mast on the Feds' flagpole. Then I won't be able to do anything for you."

As we stared at each other, the ice cream truck trolled by outside. Since last week, its version of "La Bamba" had worn down a few octaves to a funeral march.

"And what about Rivas's investigation on Lillian? What about the homicides?"

Drapiewski slowly brushed the pink sugar off his hands. "Let's just say it would be damned unusual for me to ask SAPD straight out without a reason."

We sat there at an impasse until Maia decided to help. She rested her hand on Larry's knee and smiled sadly, earnestly. "Could you find a reason, Lieutenant?"

Larry shifted uncomfortably, mumbling something to himself. He looked down at Maia's hand. His expression broke.

"Aw shit," he said. "Friday I'm doing some off-duty security work with a buddy of mine from CID. Maybe we could talk."

Maia's smile to Drapiewski was probably worth it. I was too busy watching the linoleum in the kitchen.

"And if Friday's too late?" I asked.

Larry stood up. His hand on my shoulder felt like warm lead.

"Get your ass downtown, Tres. Before Friday. And stay the hell away from Guy White."

We were silent.

"Damn it, son," he said. "There's nothing else I can do."

"You got any connections with the Blanco Sheriff's Department?" I asked. "Randall Halcomb was killed out there. I'd like to know more about the scene."

Larry frowned.

"We could go out there alone . . ." I said, glancing at Maia.

"All right," Larry grumbled. "I'm off at noon. I'll pick you up then, long as you do me two favors."

I gave him my winningest smile. "Anything for you."

"Stay put," he said.

"And?"

"Stop reminding me of your goddamn father."

40

I was hoping Drapewski would settle for one out of three. We didn't stay put and we didn't stay the hell away from Guy White.

My first mistake was trying to get through Brackenridge Park on a Sunday morning. The minute we turned onto Mulberry we were stuck in a line of station wagons and low-rider Chevies, heavily pinstriped pickup trucks with sunbathers sprawled out in the cabs. Since we weren't moving anywhere, drivers in opposite lanes carried on conversations in Spanish, exchanged beers and cigarettes, flirted shamelessly with the passengers who were invariably girls with red hair and tight black tube tops, even tighter cutoffs. The smell of barbacoa and hamburger smoke drifted through the trees as thick as fog. Picnic spots had been staked out as early as the night before along the riverbanks, so as near as I could tell the people in the cars just cruised in very slow circles, eating their Sunday lunch while they drove. Maia got several propositions and enough whistles to fill an aviary. Nobody whistled at me.

Since there was nothing else to do, I pointed out the miniature railroad tracks, the rent-a-pony stables, the place where the Great Brackenridge Train Robbery had taken place.

Maia looked at me for a translation. "The what?"

"My dad's claim to law enforcement fame," I told her. "A group of basic trainees from Lackland got let loose on Day 25, drank some beer, decided to steal a few ponies and play Jesse James. They put bandannas on their faces, laid this dead tree across the tracks, then hid in the woods and waited for the kiddie train to come by. Robbed it at gunpoint and made a getaway."

"Charming," said Maia.

I held up my hand. "There's more. My dad was a deputy at the time. Now that I think about it, that afternoon's the only occasion I remember him being off-duty and sober at the same time. I think he was taking me to the zoo. When he spotted the robbery he told me to stay put. A local station got some great footage of him, all three hundred pounds, waving his shotgun like he was Judge Roy Bean and lumbering after this group of drunk pinheads on ponies. Afterward he got drunk and gave the media a dynamite interview about bringing law to the Wild West. The next year they elected him sheriff."

"The media?"

"Basically," I said.

Maia nodded. I think she was staring at me to find my father's genetic code, trying to decide whether chasing pony-mounted bandits with a shotgun was a dominant or recessive trait. Whatever she concluded, she kept it to herself.

We finally made it into Olmos Park and turned onto Crescent. When we pulled in front of the White House, we found that Mr. White had been renovating. He'd had a presidential fountain installed in his front yard, and three workers in sweaty denim were busy digging trenches and laying down copper pipes, trying to finish the plumbing. White had also installed a three-hundred-pound Hispanic linebacker at the front door.

The new doorman looked at us with a confused expression as we walked across the lawn.

"Howdy," I told him.

His head sloped straight down into his shoulders like a lamp shade. His features were so flat they almost looked smeared. The only things that added any contour to his face were his hair and his sunglasses—both were huge, shiny, and black. He looked like he had once tried to listen to a calculus lecture and had never quite gotten over it. His eyebrows were drawn together, his mouth frowning, open.

"BeeBee," he said.

Maybe it was his name. Maybe that's as far as he'd ever gotten with the alphabet. Whichever, he didn't seem to have much to add. He crossed his arms and waited for us to go away or try climbing over him.

I looked at Maia. She shrugged.

"¿Hablas mejor Español?" I asked.

BeeBee watched me as if I were the most amazing insect in the world. If I were any more entertaining I was afraid he'd start drooling. Behind us the fountain workers were taking a break. Out of the corner of my eye I saw them toweling the sweat off their faces, watching us. One of them quietly bet five dollars.

"Okay," I said. "We'd like to see Mr. White. If you'd tell him we're here."

BeeBee seemed to be watching my mouth, trying to learn the words.

"Or you could just stamp your foot," I suggested. "Once for yes."

"Maybe if we just asked inside?" Maia said, smiling innocently. When she tried to walk through the door BeeBee's arm blocked her at the waist. Then a shape moved behind the beveled glass door. My old friend Emery opened it and stood in the entrance. He didn't look particularly thrilled to see me.

Today he was wearing a pin-striped suit that was about three sizes too big. His shirt collar was so huge it wrinkled up like an asshole around his neck when he tightened his orange tie.

I offered him my hand. "*Que pasa,* buddy?"

Emery made a sound that was somewhere between a laugh and an asthma attack. "You are one stupid son of a bitch." He put several extra syllables in the word *stupid,* just for emphasis.

"We'd like a few minutes of Mr. White's time," I said. "You remember the drill from last time?"

Emery shifted his weight from one foot to the other. "That's a good one." He looked at BeeBee for support. "Ain't that good?"

BeeBee was no help. Even though Maia had backed off, BeeBee's arm was still blocking the doorway. He'd probably forgotten why it was there.

"Mr. White isn't disposed to take visitors on a Sunday morning," Emery said. "Mr. White made it pretty clear that includes you, Mr. Navarre. I'm real sorry."

BeeBee stepped forward so I could admire his chest while Emery tightened his orange tie a little more.

"He might be interested in what we've got to say, this time."

Emery gave me a lopsided grin. "I surely doubt that, Mr. Navarre."

I looked at Maia. She smiled sweetly.

"Gentlemen," she said, "you are absolutely sure you couldn't just ask Mr. White? Really, I think it would be best."

"She thinks it would be best," Emery repeated to BeeBee. BeeBee nodded as if he might get it after a few more repetitions. Emery grinned so much his cheeks turned into canyons. "I think you should just go on back to Japan, honey, and Mr. Sheriff's Boy here can go on back to Frisco. That'd be a whole lot easier."

People always show you their impressive high kicks when they boast about martial arts. They neglect to tell you that the higher you lift your leg, the more you are telling the world: "Here are my balls. Please hit them hard." Sure, a high kick has more reach, but in truth the quickest, safest, most devastating kick, and the one that is hardest to defend against, is a good low kick to the shin. It worked wonders on BeeBee. He crumpled backward into the foyer without ever losing his confused expression. Of course it didn't help his comprehension when he cracked his head against the marble floor. Emery was less fortunate. Maia grabbed him by his orange tie and slammed his head into the beveled glass door, then dropped him on top of BeeBee.

"Japan," she spat.

I was gratified to discover that Emery was keeping the .38 Airweight in his belt these days. Maia took it. I think she would've kicked Emery in the ribs just for good measure if we hadn't had more company to deal with. We'd barely stepped into the foyer when two more linebackers came down the grand staircase that circled the back wall of the living room. Their uniform of choice seemed to be Italian suits. Their weapon of choice seemed to be 9mm Glocks.

At first they were too busy running down the staircase to fire effectively, and when they got to the bottom they had to circle to either side of a column-shaped glass-and-rosewood display case full of crystal statuettes.

"Good morning," I said. "Mr. White at home?"

I stepped forward. Nice and easy, I thought.

Maia, the calm and reasonable one, chose instead to start firing Emery's .38 at the display case. It's amazing what a beautiful grenade you can make out of some hollow tip bullets and a bunch of Waterford crystal. Shards of glass reindeer, penguins, and delicate swans turned everything in a fifteen-foot radius into a winter wonderland, including the two men's faces. They were still yelling on the steps as Maia walked up to the staircase and picked up the two Glocks they'd dropped. After I had checked for holes in my body and made sure that I hadn't soiled my trousers, I asked her: "What did you figure the odds were they'd ventilate my chest before you managed to pull that off?"

She kissed my unbruised cheek. "I didn't figure."

"Just making sure."

We tried the oak double doors on the left. Before I really knew what I was doing my arms came out, grabbing, and my waist instinctively twisted and sank into *lui* position, "pull down." The guy with the black-jack went over my knee face-first into the doorjamb.

"This way," I suggested to Maia.

At the French doors that led to the backyard, Guy White stood waiting for us, his parabellum pointed lazily in our direction. He had apparently just walked in from the patio, and was leaning against the door frame in his khakis, an untucked blue button-down, and slippers. His mole-colored hair was carefully combed and gelled, and his expression was completely peaceful.

"You are the most persistent man," he told me.

Fortunately there was no Waterford crystal to shoot at in the room. Maia dropped her three guns on the nearby desk.

Guy White smiled at her. "Thank you, my dear."

Then he lowered his Glock and waved his other diamond-bedecked hand toward his seven-acre backyard.

"I have some exceptional croissants from Pour la France," he said. "I was just reading Roddy Stinson out in the gazebo. Won't you join me?"

41

"Beau Karnau," said White. "Quite a colorful character."

He laughed without making a sound. Then he sat back in his white wicker chair and proceeded to dissect his croissant. He peeled off each layer and ripped it into small squares with perfectly manicured fingers. If the croissant had been alive I think White would've had the same unconcerned smile on his face.

"You know him, then," I said.

I drank my mimosa out of my crystal glass. It was mixed from Veuve Cliquot instead of Dom Pérignon, but the orange juice had probably been fresh squeezed by illegal aliens who had just been flown in from the Valley that morning, so I had decided not to send it back.

White said: "Only peripherally, because of my patronage to local art galleries. Why do you ask?"

"Curiosity. And the fact that Karnau's just about the only one besides you and me with an interest in the disk who isn't dead at the moment."

No reaction. White looked out over his gardens and waved his champagne glass toward the north.

"What do you think, Miss Lee?" he said. "I'm thinking about tomatoes over in that corner, next to the mountain laurels."

If Maia was trying to look hard and unapproachable, she was failing miserably. She smiled without even looking at the future tomato patch and agreed that it would be a lovely spot for gardening. I swear to God, White's eyes twinkled at her on command. When he was ready to entertain my questions again, he pushed the croissant carcass and the *Express-News* away. He leaned forward across the table, looking earnest and helpful.

"I assure you, Mr. Navarre, Beau Karnau is no associate of mine. I've only met him on a few occasions, and I found him . . . tiresome."

He let his eyes reveal just a hint of annoyance, a benign peevishness toward that quite colorful character Mr. Karnau.

"And Dan Sheff?" Maia ventured.

Guy paused momentarily, then decided to smile. I thought for a minute he would pat Maia's head.

"What of him, my dear?"

"Read your paper," I suggested. "I think the Moraga murder story dropped below the fold today, but you're still getting page one press."

I couldn't get White's attention away from his imaginary tomato patches. His tone stayed pleasantly distracted.

"As I said to you before, my boy, faulty assumptions."

"So you have no relations with Sheff Construction," I said. "No knowledge of how their business changed in the mid-eighties." I finished my mimosa. "I'd've thought about that time you would've been looking for less high-profile opportunities yourself. The drug trafficking trial, the investigation of my father's murder. It must've been very . . . tiresome."

I warranted only a strained sigh from our host, but you take what you can get.

"All I can tell you about Sheff Construction, my boy, is that Mr. Sheff, that would be Mr. Sheff, Jr., has little to do with the—shall we say the day-to-day running of business. Perhaps—" He raised a finger, as if he'd finally spotted the ideal place for some pink azaleas. "Perhaps you should speak to Terry Garza, the business manager. That might be more enlightening."

"We'd made arrangements," I said. "They were canceled last night, when we found him with an *anticucho* skewer sticking out of his neck."

That did it. White lifted his eyes off his future garden and stared at me. I think he was genuinely surprised. Then it passed.

"How unfortunate."

"Once the police come to question you, yes."

I put the photo we'd found in Garza's trailer on top of Guy White's newspaper, facing toward him.

"What I think," I told him, "is that you are either in this photo, or you know who is. Sheff Construction started some extremely lucrative and extremely questionable dealings with city construction contracts ten years ago, Mr. White, and it's an arrangement which is still going on. I would be surprised if anything that large could've escaped your notice. Either you were involved directly, or you'd make it your business to know who was."

White looked over at Maia, smiled like one parent to another when their child has said something cute and foolish.

"Mr. Navarre, I do not appreciate being scapegoated. As I told you, I went through much grief ten years ago, when your father died. Much unwarranted suffering."

"You're telling me you're being scapegoated again?"

He stretched like a cat. "Convenient solutions, Mr. Navarre."

"Help me find Karnau, then. He's got the answers."

White gave me a look I couldn't quite read. Behind the bland smile, he seemed to be deciding something.

He got out of his chair and surveyed his lawn one more time. Then he took an index card and a pen from his pocket. He wrote something on the card, folded it, and let it fall to the table.

"Good-bye, Mr. Navarre." He stretched again, raising himself up on his toes. "So nice to meet you, Miss Lee."

When Guy White was a half acre away, strolling past his newly planted verbena, Maia picked up the index card and read it.

"Try Mr. Karnau at the Placio del Rio tonight."

"That's the Riverwalk Hilton. Downtown."

Maia put her champagne glass on the table. She looked at the index card again. "Why do I feel like we've just been offered a sacrifice?"

"Or someone's unwanted ballast."

I looked across the yard at Guy White, who was now stepping carefully but easily between rows of his Blue Princess like this was his minefield and he'd crossed it many times before.

42

After that, the clean air of the country felt good.

By one o'clock we were speeding along the banks of the Blanco River in Larry Drapiewski's Jeep, and Larry was rapidly consuming the Shiner Bocks and beef fajitas we'd brought him as a peace offering.

"Three beers," Maia said. "What happened to setting a good example for your youngers, Lieutenant?"

Larry laughed. "You get as big as me, Miss Lee, then you can see what three beers does to your blood alcohol content."

Drapiewski's red Jeep seemed right at home in the Hill Country. So did Larry. Off-duty, he was wearing boot-cut Levi's and black leather Justins that must've been made from an entire alligator, a red shirt that made his hair and his freckles seem a little less neon by comparison. Howdy Doody on steroids.

"So what is it you folks are expecting to find?" Drapiewski said. "It's been a lot of years since they pulled Halcomb out of that deer blind, son. You expect something with an orange flag on it just sitting out there all this time?"

"That'd be fine," I said.

Larry laughed. The fajita disappeared in his mouth, followed closely by most of the beer. Maia looked on in awe.

Drapiewski's friend with the Blanco County Sheriff's Department had the unfortunate name of Deputy Chief Grubb. We met Grubb outside the Dairy Queen, a place he had obviously frequented over the years. His white hair had a slightly greasy tinge to it, and his upper body, once that of a football player, had swollen up over his belt buckle until it bore an uncanny resemblance to a Dilly Bar.

Larry made the introductions.

"Halcomb," Grubb said, by way of introduction. "That was a luncher."

"Meaning—?"

When Grubb grinned you could get a good feel for how much he liked his coffee. The layers of yellow on his crooked incisors were like glacial flood lines.

"Meaning we ate it, son," he told me. "Never found a damn thing."

It was a ten-minute drive from the DQ in Grubb's unit. Along the way, he told us about a slave ranch they'd closed down a week before—seventeen Mexican migrant workers kept in a barn, chained up at night, worked with a whip and a double-barrel shotgun during the day. Then he talked about the domestic disputes he'd broken up so far this week, the new Mexican restaurant in town, the high school team's chances next fall. By the time we'd driven to the site and walked through five acres of brush and live oaks, Maia and I knew every bit of gossip Blanco had to offer, including where to buy your duty-free liquor, what fields the marijuana planes landed in, and which local wives were likely candidates for a steamy affair. All I needed now was a place with cheap rent.

"There it is," Grubb said finally, wiping the sweat off the back of his neck. "Ain't much."

The blind had probably been old and abandoned when Randall Halcomb's corpse was stuffed into it years ago. Now it was just a collection of rotten planks and sheets of plywood on four wobbly posts. It had tried to fall down a long time ago but had been stopped by a nearby mesquite that was still propping it up like a sober friend trying to support a drunk. There was a frayed rope ladder hanging from the back. Even if it had held together long enough to climb, the blind would've collapsed under the weight of a full-grown man.

Grubb and Drapiewski started trading stories of gory hunting accidents while Maia and I poked around. Nothing was marked with an orange flag. Five cows were standing in a clump in the shadow of the blind, hiding from the afternoon sun. They looked at me with a kind of lazy resentment, wondering what I was doing there. I started to ask myself the same question.

I'd been hoping, maybe, to match the terrain to Karnau's photos, get a sense for where the shots had been taken from, why Halcomb's employers had chosen this site for a meeting and why Karnau might've been here. So far *nada*.

"Grubb," I called.

The deputy chief came over next to me, with Drapiewski and Maia following.

I nodded at the deer blind. "Did you determine whether this was a dump site or not?"

Grubb took off his deputy's hat and wiped his forehead on his arm.

"A lot of blood about a hunnerd yards down that way," he said. "That's where they killed him. Then they dragged him over here."

"They. As in two."

Grubb nodded. "Could be more. There were tire tracks down that way. FBI took some plaster mold footprints too. I don't recall exactly what the story was."

"Cause of death?"

"Old boy got it right between the eyes at short range.

Hell of a shooter. You know what a Sheridan Knock-about is?"

".22 caliber single shot pistol," Maia said, almost absently. "Went out of production in '62; only twenty thousand were made."

Grubb and Drapiewski gaped at her. In khakis and a white tank top, her eyes invisible behind large black sunglasses, Maia looked like a safari veteran. There was a single line of sweat running from her ear to her jaw. Otherwise the heat seemed to be having no effect on her. She'd been looking toward the deer blind until she noticed that she'd become the center of attention.

She shrugged. "Just a guess."

Larry grinned.

"A Sheridan," I said. "My dad had one, actually—got it right after Korea."

Grubb was back to swabbing his forehead. "Sure. They were popular with a lot of the vets. Target shooters, mostly. Thing was, it's a mighty strange gun to murder somebody with. Very clear striations on the bullet—easy to pin down. And by '85 they weren't what you'd call standard street issue."

I thought about a picture I'd seen in the Sheffs' house—Dan Sr. as a young soldier, off for Korea. I thought about the box of .22 ammo in Dan Jr.'s office closet.

"And you said it's a single shot."

Larry whistled silently. "You got to be pretty sure of your shooting to kill a man like Halcomb with a gun like that. Pretty damn ballsy."

"Or," said Maia, "you've got to be not really planning on murder. You might bring a gun like that along for protection to a dangerous meeting, if it's the only gun you have. Or for a little leverage if things got rough. But probably not for a premeditated kill. Either way you're not talking about a pro." She looked at me. "Not the mob. They'd come a lot better prepared."

Grubb looked Maia up and down one more time, a mixture of confusion and budding respect on his sticky forehead. "What'd you say you were again, honey? Chinese?"

To her credit, Maia left his face intact. She said dryly, "That's right, Mr. Grubb. The ones who built the railroads. You remember."

I looked back at the cows and tried to think. The cows didn't offer any suggestions.

"Is there anything else?" I asked Grubb.

The old deputy took his eyes off Maia, looked at me, and shook his head. "Just a dead end, son."

Drapiewski shrugged. He looked sorry, but not surprised.

I could've left then. I had something to go on. Our two law enforcement escorts were definitely ready to get back to the air-conditioning and the Dilly Bars of a friendly Dairy Queen. But after sweating in the sunshine and swatting the mosquitoes for a few more minutes, I started walking down toward the place where Halcomb had been shot.

There were more mesquite trees down in the hollow. The dry brush was so high we had sticker burrs as thick as fur on our pants by the time we got to the murder site. It was a small clearing barely accessible by two tire ruts that led off into the woods. It was the place in Beau Karnau's photos.

"Not a bad place for a meeting," Larry said. "Very low-profile."

He started picking the sticker burrs out of his crotch. Maia leaned against a dead tree. Grubb just looked at me, losing patience.

"What are you thinking, son?" he asked.

I wanted to give him an answer. I didn't have one.

"Who owns this land?" I asked.

Grubb thought about it. "Right now, I don't know. It was pretty much abandoned in '84. Old Mr. Baker passed on and none of the sons would move back into the house. Then in '86 the ranch burned down. It's changed hands plenty of times since. Nobody uses it nowadays except the neighbors' cattle."

"What neighbors?"

"Vivians on the north, Gardiners on the south."

Neither name rang a bell.

"A ranch house burned down?"

Grubb nodded. He told me about the big electrical storm they'd had back in '86. Lightning had caused a dozen small fires, one of them taking the old ranch house up the hill. He looked at me suspiciously.

"I reckon you'll want to see that too."

Drapiewski laughed.

"Why not?" I said.

It took a lot of compliments and the promise of a free dinner to get Grubb up that hill, but we finally made it. There wasn't much left of the house, just a thin place in the grass where the foundation had been. I couldn't figure out why it looked familiar. I made a complete circuit around the place.

"Is this gonna get us something besides a suntan, son?" said Drapiewski after a few minutes.

That's when I tripped over something large and metal. Grubb and Drapiewski came up to see while I dug it half out of the dirt—a piece of black iron piping that had been shaped into cursive writing about three feet long and a foot high. It said "Lazy B."

"Yeah," said Grubb. "I remember that. The old gates to the place. What do you know."

It took me a minute to place the name. Then something else clicked.

" 'Lazy Bastard,' " I said.

Grubb glared at me. "What was that, boy?"

"Miss Lee and I saw a photo of this place recently. Taken at night, during a meteor storm."

Grubb nodded, more hot now than interested, daydreaming of ice cream and shade.

Drapiewski and Maia looked at me, both of them trying to read my expression. My throat suddenly felt very dry.

"So this is the angle Karnau shot from," Maia said. "That only makes sense."

"No," I said. "Lillian said something before she disappeared. She and Karnau used to go on photography shoots, sometimes for days at a time. She mentioned camping out on a godforsaken hilltop in Blanco. She mentioned photographing a meteor shower."

"Funny coincidence," Drapiewski said, looking back into the hollow where Halcomb had been shot. I tried to imagine Randall Halcomb in the deer blind, curled up with a perfect red hole between his eyes, but I kept coming up with Lillian's face.

"Yeah," I said. "Funny."

43

When we got back to Queen Anne Street, Maia looked tired and angry. She lay on the futon, staring into space while I wrestled off my sticker burr-covered jeans. Finally they flew across the room and buried Robert Johnson in his bed of dirty laundry. I don't think he even noticed.

I lay down next to Maia, hugging her from behind, my face in her hair. When I reached for her hand it was a clenched fist.

After a few minutes she sighed. "Tres, get out of here with me. Destroy that damn disk if you need to, but get out of here."

I tried to pretend she hadn't said anything. I wanted to just lie there, keep my eyes closed, listen to Maia breathing as long as I could. But she pulled away. She sat up and looked down at me. The anger in her eyes watered down to frustration.

"Two men have died because of that disk, and now you've started advertising you've got it. To me that makes the rest insignificant. Even Lillian. Especially Lillian."

I shook my head. "I can't just leave it. And I can't destroy it. Not if it's about my father's killers."

"You want to get yourself killed instead?"

There was no correct answer to that. After another minute Maia lost the spirit even to glare at me. She sank back into the cushions.

"God damn you," she said.

I lay there for a long time, contemplating how else I could possibly screw things up. Mentally I started placing bets on who would be coming through my front door next with a gun.

But of course my life wasn't complicated enough. The ironing board rang. When I picked up the receiver I knew I was either listening to a rock tumbler or an aging smoker trying to breathe. Carl Kelley, retired deputy, my father's old buddy.

"Hey, son," he said. "Didn't hear from you yet. Thought I'd call."

Yet? Then I realized it was Sunday afternoon again. I'd been in town exactly one week. In Kelley's mind I'd started a tradition when I'd called him.

"Hi, Carl."

I settled in for the duration and opened a Shiner Bock. Maia watched me curiously while Carl launched into a discussion of the newest terminal illnesses he'd read about. He talked about how worthless his son in Austin was. Then he started mentioning past discussions we'd never had. He repeated himself. Finally I listened more carefully to the background noises on the other end of the line.

"Carl," I interrupted, "where are you?"

He was silent for a minute, except for the breathing.

"Don't worry about it," he said. His voice was shaky. His tone asked me to please worry about it.

"What hospital, Carl?"

"I didn't want to trouble you," he said. "My neighbor brings me in for a cold and they say I've got pneumonia. Some fucking liver disease. I don't know what all. Can you believe that?"

He started to cough so loudly I had to pull the

receiver away from my ear. When the coughing sub-
sided it took a few moments for his gravelly breathing
to start up again.

"What hospital, Carl?" I said again.

"The Nix. But don't worry about it. They've got a
TV set up for me. I've got a little money left. I'm okay."

"I'll come by," I told him.

"That's okay, son."

He held the line for a minute longer, but he didn't
need to say anything. I heard the loneliness and the fear
even louder than the hospital TV.

"What?" said Maia when I hung up.

"Somebody from my past," I said.

"Of course."

My look made her sorry she'd said it. The irritation
drained out of her face. She dropped her eyes. I dug
another handful of fifties out of Beau Karnau's retirement
fund and made sure Maia still had bullets in her .45.

"I'll be back later," I told her.

Maybe Maia asked me a question. I didn't wait to
hear it.

44

The Nix looked like exactly the kind of building Superman would've loved to jump over in the 1940s. After saying a few Hail Marys and grinding up twelve floors in the antique elevator, I found Carl's semi-private room at the end of a narrow blue-lit hallway.

I thought I'd been prepared to see Carl as an old man. I was wrong. I couldn't find his face anywhere in the thinly coated skull that looked up at me. Oxygen tubes ran from his nostrils like an absurdly long mustache. If he had been any more frail they would've had to weight him down to keep him from floating out of bed. The only thing still heavy was his voice.

"Hey, son," he croaked.

At first I didn't see how those watery white eyes could focus on me enough to recognize who I was. Maybe he thought I really was his son. Then his eyes slid back over to the TV screen and he started talking about the old days with my father. After a while I interrupted.

"Jesus, Carl. How could you not've known you were sick?"

He looked away from the TV and tried to frown. He put his hand out for mine.

"Hell, son," he said.

But he didn't have an answer for me. I wondered how long it had been since Carl looked in a mirror, or had somebody pay him a visit so they could tell him he was wasting down to a skeleton. I made a mental note to find his son in Austin and have that discussion, if I lived long enough.

"Tell me how it's going," Carl said. "About your daddy."

"You should rest, Carl. They got you on vitamins or anything?"

He opened his mouth, rolled his tongue into a tunnel, and coughed so hard he sat up. In the state he was in I was afraid he'd broken his ribs, but he just sank back into the pillows and tried to smile.

"I want to hear, son."

So I told him. There wasn't much point in hiding anything. I asked him if he remembered my dad saying anything about Travis Center, or Sheff, or even vague comments about a big investigation he wanted to do. I told him I couldn't figure out how my father would've stumbled onto the scheme to fix the bidding.

I'm not sure Carl even heard half of what I said. His eyes were fixed lazily on the television. When I was finished he offered no comments. He was staring at some Cowboy cheerleaders in a beer commercial.

"Your daddy and the ladies," he said. "I guess you never heard the stories."

"Too many stories, Carl."

His hand looked so fragile I was surprised how hard he gripped my fingers.

"Don't you doubt he loved your mama, son. It's just—"

"Yeah, he loved the ladies too much."

"Naw," said Carl. "Just Ellen."

I don't know why the name still made me uncomfort-

able. I'd heard it so many times from people outside the
family. At home it had never been an issue. No big deal,
really. Just every Thanksgiving, my father used to get a
little teary-eyed after his third bourbon and Coke. Then
he'd raise his glass and Garrett and Shelley would raise
theirs too. Nobody said anything. Nobody invited my
mother or me to ask. But we knew who they were
drinking to. That momentary cease-fire between the
three of them was all that was left of Ellen Navarre, my
father's first wife. But the name still made me feel like
an unwelcomed guest in my own family.

The studio audience cheered the winner of *Jeopardy*.

"Nothing ever took root for your daddy after Ellen
died," Carl said. "Not really."

I wished he would go back to talking about
Alzheimer's, or maybe prostate cancer. Anything but
my father's love life.

"Right before he got shot," Carl said, "he finally
thought something was working out, you know. Course
he always thought something was working out with
some lady."

I nodded politely, then realized what he was saying.
"I don't remember anybody like that."

Carl just looked at me and breathed gravel. I got the
point.

"She was married."

"Eh," he said. "They usually were."

For a minute his eyes drifted off, as if he'd forgotten
what we were talking about. Then he continued.

"Your dad was a hard-nosed son of a bitch, son. But,
Good Lord, he could turn soft over a woman. You
should've seen the roses he bought once for a Laredo
whore—"

"Carl," I said.

He stopped. I guess he saw well enough to read my
expression in the blue light of the television.

"Yeah, you're right, son. Enough said."

I sat with him for a while and watched the game
shows. The nurse brought in some applesauce and I

helped him eat it, spooning the excess up his chin and into his mouth like you would a baby.

After an hour he said: "I guess you need to go."

"I'll try and come back tomorrow."

"You don't need to do that," he said. But his hand wouldn't let go of mine. He looked at me for a minute and said: "You look just like your mama. Just like Ellen."

I didn't tell him he was wrong. I just nodded, swallowing hard.

"You find this girl of yours," Carl said, squeezing the words into my hand, "and you hang on to her, Jackson."

Maybe he was talking to me, maybe to my father. At that point it didn't matter. When I left him he was still recounting the old days, telling Vanna White what a son of a bitch my father had been.

"Roses for a Laredo whore," he told her. "Some kind of roots."

Carl Kelley held on feebly to his oxygen tubes like they were the only things still anchoring him down.

45

Maia acknowledged my existence long enough to throw a notepad at me. Then she went back to pretending to read the newspaper.

"He called about an hour ago," she said. "Right after Detective Schaeffer."

The note said: *"Carlon——5 hours and counting. Talk to me."* I tore off the note and threw it in the trash can. I missed.

"And Schaeffer is interested in talking about Terry Garza," Maia said. "I stalled him as much as I could."

"Any more good news?"

Maia dropped the paper longer this time, enough for me to see that her eyes were red. She sat on the futon with her legs tucked under her, wearing a black pantsuit with sequins. Her ponytail was tied back in a new way, with a small cluster of red and blue ribbons. It all looked slightly familiar, but not on her. I frowned.

"What else happened?" I asked. "Did you go some-where?"

She tried to look hurt. Then the tension became

unsustainable. She cracked a smile. "Your mother came by," she admitted.

My expression must've been good. She started laughing.

"You asshole," Maia said. "I'm still mad at you."

Her eyes said otherwise.

"And—what did my mother say?"

"She was mad at you too," Maia said. The smile was evil. "We commiserated. We—talked."

I sat down on the futon next to her, still frowning. I tried to look threatening. "Talked?"

She did a bad job of covering up her smile. "We buried the hatchet, more or less. She took me out as a peace offering. This was right after you left."

I looked at the pantsuit again, the ribbons in Maia's hair.

"No—"

She nodded her head enthusiastically. "We went shopping at Solo Serve."

"It's over," I said. "Homicides, disappearances, and now you're going to Solo Serve with my mother."

Maia shrugged. Then she kissed my cheek.

"I was going to tell you that I'd decided to leave tomorrow," she admitted. "I even made reservations. Now that I've seen the clearance rack, I may never go away."

I needed a beer very badly. Of course Maia and my mother had drunk them all.

"And here I thought you'd been crying," I yelled into the refrigerator. "Your eyes are just red from looking at price tags."

"Serves you right," she said. "And this is for you."

She produced a yellow plastic Solo Serve bag from under the futon, then pulled out an extra-large T-shirt that said "WELCOME TO SAN ANTONIO." On the front in neon colors was a depiction of San Antonio's one claim to heavy metal history: Ozzie Osbourne urinating on the Cenotaph in front of the Alamo.

"It spoke to us," she said. "It just screamed 'Tres.' "

"It's lovely. How do you say 'She-devil' in Mandarin?"

I guess I looked suitably angry. Maia walked up, pressed against me, and kissed my chin. "Okay, you're forgiven now."

"*I'm* forgiven?"

She smiled. "Show me the Riverwalk, Tex?"

Neither Carlon McAffrey nor Detective Schaeffer were thrilled to hear from me, especially since I answered most of their questions with "I don't know," or promises to call them back in the morning. My right ear hurt from the insults by the time I hung up, but I was otherwise intact.

After the week I'd had, it was difficult to find clothes without blood or Mexican food on them, but I still declined to wear my new T-shirt to the Riverwalk. Maia just smiled, enjoying her revenge as I searched the dregs in my closet. Robert Johnson played kamikaze, dive-bombing my clothes from the kitchen counter every time I made a pile. Otherwise he was no help as a fashion consultant.

By sunset we were driving south on Broadway, into downtown, Maia looking like several thousand dollars and me looking like spare change. The streetlamps were just coming on and the sunset was longhorn orange when we walked down the stairs of the Commerce Avenue Bridge into the crowds on the Riverwalk.

Take away the glitz and tourist dollars and the Paseo del Rio is basically a deep trench that winds through the center of downtown San Antonio. Just south of East Houston, the river gets diverted from its course and makes a huge lowercase "b," looping all the way east to the Convention Center, then back past La Villita to Main, where it reconnects with itself.

Put back the glitz and the tourist dollars, and even a native has to admit it's pretty impressive. Tonight the air was warm and the mariachi music was everywhere. Colored lights reflected off the murky green water and made the river look festive despite itself. About a hundred thousand people were strolling the flagstone banks past the fountains, stone bridges, and pricey new restaurants. The kitchen smoke of ten or fifteen different cuisines drifted up past the yellow and green patio umbrellas. Tourists with cameras and souvenir sombreros, basic trainees on leave, rich men with high-priced call girls, all happily stepping on toes and spilling drinks on each other. This is what a San Antonian thinks of when you say "river." I remember how much trouble I had reading *Huck Finn* as a child, trying to imagine how the hell that raft made it past all those restaurants and crowds, in water only three feet deep and thirty feet across, without anybody noticing the stowaway slave. Maybe that's why I became an English major—sheer confusion.

Maia held on to my hand so we didn't get separated. In one of the rare moments when there was enough room for us to walk side by side she pointed at the river and said: "I want to eat on one of those."

A dinner barge went by—a huge red shoe-box lid with an outboard motor. Fifty tourists smiled and raised their margaritas from the white linen tablecloth. The waiters looked bored.

"No you don't," I told her.

The operator in back turned the outboard just enough to avoid an oncoming barge from a rival restaurant by a few inches.

"Do they ever collide?" Maia shouted at me over the crowd.

"Only when the operators are bored, which is most of the time."

Occasionally people fell in too. My father used to keep a record of how many drunk tourists he'd personally fished out of the river working the Fiesta duty. I think he stopped counting at around twenty-three.

I was surprised how many of the older restaurants had closed. The Union Jack umbrellas of Kangaroo Court were still up. Jim Cullum's Happy Jazz Band was still swinging at the Landing like the 1920s had never ended. But almost everything else had changed. We settled for a riverside table and a mediocre plate of nachos at a place simply called La Casa. I should've guessed we were in trouble when I saw the name. I knew it for sure when I asked for Herradura Anejo and our waiter told me they didn't carry that kind of beer. Fortunately the people-watching was better than the food.

A group of blue-haired women in evening dresses and summer minks went past, trying very hard to look glamorous while the sweat was trickling down their necks. A family of Goodyear blimps stopped long enough to stare jealously at our nachos. Two nuns in full black regalia and fluted hats ran by, screaming in German, followed closely by a group of very drunk and very naked pinheads, followed closely by the SAPD beat patrol. The crowd opened and closed around the chase. A few people laughed. Then more drinks were ordered and life went on.

"Is it like this every night?" Maia asked, clearly impressed.

"Saturdays it usually picks up."

"I should hope so."

Before it was full dark we headed back toward the white tower of the Hilton Palacio del Rio. Ten stories of balconies looked out over the water, most of them lit up and overflowing with partying college kids. The main bar at river level was doing a brisk business tonight despite the entertainment, three scruffy musicians falling asleep into their microphones over a very slow rendition of "Amie."

When we got to lobby level I'd been planning to bribe the concierge anyway. It was just a bonus that I found an old high school chum behind the desk. Mickey Williams took one look at me and gave me the warm greeting I'd been expecting.

"What the fuck are you doing here?" he said.

Mickey was the closest human equivalent to the Pillsbury Doughboy I'd ever come across. He had no skin pigment to speak of, and his hair was so yellow it was almost white. He was big all over, an over-inflated kind of big, and although he looked soft, in our days at Alamo Heights I'd seen plenty of high school fullbacks bounce off Mickey's body without leaving a mark. I'd never quite gotten up the nerve to poke him in the stomach to see if he would laugh. I had a feeling he wouldn't.

Mickey had also dated Lillian for a brief time when we'd broken up our senior year. Until I'd stolen back her heart. Or, rather, until I'd stolen Mickey's pickup. Lillian's very brief flirtation with kicker dancing in general and Mickey in particular had come to an abrupt halt when they'd had to walk halfway home from the Blue Bonnet Palace in Selma.

"Mickey," I replied, grinning.

He looked at me suspiciously. His pasty face flushed red. Then he tried his line again: "What the fuck are you doing here?"

"Came to see you, old buddy."

He looked behind him. Probably he was checking for the hidden camera.

"Go away," he said. "I like my job."

"Come on," I said, "that was a long time ago."

"I didn't work for a fucking year after that time at Maggie's."

Maia smiled, not having a clue what we were talking about. I shrugged as innocently as I could.

"How should I know Ms. Pacman could pick up so much momentum going down one flight of stairs?"

Mickey appealed to Maia. "Fucker destroyed three booths and nearly killed the general manager."

"I didn't *make* you push it."

" 'Just tip this up while I look for my quarter,' " he quoted.

I shrugged and took out two fifties. I put them on his desk.

"I'll get out of your way as soon as you tell me which room Mr. Karnau's in tonight."

Mickey stared. I smiled and set down another two fifties. Mickey looked down very briefly. "You want the keys too?" he said.

46

"Karnau," said Mickey. "Room 450. Books that suite every weekend, pays in cash."

He slapped the keys into my hand. "And, Tres, you fuck with me—"

I smiled. "Would I do that?"

"Shit." Mickey shook his head like his job was as good as lost.

We watched the door to 450 from the service closet at the end of the hall. The door stayed put. The freshly vacuumed maroon rug in the hall outside was devoid of footprints.

Then somewhere around the corner at the end of the hall another door opened and closed. The man who walked across the hall and into the stairwell was wearing jeans and a striped Baja shirt with the hood pulled up. He was moving briskly.

Maia and I exchanged looks.

"A suite," she said.

"451," I said.

We raced each other down the hall. Maia's gun was

out by the time she stopped at the door. I threw her the keys and pushed into the stairwell, not even sure who I was following.

From the echoes he was about two floors below me, going just fast enough to get the hell out without someone thinking he might be running. I'll say one thing for my worn-down deck shoes—they're quiet. I managed to follow him down without giving him reason to speed up. When the blue-striped Baja exited on the Riverwalk level, I was only twenty feet above him.

I came out into a service hallway and dodged a fat tourist in a sombrero. I almost knocked a margarita pitcher out of the waitress's hand as I ran into the bar. The comatose folk trio was now doing the funeral dirge version of Cat Stevens's greatest hits. Baja Man still had his hood up. He was navigating through the patio tables outside, heading into the crowds.

I stayed twenty feet back as we moved down the Riverwalk. Baja didn't look back. The Paseo was so narrow and thick with people I couldn't get at an angle to see his face. We passed the Market Street Bridge and kept going toward La Villita. For a minute I lost Baja behind a slow-moving Oompa band. They had "Pride of Fredericksburg" stitched into their green Bavarian britches and painted on the side of their tuba, but they sure weren't in a hurry to get to whatever performance they had in mind. It's usually worth the time just to hear German spoken with a Texas twang, but not when you're chasing somebody. I finally got rude and shoved past. The guy with the hairy white legs and the bass drum almost went into the river.

"Gawdamn *scheisskerl!*" he shouted after me.

The one with "Johann" on his feathered hat tried to bean me with a handful of funnel cake. From the squeal behind me I assume he hit a nearby call girl or debutante instead. I kept moving.

The music changed from polka to full brass mariachi as we rounded the corner and crossed another bridge, then ducked through an alleyway and into the Arneson River Theater. We had somehow come up on the performers' side. There was a concert in progress, like there is most nights. The spotlights were on, the band's panchos were Technicolor, and their horns were well polished. Across the river, the old stone seats of the amphitheater were almost full. Baja stopped for a minute, considering his options. Then he sped up. So did I.

That's when I made the mistake of running into another old friend. Slamming into an old friend, actually. Carolyn Smith was directing the KSAT mobile camera on its tripod at the wrong moment to catch a particularly enthusiastic crowd response to my favorite tune, "Guantanamera." What she caught instead was my shoulder as I tried to squeeze past. That in itself probably would've been okay, but as I kept running forward she stepped back to get her balance and executed a beautiful piece of unintentional tai chi. Her leg went under mine and my foot stopped. The rest of me kept going.

A lot happened in that five seconds. Carolyn looked up and recognized me.

"Tres!" she said.

She probably didn't mean to yell it so loud, but part of that was shock as she realized a few hundred pounds of camera equipment was starting to topple. Then she realized the camera's power cord was wrapped around her ankle and she was toppling with it. I didn't even have time to wave at the other TV station's camera before the two of us and the KSAT mobile unit went headfirst into the river.

Considering it was the first day of August, the water was downright chilly. The bottom was so slick with algae I fell down the first three times I tried to stand up. It didn't help that Carolyn was trying to climb to safety over my body. As I stood up in the crotch-high water, the crowd erupted in applause. The mariachis, gratified by the response, launched into my second favorite tune, "La Bamba." I waved, feeling like a fresh mound of bat guano and smelling just about as good.

Not being deaf, the man in the Baja shirt had noticed

me. By the time I located him, he'd already decided it
would take too long to fight his way through the
crowds to the bridge. Instead he took a more creative
exit. He made the jump onto the first dinner barge and
stood precariously on the center table while fifty
tourists spilled their margaritas. The waiters and operator no longer looked bored. Since the second barge
passed only a few inches away, heading the other direction, it was a short jump to that for Baja. More drinks
spilled. Another group of German nuns in fluted hats,
possibly the same ones I'd seen earlier, looked up to see
a man on their dining table, then he was gone, sprinting
up the steps of the Arneson River Theater.

His hood came off just for a moment as he dodged
through the tourists with all the grace of a former ath-
lete. Long enough for me to notice that Dan Sheff had
gotten a hair cut since we'd talked last. Then he reached
the iron gates at the top of the amphitheater and disappeared into the darkness of La Villita.

Carolyn was yelling at me as she slipped and slid over
to the riverbank.

"What the heil do you call that?" she demanded.

The guy at the KENS camera offered a suggestion: "I
call that a take."

47

Fortunately Corporal Hearnes remembered my father. Unfortunately Hearnes was among the majority of the SAPD who had hated my father's guts. It took me some serious tap dancing and a grudging admission from Carolyn that perhaps I was not a rabid lunatic before Hearnes agreed not to lock me in Detox.

"Maybe I did step back at the wrong time," Carolyn mumbled.

"Wrong time?" I said. "Hell, I want you to teach me that move, Carolyn."

Her fine blond hair had turned into greenish licorice cords in the river. She pushed a few strands out of her face and smiled despite herself. I tried to visualize her as the reclusive computer nerd I remembered from our journalism classes at A & M. But all I saw was a TV model with a babyish face, nice lips, and fashion contacts that had come loose and were slipping into her corneas like dark blue eclipses.

"Carolaine," she corrected me.

"What?"

She tried to straighten her once-white blazer.

"I'm a media personality now, or at least I was until you ruined my spot. I go by Carolaine."

"Is it Smythe instead of Smith?"

She frowned. If she hadn't been over twenty-five I would've called it a pout. "I've heard that one too many times."

"Sorry."

I stood and made my apologies to the cameraman. He just stared at me. I thanked Corporal Hearnes for his time and compassion. I left Carolaine my phone number so we could talk about the damages.

"Hey," she said. "What the hell is your hurry?"

I looked behind me at the Hilton and thought about Maia and her .45 alone in Beau Karnau's suite. Or maybe not alone.

"Duty calls," I said.

"Great," said Carolaine. "See if I share my bath towel with you again."

It was difficult to look dashing as I sloshed down the Riverwalk, leaving a trail of puddles, but the smell cleared a path for me pretty effectively. I waved at Mickey as I jogged past the Hilton concierge desk. His mouth dropped open and stayed that way while the elevator doors closed.

The door to Room 450 was closed, but Maia opened it before I could even knock. When she lowered the gun out of my nostril and stood aside, I saw why she looked so grim.

The room decor was straight out of Versailles. Champagne chilled on the dresser in a silver bucket. The balcony curtains opened onto a perfect summer night sky and all the lights of the Paseo del Rio. The man in the bed was wearing his best velour robe and his comfiest slippers. He lay back, totally relaxed, with two black eyes and the red mark of an East Indian on his forehead. Only Beau Karnau was neither East Indian nor relaxed. He was just dead.

In Maia's other hand was a bottle of Veuve Cliquot.

She sat down next to Beau and took a swig. Then she looked at me. Only the way she breathed, shallowly from her mouth, told me that she was pretty unnerved, and only because I knew her well. Otherwise her face might've been made of polished wood, for all the expression she revealed.

I took a soggy index card out of my back pocket—the message Guy White had given us that afternoon.

I said: "Nice of Mr. White to invite us up tonight. Don't you think?"

I sat down on the other side of Beau. His ponytail had been loosened so that his hair had opened up around his head like a black and gray peacock tail when he fell back. The bruised skin around his eyes was shiny and purple. He had a slight wet smile on his face like somebody had just told him a funny but tasteless joke. Thank God his viscera hadn't loosened up yet. There was no smell.

"It was Dan," I told Maia. "I lost him."

"You still think he's not a player?"

I didn't feel like arguing the point.

On the dresser was Beau's photo portfolio, open to the first page. The article "Dallas Native Follows Dream" had been carefully removed from the plastic and stuck onto the mirror, maybe where Beau could see it when he woke up every morning. Next to that was a black and white photo of nineteen-year-old Lillian— smiling over her shoulder at the photographer, her mentor. Her eyes were full of adoration. On the floor at my feet was an open, empty CD case. It was cracked as if someone had stepped on it.

"Someone finally got what they wanted," Maia said softly. "Without a payment."

"*Half* of what they want," I corrected.

Maia handed the champagne over Beau's body. Beau didn't request any. I finished just enough of the bottle to belch the nausea out of my system. Only then did Maia seem to notice my appearance.

"You're wet," she said.

"Don't ask."

Maia nodded, not in the mood to argue, either.

"White gets us here," she said. "Dan leaves us here. And your friend Mickey knows where we are. We can't just walk away."

When I didn't respond, Maia went to the phone and calmly made three calls. First to the house detective, second to Detective Schaeffer, third to Byron Ash.

"Got any plans tonight?" I asked. Neither Maia nor Beau seemed to.

The Hilton chief of security, a large black man named Jefferies, took one look at Beau, then helped us finish off the champagne.

"I don't get paid enough," he said. Then he sat down in the Louis XIV chair in the corner and started mumbling into his walkie-talkie.

Two patrolmen arrived, then the detectives, then forensics. Tape went up, the media arrived, maids, interested guests, everybody but the jugglers, the nuns, and the dancing bear. Detective Schaeffer finally came dragging in too, looking as usual as if he'd just woken up.

"Take these two into the next room," he told a uniform. "They can wait."

And we did.

Maia's "favored" status with Mr. Ash must've been running thin. An hour after she'd called him, we discovered that Lord Byron would be declining a personal appearance. Instead a junior associate who looked about fifteen showed up and introduced himself as Hass. Hass smiled. Shaking his hand was like squeezing a damp Kleenex.

"Don't worry," Hass said, "I come highly recommended from Mr. Ash. I've handled several criminal actions."

Schaeffer decided to notice us then. He lumbered in with red eyes, managed not to bump into anything, then stared at each of us in turn. He took out a handkerchief and blew his nose slowly, meticulously.

"Okay," he grumbled. "Tell me it's a coincidence."

"Ah, before we start—" said Counselor Hass.

Schaeffer and I exchanged glances.

"He comes highly recommended," I told Schaeffer.

Schaeffer looked sour. "So did my ex-wife."

Hass smiled like he got it. We made ourselves at home in King Louie's loveseat while Schaeffer sent a uniform downstairs for a garlic bagel and some herbal tea.

"Red Zinger if they've got it," he said.

I stared at him.

"What?" he said. "You want some?"

I quickly declined.

Schaeffer made that snoring sound again and it finally occurred to me why he always looked and sounded half-asleep. It was terminal sinuses.

"Cedars?" I asked.

His nasal passages ground like ball bearings. "Damn pecan trees. That yellow stuff gets all over my yard. I forget breathing for three months. It's a healthy lifestyle."

"Now, Detective," Hass started, "if we could just—"

Schaeffer looked at him and he shut up. Schaeffer liked that.

"This guy from Ash?" he asked Maia.

Maia nodded. She tried not to smile. Schaeffer liked it even more. After that, Hass participated about as much as a tennis spectator. I had the feeling he would've held Schaeffer's handkerchief for him if asked.

"Okay," Schaeffer said, "let's hear it."

So we told him, sort of. I did a bad job feigning surprise when Schaeffer told me that Terry Garza, the man I'd been arguing with when Moraga's corpse was delivered through the wall of Sheff's office, had also been killed. I told him about the anonymous note we'd gotten to come to the Hilton and how I'd chased a guy from the room who I couldn't ID. Maia described how she'd found the body. I told Schaeffer I hadn't fired a gun since I was a kid and certainly not at Beau Karnau's head this evening. Maia asked if we were being charged with something.

Schaeffer explored his nostrils with his handkerchief one more time.

"How about stupidity," he suggested.

"Too late," Maia said. "My client's *nolo contendere.*"

"*Your* client?" objected Hass.

"Shut up," we all said.

The uniform came back with Schaeffer's tea and bagel.

"All they had was Sleepy Time," he reported.

I thought Schaeffer would demote him on the spot, but he just stared into his tea and sighed. Now he really did look tired.

"So let's run through this," he said. "A week ago you ask me to check into confidential files. You've suddenly discovered your father has been murdered, ten years ago. CID's on my butt inside five minutes for even fielding your call. Then we've got three homicides in the space of three days, and you just happen to be around for all the fun."

"Two thirds of it," I objected without much conviction.

"Yeah," Schaeffer grunted. "So there's absolutely no connection. I should just take some more Sudafed, crawl into bed, and not worry about it, huh?"

Maia and I glanced at each other. My nerves must've been more shot than I figured. I was close to leveling with Schaeffer.

"Listen, Detective—" Then my mind stopped and rewound what I'd just heard. I changed my tack. "When you said CID, you mean Rivas? As in the creep who showed up at your investigation that night at Sheff's offices?"

Schaeffer scowled.

"As in the Cambridge disappearance?" Maia added.

"As in Lillian Cambridge," I said, "the present stiff's studio partner?"

Schaeffer wadded up his handkerchief while he thought about that. Whatever he concluded, he didn't let it show in his face.

"That doesn't matter," he said. His look said the opposite. "What I want—"

Whatever he wanted, he was distracted when Jay Rivas walked into the room. Rivas sported a newly combed mustache and a silver and turquoise belt buckle the size of a grapefruit.

"Navarre," he said. "Back again. Just like a fucking yo-yo."

Rivas was in a good mood tonight; you could hear it in his voice. After he lit a cigar, over the protests of the forensics crew, he studied everybody in the room, finally nodding to Schaeffer.

"Can I help you, Detective?" Schaeffer said, without enthusiasm.

Rivas came up to me and stuck his face in mine, like I was some kind of weird exhibit. His wandering eye drifted merrily downstream. Then he sat on the arm of the loveseat directly above Maia and put his hand on her shoulder.

Maia didn't flinch. Her eyes examined Rivas's hand clinically, like she was locating all its breakable bones and pain-inducing pressure points. Rivas shifted, a little uncomfortably. The hand moved.

"Detective," Rivas said to Schaeffer, "could I get a few minutes with Mr. Navarre and his friend?"

Schaeffer stared at Rivas, then at me. Maybe he remembered what my mouth had looked like after I accidentally hit it on the door last time Rivas wanted a few minutes, that night at Sheff Construction. Or maybe Schaeffer was just pissed off because his sinuses felt like a worn-out transmission and the Hilton was out of Red Zinger. Whatever it was, he made a decision.

"I got a better idea," he told Rivas. "You could explain what you're doing in my homicide investigations. *All* my homicide investigations."

Rivas glanced at his audience. When he spoke to Schaeffer again, it was much more polite. And much colder.

"Maybe we could discuss this outside," he said.

"That's a good idea," Schaeffer said. "You go ahead. I'll be out as soon as I send these people home."

Rivas got up. "Send them where?"

All of a sudden Schaeffer looked much better. I guess

the Sudafed had kicked in. He shook Counselor Hass's hand.

"Damn fine work, Counselor. Y'all stay in town, but that's it for tonight."

If Hass had acted any more like an ecstatic puppy he would've peed on the carpet. We filed past Rivas, who seemed to be silently assessing Schaeffer as a possible rifle target. I shook Schaeffer's hand. I shook Hass's hand. I even shook the assistant coroner's hand. I probably would've shaken my old school chum Mickey Williams's hand too, but he was in the general manager's office getting a talking-to when we walked by.

"Mickey," I called. He looked up dismally.

"You need a good lawyer?" I asked. "He comes highly recommended."

48

We'd been sitting on the steps of La Villita Chapel for so long, staring at the empty building that used to be the Hecho a Mano Gallery, that I thought Maia had gone to sleep. The adrenaline had worn off. With my clothes slowly drying and my nerves shot to hell, I felt as frayed and greasy as the corn husk off a tamale.

Then we both looked at each other with something to say.

"You first," I said.

"No," Maia said. "It's just—"

"Beau waited a little too long to run," I said. "He was still trying to salvage the scam. He let somebody into his hotel room, sat down to barter for the disk, then whoever it was shot him in the face."

She nodded. "And he wouldn't be so relaxed if he was bargaining with the mob."

"So we've got a dead blackmailer," I continued, "the second disk missing, Dan Sheff looking guilty as hell, and Lillian still missing."

An elderly tourist couple walked by. The old woman smiled at us the way people do at lovers in the shadows of a summer night. Then she stared sadly at her oblivious husband. When Maia looked back at me with almost the same expression, it twisted my nerves a little tighter.

"What?" I said. "Lillian's either dead or involved, or both. Is that what you want me to say?"

She almost got angry. I wished like hell that she would. Instead she hugged her knees and stared out at the empty limestone shell of Lillian's studio.

"No," she said. "I didn't want you to say that."

"What then? You still want me to think my dad's death has no connection? The pictures of Halcomb are a coincidence? You want me to forget about it?"

She shook her head. "I was just thinking about plane tickets."

It was my turn to stare. "Tickets. As in plural, tickets?"

She took a pecanwood twig and poked at the mortar between the flagstones. The twig was so dry it broke into dust.

"Never mind," she said.

"Jesus, Maia."

She nodded.

"You know I can't just leave town."

"You never did leave town," she said. "That's the thing."

"Like hell."

I tried to believe it. The fact that I didn't made me madder. A group of Mexican nationals went by, talking about their weekend of shopping. They smiled at us. We didn't smile back.

"All right," I told Maia. "You want me to feel like shit about you and me, okay. I feel like shit. But I didn't ask for backup."

"You didn't turn it down last night," she said. "You should think about why."

Her eyes had turned to steel in the space of those two sentences. My face probably wasn't much kinder. I counted the strands of lights. I watched the cars go down Nueva. I said: "So you're leaving?"

"Tres—" Maia closed her eyes. "Why are you staying?"

"You don't want to hear this again. You saw the damn letters, Maia."

"No. I saw a carriage full of dolls in a grown-up woman's bedroom. Did it ever occur to you that you're the only piece of that collection Lillian Cambridge ever lost, Tres?"

It was one of those moments when God hands you the emotional scissors and invites you to start cutting, irrevocably. Instead I just watched as Maia stood up and walked down the stairs. I don't know why but as she passed I caught the scent of the chapel's interior smoked into the porch beams—incense and very old wax. It was the scent of confessionals and baptisms and Las Posadas candles that had been snuffed before Santa Anna ever rode through town.

When she was ten feet away, Maia turned and looked at me. Or maybe she just looked at the chapel. I felt like I'd already blended into the limestone.

"Call me when it's over," she said. "If it ever is."

She walked away slowly enough to give me time to call her back. Then she disappeared behind the outer walls of La Villita, heading up Nueva where the taxi stands were.

Another old tourist couple passed by, but this time I was alone. Nobody bothered smiling kindly. The woman took her husband's arm. They shuffled a little faster.

I got up and went across the courtyard to stare in the window of the Hecho a Mano Gallery, now filled with nothing but hardwood floors and moonlight and old ghosts.

"Now what?" I asked.

But it was a closed party and the ghosts didn't have any time to waste on me. I pulled a wad of dead man's money out of my pocket and went to find the nearest bottle of tequila.

49

When my brother Garrett called the next morning I had been asleep about fourteen minutes. Most of the night I'd sat cross-legged on the bathroom floor next to the toilet, rereading my father's old notebook and debating with Robert Johnson about the pros and cons of drinking white tequila by the pint. I don't remember who won the argument.

"You and Maia find the other disk?" Garrett growled in my ear. "I can't do shit with this one."

Once I found my vocal chords I told Garrett I had no other disk. Then I told him I had no Maia. My brother was quiet. In the background, Jimmy Buffett was singing about cheeseburgers.

"If I had legs," Garrett said, "I'd come down there and kick your stupid ass."

"Thanks for the vote of confidence," I said.

The line was silent for a few seconds. "So what happened?"

I told him.

Almost as an afterthought I read the four lines to Garrett that had been bothering me for days, the ones underneath my father's trial notes for Guy White. *Sabinal. Get whiskey. Fix fence. Clean fireplace.*

Afterward I could hear Garrett scratching his beard.

"So what?" he said.

"So I don't know. I keep wondering how Dad might've gotten mixed up with the Travis Center deal. I keep remembering what Carl told me, about some new lady in his life. You got any ideas?"

"Fuck it," Garrett said. "Get your ass back to San Francisco and forget it."

"If I had a dime——" I said.

"Yeah. You ever wonder if all us poor schmucks who care about you might have a point?"

I didn't tell him how often. Finally he grunted, probably rearranging himself in his chair, then called me a few names.

"Okay," he said. "Sabinal. Hell, he was there damn near every Christmas shooting the fucking bambis. What's so unusual?"

"I don't know. That note just doesn't sit right. For one thing, he wrote it in April. You ever know him to go up in the spring?"

He thought for a minute. "*Fireplace.* Christ. Only thing that reminds me of was the Christmas Dad stayed sober, burning the furniture in the fireplace. That was a shitter."

A memory started forming. "When was this?"

"Way before you're talking about. You must've been in fourth grade, little bro. You remember the argument about the Lucchese chairs?"

Then it came back to me.

Dad had been "between terms" as sheriff, meaning that he'd gotten voted out of office. My mom had blamed it on the booze, I guess, and Dad was making a real effort not to drink so he could get his campaign in shape for the following four years. So our first day up at the ranch for Christmas he announced this, lined up all his liquor bottles on the fence, and shot them up. After that, all I remember him getting were more deer than usual and a very bad temper. After the second day the trees outside the ranch house had more dead deer strung in them than the Christmas tree had ornaments. When that got old, my dad got his .22 and started hunting cats instead. Somebody had dropped a whole litter off in the country rather than put them to sleep, I guess, and of course they'd grown up feral and started eating all the quail on the property. So Dad went out and popped cats all day, then came home with a bloody bag full like Santa Claus the ax murderer, sank into his recliner, drank coffee, and scowled all night. By the time Garrett and Shelley joined us for Christmas dinner, Dad had just about run out of things to kill and my mom and I were starting to get nervous.

There'd been a stupid argument at the dinner table, something about who was going to inherit the dining-room chairs. They'd been custom-made for my dad by Sam Lucchese, the boot maker, right before Lucchese died. The argument ended with Garrett taking the chairs out back and grinding them up with a chain saw for firewood. In the meantime, while my mom and Shelley sat consoling each other in the kitchen, I'd watched my dad pace around in the living room. He went over to the fireplace and lifted a huge chunk of limestone off the hearth. I hadn't even known it was loose. Then he took a fifth of Jim Beam out of the hole underneath and drank it almost empty. When he turned around and saw me I was sure he was going to slap me across the back forty, but he just smiled, then put the rock back. He pulled me up on his knee and started telling me stories about Korea. I don't remember the stories. All I remember is the smell of the Jim Beam on his breath and the sound of that chain saw going in the backyard. Finally Dad leaned close and said something like: "Every man's got to have a stashing hole, son. A man tells you he's shot up his whiskey good and perma-nent, you'd best be sure he's either got a stashing hole full somewhere or he's a damn fool." Then he helped Garrett load the fireplace with Lucchese chair legs. By

the time it was over they were joking together. I never
said a thing about the stashing hole. I think I'd forgotten about it until now.

"*Clean the fireplace,*" I said to Garrett. "I'll be
damned."

"What about it?" he said.

I was probably still drunk from the night before. It
was a stupid idea. On the other hand, my other option
was to spend the day thinking about dead people,
missing people, and Maia Lee.

"What?" said Garrett. "I don't like it when you get
quiet."

I watched the water swirl into patterns as it washed
down the bathroom drain. Jimmy Buffett was still jam-
ming in Garrett's office.

"Who's got the keys to the ranch?" I asked.

Garrett swore. "I do, you know that."

I waited.

"No way," my brother said. "You're a total fruitcake."

"Runs in the family."

He was silent. "Probably. I can pick you up in a
couple of hours."

50

The Carmen Miranda took the long way, down Highway 90, Old Sabinal Road. By the time we got there I was half-stoned just from sitting next to Garrett. I'd heard *Changes in Latitudes* on CD-ROM continuous replay cranked and remixed through Garrett's computer in the back until I knew all the lyrics sideways. I'd had enough Pecan Street Ale to make my throbbing tequila hangover from the night before fade to a dull ache. There wasn't much that could bother me at that point. Nevertheless, it was hard to look at what the march of civilization had done to Sabinal.

"Oh, Jesus," I said. "There's a traffic light."

"Yeah," said Garrett. "They changed it from flashing yellow about six years ago."

I sat up a little straighter in my seat. "What the hell happened to Ogden's?"

As a kid I'd loved and feared the place. Every time we stopped at Ogden's for lunch on the way into town I used to get scolded for trying to sit at the forbidden Old-Timers' Table in the back. Once I'd had my ears pulled good; from that time on I just watched from the counter while the old men diced to see who would pay for the morning coffee. My father would order the world's greatest chicken fried steak sandwiches to go from a waitress named Meryl.

Now the diner was closed. The Hill Country mural that was painted on the glass in front was faded and chipped. The lights were off.

"Man, you are out of touch," Garrett said. "They changed the name to the Pepper Patch years ago. Then they went seasonal. No business out this way. They just open up for the hunters, now."

"How the hell do you know all this? You turning kicker on me?"

Garrett seemed to like that idea. "Sometimes I need a place to get away. It doesn't get any more 'away' than Sabinal, little bro."

We passed the Schutes' land, then a few smaller spreads of mesquites, olive-colored hills, cows. A few old ranchers leaning against their fence posts turned to watch the mound of plastic tropical fruit drive past. One of them raised his roll of spare barbed wire in a salute. Garrett honked.

The old Wagon Wheel across from the entrance to Navarre land had always been our landmark for finding which gate was ours. Now the restaurant was boarded-up. Our cattleguard hadn't been hosed out in so long it was filled three feet deep with dirt. Our cattle were walking back and forth over the bars, grazing the side of the highway at will. One of them, a Charolais mix, was right in the gateway, staring down the Carmen Miranda.

"How about honking at it?" I said.

"No way," Garrett told me. "They're tame, man. You honk your horn, they come running to be fed. You ever seen a safari bus crowded by thirty-three hungry Charolais? Ain't pretty."

"How about a red cape then?" I suggested.

Garrett just leaned out the window and had a heated discussion with the heifer. I guess it was paying attention, because it finally moved out of the way. Then we drove through, trying to find the driveway under the prairie grass.

The ranch house itself hadn't changed much since the 1880s, when it had been the homestead for the Nunley family, one of the founders of Sabinal. Just three rooms with limestone walls and hardwood floors, rough-cut beams holding up the ceiling, more or less. My grandfather had grudgingly agreed to get electricity and a septic tank when he bought the land after the original Nunley spread had been divided back in the 1940s, but neither the plumbing nor the wiring had been touched since then. These days the septic tank was called Old 90 because you could only flush the toilet or take a shower once every hour and a half without everything overflowing.

I was a little surprised to find Harold Diliberto standing on the porch waiting for us.

"He still takes care of things out here?" I asked.

"Yeah," said Garrett.

Harold had taken the job when he was still married to my sister Shelley. He'd been abusive, drunk most of the time, and not very energetic, but he'd been family, he knew about cattle, and he'd been cheap to hire. I'm not sure which was the biggest selling point for my father. That had been ten years and two of Shelley's husbands ago.

I looked at the house, the cattleguard, the lawn that had turned back to prairie grass.

"Doing a great job," I said.

Garrett shrugged. "He's okay when his friends don't get him drinking."

"What friends?"

"Me, usually."

Harold looked like he and the cows had been partying pretty hard the night before. His shirt was buttoned wrong so his collar stuck up on the right side. His jeans were half-tucked into his boots. At one point his third-grade teacher had probably told him: "You make that face at me and one day it'll stick that way." She'd

been right. Harold always looked like he was trying his
best to look ugly.

He nodded at me like he'd just seen me last week.

"Tres. Garrett."

Garrett took the stairs on his hands, then pulled his
chair up after him. The chair probably weighed fifty
pounds. Garrett used one arm without straining.

"How's the well?" he asked.

Harold scratched a rash on his neck. "Got the pump
working, but it'd been a few days. Cattle stampeded the
trough soon as it was going."

"Great."

Garrett lifted himself back into the seat and led us
through the door.

I looked around while Garrett and Harold talked
maintenance. Except for being dirtier and older, the
place had hardly changed. The Army Corps of Engi-
neers elevation drawing for Highway 90 had turned
brown on the living-room wall. The coffee table we'd
gotten for Christmas from the Klayburgs down at King
Ranch still had boot marks on it from the last time my
dad had propped his feet there. There was still a metal
pail full of Cricket lighters sitting in the corner from fifteen years before when the Western Union had derailed
in the middle of town. Before the Army Reserve had
come in to guard the trainload of new Toyotas that had
spilled unexpectedly into downtown from that accident,
everybody in Sabinal had already helped themselves to
the smaller dumped cargo—three boxcars full of
lighters. Sabinal still didn't have a single Toyota on the
streets, but it was a good place to go if you needed a
light.

I wasn't quite ready to look in the fireplace. Instead I
sat on the couch. I traced the old boot prints on the
table. Finally Harold went out to shoot a rattlesnake
he'd seen in the back field. Garrett wheeled his chair up
next to me. He handed me a warm beer out of the
chair's side pocket, then lit another joint.

"So you checked?" he asked.

"Not yet."

He took a noisy inhale. Together we sat and looked at the limestone fireplace for a while like it was getting great reception, a Cowboys game maybe, deep in the fourth. I stood up.

"Look," Garrett said, "just don't expect anything, okay, little bro?"

"Okay."

I moved the rock and looked in the stashing hole. No Jim Beam. Nothing but dark, mortar, a few daddy long-legs hanging dead. Then I stuck my hand inside. The hole was almost a foot deeper than I'd thought. I brought an old business-sized envelope into the light.

My back was to Garrett. After a while he couldn't stand the silence.

"Well?" he said.

The envelope had faded from pink to brown, but the original letter was still inside—written on pink stationery that after all these years still smelled faintly of strawberry potpourri. I read the first few lines, then turned and let Garrett see Cookie Sheff's last letter to our father.

"God damn," said Garrett.

"Does your mouth taste funny?" I asked. "Kind of like metal?"

Garrett nodded, then wheeled his chair around to leave.

"And the bastard didn't even leave us any bourbon to wash it down," he grumbled. "Fucking typical."

51

After reading the letter several times, Garrett and I either needed to get seriously drunk or do something to take our minds off what we'd learned. We opted for both.

First, Harold put us to work worming thirty-three head of cattle. I'd like to say there was something cathartic about it, but there wasn't. I had the privilege of clamping the victim's head between metal bars while Garrett pumped a wad of paste that looked suspiciously like K-Y jelly into the side of the cow's mouth. If you've never seen cattle gag, don't go out of your way.

When we were done, we sat on the porch drinking Harold's cheap booze and watching the evening come down over the plains. The sunset was orange, except when you looked at it through a liquor bottle. Then it was brown and yellow.

On the way back to town Garrett and I cranked up the Jimmy Buffett. Occasionally we'd look at each other, then decide not to talk. We both had the letter from the fireplace memorized now, and phrases of it kept gnawing at me. Protests that my father had used Cookie, searched her husband's private files, and only thus found incriminating documents about Travis Center. Pleas not to break her heart with a public scandal that would destroy her family. Promises that Dan Sheff, Sr., really wasn't to blame, that Cookie would help my father find out who was responsible for using Sheff Construction to embezzle millions. Fervent affirmations of her love, kept from open admission by her duty to her son, to her sickly husband. The letter implied that my father had made Cookie a deal: Leave her husband and have the Travis Center issue forgotten.

Garrett was bothered by it as much as I was, though his way of dealing with it was to curse at the semis on the highway and flip off the snowbirds in their RVs as he zoomed past them.

"Learn to drive, sheepdip!" he shouted at an old man whose license plates were from Wisconsin.

Garrett leaned so far out his window, with no legs for ballast, that I was afraid he was going to disappear into the wind. Then he gave the finger to another semi that wouldn't let him pass. The trucker blasted his horn.

"You ever get worried somebody's going to get pissed at you?" I asked, when the noise died down. "Somebody with a gun?"

Garrett shrugged. "It's happened. I'm still here."

We drove for a little longer before Garrett looked over at me again. This time he decided to talk about it.

"He was going to do it, wasn't he? The son of a bitch was going to ditch a major investigation for a woman. Another guy's wife, no less."

The Hemisfair Tower appeared on the horizon, sticking up from the orange glow of the city. I stared at it instead of answering Garrett's question. I wanted to deny the obvious, but the letter was pretty clear.

"Maybe he wouldn't have," I said.

"For a woman," Garrett repeated. "You know, I guess I always had one consolation, that he might've been a bastard and he might've screwed up his family, but at least he was honest about doing his job. He was the guy in the fucking white hat. Never mind."

I shifted uncomfortably in my seat. "Maybe he meant to make it public."

"Maybe he died for it anyway, little bro."

There wasn't much I could say to that. We cranked up the Buffett a little louder and rode into the smell of sulfur springs that always marked the southern entrance of either hell or San Antonio.

Gary Hales was standing in the front yard of Number 90, watering the sidewalk with a garden hose. He watched without expression as Garrett's van pulled up in front and I hopped out of Ms. Miranda's airbrushed blouse on the passenger's side. Garrett's horn honked to the tune of "Coconut Telegraph." Then the mound of plastic pineapples and bananas shuddered as he put the van into first gear and lurched off toward Broadway. It didn't seem to wake up Gary much at all.

When I walked up he raised his finger listlessly, as if he wanted to say something. After waiting for a few seconds I remembered it was August 2.

"The rent?" I said.

"That'd be fine," said Gary.

He shuffled a few steps behind me as we went into the in-law. If Mr. Hales had been harboring any last hopes that I was indeed an honest and upstanding young man, I managed to shoot them right to hell when I handed him a wad of fifty-dollar bills from my kitchen drawer.

"No checking account yet," I explained.

"Huh," Gary said.

He peeked over the kitchen counter at the drawer, which was now closed. He looked disappointed. Maybe he was expecting some assault weapons.

Then the phone rang.

"Been ranging nigh on thirty minutes now," Gary said. "I reckon I'd answer that."

Gary waited. The phone rang. I reminded Gary where the front door was. Then when I'd herded him out I picked up the receiver.

"Jesus, Navarre, where in Christ's name have you been?"

"Carlon," I said.

Behind him I could hear glasses clinking, Motown music, the sounds of a bar.

"All right, Navarre. I agreed to twenty-four hours, not forty-eight. You put me off last night, man, and two hours later Karnau gets whacked. Dead bodies cancel our deal."

My stomach twisted. "Carlon, if you've printed something—"

"Shit, man. This is getting unfunny. 'Help' does not include doing time as an accessory to murder."

"So you haven't gone to press with this?"

He laughed without much humor. "What I've done is put in some footwork for your sorry ass. So you want to know where Dan Sheff, Jr., is right now, getting himself schnockered on Lone Star, or you want me to go ahead and start the interview without you?"

"Where are you?"

"Some private dick, Navarre. You have a little patience, you do little stakeout time—"

"Where the hell are you?"

"Little Hipp's."

"I'll be there in ten minutes."

"Better make it five. I got some serious questions to ask the man and I might just—"

I was out the door before he finished the sentence, hoping that in five minutes I wouldn't have a good reason to break Carlon's face.

52

Little Hipp's wasn't so much a San Antonio landmark as it was a surrogate landmark. When L. D. Hipp's original Bubble Room got demolished to make room for hospital parking spaces back in 1980, L.D.'s son opened Little Hipp's across the street and inherited most of the Hipp's menu and paraphernalia. Despite the fact that the orange aluminum exterior made the bar and grille look like a drive-thru beer barn, the inside was faithful to the Bubble Room—multicolored bubbling Christmas lights, licenses plates, tinsel and neon, netted beach balls, and 1950s Pearl ads hanging from the ceiling. Major league tacky. You could get Hank Williams or Otis Redding on the jukebox, Shiner or Lone Star "gimmedraws" for pocket change, and shypoke eggs—round nachos with Monterey Jack whites and longhorn yokes, the jalapeños hidden underneath. The whole place was maybe sixty feet square.

The after-dinner crowd was sparse, mostly off-duty medical workers and a few assorted white collars. I spotted Carlon McAffrey at a table by the barber's chair. He was dressed in what he probably thought was camouflage—dark glasses, khaki shirt and slacks, and a tie with only three colors. As I started over, he shook his head, then pointed at the bar.

Dan Sheff occupied one of the three stools. He was hunched over a line of empty Lone Star bottles, ignoring the bartender's attempts at conversation. Dan's custom-made business suit was rumpled and one of his hand-stitched shoes was untied. He looked like he'd slept in his car last night.

A tai chi principle: If you don't want someone to run away from you, run away from them first. Become yin to make them become yang. I'm not sure why it works, but almost always they'll follow you like air filling a vacuum.

I walked up to Dan and said: "I'll be over there."

Then I retreated to a corner booth on the other side of the room from Carlon and ordered a Shiner Bock. I didn't look at the bar. One hundred twenty-two seconds later Dan slid onto the bench across from me.

He looked even worse close up. In the shadows his face looked half-dead, unshaven, the skin loose around his eyes and his short-cropped hair sickly white instead of blond. He'd been continually twisting his gold ring around on his finger until there were red grooves worried into the skin. He looked at me and tried to maintain some anger, or at least some suspicion, but it was too much effort. His expression fractured into simple grief.

"I didn't," he said.

"Beau?"

He closed his eyes tightly, opened them, then nodded. He looked around for a beer and realized he'd left it at the bar. He almost got up. To keep him there, I started telling him what had happened after he'd run from the Hilton, what I'd told Schaeffer. I didn't mention the decade-old letter from his mother that was still in my pocket. When I was finished he just stared forward like a sleepwalker.

"It's only a matter of time before they ID you, Dan. There were cameras rolling, for God's sake."

He kept turning the gold ring like it was a screw that just wouldn't tighten.

"How much do you want?" he said.

I shook my head. "I'm not Karnau, Dan."

He accepted the rejection with a listless shrug. He looked down at the checkered tablecloth.

"I—he was lying there, you know? I came in angry, saying I was going to kill him." He laughed weakly, wiping the water off his lower eyelids. "And then all I could think of was to hold the wound, but it was his head, and I couldn't—"

The waitress came up. She was about fifty, with a beer gut and a golf hat that had been through the wash too many times. She got out her order pad. Then she noticed Dan's expression.

I held up my Shiner Bock bottle and two fingers. The waitress disappeared.

"I'm supposed to be at a damn party tonight." Dan laughed again, almost inaudibly. "Mother's invited the mayor, everyone important. I'm supposed to drink champagne and dance with their wives and all I can think about is—I mean—"

He shrugged, unable to finish the thought.

"I know about the photographs, Dan. Three times I've seen you with Karnau. The second time you hit him. The third time he ended up dead. You want to avoid taking the fall, you've got to level with me."

The waitress came with our beers. When she left, Dan was staring nowhere again, getting lost in the memory of that hotel room. He got teary and drooped his head like he was going into shock. I reached across the table and pressed my thumb on the meridian point in the base of his palm. The jolt registered in his face like a cup of strong coffee.

"Tell me about the photographs, Dan."

His eyes refocused on me, a little irritated. He pulled his hand away.

"Last spring I was looking through the finances.

Garza had said something that made me angry, something about me and my mother taking up space."

"He said this to his employers?"

Dan's focus drifted down to the tabletop and stuck there, like he was trying to drill a hole through the wood with his eyes.

"Garza worked for my dad for years. He gets"—Dan squeezed his eyes shut—"he *got* a lot of leeway. Mother insisted on that. But I looked at the accounts and saw— I mean it wasn't hard to find—"

"You saw the ten thousand dollars a month that was going to Karnau."

The jukebox cranked out a Merle Haggard song.

"I couldn't believe it. All my mother would tell me is that Karnau had been threatening to publish some old photos of my father. I don't know where he got them. She said the photos could ruin us. She told me not to get involved; she wanted to protect me."

When he talked about his mother he started mumbling, head down. It was as if he were five years old, recounting to a playmate how he'd gotten in trouble.

I took out the photo from Garza's trailer and put it on the table. Dan's forehead turned scarlet.

"You've seen this before?"

"One like it. In Garza's files."

"But you don't know what it's a picture of."

Dan looked down at his beer. "No. She wouldn't tell me. She wanted—"

"She wanted to protect you."

Dan looked miserable.

"You found out right before the River Parade," I guessed. "And you told Lillian. She didn't take it well."

He swallowed. "I thought she had a right to know. She was working with this guy, for God's sake. And we were practically engaged. I'd just given her a diamond ring. I showed her the photo, explained what I knew to her. I told her I'd deal with it, but—" He shook his head, blushing. "I guess I can't blame her. She didn't want to see me anymore."

"Dan, did it occur to you Lillian might've been

shocked because she already *knew* about those photos? Karnau was her partner for ten years. Maybe she just didn't realize he was using them for blackmail. Maybe she thought they were destroyed; maybe Karnau had agreed to destroy them, then when she found out he hadn't—she didn't know what to do. Maybe—"

I stopped. I had been thinking aloud, trying to sculpt an answer I could live with. Dan was looking at me like I'd just spoken in Arabic.

"Why would she have known?" he said.

I stared at him. I probably looked as dazed as he did.

"All right," I said. "You said your mother told you to stay out of it. You obviously didn't."

Dan tried to look defiant, but his voice got quivery. "It's *my* damn company. *My* fiancée. When Lillian . . . when she told me to go away, it just made me more determined to resolve things. I confronted Beau. I told him he'd gotten all he was going to get and I wanted the photographs. I just didn't know—"

He rubbed his eyes slowly, like he couldn't quite remember where they were. A sleepless night and too many pitchers of Lone Star were catching up with him.

"You didn't know what?"

"Beau kept stalling. He asked for more money, then promised he'd bring the disk, then asked for more. He promised if I came to the Hilton that would really be it. He was leaving town. But already he'd done something with Lillian, and then that carpenter, then Garza. It just kept getting worse. If I hadn't pushed on him so hard—"

"Wait a minute," I said. "You think Karnau killed those two men. You think he kidnapped Lillian."

Dan stared at me. "It's obvious."

"Obvious," I repeated. "Who killed Karnau then? Who else knew you were going to the Hilton, Dan?"

"No one."

"Except your mother?"

He didn't respond. I wasn't sure he was even listening.

"When Lillian turned up missing," I said, "your mother talked to the Cambridges. She insisted on no police."

He frowned. "We both did. We knew it wouldn't help."

"That's not why she wanted the police out, Dan."

His eyes became unfocused. "What the hell do you know about her? You have any idea how much strength it takes—her husband about to die, some lowlife blackmailing her family, a hundred damn cousins and second cousins and nieces and nephews ready to take over the company as soon as they see the chance? She kept a million-dollar business together, Navarre. She's done that for *me*."

It sounded like a speech he'd heard a thousand times. He recited it without much conviction.

I tried to imagine the world as Dan saw it: Beau Karnau capable of shooting Eddie Moraga through the eyes, but scared enough of Dan to not try anything even alone with him in a dark alley. Dan able to save the family business single-handedly, even though he'd looked at the books maybe once. Lillian ignorant of her mentor's darker side, just too delicate to handle dating a man who was being blackmailed. The fact that Karnau was the one who'd been blackmailing the Sheff family for a year nothing but an odd coincidence. Dan's mother a frail and besieged protector of Dan's inheritance. I wondered how many of his mother's speeches it had taken over the years to make that vision of the world seem obvious to Dan. I wondered how much longer it would be before that vision caved in on him.

"I'd talk to your mother, Dan. She's been protecting you again."

The Merle Haggard song ended. Out of the corner of my eye I could see Carlon staring over at us, trying to look like he wasn't.

Dan drained his beer glass.

"Get away from me," he mumbled. "Just leave."

I stood up from the bench. I threw down a five and started to go.

"Ask her, Dan. Go to your party tonight and ask her if the blond man in the picture is named Randall Halcomb."

When I stopped at the exit and looked back, Dan was slumped over in the booth, his forehead cupped in his hands, furrows of blond hair sticking up between his fingers. The waitress with the beer gut and the golf hat was trying to console him, giving me a dirty look. Carlon had left his table and was walking toward me as quickly as he could without actually breaking into a run.

We went out together and stood next to Carlon's car in the nighttime heat. The blue Hyundai was parked on McCullough with two wheels on the curb.

"So what do we know?" Carlon said.

"We don't know much, Carlon. Just that Dan's a victim."

Carlon laughed. "Yeah, poor guy. Forced to put a bullet in Karnau's head. Give me a break, Tres."

"Dan didn't kill Karnau. He just isn't capable."

Carlon took off his inconspicuous tie, rolled it up, and shoved it in the front pocket of his khakis, never taking his eyes off me.

"I'm listening."

"Carlon, what would it take for you to give up on getting a story out of this?"

He laughed again. "You don't have that much, Navarre. This is the spiciest shit I've had since the last Terlingua Cook-off. Murder, blackmail, the mob. We're talking 40-point orange headlines here."

"I don't want it like that."

"It's already there, man. It might as well be me that pops the cherry on it."

I looked over at him. Just for the moment I wished I had a bayonet.

"Friday, then," I offered. "At the earliest. This is more complicated than I thought."

"Getting publicity has a funny way of making things unravel, man. I've still got about an hour to make copy for the morning edition."

"Look," I said, trying to keep my voice even, "if you stir things up now, if you get the wrong kind of heat onto the wrong people, somebody else is going to die. I need time to make sure that doesn't happen."

"Lillian, right?"

"Yeah."

Carlon hesitated. Maybe he was thinking about Lillian, or maybe he was thinking about the black eye I'd given Beau Karnau. I didn't really care which.

"You promise me this will be mine?" he said.

"It's yours."

"Promise me it's big."

"Yeah."

Carlon shook his head. "What is it makes me believe you when I know you're going to screw me around again?"

"Your innate benevolence?"

"Shit."

When I got home I sat down and started feeling very alone. Robert Johnson fighting with my ankles didn't help. Neither did another half pint of tequila.

I tried to push the thoughts of Cookie Sheff and my father out of my mind, but the only thoughts that replaced them were of Maia Lee. I looked around the room and saw places she had stood, or eaten *pan dulce,* or kissed me. In her hurry to pack, she'd left a few articles of clothing in the bathroom. I'd folded them neatly on the kitchen counter. I wondered where she was right now, back at work, talking to a client, cursing at a cable car operator, having dinner at Garibaldi's. Half of me was pissed off because I cared at all. The other half of me was pissed off because I didn't care enough to do anything about it. All of me agreed it was time to get out of the house.

53

My friend at the Dominion gates was learning his lessons. This time, he remembered to check the list before letting me in.

"B. Karnau," I said. "For the Sheffs."

"Yes, sir." I guess he didn't get too many VW bugs through there. He frowned at my car. "Wasn't it the Bagatallinis before?"

I smiled. "Sure. I know a lot of people here."

He nodded, his smile quivering as if he was afraid I might hit him. He checked his notebook, then looked up with great regret.

"Ah, I don't see—"

I snapped my fingers, then said something in Spanish that sounded like I was scolding myself. What I actually said was that the guard's mother had obviously mated with a learning-disabled javelina. Then in English: "No, man, they would've put it under Garza. I forgot."

He stared at me, trying to figure out how I could go from German to Hispanic in under twenty seconds. I smiled. I had black hair, I spoke the language, and it was dark. I guess I passed the inspection. He checked his list again.

Evidently nobody had thought to cross the dead man off the party list. The guard looked relieved.

"Okay, Mr. Garza. Straight ahead half a mile, turn left."

"Cool."

I shot him with my index finger. Then I kicked up as much smoke as the VW could make just to piss off the Jaguar behind me.

I won't tell you that San Antonians are the only people who love to throw a party. Garrett says Mardi Gras is great. Lillian always talked about Times Square at New Year's Eve. But in most cities they're content to have one major party season and the rest of the year is normal. In San Antonio, the normal year is about two weeks long in the middle of March. The rest of the time it's party season.

The Sheffs' party that night may have been a little classier than most, but it was just as packed and just as crazy. I could tell they were deeply in mourning for their dead employees Mr. Garza and Mr. Moraga. The walkway up to the mansion was lit with multicolored luminarias. The huge glass front of the building blazed gold, and a country band was cranking out the Bob Wills tunes from somewhere inside. A mob of rich folk spilled out the front doors and into the gravel front yard, laughing, drinking by the gallon, planning sexual escapades that wouldn't ruin their designer clothes.

I guess I stood out a little. I'd put on a fresh T-shirt and jeans, but the tequila bottle in my hand was easily the most expensive thing I had on. Or maybe it was the look on my face that made people stop talking as I walked through the front yard. I pushed past a few city councilmen, some local business leaders, a group of elderly women criticizing the younger women's dresses. A lot of the people I recognized from the old days. Nobody said hello.

I went around the side of the house, put down my tequila bottle, picked up the outside garbage bin, and went into the kitchen through the servants' entrance. The place was bustling with caterers, tortilla-makers, waiters. As I started emptying their trash cans into mine I spoke to the nearest group in Spanish.

"Holy shit, can you believe how much these *cavrons* are eating? The *ceviche* is almost gone, man. You'd better bring in another few gallons."

In a few minutes I'd put fresh liners in all the cans, whipped the tortilla-makers into a frenzy of activity, and moved across the room without anybody asking who the hell I was. I patted a waiter on the back and handed him my garbage can.

"Hold this for a minute," I told him.

Then I slipped into the hallway.

Once upstairs I only had to look in three doorways to find what I wanted. Cookie had laid out a pile of dresses on her bed. The vanity against the back wall was an explosion of makeup containers. The whole place smelled like very old strawberry potpourri. On the rolltop mahogany study in the corner, a laptop computer was waiting for me.

I didn't need Spider John's help for this one. Nothing was protected. Even half-drunk, it only took me about ten minutes. Then I went back out through the kitchen and came into the party through the front door.

Dan was nowhere to be seen, but on one of the upper balconies that looked over the living room, Cookie Sheff was laughing at the mayor's joke. Tonight her luminous blond hair was bigger than ever. Her makeup would've worked just fine with 3-D glasses. She had decided on wearing a black sequined evening gown that was probably supposed to look alluring but just made her angular body look like it had been constructed from Tinkertoys.

I headed for the side office where Dan and I had last talked. When I looked up again Cookie had noticed me. I smiled and waved. Except for the makeup, the color drained out of her face. Then she excused herself politely from the mayor and left the balcony.

The office door was locked. I took out a piece of laminate from my pocket. Ten seconds later I was inside.

Dan wasn't there either. Lillian's parents were.

The Cambridges cut short their conversation and looked up as if they were expecting someone else. Sitting behind Dan Sr.'s desk, Mr. Cambridge looked weary. He was hunched over into a pale triangle of light from the desk lamp, staring up at me over bifocals. Mrs. Cambridge stood next to him, holding tightly to her own wrists. She'd been crying.

"God damn you," said Mr. Cambridge to me. He started to get up, hands straightening his tuxedo.

"Zeke—" murmured his wife. She came toward me, her hands trembling a little. "Tres—"

I guess that's when she saw the look on my face. She hesitated. But Lillian's mother wasn't one to be stopped long by a derelict's expression and the smell of liquor. Tentatively she touched my arm.

"Tres, you shouldn't really, dear—I mean, things are so complicated right now. You shouldn't—"

"God damn you," Zeke Cambridge said again. "Don't you ever stop?"

He swept some knickknacks from the top of Dan Sr.'s desk onto the floor.

We glared at each other. It didn't feel like much of a triumph when he looked away first. He was tired, old, distraught. I was half-drunk and I didn't give a damn. Mrs. Cambridge held my arm a little tighter.

"How are things complicated?" I asked, trying to see straight. My eyes had started burning and I wasn't sure why. "Lillian's missing, nobody's doing shit about it, and you're sitting in the private study of the woman I'd vote Most Likely to Abduct Someone. How is that complicated?"

Zeke Cambridge scowled. His huge gray eyebrows came together.

"What the hell are you talking about, boy?"

"Please, Tres," Lillian's mother said.

The door behind me opened. Cookie stormed in, followed by my friend the chauffeur. Kellin was almost smiling. I don't think he would've waited for permission this time before killing me if Zeke Cambridge hadn't raised his hand.

"Zeke, Angela," Cookie crooned, "I'm so sorry. Kellin, see this person out immediately."

"Wait a minute," Mr. Cambridge said. "First he explains himself."

"Tres." Lillian's mother was almost pleading now. "There's been a murder. Mr. Karnau, Lillian's partner. The police are very concerned that—"

"The police." Zeke Cambridge spat the words out. "If the police had handled things correctly, this son of a bitch would be in jail by now."

The silver-framed photo of Dan Sr. was the only target left on the desk for Zeke Cambridge's anger. He slapped it away with the back of his hand.

Everyone was quiet. When Lillian's mother tried to speak, Cookie cautioned her with a shake of her head.

"Mr. Navarre," said Cookie, very carefully, "I believe I asked you to stay away from my home. I do not appreciate you disturbing my party, breaking into my house, and bothering my friends. Especially now. If you do not leave immediately, I will call the police."

I looked at her. Her eyes were as blue as her son's, only much smaller and a thousand times harder. They looked past me, as if they'd frozen onto one particular point in the distance decades ago and couldn't be bothered with anything closer.

"You afraid I might give them a slightly different take on the situation?" I asked.

Zeke Cambridge was watching Mrs. Sheff now, his anger getting diluted with confusion. He said: "What the hell is the son of a bitch talking about, Cookie?"

Out in the main room, the band blazed into a hyperactive version of "San Antonio Rose." Somebody did his best drunken "yee-haw" into the microphone. I felt disoriented, like someone was spinning me around for pin-the-tail-on-the-donkey.

Mrs. Cambridge took my arm again. She spoke with

the same kindly tone she'd used on numerous Thanks-givings to plead for peace at the dinner table.

"Tres," she said, "there's really nothing you can do. Please don't start this."

Her face looked blurry to me. She was crying.

"What did Rivas tell you about Lillian's disappear-ance?" I asked her. "Or did the Sheffs even let you talk to him?"

Cookie sighed. "That's enough."

Kellin knew better than to grab me this time. He just came and stood next to me, relaxed, alert, arms ready. I ignored him and kept my eyes on Cookie.

"Where *is* the future son-in-law?" I said. "He and I were just having a nice chat about Randall Halcomb over a couple of beers."

"You leaving?" said Kellin. He sounded pleasant enough. Somehow, though, I got the feeling he really wanted me to say no.

"Zeke, Angela," said Cookie. "You shouldn't be bothered with this, and I can see that Mr. Navarre is not considerate enough to cease prying. Let me speak to him for a moment."

It might've been a hypnotist's command. Zeke Cam-bridge stood up, without argument, and took his wife's arm. They drifted out of the room, looking half-asleep, Mrs. Cambridge still crying without a sound. Cookie sat down behind Dan Sr.'s desk. Then, with a look of mild distaste on her face, she waved me to the chair opposite. Kellin and I exchanged looks of mutual disappointment.

"Now, Mr. Navarre," Cookie said. Her tone foretold of restriction, loss of allowance, no TV for a week. "Perhaps we should have a talk."

54

"Kellin, I'd like a glass of red wine. I don't believe Mr. Navarre needs anything."

Kellin hesitated. She looked up at him, cold and expectant. Then he disappeared.

"Before I have you thrown out, Mr. Navarre, perhaps you'd explain yourself to me. Then I have my guests to attend to."

As if on cue, the music outside flared up into a fiddle solo. People started clapping.

"Where is Dan?" I asked.

"My son is not feeling well."

"I bet."

Cookie wasn't used to being contradicted. For an instant her eyes almost focused on me, as if I was worth considering.

"I can't make you understand," she said. "You will never be a mother, Mr. Navarre. You can't possibly appreciate—"

"Try me," I said. "Your sick husband, your years of raising Dan alone. Now here he is at the tender young age of twenty-eight, not quite ready to leave the nest but already, despite your best efforts, deeply involved in the family's shit. Where did you go wrong?"

She was tempted to get angry but to give her credit, she controlled it. She stared at the photo of her husband on the wall—young Dan Sheff, the Korean soldier.

"I have no idea what your crude comments imply, Mr. Navarre, but I will tell you this. My family means more to me than—" She faltered. "I will not allow you to—"

I'd interrupted a perfectly good chastisement by taking the faded pink envelope out of my back pocket, carefully unfolding the letter, and holding it up.

"You were saying?" I prompted. "Your family means more to you than what—an old lover who got too curious? The burden of betraying him to your husband? The guilt of knowing you got him killed?"

Cookie stared at the letter in my hands. Her harsh expression threatened to melt. Somewhere underneath the cosmetics, I think her cheeks actually flushed. I could see suddenly the remnants of a younger, more attractive woman, one who allowed herself emotions other than disdain. A woman my father might have seen as an interesting challenge.

Then she managed to refocus her eyes on that invisible fixed point in the distance. She corrected her posture.

"How——dare——you."

A row of small black mascara specks appeared underneath her eyes when she blinked. Except for that I would never have guessed there was extra moisture anywhere in her. Her bleak stare and the tone of her voice were as arid as the Panhandle.

"I will not sit here," Cookie continued, "and listen to accusations from a young man who understands nothing about my life."

I folded up the letter and put it back in my pocket. "I think I understand pretty well, ma'am. You were having a hard time ten years ago. Your husband's illness was just getting bad; he would be bedridden within a few more years. The business was deep in the red. Your son was away at college. You needed a little affection and my father was there to provide it. He must've been refreshing for you at first, before he told you he was about to start investigating your husband's company for defrauding the city, all because of papers he wouldn't have found if he hadn't been sleeping with you."

Before she could answer, Kellin reappeared at the door of the study. He walked over and handed Cookie a glass of wine. Then he picked up the small picture of Dan Sr. that Mr. Cambridge had knocked off the desk. Cookie glanced at it, then looked away. She brushed a strand of luminescent blond hair behind her ear.

"My past mistakes change nothing," she said, almost to herself. "I have my son to think of. I have done what I can to raise him well."

"To protect him."

"I am protecting him," she agreed tonelessly. "And I will not allow you—I will not allow another—" She stopped herself.

"Another Navarre to interfere," I offered.

She shook her head slowly, but there was something new in her eyes: resentment. She smoothed the belly of her sparkling evening dress with a withered hand.

"No," she said evenly. "Nothing like that."

I looked at the silver-framed picture of Dan's father, robust enough when I was in high school to flirt with countless young cheerleaders. Now Dan Sr. was upstairs somewhere, listening to the drip of the IV and the sound of dancing and Bob Wills that was rocking his floor, trying to remember his own name. I'm not sure what I was feeling for him, but it wasn't pity.

"What the hell is going on?" someone said behind me.

"Danny," said Mrs. Sheff. Her throat sounded like it was constricting. "I thought we'd agreed . . ."

The tux had made some difference in Dan Jr.'s appearance. From the neck down he looked dapper, cleaned and pressed, both shoes tied, a tumbler of bourbon in his hand instead of a Lone Star bottle. From the neck up he looked about the same—bloodshot eyes, sickly pale face, blond cowlicks slicked only partially into submission. He looked like he was probably more sober than I was now, but that wasn't saying much.

"*You* agreed to talk later," Dan said. "I want to know what's going on *now*. It's my damn company, Mother."

"Actually," I said, "that's part of the problem. It's not."

Dan stared at me. Cookie stared at me. Kellin stood behind Cookie with all the emotion of a sideboard, looking at nothing in particular.

"I'd been wondering how Sheff Construction had repositioned itself for the Travis Center deal in '85," I said. "You were on the edge of bankruptcy, then overnight you were a powerhouse again. Even to your partners who were helping you to obtain the contract, you couldn't have looked like a very safe investment. I was also wondering how Terry Garza had the balls to push the Sheff family around. After all, he was supposed to be your faithful employee. So I just checked the files on your personal computer, Mrs. Sheff."

Cookie was totally still. Dan swayed a little, looking down at me.

"What are you saying?"

"This isn't your company, Dan. It hasn't belonged to the Sheffs since '85, when your dad had dug a debt hole so big he couldn't possibly climb out on his own. You were quietly bought out, taken over, repossessed. Then you were used to make the new owner and his partners, maybe the mob, a lot of money on city building contracts. Congratulations, Dan. You're going to inherit an honorary director's title, the right to use your own name without getting sued for trademark violation, and if you're a good boy, a modest yearly stipend. You're just an employee, like Moraga and Garza. Like your mother."

Outside, the band ended its song. Applause. An announcement about a new case of champagne being opened.

Dan Sheff was swaying a little more, like he wanted to fall over but couldn't quite decide which way. His blue eyes were vacant.

"Mother?" His tone wasn't exactly angry. It was more pleading, hopeful that his mom might have a speech in her repertoire to cover this contingency.

Cookie didn't offer one.

I pushed the faded pink letter toward her. "As near as I can figure, you told my father only one thing that was true. Sheff Construction was being used. That isn't Dan Sr. getting rid of Randall Halcomb in the blackmail photos; nobody with Parkinson's, even the beginnings of Parkinson's, is going to shoot someone cleanly between the eyes with a .22 on a dark night. It wasn't the Sheff family that ordered Garza to pay the black-mail, or Moraga to kidnap Lillian so she couldn't talk. You're not protecting your son or your husband, Mrs. Sheff. You're protecting your owner."

When Dan stumbled backward, Kellin was there instantly to steady him. Kellin helped Dan raise the bourbon glass to his mouth.

Cookie was shaking her head. "All I want, Mr. Navarre, is for you to leave. My son is going to inherit his company. He will get Lillian back safely without your help, or that of the police. Then he's going to marry her."

She could've been reading from Dr. Seuss, the way she said it. For some reason that thought made me laugh.

"I can't leave it like that," I said.

Dan started to say something, but Cookie silenced him with a look. Then she nodded at Kellin.

"Good night, Mr. Navarre."

It wasn't much of a fight. Even if I'd been sober, Kellin would've had speed on his side and a score to settle. Two punches connected with my gut. Then I was lying on the Sheffs' antique kilim rug, looking at the ceiling with a funny warm feeling in my head. I think it was Kellin's boot.

We went out a side door through the kitchen. Kellin

dragged me along at just the right angle so I could admire the Saltillo tiles. The waiter tried to give me back my garbage can. A few of the cooks were telling jokes in Spanish. They got quiet as we went past.

When Kellin dragged me around to the front yard I looked up briefly into Fernando Asante's face. The councilman was just going into the party with his satin-dressed cherubs and a few tuxedoed businessmen. Asante's bow tie was bright green.

"Leaving us, Mr. Navarre?"

Somebody laughed, a little nervously.

Kellin dragged me a few more feet, then pulled me upright.

"No offense," he said.

Then he introduced my face to the gravel and walked away.

55

I'd been waiting for Detective Schaeffer at his desk for thirty minutes before he came down the hall with his garlic bagel in hand. Schaeffer looked even more tired than usual, like it'd been a busy morning for homicides.

"No time," he said. "Got a stiff to take care of. Want to come along?"

A few minutes later we were heading toward the East Side in an Oldsmobile so brown-wrapper and so obvious that some kid with a sense of humor had spray-painted "THIS IS NOT A POLICE CAR" on the sides, right in English, left in Spanish.

"Only fucking unit available," Schaeffer told me. Somehow, though, I got the feeling he kind of liked this one. We drove down Commerce for a few minutes before he said: "So what's the occasion?"

"I thought we should talk."

"I said that two days ago."

"And I need a favor."

"Lovely."

He checked with Dispatch. Yes, the wagon was at the scene. They were waiting outside the house. Schaeffer swore, then blew his nose into the huge red napkin that had been holding his bagel a few minutes before.

"Waiting outside the house," he repeated. "Lovely."

"So the smell is inside," I said.

He made a noise that might have been a grudging acceptance. "Your dad was a cop."

We turned south on New Braunfels, then left into a neighborhood of matchbox houses and dirt front yards.

"So tell me about it," Schaeffer said.

I'm not sure when, the night before, I'd decided to come clean with Schaeffer. Somewhere around 3 A.M., I guess, when I'd finished picking the gravel out of my face and had been staring at the ceiling so long I started seeing dead faces in the crystalline plaster. Maybe they'd started looking a little too familiar. Or Carlon's newspaper deadlines had started looking too close. Or maybe I just needed to make Larry Drapiewski and Carl Kelley proud of me. Whatever it was, I told Schaeffer what I knew.

When I was done he nodded. "Is that all?"

"You wanted more?"

"I want to make sure your bullshit filter is operating today, kid. Is that all?"

"Yeah."

"Okay. Let me think about it."

I nodded. Schaeffer took out his napkin again.

"Maybe when I calm down I'll decide not to kick your ass for being so stupid."

"Take a number," I said.

I don't know how Schaeffer drove with one hand and a napkin larger than his face pressed against his nose, but he managed to navigate us through the turns without slowing under thirty and without hitting any of the residents. We pulled up next to a couple of squad cars outside a two-story turquoise house on Salvador. Sure enough, everybody was waiting outside. You could tell the ones who had been inside recently. Their faces were bright yellow. A group of neighbors, mostly old men still in bathrobes, had begun to gather on the neighbor's porch.

"Someday," Schaeffer snuffled, "I want to know what it is about 11 A.M. that makes everybody want to turn up dead. It's a corpse rush hour, for God's sake."

"You got cotton balls or something?" I asked.

"In the glove compartment with the Old Spice."

I made a face. "I'd rather smell the deceased."

"No you wouldn't. One good thing about sinuses, Navarre. I can't smell a damn thing. You should be so lucky."

I opted for the Old Spice. I doused two cotton balls and put one in each nostril. When we got into the house I was glad I had.

The victim was an old widow, Mrs. Gutierrez. Nobody had seen her for a few days, according to the neighbors, until the guy next door had gotten worried enough to check on her. The minute he opened the front door he closed it and called the police.

I'd seen dead bodies, but usually not after they'd been floating in bloody upstairs bathtubs in one-hundred-degree heat for several days. Mrs. Gutierrez wasn't easy to look at. I must've needed to prove something to Schaeffer. I stayed with him while he went over the scene.

"Suicide my ass," he told the beat cop. He pointed at the slit wrist on Mrs. Gutierrez's bloated forearm. "You see any nicks on either side of the main cut?"

Just before he left to throw up, the beat cop admitted that he did not. Schaeffer put the dead hand down long enough to blow his nose, then continued his conversation with me.

"No hesitation marks," he said. "It takes two or three tries to get over the pain when you do it yourself. Somebody did this job for her."

He looked at me, for applause, I guess.

"Is this your idea of getting even with me?" I mumbled through the cotton balls.

The idea seemed to amuse him. "Come on, kid. I'll show you why I drink Red Zinger."

I followed Schaeffer downstairs. He started a pan of coffee grounds burning on the stove to help with the smell of the corpse. If I hadn't been breathing Old Spice already, it would've almost been enough to make me swear off the java too. Then we looked for the window the intruder had forced open. Schaeffer didn't believe in waiting for the evidence tech. He used a spray bottle of diluted super glue to get the impression of a dried boot print on the carpet by the front door, a hand print on the wall.

"Lesson for the day, kid. The scene doesn't lie. Went right out the front, probably in broad daylight. Probably raped the old lady too. I'd bet money."

I didn't offer any. When Schaeffer decided to go outside for a break, I was only too glad to follow. We sat on the hood of his car and waited for the coroner while Schaeffer adjusted his pants back over his belly. I thought about the way a corpse would look after a week and a half. A corpse I knew.

"So what was the favor?" Schaeffer asked.

"I want the Cambridge case done right," I said.

He squinted at the sun coming down through the pecan trees. He said: "That's not a favor. That just happens."

"But I want some leeway."

Schaeffer stared at me. "Now it's starting to sound like a favor. What kind of leeway?"

"I want to know what you've found out, and I want until Friday."

"Until Friday for what?"

"I don't want the FBI knocking down Rivas's investigation just yet. Making people nervous. If Lillian is still alive, I need a few more days to look."

"And if she gets not alive between now and Friday?"

"She's been gone for a week already. You're the expert. If she's not dead yet, what are the chances?"

Schaeffer didn't like conceding the point.

"Still no deal," he said.

"Then you look," I said. "I've tied it to homicide. Take it to the CID chief that way."

"And by Friday when the Feds are into it anyway?"

"I'll have to make it work by then."

Schaeffer almost laughed.

"What exactly are you expecting to make work, Navarre? From all I can see you've been making about as much progress as a pinball. You going to solve this by getting bashed back and forth a few more times?"

"You'd be surprised," I said.

"I'd be very surprised."

He stared at me for a minute longer. I tried to do my winning smile. Finally he shook his head.

"All right. The corpse that got driven through Sheff's office wall, Eddie Moraga—we traced the Thunderbird exactly nowhere. Switched plates, the engine block number placed it as stolen from Kingsville. It doesn't get any more nowhere than that."

"A big stop off for the cocaine trade. Might connect it to White."

"Maybe," Schaeffer said, but he didn't like the tie-in. "The fatal shot was through Moraga's heart, close range, angled down, like he was sitting and the killer was standing right over him. The bullets in the eyes happened postmortem. Weapon was a 9mm Parabellum."

"Glock, maybe?"

He shrugged. "Looks professional. Everything wiped clean. Moraga probably knew the guy who killed him, never even saw it coming."

"If it was a professional job—"

"It means Moraga really pissed somebody off, up close and personal. This bullet-through-the-eye shit— you have to screw up pretty bad to rate that."

"But you still don't like it."

He twisted the edge of his napkin. "It's too showy. The methods, yeah, professional. But these guys— they're like fucking actors."

"Like somebody imitating what they think a mob killing would be."

He didn't like that idea either, but he didn't offer another.

"Garza?" I asked.

"The trailer he rented six months ago. Wife and kids live in Olmos Park, knew nothing about it. He was killed on the scene, sometime that morning, probably around ten."

"Right after I talked to him on the phone."

"Looks that way. Garza was sitting down when he got stabbed, and he was drugged. Heavy valium in his system, couldn't put up much of a fight. You saw the blood. Slice the artery and it was over. Same problem—looks professional, too flashy."

"Karnau?"

"Not the same. Not a very smart killer, and definitely not a pro. Near as we can tell Karnau just opened the door, bought it instantly, then got displayed. Different M.O.; I'd bet money it's a different killer from Garza and Moraga."

"But the display?"

Schaeffer shook his head. "Karnau was laid out neatly, like he was sleeping. They didn't want a mess. Usually means your killer wants to convince himself nothing happened here. It's like—'I'll just comb the dead guy's hair, tuck him into bed, wash my hands, and everything's normal.' "

I thought about Dan Sheff, what he'd said about wanting to hold the wound closed on Karnau's head.

"You said the killer wasn't too smart."

"Stupid choice of guns. Very clear striations from ballistics. A pretty rare little .22 this guy used."

"A Sheridan Knockabout," I said.

"How the hell did you know that?"

I told him about the deer blind in Blanco. Schaeffer thought about it, then nodded.

"Top of the class, Navarre."

I watched the coroner's car arrive. Then two more squads. On the porch next door, the neighbors were sharing coffee. Somebody had brought binoculars. In a minute they'd start serving appetizers.

I got up. The sunlight on my skin was just starting to burn off the itchy feeling I'd picked up in Mrs. Gutierrez's house. A couple of stiff drinks and I might even forget her body in the bathtub long enough to think about a few other dead people. I looked across at the turquoise house that was just being taped off.

"I don't know how you handle it every day," I told Schaeffer. "My dad hardly ever talked about it. All those bodies on the highways, hunting accidents, bar fights."

Schaeffer blew his nose. He looked at me for a minute like he might even smile. Maybe he was going to gift me his napkin. Fortunately he only offered me a ride in the queasy beat cop's squad car back to my VW.

"I didn't know your dad," Schaeffer said. "I do know he was in the field a lot. He got shit for it too."

I nodded.

"He a drinker?" asked Schaeffer. "Religious?"

"Drinker."

Schaeffer looked at me like he was remembering every family argument the Navarres had ever had, like he'd been right there with me.

"Usually one or the other. Next time you think about him, Navarre, think about twelve or thirteen Mrs. Gutierrezes a year, maybe a few worse. See if you wouldn't rather drink it away than tell your kids about it."

We walked back over to the house. The beat cop joined us, looking almost flesh-colored again. He told me sourly that he was ready to go.

"And you?" I asked Schaeffer. "You religious?"

He shook his head. "I just talk to them."

I looked to see if it was a joke. "Who—the corpses?"

Schaeffer shrugged. "It keeps me sane. Keeps me thinking about them like they're human. Plus they're a great audience, very attentive."

I looked up at Mrs. Gutierrez's bathroom window.

"Tell her I said good-bye, then."

"I'll do that."

Schaeffer turned and patted the coroner on the back, then they went into the blue house like old friends.

56

The fountain in front of the White House was still being worked on. In fact, progress seemed to be going backward. More pipes were exposed now, more gaping holes and piles of dirt marred the lawn. The workmen were taking an extended lunch break under the shade of a live oak. One of the men grinned and gave me the thumbs-up as I walked up to the front door.

BeeBee didn't exactly smile when he recognized me, but his grunt sounded collegial. He buzzed Emery, who came downstairs within two minutes and shook my hand repeatedly. Evidently he had new orders concerning my visits. Or maybe he'd just given up. Emery's tie was dark red today, his shirt olive-colored and just as oversized around the collar.

We compared head injuries—his forehead bruises from where Maia had slammed him into the door, my swollen jaw from where Red had kicked me. Then he started telling me about his three brothers in West

Texas and how funny it was that they were all on probation at the same time.

"Shee-it," he said. "Jestin—that's the one in El Paso, you unnerstand—he made two thousand dollars just last week at cockfighting. You believe that shit? Ole Dean back in Midland, now—"

"That's great," I interrupted, trying to smile. "Is Mr. White at home?"

"Sure. He's busy upstairs at the moment, you unnerstand."

He leered at me. It wasn't a pretty sight.

"Maybe I could wait for him?"

Emery was agreeable. He even apologized when he had to frisk me. Then he led me into the study where White had almost blown my brains out. The elderly black maid brought us margaritas—made without Herradura, but otherwise acceptable. Emery talked about brother Elgin out in San Angelo. I nodded my head a lot. It was all very civilized except for Emery alternately cleaning his .38 and picking his nose while he reminisced.

After about ten minutes Guy White, tan and immaculate as always, appeared in the doorway and shook my hand. He was doing beige today—raw silk pants and an untucked broadcloth shirt open at the top just enough to show off his well-developed pects, perfectly devoid of chest hair.

He sat behind the desk, crossing his legs and leaning back, at ease. He nodded to Emery, who left. The maid brought in the refilled margarita pitcher and then disappeared too.

"My boy," White said, showing off his perfect teeth. "What can I do for you?"

I took out a page of notes I'd made after talking to Schaeffer and handed it across the desk to White.

"Edit this for me," I said.

White raised his eyebrows just slightly. He looked at the paper, then back at me. He produced a pair of silver-rimmed reading glasses from his shirt pocket.

White read my notes without comment or expression. Then he put them down and smiled.

"Flattering," he said.

"That wasn't the first word that came to my mind."

He laughed without sound. "I mean that I should still be taking up so much of your thoughts. But regrettable that you could be so mistaken."

He patted the paper like it was the head of a puppy. At the moment I wanted very much to stick that well-manicured hand into the nearest food processor and see how well White could maintain his smile.

"Three men are murdered," I said. "Two look like professional hits and the third is probably shot with the same gun that killed Randall Halcomb, the only real suspect, besides the mob, in my father's murder. The press is already loving the mob angle. And that doesn't concern you at all."

"On the contrary," he said easily. "It concerns me a great deal. But it doesn't change the fact that you are still mistaken about my involvement."

He met my eyes level and calm. I sat forward.

"The thing is, Mr. White, for every question I keep asking myself, you keep coming up as a very good answer. It's possible you're the person who took over Sheff Construction in the mid-eighties, bailed them out of debt and put their resources to work on illegally contracted city projects. If not that, it's equally possible you worked with whoever the new owners were to rig the bidding process at City Hall, in exchange for a cut of the very considerable profits. There were two people with Randall Halcomb in Karnau's photos—both of them saw to it personally that my dad's killer was eliminated; both profited from Travis Center then and are interested in profiting from the new fine arts complex now; both had a lot to lose when Karnau started his blackmail last year. You could be either one of those people."

White dabbed the salt away from the edge of his margarita and took a sip. I'd like to say I was rattling him, throwing him into a nervous fit, forcing him to make careless mistakes. Unfortunately the only thing I seemed to be making him was late for his next tanning session. He checked his watch, trying to be polite about it.

"All very imaginative." He looked at me with a half smile. "But really, my boy, you don't believe a word of it. Allowing myself to be photographed at a murder scene, much less one done by amateurs. Kidnapping Ms. Cambridge. Disposing of people by such sloppy and obvious means. You give me more credit than that."

The margarita was now waltzing pleasantly through my circulatory system, turning my limbs to lead. It took away some of my will to get out of my chair and strangle Guy White with his Gucci belt. What irritated me was that he was right. As much as I might want to, I couldn't really see him being at the center.

White nodded as if I'd assented out loud, then gazed off toward the ceiling. He looked like he was thinking about rose arbors, philanthropy, anything but decade-old murders.

"Your father was a great rattler of cages," he said after a while. "I would think twice before following that family tradition, my boy."

The words sounded like a threat, but White's tone conveyed something different. It took me a minute to interpret.

"You respected him," I said.

White examined his perfect fingernails. "It saddens me when a man of talent is brought down by men with less talent, even if that man is my enemy. It saddens me more when those who are supposed to represent the public interest use my name to cover up their own crimes."

His eyes drifted toward me.

"Asante," I said.

White looked gratified. He refilled his glass from the margarita pitcher. "The more dangerous I appear, the more the politicians have to campaign against. Unfortunately, Mr. Navarre, contrary to popular belief, I've found that direct retaliation against such people is most often . . . counterproductive."

There was a knock at the door. White uncrossed his legs. The audience was concluded.

"And now you'll have to excuse me, Mr. Navarre. Either you will choose to believe me, that I had nothing to do with your father's death—"

"Or?"

"Or you will not. Nevertheless, my boy, there's nothing more I can tell you. I have a keynote address to deliver in exactly twenty minutes."

I decided something. "You don't have it—the other disk."

White almost played dumb. I could see him change his mind just as he opened his mouth. "No," he said. "I do not."

I tried to stand up, and was surprised to find I actually could.

"Assuming I believe you," I said, "assuming Asante was Sheff's partner inside City Hall on the Travis Center project, that still doesn't tell me who the other side is—the ones who control Sheff Construction."

White gave me a look I couldn't read. Sadness. Maybe even pity.

"As I said, my boy, some cages are better left unrattled."

We studied one another. Maybe that was when I had the first glimmering of understanding about where it was all going. Maybe that's why I chose not to push him any further.

When I left, Guy White was listening to Emery's rundown of their afternoon schedule—benefits, cocktail parties, an award for good citizenship from a local nonprofit. Emery was cleaning another gun as he talked. Guy White was staring out the sunny windows at his gardens, smiling a little sadly now.

57

When I looked out my living room window the next morning, Ralph Arguello's maroon Lincoln sat in front of Number 90. When I came up to the driver's window the black glass rolled down and mota smoke rolled out. Ralph grinned up at me like a happily stoned *diablo*.

"Do I know you?" I said.

"Get in."

I didn't ask why. We drove into Monte Vista on Woodlawn, past rows of dying palm trees that leaned over the boulevard like they hadn't quite woken up yet. Mansions squatted next to shacks. The signs and storefronts gradually turned bilingual. Finally Ralph looked across at me.

"I'm meeting a guy at eight-thirty," he said.

"Yeah?"

He nodded. "Business deal, *vato*. New territory."

We pulled up in front of a dark blue building that had been plopped down in the middle of an acre of asphalt on the corner of Blanco and French. The yellow back-lit sign in front promised "Guns N Loans." At least that's what it used to say before half the letters had been broken out with rocks.

A tall Anglo man in a wrinkled black suit was waiting at the door, smiling. From the bruises on his face I wondered if he'd been pelted at the same time as his sign. Most of the marks were fading into yellow around his cheeks and neck, but he still had a blue-black knot the size of a pecan over his left eyebrow. The smile just made him look more grotesque.

"Mr. Arguello," the tall man said as we got out of the car. When he swallowed, his Adam's apple went up a few inches and stayed that way. He shook Ralph's hand a little too enthusiastically.

"Lamar," said Ralph. "Let's see it."

Lamar fumbled with some keys. He unlocked two rows of burglary bars first, then the main door. The inside of the pawnshop smelled like cigars and dust. Grimy glass cases filled with guns, stereo parts, and jewelry made a "U" around the back walls. A few beat-up guitars and saxophones had been lynched from the ceiling.

Ralph inhaled, as if to get the full atmosphere of the place into his lungs. Lamar smiled nervously, waiting for his approval.

"Books," said Ralph.

Lamar nodded and went to open the office. I plucked a string on one of the convicted Yamaha guitars. It rattled loosely, like a Slinky.

Ralph looked at me. "Well?"

"Sure," I said, "some lace curtains, a loveseat or two. I can see it."

Ralph grinned. "Ethan Allan, maybe."

"Levitt's."

"I'm sold. You can do all my shops, *vato*."

Lamar came back and spent a few minutes with Ralph over the books. I looked at the guns, then watched the traffic in and out of the flop house across the street for a while. Finally Ralph shook hands again and Lamar handed over the keys. Lamar started to leave but on his way out he looked at me, hesitated, then came over. He was so nervous his Adam's apple disappeared above his jawline. The yellow bruises turned pink.

"I just—" he started. "Hey, man, it just wasn't necessary. That's all I got to say."

Then he left.

I looked at Ralph for an explanation. His eyes floated behind his round lenses, impossible to read. The smile didn't change.

"*Loco,*" Ralph said. "I guess he thought you were somebody else, man."

"I guess."

We went back to Ralph's new office, a cheaply paneled closet with a window AC unit, two metal folding chairs, and an unfinished particle-board desk. Ralph sat down and started looking through the drawers.

"You always do property deals in under five minutes with no paperwork?"

Ralph shrugged. "Details, *vato*. That's for later."

He fished out a half-empty bottle of Wild Irish Rose and a few .38 rounds, then a stack of ragged manila folders. When he was satisfied there was nothing else, he sat back in his chair and smiled at me.

"Okay," he said. "So tell me about it."

"What do you want first? You've got your choice of three murders, blackmail, several pissed-off policemen—"

Ralph shook his head. "I know all that. I mean the Chinese woman. Tell me about her."

I stared at him for a few seconds. I guess I'd forgotten who I was talking to. Ralph would've heard just about everything that had happened to me over the last week. He'd know about the dead bodies, the heat, the people I'd talked to. But the question about Maia took me off guard.

I must've looked pretty irritated. Ralph laughed.

"Come on, *vato*. All I want to know is this—are you still looking for Lillian or aren't you? 'Cause if you're not, that's cool. I can take you home and save us some trouble."

"Some trouble?"

He shrugged.

"And if I'm still looking?"

He thumbed through the stack of manila folders. The action sent puffs of dust up in front of his face. He kept looking at me. "Is that a yes?"

"That's a yes."

He shook his head, like I'd made a bad business decision. "Then this is between you and me. A couple of people came up to me over the last two days, telling me about this guy that turned up dead, this *pendejo* Eddie Moraga who took Lillian that Sunday."

"You've been sitting on information for the last two days?" I tried to keep my voice even.

Ralph leaned forward and spread his hands on the desk, palms up. "Hey, *vato*, every time I come to see you, I find the Man there. Or you're with him. It kind of cuts down on the quality time I want to spend with you, you know?"

I nodded for him to go on.

"Okay, so first I talk to this guy, old friend of Eddie's. He's pretty shaken up about it all being in the papers Friday morning. So fifty dollars later and he says, yeah, he talked to Eddie on Monday night. He was all alone at this bar down on Culebra, talking about this hot date he'd had the night before. A date, *vato*, like this rich white girl would go out with him."

I couldn't talk. I was remembering a rapist I'd brought down for a client of Terrence & Goldman two years ago, a rapist who'd talked about his "dates" with his victims, two of whom later turned up in garbage cans.

Ralph must've thought that through too. He'd been on the streets long enough. He looked at my expression.

"Hey, man," he said. He probably wanted to say something consoling. He shifted in his chair. "Like I said, if you were with this other lady, I could have just walked from this, *vato*. This isn't easy shit—"

"Keep going."

For a minute we both stared at the bottle of Wild Rose, almost tempted. Then Ralph sighed. "Yeah, anyway, so Eddie was talking about coming into some money from this lady. I don't know, man, maybe not like she was paying him, maybe he was just making a joke, like he was getting paid to take her away for somebody else. Anyway, Eddie said that this lady was a fire-eater, like you couldn't turn your back on her or she'd either steal your shit or kick you in the balls. That's what he said. And check this out, *vato*: He said they went to this place he knew, a construction site he worked at, real intimate."

I shook my head. "There's only a few thousand of those, Ralph."

"No, man," he said. "I'm not finished."

"What else?"

"Like I said, some other people talked to me. Some people who like a low profile. Keep that in mind."

I thought about Ralph and his .357 Magnum. "Low profile like you?"

"More than me, *vato*. These people, they're in the car business, you know?"

"As in chop shop? S.A., second highest auto theft rate in the country?"

Ralph shrugged. "I wouldn't know, *vato*. But I wouldn't tell these people they're in second place, man. It might offend them."

"Okay."

Ralph nodded. "So anyway, I ask around about this green Chevy Eddie's supposed to drive. His friend tells me it's a '65, fully restored. So I think, sure, the police are just going to find this Chevy sitting around on the streets after a week."

"So your friends just happened to come across it, strictly legit."

"They were about to paint it white, man." Ralph's frown told me he didn't approve of the color choice. "So I told them to wait awhile, leave it like it is."

"And how was that?"

He looked at me, grinning again. Then he took out a brown paper bag from his pocket and poured the contents onto the desk. White powder. I didn't even have time to misread it as cocaine before Ralph shook his head.

"No, *vato,* check it out."

I looked closer.

"It was all over the wheel casings, man. The outside was washed off but it was caked on thick inside. You know that rainstorm that came through last week?"

I smelled it. I tasted it. It seemed to be powdered rock.

"I give."

Ralph shook his head, disappointed.

"Oh, man," he said, "you didn't live there. You didn't go to Heights with your shoes covered in it. We lived in it, *vato.* Mother of God, my old man's lungs collapsed because of this shit. It's lime powder, man, pure lime."

It took a minute for that to register.

"As in the stuff they make cement from," I said.

"Okay, *vato,*" he said, trying to lead me to what he was thinking.

"Couldn't that be *any* construction site?"

Ralph laughed and started repacking his desk.

"You goddamn white collars. No, man, who mixes cement on site? That much lime only comes from the factory."

As usual, the answer was something under my nose, something I'd lived next to most of my life. When I put it together I almost couldn't believe how ridiculous the idea was, which probably meant it was the truth.

Ralph and I looked at each other. God knows I didn't have much to smile about. All I'd probably learned was where to find the body of the woman I thought I loved. But I looked at Ralph grinning like a fiend and I started smiling anyway.

"It's pretty slim, man," I said.

"It ain't goin' to get any fatter, man," Ralph said. "You got to jump on it."

"Goddamn Cementville," I said.

Ralph grinned. "There's no place like home."

58

The sign on the fence outside the factory said "Sheff Construction—Keep Out."

There was no movement inside the barbed wire. No trucks, no lights in the broken windows of the old factory. Ralph and I sat in his car for a while and just watched while the Cadillacs went by, old men going to the golf course, women going to shop Albertson's and SteinMart. The new subdivision, Lincoln Heights, had its own private security, and after the same patrolman drove by us twice, real slow, Ralph and I decided it was time to move on.

"Tonight," I said. "I can't do anything until then without being seen by half the North Side. Neither could they."

Ralph followed the security car with his eyes until it was out of sight. "How you know who 'they' is, man?"

"One way to find out."

As if he were reading my mind, Ralph reached into his backseat and produced a cell phone. I dialed a number I had memorized from Lillian's datebook and got an answering machine.

"I'm thinking about visiting Cementville," I said.

Then I hung up.

Ralph started the Lincoln and pulled it into traffic.

"You got the right person, they got to move her tonight," he said. "Or at least they got to look."

"Yeah."

"You want some backup?"

I started to say no, then I decided not to be hasty. "I'll call you."

Ralph nodded, then handed me a card.

"Two numbers," he said. "Cell phone and beeper."

"A beeper?"

Ralph grinned. "Hey, *vato*, the doctor is *in*."

When Ralph dropped me at home it was early afternoon. Several hours until dark, when I could actually do something. Rather than go crazy watching Robert Johnson run circles around the living room, I took my sword and walked down the street to the edge of Brackenridge Park.

The cicadas were the only thing stirring. Nobody was stupid enough to walk over a block in this heat, much less exercise in it. I crossed Broadway and jogged over to the Witte Museum where the old iron gates of the Alligator Gardens were hanging off their hinges. One of the less successful tourist attractions in San Antonio, the Gardens had seen ticket sales to the public schools drop off dramatically after the alligators had eaten a few hands off the trainers. Then the place had faded into obscurity and eventually closed. The gates were easy to climb, though, and the dried basin where the gators had been kept made a perfect shady tai chi surface.

I did an hour and a half of high stance until I was sweating and about to pass out from the heat. Then I rested for a few minutes and did another two hours of sword. By the time the sun started going down, I had cleared my mind and worked the kinks out of my body. I knew what the plan was.

I bought some provisions from the Lincoln Heights

Albertson's, then I drove down to Vandiver and traded cars with my mother. More or less. Actually she'd taken her Volvo somewhere so I had to leave the keys to the VW in her mailbox and hot-wire Jess's truck. With luck he'd need to run for beer between TV shows and would find it missing long before I could get it back to him. My evening was starting to look up.

Jess's monstrous black Ford must've known I was not wearing the obligatory Stetson and boots required to ride such a beast. It bucked and kicked all the way down Nacodoches until I pulled it over into the scrub brush on Basse, just behind the old freight entrance to Cementville.

"Whoa, Nelly," I told the truck.

The engine shuddered resentfully and died. Just as well. Another few blocks like that and I would've had to shoot it anyway.

I waited outside the fence for a couple of hours. What I was looking for didn't materialize. I ate an Albertson's deli sandwich. I had some terrible Italian bottled water. On this side of the old factory there were fewer high-priced new homes, which meant there were fewer nervous security guards. After dark, traffic died down to almost nothing. Nobody seemed to care about me and my semi-stolen truck.

It was full dark when the Sheffs' cherry-red Mustang passed me and slowed down a quarter mile up the road, right outside the old loading docks. I couldn't see the driver very well when he got out. He unchained the gates, got back in the Mustang, and drove through.

I was about to drive back to the Albertson's pay phone when I noticed the cargo holder by the stick shift. No chance, I thought. I opened it anyway and found Jess's deep dark yuppie secret. The real cowboys would've laughed him off the open range if they'd known. Suddenly liking Jess more than I cared to admit, I picked up his cellular phone and dialed Ralph's number.

He picked up almost immediately.

"Annie get your gun," I said.

The line was silent for a moment. "Give me ten minutes." Ralph hung up.

Exactly eleven minutes later the maroon U-boat slid to a stop behind the truck. Ralph stepped up to the shotgun window and leaned his head into the cab.

"Nice wheels, vaquero. You chewing Red Man, yet?"

"The gun rack wouldn't fit on my VW."

"No shit."

Ralph had changed into work clothes—Levi's and a loose black shirt, untucked. I didn't need to ask what he was carrying underneath. I pointed out the red Mustang up ahead, now dark and silent just inside the chain-link fence. Ralph nodded.

"Meet you up there," he said. Then he disappeared.

By the time I got out of the truck and followed the fence up to the gate, Ralph was crouched in a patch of wild cilantro. He had his straight razor in one hand. In his other hand were four severed tire valve stems. He held them up, grinned, then tossed them through the fence.

We watched the old factory for a while—the weed-covered shipping yard, the storage silos, the grimy windows with most of the glass broken out. The only thing moving were the fireflies. They were everywhere tonight, pulsing off and on in the hackberry bushes around the fence like defective Christmas lights.

Ralph nudged my arm. We watched the yellow cone of a flashlight, aimed from the factory roof, slide up the right side of one of the huge smokestacks and illuminate a metal rung ladder that led up to the wraparound catwalk just below the red "O" in ALAMO. The light clicked off abruptly.

I could hear Ralph swallow. "There's a small maintenance room up there where they wired up the sign," he said. "I think."

His voice sounded like it was closing up all of a sudden. I couldn't see much in the dark, but I could've sworn he was turning pale.

"Ralphas?"

"Heights, man. I can't handle them."

There was a quivery tone to his voice that might've been funny under other circumstances, like Ralph trying to imitate somebody who was really scared. But you don't laugh at your friend's phobias. At least not when your friend is holding a straight razor.

"Okay," I said. "We'll deal with it when we get there."

"Shit, *vato*, I didn't think—"

"Forget it, Ralphas. Any other chained gates between her and there, you think?"

Ralph showed me a small but wickedly sharp set of metal cutters. His grin came back slowly.

"Not anymore, *vato*."

Minutes later we were crossing the train tracks under the shadow of the factory walls. The ground was littered with dried globs of cement, old railroad ties, scrap metal, dry sage grass—none of it conducive to sneaking around in the dark. It was my turn to be embarrassed. When I stumbled the second time Ralph had to grab me by the shirt to keep me from sliding face first into a quarry pit. The sound of the loosened gravel skittering into the hole echoed off the building like a standing ovation. We froze. No sounds, no light from above.

Ralph's childhood memories came through. He found a set of metal doors around the side of the building that were standing wide open. What moonlight there was fell in a square over the bottom steps of a spiral stairwell. We went inside.

"This goes to the roof," he said. "I guess—yeah, there was talk about saving the old smokestacks for a restaurant or something. You could store something up there for a long time and none of the workers would think to bother it."

I looked up at the rickety stairwell.

"You okay with this?" I whispered.

"Don't ask, *vato*. Just start climbing."

By the way every creak and groan of the staircase echoed around as we ascended, I figured the interior of the building must've been one massive chamber, stripped to a shell when the plant shut down. I gave up counting steps when I got to a hundred. I gave up counting missing bolts that were supposed to secure the stairwell to the wall when I got to one. More I didn't want to know.

Somehow Ralph stayed behind me. After what seemed like a thousand years we came to a door that was open to the roof. I stepped out and immediately flattened my body against the wall of the roof house to avoid making a silhouette. Ralph crawled out and sat down, breathing heavily.

"I'm not getting up," he said. "No way."

The view was tremendous—to the south, the lights of McAlister Freeway snaking through the darkness of the Olmos Basin, then emptying into the hazy glow of the downtown skyline. The buildings there were all lit up gold except for the stark white Tower of the Americas, the proverbial needle in the haystack. In the opposite direction, Loop 410 made a glittering curve of hotels, malls, singles apartment complexes around the North Side—"Loopland" as it was not-so-affectionately called. Beyond that was the dark rise of the Balcones Escarpment, and more storm clouds rolling in. Ralph was not impressed. He sat cursing the horizon quietly in Spanish.

After being in the dark of the building, the moonlit roof was easier to see across. A few yards away to the south, the tar had sagged and caught a sizable lake of rainwater from the last storm. It had almost evaporated after several days in the sun, but not quite. There was still enough moisture around the edges to track footprints—at least one set, leading toward the edge of the roof. From there an old steel catwalk spanned thirty yards of empty space to the ladder on the side of the smokestack. About one story up, the ladder dead-ended at an oval door that resembled a submarine hatch. The door was ajar, with light seeping out from behind it.

I looked at Ralph, who was either invoking God or preparing to throw up.

"I'm okay," he croaked.

Then I looked back up and saw the door open, a familiar face in the portal.

"I wish I could say the same," I said.

59

With the light behind her, her hair looked disheveled, like straw. She was wearing an old T-shirt and black sweatpants smeared with paint. I couldn't see her face well, but she was moving slowly, like a sleepwalker.

Kellin hadn't even changed out of his black chauffeur's outfit. He got onto the ladder first and guided Lillian down onto the rungs, cradling her with his body so she wouldn't fall. It took them a long time to descend to the catwalk.

"Thank God," Ralph whispered. He said a prayer to the patron saint of acrophobics, then crept around to one side of the roof house while I crept to the other. We waited.

Lillian started talking as they approached, but it didn't sound much like her. She giggled, then spoke in a low voice. Kellin shushed her the way you would a child. I made a silent promise to force-feed Kellin whatever the hell they'd doped her up with.

Then they were at the doorway, close enough for me

to catch Lillian's scent—her perspiration, the way her skin smelled on a hot night. Maybe that's what tripped up my timing.

Whatever it was, Kellin froze. It should've been over when Ralph stepped around, bringing the .357 over his head. Instead, Kellin pushed Lillian into him, then knocked Ralph's arm away. It's hard to send a S & W Magnum flying; it's not exactly a light gun. Nevertheless, it flew.

Lillian said something like "Whoops" as she toppled into Ralph. Only Ralph's sheer terror of falling back into the stairwell kept them both on their feet.

The .357 skittered across the tar and came to a stop somewhere in the shadows off to my left. I stepped out and immediately had to duck Kellin's right cross. So much for the surprise factor.

I didn't think he was carrying, but I couldn't give him time to pull a weapon. Kellin stepped back and I stuck to him like glue. That's the most disconcerting thing about fighting a tai chi opponent: you step back, they step forward; you advance, they retreat; you swing right, they disappear to the left. The whole time they're only a few inches away, but you can't connect a punch. And they touch you almost the whole time—there's a hand on your shoulder, maybe, or fingertips on your chest, feeling exactly where the tension is, where you're going to move next. It's very annoying.

"Motherfucker," Kellin grumbled.

I let him swing at me for a while—missing. We moved across the roof, into the water, back toward the roof house, back into the water. Meanwhile Ralph got Lillian down the stairs—that was all that mattered. And Kellin was losing his cool.

"Get your goddamn hands off me," he yelled.

A left uppercut. I wasn't there. I kept moving with him, waiting for the right opening. It was going fine until I fell for a feint so obvious Sifu Chen would've kicked me out of class for missing it. Kellin was learning his lesson. He jabbed right, got me to turn, then turned with me and embedded his left fist in my kidneys with the force of a twenty-pound champagne cork. With a few seconds preparation, it is possible to compress the chi in your diaphragm and take a hit like that with almost no pain at all—if I'd had a few seconds. Instead I went down, just managing to hook Kellin's leg as he stepped back. He joined me in the dirty rainwater.

We were both flat on our butts for a moment, cursing, but unlike me Kellin wasn't cradling a hot bowling ball in his intestines. By the time I stumbled to my knees he was on his feet and running.

I wiped the roof sludge out of my eyes and looked back at the door to the stairwell. No Kellin. Just an empty doorway. I heard Lillian's giggles echoing from somewhere down below.

Wait a minute. Feet banging on metal.

I turned. Kellin was just reaching the far side of the catwalk. My body was telling me to stay doubled over, to curl up in the rainwater and take a nap. Instead, I forced myself to get up and follow.

I didn't have Ralph's phobia—not until I stepped onto the catwalk and it started bouncing up and down, creaking under my weight. Below there was nothing but five stories of blackness. The smokestack loomed out of the void, white and huge; its diameter was big enough to house a tennis court. Above me it rose another five stories like some massive antiaircraft gun. Kellin was only a few feet up the ladder now. He seemed to be having trouble with his right ankle.

I made it across. The concrete sides of the smoke-stack were surprisingly smooth and cold. The ladder rungs were wet. Kellin was breathing hard above me, still cursing. His hand was about two rungs below the bottom of the door.

I didn't know why he wanted back in that room. I just knew if it was more important to him than fighting over Lillian, I couldn't let him get there.

I got his ankle, the right one, as he was pulling himself into the doorway. He kicked back, reflexively, and I twisted, using his own kick to bend the joint. He screamed. It would've been perfect if I hadn't lost my balance.

For an instant I was hanging on only by my left hand, my feet dangling freely over nothing at all. My other hand let go of Kellin, then grabbed for a rung. I scraped against concrete instead. I felt my fingernails rip.

I was watching the Tower of the Americas tilting sideways in the distance, wondering why it was like that. I wondered if that revolving restaurant at the top of the Tower was still open, the place my dad used to go for his birthdays. I was also thinking what an inane final thought that would be. Then my foot found a rung.

Kellin could've kept me out of the doorway easily if he had been there. He wasn't. When I pulled myself into the tiny cement chamber he was limping off to the left, toward a milk crate full of hanging files that was sitting on the floor next to another metal door. On top of the files was a revolver.

The maintenance area wasn't much more than a hallway. It was only about six feet deep, but lengthwise it curved around with the circumference of the smokestack, ending in a metal door ten feet down on either end. The fuse boxes and metal cables along the inner wall were probably once used to light up the "ALAMO CEMENT" signs on the sides of the stacks. There was also some bedding on the floor, an open wicker picnic basket, some clothes scattered about.

Kellin heard me behind him and turned. His uniform was covered with sludge and white dust from the side of the smokestack. His short-cropped hair looked like a Brillo pad that had just been used. And his face, for once, was anything but impassive. I suddenly realized that he was much older than I'd first thought—closer to fifty than thirty. He was pointing the gun at me now.

You can never be faster than a squeeze of the trigger, no matter how fast you can hit or kick. I knew it, he knew it. I wasn't stupid. I smiled and spread my hands, admitting defeat. He smiled back at me.

Then I kicked the .38 out of his hand.

The shot went past my left ear and tore a chuck of concrete out of the wall. The gun landed in the corner.

For a second Kellin looked amazed at how stupid I had been, right before I pulled him forward and flipped him onto the concrete on his back, hard.

I'll give Kellin credit. He got up.

My right hand was starting to get sticky from the blood. The ruined fingertips throbbed so bad I was afraid to look.

"Is the lady of the house in?" I asked Kellin, who was now backing up to the exit.

He wiped the grime off his forehead with the back of his hand, then glanced over at the gun. He smiled at me.

"No offense, man," he said. "But you don't know shit about what's going on here."

"Fill me in."

He shook his head. "I was there," he said, still smiling almost pleasantly. "With that stupid shit Halcomb we set up for the fall. I was driving. Pretty damn funny watching Randall plow that fat fuck into his front lawn. Your face, man—"

He started laughing. Then he went for me, figuring I was disoriented.

I was. Tai chi would've demanded that I use his own force to send him into the wall behind. I didn't. I pushed back—force against force, a totally incorrect approach. Kellin was obviously appalled. At least he looked that way when he went out the door. His hands kept reaching for something, but there wasn't anything there. There was no sound at all until he reached the bottom and even then nothing much—a faint metallic clap like the echo of a snare drum, nothing nearly as loud as my heartbeats.

I sat down on the blankets. I wrapped my bloody hand inside one of Lillian's old T-shirts. I needed to get out of there. Instead I sat and stared out the door.

I must've gotten up and looked around after a while. I remember looking through a few of the files in the milk crate, learning all about the real owners of Sheff Construction.

All I really needed to do was look in the picnic basket. There were a few slices left, wrapped in a linen napkin and smelling wonderful. Obviously fresh baked today. The lady of the house had not been in. But she'd sent some banana bread.

60

It was a long ride to the West Side in Jess's pickup truck. The engine was bucking resentfully, my hand was bleeding, Ralph was still shaking from acrophobia too badly to drive, and Lillian was sandwiched between us mumbling lines from Dr. Seuss. So far she had not recognized either of us, but she seemed perfectly happy to go for a ride.

After her second complete and flawless recitation of *Green Eggs and Ham,* Ralph and I looked across at each other.

"*Hijo,*" he swore.

"Yeah," I said.

I tried to force my mind not to think about what I'd learned up there in the Alamo Cement smokestacks. It didn't work. By the time we pulled up in front of the Arguello family home off McCullough, I'd put it all together and I was trying like hell to deny that the pieces fit. But they did.

Mama Arguello was quite possibly the shortest, widest person in the world. She was standing in the doorway, the entire doorway, when we drove up. Her faded plaid dress barely managed to contain her awesome cleavage. Her hair was pinned up in a black wedge; her eyes, like Ralph's, were hidden behind thick prescription glasses. The fact that her hands were covered in flour didn't stop her from grabbing Ralph by the cheeks and dragging his face down to kiss hers.

"Ay," she said, "is my boy in one piece? An amazing thing."

Then she came to hug me. Maybe she remembered me from high school. I'm not sure. I think she would've hugged me anyway. Her neck was bristly and smelled like chocolate. Then she hugged Lillian, who giggled.

Mama Arguello looked at Lillian again, more critically this time.

"Ay," she said, "what kind of drugs are these?"

I showed her the family-sized bottle of valium I'd retrieved from the smokestack.

She scowled, gave it back to me, and asked me to read the label. I did. Finally she announced her remedy: "Raspberry leaf tea."

Then she was gone.

Ralph and I got Lillian to lie down on the plastic-covered couch. She was frowning now, yawning, starting to look around in confusion. I decided to take that as a good sign. I sat and spoke to her for a minute while Ralph used the phone. He had some friends who were extremely interested in retrieving his car for him, especially since it was right next to a beautiful red Mustang that just needed some new tire valve stems. Then I used the phone. I called and asked Larry Drapiewski a favor.

When I came back I stroked Lillian's hair until her eyes closed and she started snoring lightly.

"What do you think, *vato*?" Ralph asked.

I looked down at Lillian asleep. With her face relaxed, her reddish-blond hair tousled, and her freckles dark, she looked about sixteen years old. And I should know—I remembered her at sixteen. And twenty. And now—Jesus. Half my life I'd either been in love with her or convincing myself that I wasn't. Which made it strange, now.

I kissed her forehead one more time, then asked Ralph: "Will your mom mind taking care of her for tonight?"

Ralph grinned. "She'll have her up and helping with the cleaning in no time, *vato*. You watch."

"Will you stay with her?"

"You look at yourself in the mirror lately, *vato*?"

"It's easier if I take it alone from here. And I want Lillian to be with somebody she knows if she comes around."

He didn't like it. "Take a piece, at least."

"Not where I'm going, Ralphas."

He shook his head. "Jesus, man, you're a hardheaded *hijo-puta*."

That's when Mama Arguello came back in with the tea and smacked Ralph on the arm for bad language. I tried to leave, but Mama Arguello insisted on bandaging my hand first and cleaning my face with a dish towel. She fed me homemade tortillas until my stomach stopped revolting. By the time I got out of her living room it was almost 10 P.M.

"We'll take care of her for you, Mr. Ralph's Friend," Mama insisted. "You don't worry."

Then she went back inside to force-feed Lillian some raspberry leaf tea. Ralph walked me out to the truck.

"Sorry, Ralphas," I said.

He just shrugged. "Eh, man, just means I got to be here when my stepdad gets home. He comes in drunk, I'll try not to kill him in front of Lillian."

"I'd appreciate that."

"Yeah."

I started the engine, which came out of the stall already bucking mad. Ralph shook his head and grinned.

"Some sorry wheels, man. You even know who you're going to see?"

"Yeah. The ghost of a father."

I looked back in the pickup bed, where a milk crate

full of old files was rattling around. That's when Ralph's stepdad drove up, parking his Chevy half on the curb.

"Yeah, well," said Ralph, looking over. "If it turns out to be mine, let me know. I kind of miss the old man."

Then he turned away and headed up the steps of the front porch. I think he locked the door behind him.

61

I almost decided to scrap my plans when I saw the car in the driveway.

Dan Sheff's silver BMW was parked crooked, pulled so close to the house that its nose was buried in the thick pyracantha bushes. Someone hadn't closed the passenger door hard enough to turn off the dash lights. As I got closer I could hear the BMW complaining about the situation with a muffled "eeeee——"

The house's porch light was off. I tried the black iron handle of the front door and found it securely fastened. At the far end of the house, where the study was, one heavily-curtained window glowed orange around the edges. Otherwise no sign of life.

I took the side path around the house, crouching under hackberry branches and trying not to trip on the uneven flagstones. The poodle in the neighbor's yard yapped at me once without much enthusiasm. I jumped a short chain-link gate, then did a little searching on the back porch. The spare key for the kitchen door was still underneath the plaster St. Francis on the third step where it had been ten years before.

Inside, the kitchen smelled faintly of banana bread and fresh-brewed tea. The microwave door was open, giving off just enough light to make the copper baking molds and the olive-green counter tiles glisten.

I walked down the hallway, turned left into the main bedroom, and found what I was looking for with no trouble at all. The gun was in an unlocked nightstand drawer on the right-hand side of the bed. It was loaded too. No points for safety awareness. I continued down the hall toward the voices that were coming from the study.

Five feet from the lighted doorway, I heard one of the people inside say: "You did the right thing, kid."

The voice belonged to Jay Rivas, my best buddy at the SAPD. That made things just about perfect.

The ripped fingernails on my right hand were starting to throb against the bandages. My stomach ached. When I tried to move closer toward the entrance my feet wouldn't cooperate. I found myself staring at family photos on the hallway wall—daguerreotypes of Victorian ancestors, Easter-egg-colored Sears portraits from the sixties and seventies, a recent panorama from a family reunion. There was a time when I'd imagined my wedding pictures hanging here, maybe even pictures of kids, happily accumulating dust and the odors of Thanksgiving dinners over the years.

Looking at that photo collection now, I felt as if I were holding a hammer to it, about to cause a lot of noise and broken glass that wouldn't make me feel a damn bit better.

When I stepped into the doorway, Zeke Cambridge was the first to notice me. He'd apparently had a hard day at the office. His black suit was rumpled, his collar loosened, and his tie twisted with the tag side out. His unshaven whiskers made a dark gray sheen along his jawline. He'd been pacing in front of the baby grand piano at the far end of the room, and had already been looking at the doorway before I appeared, as if he were anxiously waiting for someone. I was not the person he was expecting.

A few feet closer to me, Mrs. Cambridge and Dan Sheff sat on the couch, consoling one another. Dan had his back to me, but Mrs. Cambridge saw me. Her hands slipped off Dan's knee. She stood up. Her bright yellow sundress and Day-Glo plastic earrings seemed absurdly incongruous with her pinned-up gray hair, her pearl necklace, her white liver-spotted shoulders, and her morose, weary face. She looked like she'd been the victim of a failed makeover attempt by a much younger woman.

Surprisingly, Dan looked better than I'd seen him in days. He was freshly showered and dressed—his blond hair gleaming with gel, his khakis creased, his white Ralph Lauren button-down neatly starched and tucked in. Only his miserable expression hadn't changed.

Jay Rivas stood behind Dan. Rivas looked better than I'd seen him in days too, though for Jay that didn't mean much. He was sporting brown double-knit slacks and his usual silver and turquoise belt buckle and a white polyester shirt so thin that his armpit hair and the lines of his undershirt showed through. The real fashion statement for me, though, was the side-holstered 9mm Parabellum, the same kind of gun that had drilled holes in Eddie Moraga's eyes.

The second disk, the one that had been taken from the Hilton over Beau Karnau's dead body, was sitting casually on top of a *Country Living* magazine on the coffee table, next to an untouched plate of banana bread and a pot of tea. Dan was staring at the CD, but he was so engrossed in his own thoughts I think he would've stared at anything. Nobody else seemed to be paying the disk much attention.

Jay patted Dan Sheff's shoulder roughly and said again: "You did the right thing."

Then Rivas saw me out of the corner of his eye. He registered my face, then the .22 in my unbandaged left hand. His hands stayed where they were, one on Dan's shoulder, one hooked in his belt about an inch away from the handle of the Parabellum

Dan was the last to notice me. When he finally looked up he didn't seem very surprised. He spoke as if we were continuing an old conversation.

"I told them about my mother. They had to know."

The Cambridges both looked at me intently, not saying a word. Even Rivas was silent.

Dan glanced at each of them, frowning when he realized he was no longer the center of attention. Everybody else kept looking at me, at the single-shot Sheridan Knockabout I was holding.

"I'm going to set this right." Sheff tried to put some steel into his voice. "I don't care if it *is* my mother. I—I called Lieutenant Rivas. I've told him everything."

My own voice sounded papery. "Must be a real load off your conscience. I suppose the lieutenant suggested you talk with Lillian's parents. Rivas wanted to be present, of course."

Dan sat up a little straighter. "My mother lied to them about Lillian. She tried to keep the police away. She might have even taken Lillian herself. She lied to me and I can't—I can't just—" He made it that far without taking a breath, saying each sentence with the intense concentration of a toddler trying to stack blocks. Then his composure dissolved. He shut his eyes, his nostrils dilated, and he curled himself inward until his forehead was resting on his knees. He let out a single quivery sound, like he was trying to match his pitch to a tuning fork.

He cried for about a minute. Nobody comforted him. Very slowly, Rivas let his hand slip off of Sheff's shoulder.

"You're breaking and entering, Navarre," Rivas said. It was the most calm, reasonable tone I'd ever heard him take. Somehow that didn't comfort me any. "You're holding a gun in somebody else's house and there's a police officer present. I'd be very careful if I were you. Fact, unless you shoot real well with your left hand, I'd set that gun down on the carpet before I said another word."

"Tres," Angela Cambridge said gently, "if you care for Lillian—"

Zeke Cambridge told his wife to be quiet. The banker's watery eyes were staring intently at my forehead. Maybe he was imagining a bullet hole opening there.

Dan sat up. I could see him slowly stacking those mental blocks again, trying to get control over his face, his emotions, his voice. Finally he wiped his wet cheeks with the base of his palm so forcefully he left scratches from his gold watchband. "Go ahead, Navarre. You're here to get even with me, this is your big chance. Tell them how stupid I was. I thought I could handle Garza, then Karnau—"

"I'm not here to talk about your mistakes, Dan."

"I put Lillian in danger and probably got those other people killed and all the time my mother was—she was telling me—" He faltered, looking at Mr. Cambridge. "At least believe me that I didn't know. If I'd known about her—about her and the mob—"

Mr. Cambridge's cold expression didn't change. "Don't be too hard on yourself, son."

"Absolutely," I said. "Don't be too hard on your mother, either. Her biggest mistake was confiding in the wrong people, Dan. Like you are."

Dan's blond eyebrows knit together. His body was swaying just slightly, counterclockwise, like he was magnetically correcting for true north. "What are you talking about, Navarre? Lillian's parents deserve to know what's going on. It's my responsibility to tell them."

He turned toward Zeke Cambridge for support. Cambridge offered none. Dan looked away, eyes a little hungrier. It reminded me of the time I was eight, watching a javelina die in the woods and wondering if skinning the ugly thing would finally merit a positive response from my dad's impassive face.

"He can't give it to you, Dan."

Dan looked at me, puzzled.

"Approval," I said. "Somebody to pat your head and

give you permission for what you did and tell you how proud they are. Mr. Cambridge can't give you that. Go ahead, Lieutenant, tell Dan he did the right thing a few more times. Call him 'kid.' He needs the safety net."

Rivas's hand stayed relaxed next to the Parabellum. The only sign that Jay was tense was the tendon on the left side of his neck, which pulsed out every few seconds.

Dan was swaying a little more. He brought his hand up to his cheeks, absently, and ran his fingers along the scratches, like he was just realizing they were there.

"How do you know your mother went to the mob?" I asked him. "How do you know that's who she's protecting? Did she tell you that?"

Dan closed his eyes tight. "She didn't need to, did she? After seeing Beau Karnau in the Hilton like that, after what you said—it's obvious."

"You told me what was obvious when we talked at Little Hipp's, Dan. Turned out the obvious was wrong."

Mr. Cambridge was still boring an imaginary hole through the center of my head. Angela Cambridge was crying silently.

I raised the Sheridan Knockabout. "This is the gun that killed Randall Halcomb and Beau Karnau. Single-shot pistol, Dan, out of production since 1962. Not the kind of weapon a serious violent criminal would favor, but it works all right for an old Navy marksman who wants personal protection, or some target practice, or an occasional murder when his back's against the wall." I glanced at Mr. Cambridge, then at Jay Rivas. "You folks jump in anytime you want."

Dan had his hands out, like I was about to rush him. "Wait a minute . . . you can't stand there and tell me . . ."

"I took out the first disk, the one that Maia and I had found in Lillian's statuette. I held it up. "This is half of what you were trying to get from Beau Karnau. The other half is sitting on the Cambridges' coffee table. What does that tell you?"

The muzzle of my borrowed Sheridan swung toward the right, almost by itself. I hadn't seen Rivas move, but somehow he had his 9mm in hand. He was aiming it at my chest.

"It tells me I'm using my good hand, Navarre. And I got eight rounds. How many you got?"

I opened my left hand and let the .22 drop.

For the first time in the fifteen-some-odd years that I'd known him, Zeke Cambridge smiled.

62

"I should've shot you the first time you left my daughter."

Mr. Cambridge sounded apologetic, smiling a sour little smile, like he was regretting a practical joke that went awry fifty years ago. "I wanted to track you down and kill you for breaking her heart, Tres. I should've done it."

"Don't feel too bad," I said. "You had other things to worry about—the S&L crisis, the bad investments Lillian used to blame your foul moods on. Sheff Construction, for instance."

I tried to keep my voice even, unconcerned. I'm not sure I managed it. I had to drop the CD so it wouldn't be quite so obvious how badly my hands were shaking.

Angela Cambridge stepped next to Dan and took his arm.

"Dear, why don't we—" she started to whisper before he pushed her away.

The muscles in Dan's face seemed to be conducting a system-wide test. His cheek twitched slightly, then his jaw, eyebrow, nose. He was staring at me with a look I would've called anger if his eyes hadn't been so empty.

"You can't tell me . . ." he started. He opened his mouth for the next word but it didn't come out.

"You get it, don't you, Dan?" I asked. "About the time your dad was making those hefty college tuition payments to SMU, Sheff Construction was so deep in debt they were on the verge of dragging their main creditor, Crockett S&L, into bankruptcy with them. Until the Cambridges assumed control of the company, that is. Then they turned their liability into a gold mine. With a little help from Fernando Asante at City Hall." I looked at Mrs. Cambridge. "How many millions did Travis Center make for your husband, Angela? How much was he figuring on making this time around, with the fine arts complex?"

She wasn't bothering to wipe away the tears anymore. They made her face looked glazed, like a very old pastry.

"Angie *Gardiner*," I said. "When I saw the picture of you with the fighter pilot, your maiden name didn't mean anything to me. Then I went out to Blanco—the ranch where Randall Halcomb was killed, right next to land owned by the Gardiner family. That's why Lillian and Beau happened to be out there that night. Your husband and Lillian both had the unfortunate idea of using the family land that weekend, for different reasons."

Behind her, Mr. Cambridge was absolutely still. His smile had faded.

For his part, Rivas looked content. He was half standing, half sitting on the backrest of the couch, resting the butt of the 9 mm on his knee. He didn't appear to be in any hurry to shoot me. Probably he didn't get to hold people at gunpoint as often as he'd like.

"Danny Boy," he said pleasantly. "Be a pal and get that disk at Navarre's feet. Leave the gun alone, you hear me?"

Dan didn't seem to. He stayed where he was, staring in my direction with bright, completely unfocused eyes.

"You're lying, Navarre," Dan decided. "You've been angry at the Cambridges for years and now you're trying to blame them for everything that's happened. That's it, isn't it?"

His voice was anything but confident. He looked at the Cambridges for some confirmation—a nod, a smile, a "yes." They didn't give him any. Dan turned to Lieutenant Rivas. "You're going to arrest him or something, aren't you?"

Rivas nodded. "Or something."

Dan's face started doing its muscle tests again. He looked at me uneasily.

"My father made a big mistake, Dan," I told him. "Ten years ago he let your mother know what he'd found out about the Travis Center scam. Maybe when you're old enough—forty-five or so—these folks will tell you how my dad stumbled across the information in your mother's bedroom. When Cookie found out, she ran straight to your father, who was still healthy enough to recognize the danger, and he ran straight to his new bosses." I looked at Zeke Cambridge. "Whose idea was it to use Halcomb for the killing—yours or Asante's?"

For a moment Zeke Cambridge's eyes darkened, taking on a little of the old ferocity that had frightened me as a teenager. "You think you really knew your father, boy? He ruined people's marriages, their careers, his own damn family. You think he's worth defending?"

"No," I said. "He probably isn't. Fortunately, this isn't about knowing my father. It's about people telling me for ten years that I couldn't do anything about his murder, and me knowing it wasn't true. Sooner or later I had to come back and try. Whether or not my dad was worth the effort isn't really important. Maybe instead we should talk about how you shot Randall Halcomb while Fernando Asante looked on, how your daughter happened to be watching from the hilltop nearby, how she's lived with that knowledge for ten years, hiding it from you and everyone else because she couldn't turn in her own father. You think *you* were worth defending?"

"That's enough." Mr. Cambridge tried to put the old tone of command back into his voice. It failed him.

I looked at Dan. "I suppose you get to a point where you can't do anything more about a problem, Sheff, and then you just have to acknowledge the brick wall in front of you and let it go. Maybe you're at that point. You keep thinking you can set things right with your family; you keep screwing up. Maybe you just need to admit that the situation is out of the scope of things you can fix. If that's where you are, I feel sorry for you, because either you won't live long or you're going to live exactly the way these people want you to."

Mrs. Cambridge looked like she wanted to hug me. Her eyes had gotten paler as she cried, like all the green was being washed out. "You don't understand, Tres. Zeke didn't intend—he was trying to save his own family, dear. He never thought—"

"Shut up," Mr. Cambridge said.

Rivas cleared his throat. "I'm still waiting for that disk, Danny."

Dan lifted his hands, moving them in front of him uncertainly as if he were trying to remember just how big a fish he'd caught. He looked bewildered.

"I won't believe any of this," he told me.

"Sure you will," I said. "You believe it already. You're remembering how violently Lillian reacted when you told her about the blackmail, and you suspect it wasn't just the shock of finding out you had a dirty family secret. It was *her* secret, Dan, and you let her know it was blowing up in her face after all these years. No wonder she wasn't happy with you—she probably thought those photos had been destroyed. Beau would've promised her that. He would've agreed to keep the secret, even to get rid of the negatives of Halcomb's murder, only he couldn't make himself do it."

"Karnau was scum," Mr. Cambridge said almost to himself.

I shook my head. "Scum would've cashed in on those photos immediately, knowing what they were worth. Beau cared enough about Lillian not to use them for a long time, until year after year he got more obscure in the art world, more dependent on Lillian's social connections and money for any kind of exposure at all, while Lillian grew less and less enamored with him. That can make a guy like Beau bitter. Then last year Lillian told him she wanted to move on. Beau got violent. It got so bad Lillian asked for a restraining order against him. Eventually they reconciled, for a while, but Beau had already started taking his revenge. He'd started sending you and Asante copies of the old prints, demanding payments. You both must've had coronaries when you opened up that first blackmail letter, especially since you'd just started planning your encore performance—the fine arts complex."

Dan turned toward Mr. Cambridge, imploring him one more time for an alternative answer.

Mr. Cambridge tried to soften his expression, but it didn't come easy for him. "You'll have your company back, son. Don't you see that? You can marry Lillian, bring the families together. We're doing this for both of you, to protect your future."

"Protect my future," Dan repeated. His voice cracked when he laughed.

"Everything prearranged," I said. "You get to carry on the traditional family scam and if Lillian doesn't cooperate maybe they'll let you keep her doped up, locked in a room somewhere so she doesn't cause you any social embarrassment. How's that sound, Dan?"

Rivas raised his 9mm Parabellum. He seemed to be picking just the right spot on my face. "Enough. Danny Boy, get the fucking disk."

"No, Daniel," said Zeke Cambridge. "Leave the room now. Let us handle this."

Dan still didn't move. He was looking at me, working something out in the back of his mind. "What do you mean about Lillian?"

"They had to hide her away," I said. "The Cambridges had to protect her after she'd screwed things up between them and Asante. What was your deal with Karnau, Zeke—a year of payments maybe? Then Beau gives you and Asante each a disk. Beau gets out of town a wealthy man, and with the photos scrambled neither you nor Asante could double-cross the other. Is that it? Only Dan found out, and once Lillian learned about the blackmail from him, she had to do something. She had no one to turn to—not Karnau, not her parents, not the Sheffs. The only thing she could think of was to bring in someone who had just as much of a stake in setting things right as she did—me."

The veins on Zeke Cambridge's nose were turning scarlet. "My baby girl has nothing to do with this."

He said it to me but he was looking at Rivas.

"Sure," I said. "Keep saying that and maybe the lieutenant will start believing it. Lillian *did* make it to dinner last Sunday night, didn't she? She'd just given me the disk she'd discovered, just gotten up the courage to break off from the gallery again, and Sunday night she must've confronted you—told you what she'd seen ten years ago, probably told you she was going to do something rash, like go public. That's when you knew you had to put her away for a while. Asante wouldn't be so understanding with her. He might send Rivas to make sure that Lillian kept quiet for good."

"Tres," said Mrs. Cambridge, still crying, "Lillian loved you so much . . . she wanted a second chance with you. Don't—"

"She was very alone," I corrected. "She needed someone to solve the problem for her."

"And you did a hell of a job," said Rivas. "Now, Danny Boy, at the count of five I want that disk. You can bring me the one on the coffee table, while you're at it."

Zeke Cambridge's eyes, which had been getting watery, now turned hard as sapphires as they focused on Rivas. Cambridge took one step toward the couch. "Wait just a damn minute."

Rivas trained the 9mm on the older man. "Wait for what, Mr. C.? What are you going to tell me that's going to make this better? We kept our part of the bargain. We paid good money for that little statue, then Karnau tells us Little Miss Cambridge swiped it. He tells us she's going to spill what she knows about Travis Center, pin it all on your partners to get you off the hook. And we say: 'No way, not good old Zeke Cambridge. Old Zeke's too smart for that.' Only then we find out you've taken your precious daughter out of commission, got your people searching for both disks like you're getting greedy on us. That's a real pisser."

"Which is why you killed Moraga and Garza," I said.

Rivas flicked ashes onto the couch. "I'm counting to one, Danny Boy."

Dan suddenly became very calm, very composed. The change made me uneasy. His face closed up with a kind of frozen dignity that reminded me uncomfortably of his mother. He took the disk off the coffee table, then started walking toward me.

"We had an arrangement that is still valid," Zeke Cambridge insisted. "Daniel is no part of this, nor is Lillian. You can't ignore ten years of solid profits just because—you can't seriously think—"

Rivas shrugged. "There are other construction firms ready to make those kind of profits, Mr. C. Maybe you get whacked, it goes down as another mob killing, Mr. Asante gets a law-and-order speech ready to go in the morning. He can ride this one all the way to the mayor's office. I'm counting two, Danny Boy."

Dan knelt down in front of me and got the other disk. He kept his hands in plain sight, well away from the Sheridan Knockabout. When he stood up, though, I saw in his eyes what was coming. I tried my best to tell him "no" just by the way I looked back at him, but he'd already turned away.

I said: "You don't get Lillian, Jay. You don't get any assurance that the disk I brought tonight is real. You kill me, you're leaving loose ends."

Jay grinned underneath the mustache. He pointed the gun at me.

"It's worth it, Navarre. Loose ends we can handle later."

"I should also mention—some friends of mine from the Sheriff's Department are on their way here."

"Then we'll just have to make it a quick good-bye."

Dan was back where he'd started, standing next to Rivas with the couch between them. Dan dropped the two CDs on the cushions.

"Good boy," Rivas said. He still had the gun trained on me. He didn't notice Dan's face, the tension in Dan's shoulders.

I wanted to yell *no* but it wouldn't have helped.

"What now?" I asked Rivas, trying to keep his eyes on me. "Asante finally gets you that promotion to captain?"

Jay looked like the idea pleased him.

Whatever he was going to say next, it never got said because Dan grabbed his gun. It was an extremely stupid move, done exactly wrong. Dan seized the 9mm by the barrel and made the mistake of pulling it down, toward his own body. I don't remember actually seeing the force of the discharge take off the edge of Dan's right hand, or the bullet ripping an exit wound out the back of his thigh. I just remember the new red spray pattern that appeared like magic on the flowery pillows of the couch and on Mrs. Cambridge's yellow dress, and the way the back of Dan's khakis were suddenly dark and slick as he charged headlong over the sofa into Rivas. The Parabellum went off again but by then I was already in motion.

Nothing else is very clear, looking back on it. I remember a sound like a watermelon rind snapping when I brought the butt of the old .22 down on Rivas's head. I remember a lot of blood seeping between my fingers as I tried to keep pressure on the large hole in Dan's leg, yelling at him to keep still as he writhed around on the carpet, clamping what was left of his right hand between his legs. I vaguely recall the sirens and the paramedics coming in to relieve me, and later as I crouched in the corner, I remember Deputy Larry Drapiewski calling my name and gently taking away the Sheridan Knockabout that I was cradling against my cheek.

63

I woke up with Larry Drapiewski waving a cup of coffee under my nose.

It took a year or two for me to remember where I was.

I was in my underwear, on a cot on a screened-in porch. The breeze from the ceiling fan above me was chilly on my bare skin, but the August sunlight was pouring in hot and low from the west, and the noisy refrigerator I'd been dreaming about was actually cicadas, humming by the thousands in the huisache trees outside. There was a grass fire burning somewhere. A brown and white heifer lay in the mottled shadow of a cactus patch twenty feet away, watching me. I was at the ranch in Sabinal. It must've been about three in the afternoon.

I felt dizzy as hell when I tried to move. With some difficulty, I lifted my head and saw my brother Garrett in his wheelchair at the foot of the cot. Or rather I saw Garrett and Jerry Garcia and Jimi Hendrix all blurred together. Until my vision cleared the two airbrushed faces on Garrett's T-shirt floated around with Garrett's own like some tie-dyed Holy Trinity.

"Come on, little bro," Garrett said impatiently, "we're waiting to flush the toilet."

I squinted and swallowed a taste like dead frogs out of my mouth. "What?"

"We haven't been flushing all day, man, so you'd have enough water pressure from the tank to take a nice hot shower when you woke up."

Larry handed me the coffee. The bags under his eyes and his uncombed hair told me Larry hadn't gotten much sleep last night, though he'd changed his deputy's uniform for jeans and a denim shirt. "You've been out for thirteen hours, son. We were starting to get worried."

It was another hour before I could stand up steady enough to take that shower. There was an overnight duffel in the bathroom that I'd apparently packed for myself the night before, though I remembered nothing about going by Queen Anne Street. Inside I found some reasonably clean blue jeans, my City Lights T-shirt, my toothbrush, and my father's old notebook. Some letters spilled out when I picked the duffel up. I put them carefully back inside.

Once I was dressed, Garrett and Larry gave me the courtesy of some time to myself. I rummaged around the kitchen for some potential breakfast. The candidates were two bottles of whiskey, one egg that had crystallized into a geode, a tangerine of unknown age, a jar of Sanka, and a variety pack of lunch-bag-sized snack chips. I wondered if whiskey poured over Fritos would make an acceptable breakfast cereal. I decided to opt for the tangerine instead.

While I ate the tangerine and drank instant coffee, Larry and Garrett sat in the living room with Harold Diliberto, our trusty overseer, and discussed the pros and cons of legalizing marijuana. Garrett was predictably in favor, Larry was predictably against. Harold seemed to think the whole issue was those damn Californians' fault and both Garrett and Larry seemed comfortable with that.

I must've been washing my hands in the stainless-steel sink for a good three minutes before I realized what I was doing. I kept separating my fingers in the water, watching it flow through, thinking about the sticky consistency of Dan Sheff's blood.

Finally Larry called from the living room: "You okay, Tres?"

I told him I was. Then I shut off the faucet and looked for dish towels. There were none.

When I joined Larry on the leather couch, he was pouring whiskey into four glass tumblers that all said JACK. Garrett was smoking a joint and looking out the screen door at the fading afternoon. I asked Harold if he'd get some wood for the fireplace.

Larry and Garrett looked at me strangely, but they didn't say anything. Harold went out to the wood pile.

By the time Harold had stacked the wood and started the fire with one of our Bics from the bucket-o-lighters, I was on my second glass of Jim Beam and the shivery feeling in my gut had just about faded. The fire burned it away completely. The mesquite wood, left over from last winter, was so dry after three months of summer that it ignited instantly and burned like a forge. The room got uncomfortably warm, until my fingertips felt almost alive again. I didn't even mind the smoke rolling out the front of the mantle from the poorly working flue. Harold excused himself to go work on the water pump outside. Sweat started beading on Larry's forehead, but he didn't complain. Garrett wheeled himself a little further away and sat watching the flames.

After finishing my second drink, I got up, went to the bathroom for my duffel bag, and came back out with my father's notebook. I removed the letters and set them aside. Then I squatted down and propped Dad's notebook against one of the burning logs.

Nobody protested. The smoke rolled through the pages of the binder, sucked inside by the cooler air. One canvas corner caught fire. Then the outside cover fell open, letting one page burn at a time, each blackening at the edges and curling inward to reveal the next.

Dad's handwriting looked lively in the red light. The pictures he'd drawn of Korean planes and tanks for my bedtime stories seemed to jump right off the page. After a while the binder was reduced to a mass of black cotton candy at the edge of the fire.

When I turned, Garrett saw my eyes watering.

"Smoky?"

I nodded.

Garrett squinted, then blew pot smoke toward the ceiling. He kept looking up at the cedar rafters. "Yeah. Me too."

Larry poured us all some more whiskey. "I suppose that notebook might've been potential evidence."

"I doubt it," I said. "But maybe."

Larry grunted. "I suppose after what I helped you do last night, I shouldn't complain."

I had to think for a moment. Then fuzzy snapshots started coming into my head—Drapiewski getting me away from the investigation early, the two of us taking a long drive into Olmos Park, me having a conversation with someone on Crescent Drive, making a deal. I reached for my wallet, opened it, and found the hand-written piece of paper still inside. I put it back.

Larry propped his boots up on the coffee table. He stared at the fire, then started laughing easily, as if he were remembering all the clean jokes he'd heard that week.

"Last time I was out here with your daddy, boys, Good Lord it must've been '82 . . ." He proceeded to tell us about the big tornado that had ripped through Sabinal that year and how Dad had invited Larry out to help inspect the damage. The ranch house had been spared, but my father and Larry had spent the afternoon trying to extract a dead cow from the top of a mesquite tree with a chain saw. Larry thought it was so funny I couldn't help but laugh along, although last time I'd heard the story it'd been a horse in the tree, and a hurricane instead of a tornado that had done the damage.

Finally Larry raised his glass. "To Jack Navarre. He was a lovable bastard."

"He was a bastard," Garrett amended. But he raised his glass too.

"To Dad."

I drank my drink, then took the stack of letters off the mantel and held up the one on top—a pink envelope that had faded to brown. I set it in the fire and watched the old love letter flutter restlessly while it burned. It was gone in no time.

Larry nodded as if he were agreeing with something I'd said. "I didn't see that. That was most definitely an evidential document and I didn't see you burning it."

"We both know this isn't going to get resolved in the courts," I said. "It couldn't be. Rivas will be sacrificed for the new murders. The people who count will hire the expensive lawyers. Their defense will have a field day with the lack of clean evidence."

"Huh. Whose fault is that, son?" But he couldn't seem to muster up much annoyance. The deal we'd made last night still didn't sit right with him, but I suspected he knew it was the closest we'd get to justice.

In the firelight Larry's red freckles were invisible, perfectly camouflaged so his face looked clearer and whiter and more open than I'd ever seen. He looked nineteen years old. I suppose some people are naturally born to be thirty; it's the ideal age for their temperament. Other people are born to be twelve, or sixty. For Larry, nineteen seemed just about right.

"Your dad was a good man," he said. Then he added grudgingly: "You did right by him, Tres."

"Good man, huh?" Garrett wondered. He looked at me apprehensively. "I don't suppose you found out."

I knew what he meant. Would Dad have covered up the Travis Center deal? If Cookie Sheff had agreed to run away with him like he asked, would he really have turned a blind eye to that much graft?

"No," I said. "Meaning no, I didn't find out. There's no way I could. You'll just have to credit Dad with as much virtue as you can, then predict how he would've acted."

Garrett scratched his beard. "That's what I was afraid of."

I stood in front of the fireplace for a while, looking at the remaining letters in my hand. There were eleven envelopes of blue marbleized paper, the first postmarked in May and the most recent two weeks ago. All of them were addressed to my old Potrero Hill apartment. All were written in that familiar, rounded, backward-slanting cursive I'd loved since junior high.

I kept looking at the letters and feeling the whiskey knit itself into my joints. I was thinking about my dad stashing things in a mantelpiece hole because he couldn't quite make himself get rid of them. I was thinking about him chasing kiddie train bandits with a shotgun and chainsawing cows out of trees and telling stupid jokes with Carl Kelley. It took me a while to realize that the memories, for the first time, weren't all overlaid with the image of him sprawled on the sidewalk in front of his house, that old gray Pontiac pulling silently away. I liked the way that felt.

I reached down and stuck Lillian's letters carefully between two burning logs, so they wouldn't fall out. When Harold Diliberto came back inside, I told him he could cement up that hole in the fireplace whenever he got the chance.

64

For once, Garrett seemed in no mood to speed. We started following Larry's red Jeep back toward town, but quickly lost sight of the deputy's taillights when he turned onto Highway 90. The Carmen Miranda drove on leisurely while a brilliant Texas sunset flared up over the edge of the plains.

When Garrett dropped me back at Queen Anne Street, I found a courtesy copy of today's *Express-News* on the doorstep. I took it inside and tried to read the front page while Robert Johnson, after one unenthusiastic "roww" of greeting, began practicing his "slide-into-home-plate" routine with the other sections, seeing how many square feet of the living-room carpet he could effectively cover with paper.

"Don't you have anything better to do?" I asked.

He looked up, wide-eyed, like he was shocked by the very idea.

The *Express-News* said that Dan Sheff, Jr., heir to Sheff Construction, had apparently uncovered a scheme by his own family and their associates to defraud the

city of millions in bond monies for the proposed fine
arts complex. Dan Jr. had, in the process of heroically
confronting the alleged conspirators, been shot once. A
policeman was involved in the incident, name not yet
released, and there was some indication that the construction scam might extend back as far as ten years.
The mayor was already being hounded for an extensive
investigation to ferret out any wrongdoing on the part
of local officials. I was mentioned briefly as being at the
scene of the shooting. The article said Dan was
presently in critical but stable condition at the Brooke
Army Medical Center, where he was receiving flowers
and praise from a number of well-wishers. The location
of Lillian Cambridge, who had been missing for several
days and whose parents were implicated in the scheme
to defraud the city, was still unknown.

I threw section A to Robert Johnson. He used it for a
triple play.

When I pulled down the ironing board and checked
my answering machine I found about half an hour of
messages. Bob Langston, Number 90's former tenant,
claimed he now had enough pinhead friends together to
effectively kick my ass. Carlon McAffrey warned me I'd
better get him that exclusive interview with Dan Sheff
soon in case Dan decided to die. Carolaine Smith, the
TV news lady I'd knocked into the river, said KSAT
was willing to forgive the whole incident in exchange
for an interview with Dan Sheff, if I could arrange it.
Detective Schaeffer from the SAPD had left several messages—wondering where the hell I'd disappeared to last
night, letting me know that the Cambridges had signed
a testimony about some disks that had turned up
missing at the scene. Schaeffer wanted to know if I had
any ideas about the disks or if he just needed to arrest
me. One message from my mother, pleading for me to
come over to dinner and please bring Jess's truck back
with me. One from Ralph that simply said: "She's fine.
Que padre, vato."

The only person I called was Maia Lee.

It was six o'clock San Francisco time. Maia was just

about to go to dinner. At least that's what the man who answered her home phone said.

"You want me to get her?" he said.

"Just tell her Tex called. She asked me to let her know when it was over."

The guy made a small grunt, like he was leaning over to tie his shoe, or maybe finish straightening his tie.

"*What's* over?" he asked.

I hung up.

The sunset was almost gone when I drove into Monte Vista, to an address I knew only by reputation.

It was a gray adobe house, three stories high, with two Cadillacs in the drive and a huge live oak in the front yard sporting a homemade plywood treehouse. A little Hispanic boy was grinning down at me from the top, pretending to hide. He had his father's smile. I pretended to shoot him as I walked by underneath. He giggled hysterically. When I got to the door I could smell homemade tamales cooking inside.

When Fernando Asante came to the door, dressed in his jeans and a Cowboys jersey, I said: "Is there a place we can talk?"

His other child, a little girl, came up and hugged his thigh. Asante glanced at me, then motioned me inside.

"What is it, Jack?" he said after we were seated in his office.

Asante was a football fan—even the light on his desk was a Cowboys helmet, the kind of thing a kid might keep in his room. The room was cozy, a little messy. It wasn't what I'd expected.

Asante looked almost sleepy now, no trace of the politician's smile.

"I don't like loose ends," I told him.

He laughed, shook his head. "After the last two weeks, after the last ten years, you say this, son."

I took out a piece of paper I'd received last night when I'd conducted some business in Olmos Park. I held it up.

Asante looked unimpressed. "What is it now? More old notes from your father's grave?"

He tossed me the front page of the morning paper.

"Already seen it," I said.

Asante smiled. Asante could afford to smile—there was as yet no mention of him.

"Here's what I think, Councilman. I think you're going to weather the storm."

Asante's eyes were like black marbles. He might've been blind for all I could read in them.

"I think you can pull in enough favors and manipulate the investigation enough to get yourself off the hook. I helped out by tampering with most of the evidence myself—your lawyers will have a great time with that. Unless those CDs show up, and you know they haven't yet, there isn't enough legally obtained direct evidence to implicate you in anything. The Sheffs and the Cambridges may or may not go down for defrauding the city, they'll try to take you with them, but I'm betting you'll survive. Unless those CDs show up."

"Let it rest," Asante told me. "You're going nowhere with this, son. If you had any such evidence, you'd've brought it to your own friends in the police department by now. Then we'd just have to let justice prevail in the courts, wouldn't we, Jack?"

I shrugged. "Maybe."

Asante looked at the piece of paper I was tapping on the table. His smugness wavered, just for a moment.

"And what have you got there, son?"

There was a knock on the door. Asante's son scampered into the room, around the desk, and into his daddy's lap. Suddenly shy, the boy hid his head in his hands. Then he whispered something in his daddy's ear, got a kiss, and ran off.

Asante's face softened as he watched the boy leave. Then he looked at me again, his eyes hard.

"My dinner is ready," he said.

I nodded. "Then I'll be brief. I couldn't sit around waiting for you to come claim the disks from me, Mr. Asante. Eventually you would try. Even if I destroyed them—you'd never be sure. For your own peace of mind, you'd come looking. I could've turned them over to the police, but I somehow don't trust the police or the courts with this one. They never did much good with my father's murder the first time around, did they? That's why I decided to make a deal."

I unfolded the piece of paper. I slid it across the desktop to him.

Asante looked at the signature, frowned, then tossed it back on the desk. He didn't get it.

"And this is?" he asked.

"A receipt for my disks. Guy White always writes receipts. It's one of the few ways he's decent."

Asante stared at me for a minute, still not comprehending.

"White's been pretty mad at you for ten years," I explained. "Sending all that heat his way about my father's murder, then trying to do it again with Garza and Moraga. So we made a deal. Mr. White and I have just bought controlling interest in Fernando Asante."

As it started to sink in, Asante's face went pale. That was all I wanted to see. I stood up to leave.

"I don't know what Guy White's demands will be to keep these disks from going into circulation, Councilman, but here's mine, for now anyway. Tomorrow morning you call a press conference and renounce any plans to run for mayor. You're going to tell them you're happy right where you are—a frustrated little man in a little job. I'm not sure what else you're going to do yet, but you'll hear from me. You can plan on that for the rest of your life."

"Tres—"

Asante spoke my name as if he were just now realizing which Navarre I was. I liked the way he said it.

"Enjoy your dinner," I said.

I left him staring at his Cowboys helmet desk lamp, with his children screaming for him to come to the table. His wife, a pleasant-looking fat woman, smiled at me on my way out. The table was set, and the kids were jumping up and down in their seats, anxious to say grace. I'd never smelled better homemade tamales in all my life.

65

"Do I look all right?" Lillian asked.

We both knew the answer to that was "yes," but I confirmed it for her anyway.

We'd just made it past the security guard and the journalists in the lobby and were now in the Northeast Baptist elevator, going up. Lillian and I were both wearing black for what lay ahead this afternoon, so I was grateful to be out of the noonday sun for a while. Even after several minutes in the hospital's industrial-strength air-conditioning, the inside of my linen jacket felt like the liner for a bag of microwave popcorn.

I made a conscious effort not to imagine what the inside of Lillian's clothes felt like. She was wearing a black sheath, Jackie O. style, with no stockings and black sling-back leather pumps. Her coppery hair was pulled back with a wide black grosgrain ribbon. Around the scoop neckline of her dress she wore her mother's pearl necklace, the one Angela Cambridge had worn the night Dan got shot. The last was a fashion choice I could've lived without.

After a week of recuperation, Lillian's color was healthy again. The summer tan showed off the freckles on her shoulders, chest, and face. Her bare legs looked just fine.

It was hard to pinpoint exactly how I could tell, just from looking at her, that she'd spent the last week crying, some of it yelling and breaking things, but I could. Her eyes weren't red, nothing about her looked shaken or distraught, yet there was a kind of post-flood quality to her. Her features looked harder, weathered, as if her face had been scoured of everything that wasn't absolutely essential.

The elevator door slid open on the second floor. We followed signs to the orthopedics wing, down a fluorescent-lit corridor that was an obstacle course of wheelchairs and food carts. Toward the end of the hall, one of the private rooms had a security guard in front of it.

As we headed that way, Lillian took my hand and squeezed it. "Thank you for coming with me."

I squeezed hers back, then released it. "You'll do your part of the deal later."

Lillian managed a smile. "It's funny. *Dan's* the one I'm nervous about seeing. You'd think . . ."

She let the thought go.

The security guard let us through with no problem. Inside, Dan Sheff was lying in bed in the middle of what seemed like a commercial for springtime. The drapes had been pulled back, so the white walls and newly mopped tile floor glowed with huge squares of yellow Texas sunshine. Multicolored flower arrangements exploded all over the windowsill. Dan's built-in bedside radio was playing Vivaldi or Mozart or something equally peppy—it wasn't Lightin' Hopkins, that's all I knew. The usual hospital odors were overpowered by warm flowers and Polo cologne. Everything about Dan's bed was white and crisp—his pajamas, his neatly turned down sheets, the thick gauze bandages that encased his right hand and leg. Even his IV looked like it had been recently polished.

Dan didn't look quite so good as his room. His complexion was pasty, the lines around his eyes tightly drawn from days of lying around in pain. His hair was all canary-wings. The way he focused on us, slowly and with great effort, made me suspect he was on some pretty serious medication.

His smile seemed genuinely friendly, though. "Hello, Lillian, Tres. Come to see my Purple Heart?"

He wasn't kidding. Somebody had brought him an old Purple Heart medal in a little display case and set it on his nightstand, next to a vase of daisies.

I came up to the side of the bed and shook Dan's good hand. Lillian came around on the other side. I looked at the war medal.

"Your dad's?"

Dan smiled sleepily. "Mother had one of my cousins bring it to me. I guess it was her idea of a reminder— where I come from, where my loyalties are."

"Or it could be a peace offering," I suggested.

Momentarily, anxiety and anger tightened up his face, making him look once again like the Dan Sheff I knew. Then the tension unraveled. Maybe it was the drugs that kept Dan so content. If so, maybe he'd agree to lend me some for the rest of today.

"A peace offering." He sounded dryly amused. "Fat chance."

Dan started telling us about his condition. He didn't sound bitter. He talked about the surgeons at BAMC removing the destroyed bones in his hand, closing the hole in his leg, telling him he was very lucky considering the amount of blood he'd lost. The Sheff family doctor had then arranged a transfer to Northeast Baptist for recuperation and daily antibiotic cocktails. Dan was due for reconstructive surgery in a week, then a transfer to Warm Springs Rehab for several more weeks of rehabilitation, learning to walk with crutches and to use a right hand that would only have two fingers. About halfway through his story, Dan reached over and pressed the little button that self-administered his morphine.

While Lillian listened, her face readjusted itself several

times. She had the alert, almost alarmed expression, the flickering eyes of a professional juggler who was being thrown a new knife every fifteen seconds. All her effort went into not losing control, keeping everything just barely balanced.

"I don't know where to start with the apologies," she said finally.

Dan shook his head. "Maybe I should start. I should tell you—the D.A. visited me this morning. I plan on cooperating."

Lillian's expression stayed tightly controlled while she readjusted her interior rhythm to that new knife in the air. "That's all right."

"I have to try to salvage something of the company," Dan explained. "If I can do that by striking a deal—"

"It's really all right, Dan."

Lillian said it with conviction, like she was almost glad. She'd spoken with equal conviction this morning when she'd told me she wouldn't press her own charges for the abduction, wouldn't volunteer any information for the case against her parents. She had even helped her mother find a good lawyer.

Dan was probably wondering the same thing I was. Lillian looked at both of us briefly, seemed to hear the questions we weren't asking, then tightened her lips into a perfectly straight line. When she spoke she addressed Dan's IV bottle.

"I've had ten years," she said. "The first two or three of those, I almost tore myself apart with mood swings, private screaming fits—I didn't know whether to be resentful that my parents had put me in this position, or angry that they weren't the good people I'd thought, or guilty because I still loved them, or scared because my father was a monster. Beau—" She stopped, took a few heartbeats to regain her balance. "Beau actually helped me with that a lot. After a few more years I learned to build partitions. To stay sane I had to learn how to love my parents and resent them at the same time." She looked at me, reticently. "Do you understand that, Tres? I've been defending and prosecuting them simultaneously in my head for years. It's stopped being a contradiction for me. I know they're guilty; I'm glad they'll be tried for what they did. But it's a relief to be able to give up that side to someone else. Now I can just be the defense, just concentrate on the side of me that forgave them a long time ago."

Dan's eyes were drooping. The morphine had kicked in.

"I can't even think about forgiveness." His tone was oddly pleasant, like the Vivaldi soundtrack that was still playing merrily along in the background.

"You'll be testifying against your mother as much as the Cambridges," I said. "Have you told her?"

"I won't see her," he said. "I know I can stand up to her now. It's just . . ."

"You're not sure you want to test it, yet."

Dan looked uneasy. "I've had the same relationship with my mother for twenty-eight years, Tres. It's going to be hard not to fall into an old pattern. If that happened . . . I think part of me would feel like this was for nothing." He looked down at his bandaged hand affectionately, like it was a pet curled up at his side. "It's funny. I should've gotten myself shot a long time ago."

Dan smiled. He'd spoken with a kind of brave, self-deprecating humor, but there were undercurrents in his tone that I'm not even sure Dan was aware of—fear, bitterness, uncertainty, loathing. I knew it was only a matter of time before those things became more than just undercurrents.

"We should probably let you get some sleep," I said.

Dan nodded. "All right."

Lillian put her hand on Dan's shoulder. She hesitated, then leaned down to kiss his forehead. She straightened up again so quickly her pearl necklace almost hooked itself on Dan's chin.

"I'm sorry, Dan," she said. "I'm sorry that you got involved the way you did. Until you told me about the pictures being sent to your family, I didn't know. I didn't see the connection, why our parents were so insistent on us dating. I blew up at you."

Dan had closed his eyes as if he were trying to identify a particular instrument in the classical music playing. It apparently wasn't an unpleasant task, but it did take his full attention.

"Nothing to apologize for," he said.

Lillian pushed a stray lock of coppery hair behind her ear. Her fingernails were painted red. I tried to think whether I'd ever seen her fingernails painted before.

"Your mother must've been pushing you toward marriage as hard as my parents were pushing me," Lillian said, almost hopefully.

"That's true." The way Dan said it, he knew it wasn't true and so did I. If Lillian believed it, it was only because she was trying so hard.

"Get better," she said.

Dan nodded. "Do you mind going ahead? I'd like to say something to Tres."

I thought about the first time Dan and I had tried to say something to each other without Lillian, on the front of her lawn. Lillian's reaction this time was perhaps not as angry, but every bit as uneasy.

"Of course," she said, then to me: "Meet you at the elevator."

She turned and walked away as if she were conscious that our eyes might be on her. They were.

When she was gone, Dan sighed and let his head sink into his pillow. His hair made a spiky blond aura against the white linen.

"I wanted to ask about that night," he said. "What you told me about coming up against a brick wall."

"Yes."

Dan looked half-asleep, like one more bedtime story would do it.

"I felt that," he said. "I knew there was nothing I could do, but I did something anyway."

"You almost died because of it."

"I know." He sounded content. "That's not my question. I just wanted to know: Would you be able to do it?"

"Do what?"

"Realize when you've hit a brick wall."

"I think so."

"Would you be able to let go of it, like you said, and walk away?"

"Probably not."

He laughed with his eyes closed. "I think I'd rather get shot."

When he was asleep, he looked content, but his mouth kept moving, changing expressions, knitting and unknitting the frown that used to be the main feature of his face.

66

If funerals came in sizes, retired Chief Deputy Carl Kelley's was extra small. It was me, Lillian, the priest, Larry Drapiewski, and Carl. No son from Austin. No other friends except those Carl was about to be buried next to. The only thing Carl left behind him was the brooch he'd given me just before he died, three nights ago in the Nix, with directions to give it to his son. I planned on keeping that promise. If I ever found the bastard, I planned on giving him a lot more than just the brooch.

After Drapiewski's red Jeep drove off, taking the priest back to his church, there was nothing stirring in the cemetery except the cicadas. They droned so persistently I started to doubt my own sanity at those moments when they suddenly stopped.

Lillian and I sat in a little gazebo outside the Sunset Mausoleum. It was a hundred degrees in the shade, a hundred and ten inside my black suit.

It was my turn to say: "Thank you for coming with me."

Lillian had her hands folded in her lap and her legs extended, crossed at the ankles. She looked distracted, like she was trying to read a tombstone several acres away.

"Really," I told her. "If you hadn't been here we wouldn't've had a quorum. Carl wouldn't have been legally able to die."

Lillian looked at me, still following her own line of thought. "I wonder if it's true, that we all turn into our parents as we get older."

"Thanks," I said. "That cheers me right up."

"I'm serious, Tres. It bothers me. It's one of the reasons I haven't been able to apologize to you yet."

"What do you mean?"

She ran her thumb inside the arm opening of her black sheath dress. Even with her base tan, it looked like Lillian's shoulders were reddening from being outside so long.

"I mean the way my father scares me . . . the amount of violence he's capable of. Sometimes what really scares me is I see that in myself."

"You're not going to kill anyone, Lillian."

"No. No, that's not what I mean."

When she exhaled she shuddered. I hadn't realized how close she was to crying. She managed to contain it, just barely.

"I need to tell you," she said, with difficulty. "I need to tell you that part of me was glad you were hurting all those years. By the time I realized who my father had killed, how it related to your father's murder—by that time you had left me, Tres. And in a way, it made me feel better, knowing that I was hurting you by not telling. I know that's horrible—it scares me, that I could feel that way."

That was my cue to tell her it was okay. Foolishly, I found myself staring at Lillian's legs instead, studying the way the black leather straps of her pumps cut just slightly into her calves.

Lillian sighed again; this one was a little less shaky. "I wasn't just inviting you back here to *use* you, Tres. As hard as it may be to believe, I really do love you. But there's that other side of me, the side that scares me, that reminds me of my father. I keep asking myself if I was dragging you into this to deliberately hurt you some more."

My heart was trying to compress itself into something the size of a marble. The blood didn't seem to be flowing right into my fingers. Here it was a hundred degrees, and my fingers felt cold.

"I'm telling you this because I'm trying to work through it," Lillian said. "I still love you. I'm trying to discard the other things and concentrate on that, but I need to know from you if it's still worth me trying."

Contrasted with her black dress, her green eyes with their multicolored flecks looked especially brilliant. They were watering just a little, but there was a desperate fierceness to them. I saw what she needed me to say.

"Maia Lee was right. I just wasn't listening."

Lillian's expression rearranged itself when I said Maia's name—the emotional equivalent of a strategic withdrawal. "She was right about what?"

"About you, and why you needed me back."

Lillian looked even more uncertain. "Does that mean—"

I shook my head. "No. I'm not going back to her. San Antonio is home."

"Then what?"

I rubbed my hands, trying to get some feeling into them. "I think there's something else you're afraid of. Something even more scary than turning out like your father."

Her face was already closing up, preparing for the blow. "What would that be?"

"Turning out like your mother—an old woman with a shoe box full of photos of a former lover who you can't get rid of. I think you're terrified of becoming that person."

Lillian stood up, hugging her arms. She wouldn't look at me.

"The hell with you, if that's what you think."

She said it with as much coldness as she could muster, but her expression was the same as it had been when Dan Sheff had lied to her in the hospital room—concealed relief.

"You couldn't let go of me because of the secret you were carrying around," I said. "Now for the first time, that secret is gone. You've got to either try reconstructing our relationship so you don't have to deal with a ghost, or end it for good and hope you can move on to something totally new. Either way, you're terrified that it won't work, that I'll keep poisoning your life."

She spoke with surprising softness. "Two weeks ago you were sure we'd still be perfect together. You were willing to come back and try after all these years."

"Yes."

"You're telling me now you're going to shut out the possibility? You're so sure it wouldn't work?"

"Yes," I lied. "I'm sure."

She stared at me, looking for chinks in the armor. I didn't let her find any. Slowly, the tightness in her shoulder muscles relaxed.

"All of that," she said softly, "just for you to leave me again."

She waited for a response. It was hard, it was very hard, but I let her have the final word.

Then she turned and walked out of the gazebo, down to her mother's empty black Cadillac. It was much too big, much too formal a car for her, I thought. But as she drove off, she looked as if she were learning to be at home behind the wheel.

I took my suit coat off, then walked down to the corner of Austin Highway and Eisenhower, letting the sun turn me into a walking water fountain while I waited for the bus. There was a vendor on the corner selling fresh fruit next to black velvet paintings of Aztec Warriors and Bleeding Jesuses. I guess I looked like I needed something. He smiled crookedly and handed me a free slice of watermelon. I thanked him for not giving me one of the paintings instead.

"Hey, *vato*," someone said behind me.

I turned and saw Ralph leaning out the window of his maroon Lincoln and grinning like a fiend.

"You lose your wheels, man?"

I shrugged. "More like I lost Jess's. They're denying me visiting rights to the VW."

Ralph laughed and showed me a bottle of Herradura Anejo and a six-pack of Big Red.

"You still need friends like these?" he asked.

"Only more than anything," I told him, and I got in the car.

About the Author

RICK RIORDAN is the author of four Tres Navarre novels—
Big Red Tequila, winner of the Shamus and Anthony Awards;
The Widower's Two-Step, winner of the Edgar Award; *The
Last King of Texas*; and *The Devil Went Down to Austin*. A
middle-school English teacher by day, Riordan lives with his
wife and family in San Antonio, Texas.

Visit the author's website at www.rickriordan.com.

If you enjoyed Rick Riordan's BIG RED TEQUILA, you won't want to miss any of the novels in this sizzling, award-winning series.

And turn the page for a preview of Rick's latest Tres Navarre mystery, THE DEVIL WENT DOWN TO AUSTIN. Look for it at your favorite bookseller in hardcover from Bantam Books.

THE

DEVIL

WENT DOWN TO AUSTIN

RICK RIORDAN

Date: Wed, 07 June 2000 19:53:16 -0500
From: <host@ashield.com>
X-Mailer: Mozilla 3.01 Gold (Macintosh; I; PPC)
To: <host@ashield.com>
Subject: drowning

The first time I knew I would kill? I was six years old.

I'd snuck some things from the kitchen—vials of food coloring, Dixie cups, a pitcher of water. I was in my bedroom mixing potions, watching how the dyes curl in the water.

That doesn't sound like much, I know. But I'd spilled a few cupfuls onto the carpet. My fingers were stained purple. It was enough to give the Old Man an excuse.

He came in so quietly I didn't hear him, didn't know he was standing over me until I caught his smell, like sweet smoked beef.

He said something like, "Is this what we clean the house for? We clean the house so you can do this?"

Then I realized water was running in the bathroom. I remembered what my friend had said.

I tried to apologize, but the Old Man caught my wrists, dragged me backward, using my arms as a harness.

CHAPTER 1

Lars Elder looks like a banker the way I look like a private eye, which is to say, not much.

He was waiting on the porch of my family ranch house, flicking a switchblade open and closed, a computer disk and a can of Budweiser next to him on the railing.

Lars' hairline had receded since I'd seen him last, but he still sported the earring, the Willie Nelson beard. His shirt, vest, and jeans were faded to the colors of a dust storm, and his eyes gave the same impression—dry and turbulent.

"Tres," he said. "Thanks for coming."

"No problema."

What I was thinking: The Navarre family banker drinking beer at ten in the morning is not a good sign.

Lars closed his knife, looked out toward the wheat fields.

Fifty yards away, past the tomato garden, the ranch caretaker was putting hay into the cattle feeder. Harold Diliberto stopped to watch us, his pitchfork suspended, dripping straw.

"Harold showed me the work you've been doing inside," Lars said. "You've been spending a lot of time out here."

"Some," I admitted.

I tried not to feel irritated, like Harold had betrayed a confidence.

Truth was, I'd been out at the ranch every weekend since the end of April—scraping old paint, filling in the spreading cracks in the original section of the house that had been my great-grandfather's homestead in the 1880s. I'd neglected both my jobs in San Antonio, ditched the cell phone, dropped out of my social life with little explanation to my friends.

"Place was overdue for some maintenance," I told Lars. "You ask me out here for the Home Beautiful tour?"

He didn't smile. "Talked to Garrett recently?"

"Maybe four, five months ago."

"But you'll see him soon. You're teaching that summer class in Austin, aren't you?"

Another surge of irritation. "British lit, for six weeks. May I ask how the hell you know about it?"

Lars brought the switchblade up like a conductor's baton. "Look, I'm sorry. I had to talk to you before you left. You know what Garrett's been up to?"

"You mean like Buffett concerts? Smoking pot?"

"His programming project."

"Must've missed it. I tend to phase out when Garrett talks about RNI."

Lars winced, like I'd just told him the price of an expensive gift. "Tres, Garrett isn't working at RNI anymore. He quit over a year ago."

I stared at him. My brother had worked at the same software company for sixteen years. He practically ran the place, took all the days off he wanted, had a retirement package.

"Got himself involved in a start-up company," Lars told me. "That was two years ago—spring of '98. Then last year, May of '99, he decided he couldn't keep working both jobs anymore. Garrett just left RNI—no severance, no benefits."

"Not possible."

"He's working the start-up with Jimmy Doebler."

I studied Lars' eyes, tried to tell if he was joking. Apparently, he wasn't, and beer for breakfast started sounding like a good idea.

Last I'd heard—maybe three years ago—Jimmy Doebler and Garrett hadn't even been speaking to each other. When they were speaking, they got along about as well as electricity and gunpowder.

"You're sure?" I asked him.

Lars picked up the computer disk, handed it to me. "Some files—things I was able to find on the Internet. They're calling themselves Techsan Security Software. Three principals in the company—Jimmy, his wife, Ruby, Garrett. They've been designing an encryption product. The beta-testing started in January."

I wagged the floppy. "It's news to me. Why the dossier, Lars? What's your interest?"

He rubbed his beard with his knuckles.

"I've known Jimmy and Garrett for a long time. I was around when Garrett—" He faltered. "Well, you know. I was around for the bad times. But when I called Garrett last week, I'd never heard him sound so bad. He and Jimmy are fighting again. Jimmy and his wife have separated—all because of this company they've started. I asked Garrett how they were holding up financially. He just laughed. The last few days, he won't even return my calls. I thought maybe you could talk to him."

I looked over the split rail fence, down the pasture toward the woods. The Charolais were grazing in the dry bed of Apache Creek. The water tower glistened gray.

I thought about the hundreds of times I'd watched the sun come up over the Balcones Escarpment from here, the topography like an onion, layer upon translucent layer—my first hunting trip with my dad, a dozen Thanksgiving dinners, my first night with a woman, three hurricanes, two fires, even a snowstorm. I remembered my grandfather, over there by the northern property line, digging holes for fence posts.

And even after six weeks of manual labor, rebuilding my relationship with the ranch, I could still feel that Sunday afternoon last April, down in the clearing, when I'd almost died at the hands of an old friend.

All I wanted was a few more weekends, time to scrape paint.

"Look, Lars, I won't say I'm not worried. But Garrett and Jimmy—what you're describing. Unfortunately, it sounds pretty typical. I appreciate your concern . . ."

"You don't understand," Lars said. "Garrett needed capital for his share in the Techsan start-up. A *lot* of capital. With his financial record, nobody else would help him. I hate even talking to you about this, Tres. I know you don't have a lot of money."

I tried to hand back the computer disk. "If you made my brother a loan, I'm sorry, Lars. I don't see how I can help you."

"I couldn't talk him out of it," he said. "The deed is in his name. He made me promise not to worry you, but when he signed the papers he still had a steady job. Now . . . He hasn't made a payment in over a year. It's just—I don't know what I can promise, come July 1st. My boss is breathing down my neck."

My heart twisted into a sailor's knot. "July 1st?"

I wanted to ask what he meant, but unfortunately, I'd begun to understand.

Lars pinched the blade of his knife, threw it toward an old live oak stump, where it stuck straight up.

"Garrett mortgaged this ranch, Tres. And unless I see something—a sign of good faith by the end of this month, I'm going to have to foreclose."

CHAPTER 2

San Antonio and Austin are like estranged siblings.

San Antonio would be the sister who stayed home, took care of the elderly parents, made tortillas by hand in the kitchen, wore cotton dresses until the colors faded. She's the big-boned one—handsome but unadorned, given to long afternoon siestas.

Austin is the sister who went away to college, discovered rock 'n' roll and dyed her hair purple. She's the one my mother would've warned me about, if my mother hadn't been an ex-hippie.

That afternoon I figured out why God put the two sisters seventy-five miles apart. It was to give irate siblings like me a cooling-off period—an hour on the road to reconsider fratricide.

Around two o'clock, I finally tracked down my brother. A friend of a Hell's Angel of a friend told me he was staying at Jimmy Doebler's place on Lake Travis.

Sure enough, they were down by the water, bricking in a shed that looked like the third little pig's house. It was a kiln—pottery being Jimmy's second oldest hobby, next to getting Garrett in trouble.

From fifteen feet away, Jimmy and Garrett hadn't noticed me.

Jimmy was hunched over, tapping down a line of bricks.

Garrett was up on a scaffold, five feet above, doing the chimney. His ponytail had flipped over the shoulder and gotten stuck in a splot of wet mortar. Sweat glistened in his beard. He made an odd sight up there, with no legs, like some sort of tie-dyed polyp grown out of the board.

The afternoon heat was cooking the air into soup. In the crook of a smoke tree, a jam box was cranking out Lucinda Williams' latest.

"Garrett," I called.

He looked down as if he'd known I was there all along, his expression as friendly as Rasputin's.

"Well," he said. "My little brother."

Jimmy wiped his hands on his tattered polo shirt, straightened.

He hadn't aged well. His face had weathered, his mop of sandcastle hair faded a dirty gray. He had the sun-blasted look of a frat boy who'd gotten lost on Spring Break thirty years ago and never found his way out of the dunes.

"Hey, man." He cut his eyes to either side, wiped his nose. "Garrett said you wouldn't be up until your class started."

"Wasn't planning to," I said. "Then I talked to the family banker. That kind of changed things."

Garrett stabbed his trowel between two scaffold planks. "This ain't the time, Tres."

"When would be the time, Garrett? Next month—when they stick the FOR SALE sign on the front gate of the ranch?"

Lucinda Williams kept singing about her mamma. The bottleneck flew across her guitar.

"What do you want?" Garrett asked. "You want to take a punch at me?"

"I don't know. Are you filled with money?"

Garrett climbed down from the scaffold—one hundred percent upper body strength. He settled into his Quickie wheelchair—the deluxe model with the Holstein hide cover and the Persian seat cushion. He pushed himself toward me. "Come on. You've driven all this way pissed off at me. Take a swing."

He looked terrible. His skin was pasty, his eyes jaundiced. He'd lost weight—Christ, a lot of weight. Maybe fifteen pounds. He hardly had a gut anymore.

I said, "I want an explanation."

"It's *my* ranch."

"It's *our* ranch, Garrett. I don't care what it said in the will."

He puffed a laugh. "Yeah, you do. You care a whole *shitload*."

He jerked the macramé pouch off the side of his wheelchair, started rummaging through it—looking for his marijuana, his rolling papers.

"Would you not do that?" I asked.

"Do what?"

I grabbed the bag.

He tried to take it away from me, but I stepped back, felt how heavy the thing was, looked inside. "What is this?"

I came out with a handgun, a Lorcin .380.

"What did you do—buy this on the street?" I protested. "I took one of these away from a fourteen-year-old drug dealer last week. Since when do you carry something like this?"

Complete stillness. Even Lucinda Williams paused between songs.

"Look, Tres," Jimmy said. "Back off a little."

I checked the Lorcin. It was fully loaded. "Yeah, you're right, Jimmy. Garrett's got you on his side now. Everything's under control."

It was a cheap shot.

Jimmy shifted his weight from one foot to the other. His face turned the color of guava juice.

"We're working things out," Garrett told me.

"With a gun?"

"Jimmy and I made a pact for the day, man. No arguing. You want to stay here, abide by that rule."

His tone made me remember trips to Rockport when I was in middle school, Jimmy and Garrett college kids, forced to baby-sit me while my dad got drunk down on the jetties. Garrett had resented me tagging along, told me to shut up so they could meet some girls. The memory brought back that irrational anger, shaped in the mind of an eleven-year-old, that this was all Jimmy Doebler's fault—that he had always inserted himself into our lives at the wrong time.

I shoved the Lorcin back into the bag, tossed it back to Garrett. "Lars Elder passed along some headlines you've been making in the high-tech magazines. Beta-testing problems. Glitches in the software. I didn't understand half of it, but I understood *several million in debt. Millions,* Garrett, with six zeroes. And your friend here wants me to *back off*?"

Jimmy said nothing.

Garrett rummaged in the bag, found a prerolled joint, stuck it in his mouth. "If we thought it was your business—"

"You pawned the ranch."

"And Jimmy got divorced today," he yelled. The joint fell out of his mouth, into his lap. "Okay, Tres? So shut the fuck up."

His voice wavered, was closer to breaking than I'd ever heard.

Jimmy Doebler stared down at his unfinished brick-work.

I remembered years ago, seeing heat tester cones in Jimmy's old portable kiln—how they turned to pools of liquid rock in the fire. Right now, Jimmy's eyes looked a little hotter than those cones.

"All we want to do," Garrett told me, "is build this damn kiln. You want to help, fine. You want to criticize, get your sorry ass home."

I looked at the half-built little pig house.

I looked at my brother's fingers, scarred and bleeding and crusted with mortar.

My anger drained away, left a taste in my mouth not unlike a TV dinner tray.

I said, "Hand me a trowel."